Don't Let My Baby Do Rodeo

Don't Let My Baby Do Rodeo

A NOVEL

Boris Fishman

HARPER

An Imprint of HarperCollins*Publishers*

HarperCollins books may be purchased for educational, business, or sales promotional use. For information, please e-mail the Special Markets Department at SPsales@harpercollins.com.

Grateful acknowledgment is made to Ludmila Chorekchian for permission to refer to and quote from *The Revelation of a Russian Psychotherapist on the American Land*, Vantage Press, 2002, on pages 106 and 108–12 of this novel.

FIRST EDITION

Designed by Fritz Metsch

Library of Congress Cataloging-in-Publication Data has been applied for.

ISBN: 978-0-06-238436-2

16 17 18 19 20   OV/RRD   10 9 8 7 6 5 4 3 2 1

For my mother

For West is where we all plan to go some day. . . . It is where you go to grow up with the country.

—ROBERT PENN WARREN, *All the King's Men*

The conquest of the physical world is not man's only duty. He is also enjoined to conquer the great wilderness of himself.

—JAMES BALDWIN, *The Price of the Ticket*

I

East

1

Maya had been early to pick up Max the day he didn't come home with the school bus. Usually she was still powering up Sylvan Gate Drive when the old yellow bus sputtered to its crown, the doors exhaled, and Max tumbled out, always before the Kroon girl because Max always took the front seat. Even in the family Corolla, it was Alex at the wheel, Max in the passenger seat, and Maya in the back. Maya had gathered that the popular children sat back of the bus. She had asked Max once why he wasn't among them. "There's too much noise in the back," he had said, and she had felt a hidden satisfaction at his indifference.

That day, after a week of disabling warmth premature even for New Jersey in June, a note of unhumid reprieve had snuck into the air—Maya had caught it on her drive home from the hospital—and so she had walked out of the town house early. On the rare occasions Alex was home early enough to collect Max, he drove the thousand yards to the head of the drive—Alex enjoyed the very American possibility of this convenience. But Maya walked. She was on her feet all day at the hospital, but she shuttled between three rooms and it was all indoors.

In Kiev, Maya's mother had always awaited her by the school doors, painted and repainted until they looked like lumpy old women. The walk home was time alone for mother and daughter; by the time they reached their apartment, Maya's father would already be at the kitchen table slouched over the sports section, the only part of the newspaper where things didn't have to be perfect. Maya's mother would begin their walk by asking all the questions a mother was required to ask of a daughter's school day—even as an eight-year-old, Max's age, Maya understood this as a formality—but then, after a discreet pause, Galina Shulman would bring her daughter up to date on the indiscreet doings of "the great circus" of their thousand-apartment apartment building.

Maya was exhilarated by these walks for she felt her mother spoke as if Maya was not present, or if she were, then as an equal, a friend, not a daughter to whom convention described responsibilities. So—a silent hello to a woman now five thousand miles away—Maya picked up Max from the school bus. It wasn't particularly necessary—the danger was not in the distance Max would have to cover down to their town house, but in his time out in the world. But it was Maya's only time alone with her son. She used it to try to understand why she couldn't always speak with Max in the same easy, unspooling way her mother had spoken with her. Maya did not have her mother's imagination; that was part of it, certainly. Nor did she have her mother's curiosity about her neighbors, though Maya knew that this was a failure of her looking, not their living. But none of that seemed the answer. Maya asked her son about school, questions he answered politely and briefly—she never failed to marvel at the unkinked Russian speech of her not-Russian son—and then both fell silent. All she could think was to take his hand, and he let her hold it. She felt she was failing him in some way. Failing him, and couldn't say how; she felt thick and graceless.

They had been lucky, the adoption supervisor had kept reminding them, as if he worked on commission. American parents often had to go abroad to find children: Malaysia, Korea, Romania. Bribes, endless waiting, no medical records. Whereas the Rubins got an outright American. Who got an American any longer, and a brand-new baby instead of a child old enough to have been terrorized by somebody else? Maya had the ungrateful thought that she did not want an American: She felt that she would have more to say to a Romanian child. In the sleepless hold of another intermi-

nable night, she had shaken awake Alex and said so. He closed his
fingertips around the knob of her shoulder, as if she were a loose
lightbulb: "He's a newborn. Was New Jersey familiar to you when
you moved here? This house? But now it's all home." He turned
onto his side, cupped one of her breasts from behind, and said:
"Sleep, Maya—please."

She had picked out the weary magnanimousness in his
voice—he had to indulge not only her willingness to adopt, but
her anxieties over it. Only who wanted a child more than he did?
However, a biological solution being impossible, Alex's desire had
just one condition—that he not be made to confess it. And so she
carried on as the secret advocate for them both. His contribution
was to disparage the woe conjured up by her railroad mind at two
in the morning. "Railroad mind"—that was Alex's term for the
hive of Maya's brain. Railroads made him think of motion, steam,
frantic activity. What he really meant was that she was like some
Anna Karenina—superfluously melodramatic. And Maya understood what he really meant only because she had a railroad mind.

Alex had been ten years younger than Maya's eighteen when
his family had come to America; the Rubins had come for good,
whereas Maya had come on an exchange program in 1988, the first
year such things were possible. After college, Maya was supposed
to return to the USSR—a plan altered by her love affair with Alex
and the end of the USSR. Alex had taken to America—he spoke
with confidence about Wall Street, the structure of Congress, tech-
nology. Maya conceded his authority. Only once had she exclaimed
that in twenty years he had almost never left New Jersey, so what
did he know? Alex had looked at her as if at a child who doesn't
understand what it means to say things one will later regret, and
retreated upstairs. He did not speak to her for three days, their
sullen meals spent communicating through Max and his grandparents, and Maya never said that again.

Was this acceptable to discuss with an eight-year-old? Maya
laughed at herself and rehearsed her to-do list: Max needed a ride

to Oliver's on Saturday, and they had to find time before the end of the month to update two of Max's vaccines—she would have to pick him up from school and rush back to the hospital before that office closed at four. She sniffed at the festively mild afternoon. The briefly unfevered air grew fevered inside her all the same due to the exertion required by the hill. The sweetness in the air would not last the night.

The Kroon girl was first, swinging her arms. This was new. This was something she and Max could talk about. Today, he had decided to sit in the back, just to see how things looked from back there. Perhaps he had made some new friends; he had one friend in the world, Oliver. Maya smiled at the Kroon girl, who ignored her, and looked up expectantly at the driver, who never chatted with Maya, which made her feel snubbed though she tried to persuade herself it was because he was grave about his responsibilities. He nodded and yanked the door lever.

"Wait!" Maya shouted. She laid a soft fist into the glass. The driver looked up reproachfully and the door folded back in.

"Please don't hit my bus," he said.

"But where is my son?" Maya said. She heard, as always, her slight accent, like a hair under the collar. She spoke with resentment—all those times the bus driver had not acknowledged her.

"The young man was not on the bus," the driver said.

"It's Max," she said.

"Not on the bus," the driver repeated.

"But he went to school," she opened her hands. She took in the driver's gray T-shirt, swollen by the half globe of a gut, the blue sweatpants and brown sandals.

"Call the school?" he said. "But I've got to move now." He checked the mirror for traffic.

Maya's chest emptied out and she leaped onto the first stair of the bus. The driver looked on with astonishment.

"Children!" she yelled at the bus. The small heads poking out of the green rows gave her attention, even the ones in the back. "My son, Max. He takes this bus every day."

They stared at her silently.

"Ma'am," the driver said.

She swiveled to face him. "You might put on something more decent to set an example for children."

His head retreated slightly, and a look of sleepy alarm came over his face.

She turned back to the rows. "Does anyone on the bus know who my son is?" They gazed at her stubbornly. They were not going to give anything up and they felt pity for her.

"You know Max," the driver called out from behind her. She felt gratitude—he knew her son's name. Then she remembered that she had just used it. "This is his mom."

A hand shot up from a row midway down the aisle.

"You don't have to raise your hand," the driver said.

"Max took another bus," the voice came. It was a girl's voice. Maya surged down the aisle.

"What other bus?" she demanded. The girl—unattractive, a pug nose, Maya disliked her instantly, as if she were responsible for Max's disappearance—shrugged.

"Was it a school bus?" the driver said. "Yellow."

"No," the girl said.

"Town bus? With purple stripes."

The girl nodded.

"I don't suppose you saw the number," the driver said.

"It stops by the flagpole."

"That's the 748," he said. Maya turned toward the driver. "That one goes north," he said. "Toward the state line."

"What state!" she exclaimed.

"New York State," he said. His face folded, concern rising in it like color. Until a moment before, Maya had wanted to see it, and now she did not. "I'll radio the school."

Maya raked her temples. She heard the rumbling of the vehicle and the silence of the children. The back of the school bus was sticking out into Brandenburg Turnpike, cars backing up as they funneled into a single line to avoid it. The driver lifted a wired receiver, which crackled like a radio between stations, and murmured into it. Some of his belly rested on the lower part of the steering wheel.

"I can't get them," he said, exhaling contritely. "They're busy with buses. But I'll get 'em. He'll turn up."

Things had improved between them, between her and the driver, and Maya tried to take this to mean that good things were possible and her son would return. She stared out of the open doors down at the drive, its familiar plunge suddenly malevolent and abundant with risk. Without turning back to the driver, she rushed the steps down to the ground and ran toward home, the pavement going off in her knees. Behind her she heard sounds belonging to other people in another world: the bus doors sliding shut, the brake coming off, the bus shuddering off to the next residential development, where children would be disgorged into the hands of their mothers, an unremarkable ritual made remarkable only by its failure to take place.

+

Maya was unvigilant about her cell phone. She would be serving dinner to Alex and his parents, who almost always ate alongside their son and his wife, and hear that each of them had left multiple messages earlier. This information was relayed to her with exasperation covered with feigned amusement. Now, predictably, her handbag, emptied out on the dining table, gave up nothing. She ran for the landline. At Max's elementary school, she demanded the principal's office. The man himself came on the line once word traveled why she was calling. Maya was too troubled to feel nervous about speaking to him. He listened to Maya's news with a strange disappointment, as if she and not he had failed to keep an eye on her son. "I'll stay late and make inquiries," he said flatly. She admonished him that she was about to call the police, but it failed to have the intended effect: "Good idea," he said noncommittally. She wanted more from him; he had lost her son. How could a child wander off school grounds and climb aboard a regional bus line? But she heard herself only thank him.

She walked the kitchen, trying to think of whom else she could try before Alex and his parents. There was no one. She called the police and was reassured by the temperate way with which her information was received by the dispatcher. Temperate meant that such things ended positively all the time—it had to mean that. Finally, she hit the buttons for Rubin Trading. The line strafed and buzzed. When the secretary's voice came on, Maya burst into tears.

Alex and his father drove home in a mourner's silence. Alex's mother, who was taking her afternoon swim, was summoned by loudspeaker from the pool. Wary of all singling out, Raisa Rubin waited some time in the slow lane before making sure she had to come out. She did just in time for her husband and son to pick her up from the YMCA, and the three of them set off to receive Maya's terrible news. When the bell rang, Maya ran for it, but on the other side of the door she discovered not her son but a mournful trio of Rubins, gazing at her as if her discovery of their child's disappearance meant that she had lost him as well.

+

The elder Rubins lived right in Sylvan Gate, though enough properties away to be out of view in deference to American ideas about privacy. A forty-three-year-old son, and they weren't seventy yet, Eugene still practically full-time at his food-importing business, all of which allowed the senior Rubins to feel a sense of youth and modernity. Of necessity, also: Where would Maya and Alex be without their aid? They had encouraged Maya to move from mammography to pharmacy—pharmacists earned in the six figures, with another half on the side if she wanted—but Maya was not proactive like them. Alex had tried investments, but if he had earned for himself a fraction as much as he earned for others, it didn't show, and his father had persuaded him to become the second-in-command at Rubin Trading.

"Someone's laid a hex on us," Raisa said grimly. The four Rubins, two by birth and the others by choice, were leaned over the kitchen table in a tight, anxious circle.

"When I was a boy, I ran away, too," Eugene said. "My father laid the strap to me. I didn't run away again."

"So why didn't you do it to me if it was so effective?" Alex said.

Eugene looked up. "You didn't need it."

"I don't understand why you called the police," Raisa said to Maya. "People will find out and think he's some kind of runaway!" The other Rubins looked at Raisa in such a way that she did not try this line of argument a second time.

Eugene shook his head. "I always said this was a bad idea. I've always known something would go wrong. It was only a matter of time. I kept quiet only because I didn't want to upset you. But I was waiting for this day."

"Please don't go back to that," Alex said. "He's a boy. Boys act up. It's nothing."

"You like to bury your head in the sand," Eugene said. "Your mother set you up nicely for that." He cast a disparaging look at his wife. "But problems don't fix themselves. Customs is not going to wake up tomorrow and realize they made an error and expedite my honey. Philadelphia is not going to get why Bulgarian feta is just as good as Greek fucking feta unless I go down there, and I open the buyer's mouth, and I put a square of Bulgarian feta in it—"

"Zhenya!" Raisa exclaimed.

"And he chews it, the cow," Eugene barreled on, "and slowly the dawn comes on his face—'you're right, Rubin, this isn't bad, and two dollars less per pound, you say. Well, you've been saying it on the phone for two months, haven't you'—"

"What are we talking about?" Alex said. "What do you propose?"

"You want to adopt, adopt a child from a place that you know," Eugene said. "Adopt a"—here Eugene stretched the corners of his eyes to indicate an Asian child. "Those, at least, have good genes for school."

"Where was this help eight years ago?" Alex said. "Or did you not want to upset us?"

Eugene twisted his nose. "An Aryan they get, from Montana. Where? Who? People fuck sheep over there. There aren't any women. Sheep, goats, whatever's at hand. Of course those parents sprang him on you the way that they did." Eugene slapped the tablecloth. "And got away without ever telling you why. Rodeo?" he laughed in an ugly way. He was finally saying things he had kept back because he was kind. "What is that? A lie. But you ate it." He stared at Maya and bellowed, "What didn't they tell you?"

Maya's chair retreated from the table, her hand over her mouth.

"What didn't they tell you?" his voice followed her out of the kitchen.

Alex leaned into his father's face. "If you speak that way again, you are not welcome in this house."

"Is my money welcome?" Eugene said, and they descended into a terrible silence. It was interrupted by the plink of the doorbell. They looked at each other and leaped out of their chairs, Maya finding the door first as the other three arranged themselves behind her in a hopeful file. But it was the police. The two officers, lean and tidy and queasy to behold on the other side of their threshold, fanned out through the house, as if Max were in a corner somewhere and the Rubins had merely failed to look. Maya realized that the policemen were forced to consider the possibility that the parents themselves had done something to the child. They were looking for evidence. Her blood ran cold, and she was filled with an unbearable sense of futility.

Eventually, the uniformed men sat with the Rubins at the kitchen table and took down the information that no parent wishes to give. A bit over four feet, a bit under fifty pounds—thin for his age. Hay-yellow hair, straight like pine needles—it fell over his head like a cap except for a little part on the side. Which side—left side. *His* left. The ears stick out a little, not that you really see it under the hair, and he blinks twice very quickly when he's nervous. Green eyes, flecks of gray. Beautiful, beautiful eyes. Maya sought out, in the officers' expressions and gestures, hints of sympathy and reassurance, but then she understood that they had to be like the doctors in her hospital. They had seen too much despair to be able to give anything of themselves to it. If they did, she would never stop taking.

Grateful for an assignment, Maya went off to look for printed photos—for years everything had been on their cell phones. Well behaved, shy, orderly, and obedient, Raisa pressed the police officers as Maya walked away—needlessly; they wouldn't find him by his personality. Any other significant details? Maya turned back. She hesitated. He's adopted, she said. He doesn't know. The other Rubins stared at her with dismay.

+

As they waited for news, the Rubins dispersed to disparate corners of their panicked home and explored the forms waiting could take.

Maya Rubin née Shulman was one of those women who, at forty-two, continued to look more or less as she had in her twenties. In her case, her body had never been distended by a child, though the women evaluating her—if they were up to candor— would have admitted that this would have made no difference. These subtleties were lost on men, who focused on the slimness of her hips; the unspeckled smoothness of her legs, save for a long vein thick as a guitar string down one thigh; and the small breasts that seemed boyish at first and then impossibly erotic. Her face confounded them: a strong nose above full lips, framed by soft, jutting cheekbones that had missed their time by a century. To some, the face was ordinary, and in others it caused an arousal no less severe for being not very explicable. In their own way, the men arrived at the same impression as the women: sufficient miscalibration to conjure a subtle, irresistible beauty.

Her husband, possessed of a handsome wide face that remained olive-colored even in winter, was soft where Maya was slight, as if life had padded him against misfortune. And if not life, then his mother—Alex had been stocky from boyhood and finished his plate every time. He paid attention to his closet, never went to work without a blazer, and spent part of the weekend shearing coupons to Lord & Taylor and Nordstrom. His soccer legs and tennis waist—Alex's parents had insisted on sports, though Alex was left free to choose which—had filled out, but democratically, in equal parts everywhere, as if according to blueprints.

The mother and father were an inversion of the children: the father thin as straw, the mother heavyset despite a youth in swimming. (A photo in burnt-brown tones left on the children's mantelpiece by Raisa showed her as a young woman just out of the Minsk city pool, the rubber cap still tight on her ears, lipstick already on her lips, a single gold tooth watting up her smile.) Raisa could pile into Eugene what she wanted and still the shoulders stayed knobby, the collarbone so taut you couldn't look at it without thinking of the bone cutting right through its poor membrane of skin. Eugene had more hair in his eyebrows than some on their heads, and in youth Raisa called Eugene her gypsy even though his parents and grandparents were light as Slavs. The mystery of inheritance.

Maya sat on a settee by the window and looked longingly toward the kitchen. In the afternoons, after she and Max walked through the door, they worked on dinner. It was Maya's favorite part of the day. This she knew how to do, and could show Max without second-guessing herself. Max did all the prep that required no knife work—prying from the root the onion scales Maya had julienned, mashing potatoes (Max clutched the masher so hard his fists shook). Within a year or two, she planned to start him on knife work.

Maya turned back to the driveway, watching the extended daylight of even this day forced to end. Is there a time of day more frightening to a parent whose child has vanished? She was grateful that her son had chosen to run off in June instead of December; the air was greasy with a slack, twinkling leisure that made it impossible to imagine a person coming to harm. Once in a while, this optimism was ruined by the sight of a car driving too quickly down their street: because it was going too quickly to avoid mowing down a child in the gathering dark, and because, moving so fast, it couldn't be a car returning their son.

Alex rose, the sofa giving him up with a sigh, and the others checked sluggishly in case his movement indicated some new insight. But he was going off toward the kitchen. They heard him working the kettle—he emerged with a cup of steaming water with three slices of lemon for his wife. How she liked it, just hot water and lemon, even in hot weather. Her gaze fixed on the window, she winced when he touched her shoulder, the cup trembled in his hand, and a gulp of it sailed onto the wood of the floor. They all stared at the spot—something dropped meant news on the way. Alex folded his lips with reproof. Maya smiled with pained gratitude.

"We should look in his room," Eugene looked up from the hands netted in his lap. Maya stared absently at her father-in-law. "Maybe there's a note, for God's sake," Eugene went on. "Has anyone been up to his room?"

"I looked in his room," Maya said feebly.

"Let's look again," Eugene said.

Grateful for something to do, Raisa rose, followed by Eugene. Maya tried to signal Alex—his parents would see what she and Alex saw every night. But Alex only looked at her blankly. Perhaps he was disabled by worry.

"Would Max like it if we looked in his room without him there?" she tried.

"I don't think he minds when you go in there with a vacuum cleaner, am I wrong?" Eugene said.

"Don't say that, Eugene," Raisa said. "Maxie is so neat."

Maya couldn't think how else to distract them and gave up. To remain alone downstairs after having been doubted would have expressed a greater objection than Maya felt up to. She followed. They took the stairs in a line, like a team of emergency workers. The four of them stood at the furry threshold of Max's room, hesitant to find the clues they wanted to find.

"I'd run away, too, if my parents painted the walls of my room the color of hand cream," Eugene said, but the joke didn't take. He persevered defensively: "I didn't have these concerns as a child—my brother and I slept in the same bed."

One wall of Max's room was covered with a map of America Alex and Max had hand-drawn across a quilt of printer sheets; shelves ran the height of the next: Max's books; two menorahs and a stuffed doll in a Purim costume, halfhearted Jewish gestures whose makers hoped their ancestral religion would take better root with Max than with themselves, even though he was the only non-Jew among them; and the Indian masks Max always wanted when they went to the Riviera Maya on vacation. Just now, the one with two red lightning bolts in place of eyebrows and a snake coiling out of its mouth communicated all their unease.

Eugene stepped inside and nodded toward the bedding, in a neat pile on the floor. "This was you, Alex," he said. "You never had to be disciplined or told to clean up." Maya swallowed, eager for him to misunderstand why it was all on the carpet. With satisfaction, Eugene ran a finger across the top of the dresser: no dust. He went over to the window and forced it up, sighing with the pleasure of his muscles at work, and stuck his nose into the evening air. The humidity was on its way back. The other three stood awkwardly in the middle of the room, looking around. What were they looking for? Everything seemed in place; there were no empty hangers in the closet. That could be good news because Max meant to return, or bad because Max had meant to return and had not.

Eugene turned back to them from the window. "To voluntarily

sleep on the ground." He shook his head. "Even on the night of a Cossack pogrom a hundred fifty years ago, a Rubin slept off the ground. Maybe on a haystack, but not on the ground." He meant the pup tent in the backyard, where Max was allowed to sleep on weekends when the weather was warm. Alex and Max spent afternoons there. Home from work, Alex changed into lawn-mowing clothes, and father and son journeyed outside. Maya did not resent losing her sous chef to her husband, as if, eight years later, she was still checking the glue between them. By the time she saw, through the kitchen window, her men reaching the tent, gold on the inside and forest-green on the out, like a leaf in two seasons at once, they were stumbling back to base camp after losing their men to hostile Siberians who rode wolves. Or they were on a new planet and Alex had to leave outside the flap the crystal lowball with two fingers of cognac that he sometimes brought with him because liquids turned to gas on Planet Chung. ("Why Chung, Maxie?" "I can't tell you.") Surgical masks Maya had been made to bring home from the hospital enabled father and son to survive the bad gas. Then—a star popping softly in the black ether—the faint call for dinner would come.

Eugene slid his head back inside and stared at the bedding on the floor. "That's not for laundry, is it," he said ruefully, understanding. "It's folded too neatly. Your son sleeps on the floor. And you know." He stared at his son and daughter-in-law. Betrayal appeared on his face. "What else have you concealed about my grandson?" He looked at his wife. "Did you know?"

"No," Raisa said without joy. Alex and Maya did not answer, but Maya sought support from the wall.

Eugene sat down on Max's bare mattress and stared at the bedroll. "Maybe our boy is off on some adventure," he said without believing it. "Maybe he'll be home before long for a nice scolding."

"Why don't we return downstairs," Raisa said.

"Genes are not water," Eugene said. "Biologically, he is and always will be the child of those people. And the people who made them. It's a miracle you're seeing this only now. He came to us with programming; you can spend your whole lives changing the code, and still you are going to rewrite only fragments. I knew my great-grandparents. And who am I if not their great-grandson, buying for ten cents and selling for twenty? Faxes, e-mail, zip drives, okay. But it's the same game."

His audience stood silently. Maya felt the wall with her hand. It was cool to the touch. She tried to fit all of herself into the feeling. She was a palm against the cold wall.

"I ship everywhere," Eugene said. "Denver, Las Vegas, San Francisco, Seattle. I like cities that end in consonants, strong names. Denver. Boston. Washington. New York—the "k" is like a nice flick in the eye. Miami, Philadelphia—feminine names. Montana.

"They don't have philharmonics out there. The Metropolitan Museum of Art, the ballet, buildings taller than a barn. They don't have that."

"And, what, you go to the ballet?" Raisa said.

"No, but I can go whenever I want," Eugene said. "I can go this very evening."

"Come on, Zhenya," she said. "Don't get upset. Let's go downstairs. I'll make a cup of tea."

"They have horses, and rivers, and grass, and then nothing," Eugene said. "I know because that was my village—why did I run away to the city before I finished ten grades? The countryside is for poor people. Drunk people. They subsist on drink instead of turning ten into twenty."

They observed one another gloomily. Outside, the light was letting go of the day.

"You've called the school," Raisa said finally, redundant in a wish to turn back the conversation.

"Mama," Alex said wearily.

"The school is responsible for him until two forty-five," Maya said. "He went outside with the rest of his bus, and then he must have walked off."

"The school is responsible for him until two forty-five!" Eugene exclaimed. "And if a murderer shows up at two forty-six, they'll just fold their hands and watch with regret? No, this is a lawsuit. The school is guilty of negligence."

"When I was little and playing in the sandbox with Sasha, and those men stopped to ask directions to school?" Alex said. "I knew you weren't supposed to talk to strangers, but I not only talked to them, I walked them to the school. Children do mysterious things."

"This is supposed to make me feel better?" Maya said. "Your father had to rescue you at the last moment."

"I don't think it's the best example, son," Raisa said.

Eugene rose heavily, and his ankle nicked a board peeking out from under the bed. His knees cracking, he leaned down and pulled it out, a bulletin board, its symmetrical rows of tacked plastic pouches pleasing to the eye. Each pouch had a label: Fescue. Timothy. Zoysia. They were grasses. The fescue was tufted, like the back of a porcupine, the timothy like grass everywhere. He looked up at Alex and Maya. They stared at him woefully.

Until now, Eugene had not known that there was more than one type of grass in the world: grass. It looked like a science project. As his family watched him, Eugene fished out a faded clump from the pouch labeled "timothy" and sniffed it. He didn't get anything except the smell of old sun. He looked again: The tawny grass looked chewed. Eugene noticed tooth marks on the other grasses. Not all; some. They had been chewed and placed back in the pouches. Some of the pouches held more grass than others, as if some of the grass had been not only tasted but eaten. Feeling foolish, Eugene looked around, as if to confirm that he was where he thought he was—a suburban bedroom where the carpet had been vacuumed recently enough that the lines remained visible. No animal had climbed to the second story and delicately pawed its way inside the pouches of grass without shredding the plastic. No, his grandson had eaten the grass. He dropped the board like a cursed object.

"About this we didn't know," Maya said fearfully.

"So he chewed some grass," Alex said unpersuasively. "When a boy . . ." he started and trailed off.

"He went and picked twenty pouches of grass," Eugene said, opening his hands.

"It was a science project," Maya said. "I walked around with him. I didn't know he was—he was—"

"You didn't know you were turning your son into an animal."

"Stop, Papa—please," Maya said. Now Raisa gave up and sat down on the bed.

Maya pushed herself away from the wall. "I'm going to ride the bus."

The others turned. "What bus?" Eugene said.

"The 748," Maya said. "The bus the girl said he was on."

"He's not on the bus *now*," Alex said.

"If he took the bus to go there, maybe he would take the bus to come home," Maya said. "Maybe I'll see something."

"At least she wants to do something," Eugene shook his head.

"But if he will take the bus to come home, he's going to come home," Alex said. "What will your showing up on the bus do? It's a futile gesture—do something just to do something. We're at his mercy. Four adults are at the mercy of an eight-year-old."

"So your proposal is to do nothing," Maya said.

"You are all so certain he's going to come back from where he went off to?" Eugene broke in. "To his mama and papa, who rescued him from the excellent life he had coming to him in Montana? Yes, he's *very* concerned about you."

"My proposal is not to do things just to do things," Alex said. "The school doesn't know where he is. The police are looking. Until then, we wait."

"I am going to ride the bus," Maya repeated.

"Please don't give me a look that says I don't care," Alex said. "I am trying to think rationally."

"Please drive me," she said.

They remembered that she did not drive past the mall. Alex,

unwilling to feel as churlish as refusing would force him to feel—
the upper hand was tricky that way; truly, power was with the
needy and meek—nodded cumbrously.

"Into the night, you're going," Raisa remarked sorrowfully. In
Raisa's view, darkness uncloaked the world's essentially hostile
nature, and brought about only traffic accidents and loss-filled
reflections. In the evenings you stayed at home with loved ones,
hunkered down against the unreliable blackness.

"Take the Escape," Eugene said charitably.

"We'll be fine in the Corolla," Alex said.

After the young parents walked out, Raisa slapped her hands
together. She could have made a sandwich for Maya to take on the
road. Her head was not on her shoulders.

+

The air was humid again, the evening panting out a plush weariness. Maya waited for Alex by the car. He climbed in and unlocked
her door. It's open, she heard dimly from inside. She didn't want to
ride in her son's seat. She wanted Max to come home and take his
seat, to tumble out of the school bus first, even if it meant he never
interacted with the popular children. Damn the popular children.
And the bus drivers who wore sweatpants to work. The fat Italians
everywhere, the polo-shirted men braying about sports teams and
the plucked women in velour zip-ups with immaculate nails.

"Maya?" Alex's face was peering up through the window of the
passenger side. She climbed in.

Alex switched on the air, but Maya kept her window down, the
inside of her palm meeting the night as they drove. She counted
until Alex asked her to roll it up—she was wasting air-conditioning.
She had counted to thirty-seven—he was trying. Acrewood Township finished the day early, even in summer, and by this hour they
passed only the occasional car, otherwise televisions flickering
blue on the other side of air-conditioned curtains, the Valley Hill
mall sewn up in silent languor, the night-covered trees swaying

slightly as they communicated with each other. The town had taken its business inside; Acrewood belonged to the Rubins and their dread. The Corolla ate up the smooth slab of the road. This part of Bergen County had some of the highest taxes in the state, but they went to work; Alex didn't need road signs to know he was in Passaic County because suddenly his tires were bouncing. Maya was comforted by the scratchy gray hide of her seat. Eugene was planning to change this model for an update, with a rearview camera and leather seats; she imagined her skin sticking to the leather, the bad feeling of having to find comfort in clothes too festive and crisp.

"You hear what the brakes are doing," he said.

"What?" she said.

"That huff-huff-huff sound," he said. "Every time that I brake."

"I don't know when you're braking," she said. "I'm sorry, I don't hear it." She stared away at the window.

"I'll take it in," he said. "Though we're well shy of a year." He tapped the inspection sticker. "When you drive it, please—the brake goes down in a glide. Don't jam."

She stared at him, mystified, then looked away once more. They rode in silence.

"Did you really not know about the grass?" he said.

"No," she said, but felt she wasn't believed.

"Nothing's wrong with Max," Alex said. "It's primitive out there, that's all Papa meant. He's going to roll up Max's tent. From the floor to the ground to a haystack like a country idiot—it's a natural progression. I've let my attention wander, Maya. I've been too quiet. I am always trying to please you."

"So you see it the same way," Maya said.

"For my father, there's no gift without a con wrapped around it. You divide what he says by half and subtract, and you start getting closer. He speaks in Fahrenheit, but the truth is closer to Celsius."

"But you don't disagree."

"Why don't *you* disagree with him, Maya? There's a great saying in English: 'A broken clock is right twice a day.' Max is what we make of him. And if there's something sitting inside him—"

"Sitting inside him?" Maya said. "Are you really speaking that way? That's village superstition. The same village that Eugene wants to leave behind so badly."

"Genes are a superstition to you?" he said. "A medical worker?"

She turned away and watched the blue evening scroll by. "I wanted to live in the city, Alex," she said.

Alex grasped the steering wheel at ten and two like a smothering pillow. "Sometimes, I think *you're* my father's child. Both of you love to panic."

"When is it panic and when is it attention?" she said. "You're so certain it's nothing."

"So we are giving it attention. We're going to roll up the tent, and we're going to take down all those masks. Also, it's time to say good-bye to Oliver. I want him to have normal friends."

She was expected to understand what he meant—Oliver had a cleft palate; for Alex, this meant that Max's best friend was a cripple, marked by ill fortune.

"You're his father," she said. "Why don't you tell him that he's no longer allowed to see his one friend because he doesn't look like a child in a greeting card? You want me to do it."

"Why does our son have only one friend?" Alex said.

"Maybe he's not normal," Maya said vindictively.

"What does that mean?" Alex demanded, distaste in his voice.

"You said why can't he have normal friends," she said.

"I didn't say that," Alex said. "He's not normal or abnormal. He's what we make of him. And when he goes to play with a boy who looks like a—you know, I wish Oliver all the health in the world—"

"Alex, do you really think Max will walk through the door as long as we decide to get rid of Oliver?"

"No, you're going to find him on that bus," Alex said acidly.

Embarrassed, Maya turned away and stared out the window. She counted the lights that craned over the roadway. The earth did not begin to rise until you got well north of Acrewood—some parts of the state rose to three thousand feet; Eugene skied there every winter, e-mailing Alex, Maya, and Max photographs of himself, ski-suited and goggled like an Austrian, and of his wife, set up by the lodge fireplace with a book and a sour-apple martini—but even in Acrewood you had an intimation of approaching foothills. The Corolla climbed a short hill; a row of streetlamps came into view; Maya counted them until the road dipped again; and they disappeared once more.

2

1992

As in all such stories, Alex and Maya almost did not meet. Alex, just a year out of college, was living in south Brooklyn with his parents. The Rubins had been in the country more than a decade, Eugene already pressing pickles and jam on the American public (these Turkish, but with the dissolution of the Soviet Union two months before, the time was ripening for inroads into their former homeland). Alex was with his friend Dima, who lived on the Upper West Side, a year older and Russian, meaning not Jewish, which made Alex want to know how Dima's family had gotten out, and years before the Rubins too, but Alex never asked. They played hockey in Riverside Park every Saturday with a spontaneous assembly of Russian programmers and restaurant Hispanics. That day, Alex watched their train roll past the 110th Street subway stop and turned questioning eyes on Dima. "I left my lucky puck at Maya's," Dima said idly, setting off in Alex a customary irritation at his friend for dispensing information as if to an employee. "You'll get to meet her, finally." Dima picked his nose.

Can't play hockey without pucks. Alex had played once in Minsk using a rubber ball, which bounces rather than slides, becoming much easier to miss, but the aluminum hockey stick keeps slicing through the air until its toe lands in Alex's astonished mouth, excavating two incisors, leading Alex's mother, Raisa, to burst into the bathroom, where Alex stands under a hot shower tonguing the new grooves in his mouth, and demand to know whether the boy who hurt him was Jewish, and only upon being told yes he was Jewish does she relent and return to the kitchen to cry into her fist instead of rushing into the yard to avenge her son. And Alex understands for the first time, a six-year-old, the value of pragmatic deceit, for the boy was not Jewish but he had hardly designed to hurt Alex.

Outside, in the yard, where older boys sometimes appear demanding last names, which helps them determine who to beat on for sport, Alex must pretend he isn't a Jew. He has a Russian Orthodox last name ready just in case, and God help his friends if they raise their eyebrows when he offers it. Meanwhile, here in the apartment, Alex must lie in the opposite direction and insist to his mother that those who abuse him out there *are* Jews, so she doesn't embarrass him by flying outside with a broom. These are important, heavy, turgid lessons for a six-year-old mind. The two front teeth grow back, though one grows back crooked, and sometimes Raisa props open her son's mouth so that she can try to force its edge straight with the pad of her thumb, saddling her son with a complex—otherwise he grows up to have white teeth, veined arms, perfect skin—until Maya Shulman tells him that it is her favorite part of him, that one renegade tooth in pursuit of its own ends, and when she learns the English word *snaggletooth*, it becomes her nickname for him, which annoys him because it highlights the flaw, so she gives it up.

A puck—it is nothing, but to Alex it is a lead pulley on his heart, the things that lovers leave in each other's homes to say: Part of me lives here now. And so Alex declines to accompany Dima upstairs, to press his face even more tightly against the window of the joy in which others live; it is enough to hear his mother wonder when a girl deserving her Alex will finally appear in his life, which is an acceptable way of asking Alex when he will finally bring home a girl deserving of his mother's attention. Alex is all of twenty-three. His American friends are at work on their careers, or on the girls who frequent their neighborhood bars, but none have marriage in mind. But Alex—Minsk Jew, a Rubin, only son—checks a different timetable.

Dima badgers his friend to come upstairs. His friend says that if he joins Dima, Dima will take forever, but if he remains downstairs, Dima will feel guilty for staying upstairs too long. But if you stay downstairs, I might get distracted by my girlfriend and stay even longer, Dima says, emptying another vial of despair into Alex's heart. Dima's girlfriend, Maya, is hosting some kind of dinner—she cooks, that's her thing, she's always at the stove, dipping and measuring—and so she'll be busy, in any case. *It's freezing out here. Come on.*

As Alex walks with Dima into the vestibule of the building, the lead pulley briefly lets go because how can Dima abscond to a hockey game if Maya is in the middle of preparing a dinner? Is Dima not expected at dinner? Is Alex to take this as a sign of intimacy (Dima and Maya are so flawlessly united that they hardly have to perform kindnesses for each other), or of subdermal friction? Alex notices himself wishing for the latter despite never having met Maya.

As they ride the elevator to the sixth floor, the smell of urine filling their nostrils, Alex observes that Dima's girlfriend did not have to leave Kiev if she wished to live in a building whose elevator smells like urine and rumbles like it is about to snap off its cables. Dima reminds his friend that his girlfriend doesn't have a father in imports; she's in the fourth year of a four-year college visa, and her parents are now jobless because what was up is now down in Kiev, Ukraine, two months after the Soviet Union's offed itself. Her father has found several hours a week tending a boiler in the basement of an infectious-diseases hospital—that's it. Chastened, Alex asks informational questions: How old are her parents? What will Maya do when the school year is finished? Dima shrugs: Go home. She can't obtain a visa extension? Alex insists, his sympathy now engaged alongside his guilt, a powerful pairing. Dima shrugs. He hasn't thought about it, it seems, and again Alex marvels at his friend.

But then Dima's face casts aside the heaviness forming between them. "You're such a burden of gloom, Rubin," he says, a loving sneer on his face. "Don't make me regret asking you up." And as the elevator completes its ride to the sixth floor, its bell emitting a tired, old-fashioned peal, Alex thinks that this is why he keeps close to Dima, even if Dima doesn't know it and even if there are things about Dima that set Alex on edge—he envies the way Dima can gently unburden any load (onto the ground, onto Alex's shoulders). And just walk off. And just walk on.

On Maya's landing, they are assaulted by a screech from somewhere on the floor, adding to Alex's sense of having left Manhattan for a dismal high-rise in a muddy Ukrainian city. Alex is hard-pressed to name the animal; the cry is strangled, a last appeal from a besieged corner. A half minute passes and they hear it again.

"They raise parrots for kid parties," Dima nods across the hall, then shoulders open the door to 6E.

Following Dima, Alex steps from a cold, dusty stairwell with a burned-out lightbulb into heat, aroma, and light. The aroma is familiar: Alex's Belarus and Maya's Ukraine cook the same things, only call them by different names. Alex makes out onions, garlic, vegetable oil. He even sees a cloud of steam roll out of the kitchen doorway as if belched by a dragon. He thinks uncomfortably of the parrot once more, and as if on cue, another shriek—drawn-out, lordly—reaches them from the hallway.

Even though the hallway is lit up, the kitchen is dark, and from its doorway Alex can make out only the silhouette of the girl at the sink, her ear jamming the crescent of a telephone. She wears black gym shorts and a man's A-shirt, Alex jealously wondering is it Dima's, and only one of her feet is solid with the floor, the other inclined as if she is about to lean for something. *Znayu, znayu,* she says to the other end of the line, stifling irritation—"I know, I know"—as the pot in her hands bangs the walls of the sink. The kitchen has been ravaged: Every inch, including the floor, is taken up with used pots, used cooking utensils, used cutlery. As Maya talks, a cigarette finishes smoking itself in a tin plate on the windowsill. The window is cracked open, and the cold air eats a little ash off the cigarette with each gust, scattering it on the linoleum. Alex wants to walk over and ash the cigarette.

On entering the kitchen, Dima heads for the fridge without even greeting Maya. Alex's heart swells at this encouragement: There is distance between them. But then Maya, also not turning to face them, in fact initiating a new round of assurances of the person on the phone, snaps her fingers by the back of her thigh, where Alex is only happy to look. There, on the edge of the kitchen table, between an enamel bowl and a cutting board heaped with what looks like cured pork, he sees two sandwiches and a thermos. Despite her chaos, Maya has made them food and something warm for after the game. Alex's heart falls. She and Dima do not even need to say hello, they are so close with each other.

But Alex also feels an agreeable warmth: Twenty minutes before, when he was hurtling uptown in a subway car, when Dima's girlfriend Maya was as meaningful to him as a deli cashier, her mind was on him as she fixed him a sandwich. No, not him—some friend of Dima's named Alex—but that was him too, wasn't it?

Dima knocks over his daydream: He walks to Maya, palms the sandwiches, *leans down to kiss the back of Maya's thigh*, and, still not having exchanged a direct gaze with his girlfriend, brushes past Alex on his way out of the kitchen.

Alex's discouragement is so absolute that he is surprised even more than Dima when he says, to Dima's back, "We should stay." In the hallway, Dima hoists his hockey bag back onto his shoulder and gives his friend a confounded look. Alex repeats, his heart pounding: "She needs help." Dima regards Alex impatiently. "Let's *go*," he says. "We'll be late." "*Dima*," Alex savors his objection. "She needs help."

Maya has clicked off her call, and listens to their conversation with amusement, a little insolent like Dima's. "So help," he hears Dima say in exasperation. "I have a hockey game." And with that Dima waddles through the door, the hockey bag banging the doorjamb, and Alex and Maya are left alone.

Alex's mind rushes to take hold of the events just elapsed because he has been no less of a bystander to them than Maya. In better light, she is pretty, but not so pretty that Alex must hide his crooked tooth while speaking. Her face is young, too young for twenty-two, two little coals blinking out of it with mockery and surprise, two brows that would make an Armenian girl proud, one pigtail. Typically, the Russian girls to whom Alex is introduced by his mother cause a mixture of itchiness and despair, so why this behavior now? For Maya is one of them—the enamel cooking bowls, the row of house slippers by the front door, the grandparent photos on the living room mantel all prove it. But the Russian girls Alex has met have been brought to him by his mother like a bird dog trudging back with prey in its mouth. This girl Alex has found on his own. But he didn't find Maya on his own. She's Dima's girl-friend. He remembers Dima—when he walked out the door, he walked out of Alex's mind—and a sweat starts at his hairline.

Maya breaks through the glazed silence. "They say the mark of a professional chef is not the food that he makes, but how many dirty dishes he leaves," she says. She flicks an empty measuring cup off a chair, flour scattering from its edges; plops down so that Alex sees her thighs flutter in answer, a long blue vein running down one of them; plucks the cigarette from its tin nest on the windowsill, and draws hungrily only to find it long dead. She waves it at him and nods cynically: See? Even the cigarette's dead.

"Well, you're not a professional chef," he says, meaning to soothe.

"Oh, no?" Maya says, stretching out her legs and wriggling her toes. He marvels at her lack of self-consciousness in front of a new person. "That was the idea."

Alex stares, puzzled. "You're in college," he offers hesitantly as evidence.

She confirms this with a dark dip of her head. The pigtail slides over her shoulder. "I'm in college," she affirms. "But I don't want to be a doctor in Kiev. I want to be a cook in New York."

Alex isn't sure what to say. Short, stubby, smiling Mexicans cook; the Hispanics with whom he and Dima play hockey cook;

not underweight girls. He imagines telling his parents that he is dating a girl who cooks on a line, sweat on her neck and grease on her forearms.

"A cook of what?" he inquires. "Ukrainian food?" he jokes.

"Why not?" she says, and Alex gets his first glimpse of Maya sans playfulness. "To us it's familiar, but the Americans don't know it. There are two Ukrainian restaurants in Manhattan, both like you're eating boiled shoe lost in corn oil. Imagine a place with a cool feeling, like a lounge instead of your grandmother's house, cool art, like maybe Gogol's face in neon. Café Gogol." She lets this sink in, then adds: "Maya Shulman, chef." She is so taken by the fantasy that the distress temporarily vanishes from her face and she snatches up the used cigarette and tries to smoke it once more. Once more apprised of its uselessness, she flings it into the sink with a bruised irritation that makes Alex want to touch her shoulder. Suddenly, Maya throws herself to the linoleum and starts sweeping up ash and flour with the side of her palm. Somewhere beyond the front door, Alex hears the parrot again.

"So you're not going back when the school year is over?" Alex says hopefully.

"I can stay for one extra year," she says from the floor, "but only in my major. In a medical job."

Alex can't quite make sense of the information. Café Gogol? Setting aside the visa issue, where does she plan to get the money for something like that? A café, like a seedy boulevardier in a second-rate town in southern Russia, whiling away the day between too many coffees and too many cigarettes at a front table done up in fake marble in pathetic imitation of a Parisian café? Actually, for a man, the role is more or less imaginable, but for a woman? Alex smiles at Maya in embarrassment, hiding his thoughts. He feels relief, too: This silliness makes her less daunting. Then Alex chides himself: She is new to the country, how can she know? Wanting to be kind, he changes the subject.

"So you keep cooking, and I'll clean," he says. "What's the occasion, anyway?"

"Are you hungry?" she says.

"It's true, he left with both sandwiches."

"Let me show you the apartment. I can't show you the other girls' bedrooms, but the living room has nice windows."

The obligatory walk through the premises: a Soviet habit. Following Maya out of the kitchen, Alex for some reason imagines himself in his mother's home when *she* was twenty-three, just a year before Eugene Rubin walked into her life. A shamefully obvious notion follows: *Once, my mother was my age.* Alex tries to picture Raisa as a young woman but can't, even though he has been shown many pictures in many albums; Raisa's present rolls and tiers insist on the view. Attempting to do the same with his father, all Alex can conjure up is Eugene at his present age, fifty, crouching; that is the way Alex manages to translate him to a younger size.

After the tour, Alex obliges with a taste of Maya's *grechanniki.* When the patty—ground pork and chicken mixed with buckwheat and stewed carrots, a peasant's meal—meets his tongue, he stops speaking and closes his eyes. His mother does not make *grechanniki,* but he does not need the direct comparison. The comparison is between someone who plays hockey in Riverside Park and the great Slava Fetisov. After Alex is finished stuffing himself (Maya has to ask him to stop so something is left for the table), they work. Alex stands at the sink, soapy to the forearm, and she bustles behind him, next to him, under him. The kitchen is so terribly cramped—at one point, Maya sets up a cutting board on the floor—that no movement leaves her more than a foot from him, and from this he takes solace even though he knows he shouldn't. He tries to keep his eyes on the caked Dutch oven in his hands, but he can hardly ignore the appearance of her mouth just inches from his thigh, all the skin her shorts and A-shirt fail to conceal (it's

twenty degrees outside but a hundred in the cubbyhole kitchen),
the way house slippers stay on her feet as they never do his.

"Whom is the dinner for?" he asks again.

"A friend has a friend who puts money in restaurants," she says,
sending a pan of beef chuck de Gaulle into the oven, briefly envel-
oping Alex in a fogbank of heat. Alex wonders about the purpose
of such an investment if she has to go home in three months, but
keeps quiet.

"Are you worried about things back home?" he says, not wanting
to remind her directly of her impending return. Nor himself—if
he does not speak of it, it does not have to be real, at least for the
duration of this visit. And while the visit has to end, it will not do
so for a very long time; there is still so much to be done before
dinner is ready and the kitchenware has been cleaned. Never has
Alex been such an enthusiastic, deliberate washer of dishes.

"It's no longer home to you?" Maya says.

"It's different for you," he says. "We left without a return ticket.
There was a day two years ago after which I've lived more of my
life here than there."

"That doesn't mean anything," she says, and Alex hesitantly
admits a reservation into his moonings about Maya. He doesn't
like the declarative way that she speaks, so flauntingly indifferent
to his opinion.

"Do you want to return, then?" he retaliates.

"My parents are there, of course I want to return," she says,
then curses because her thumb has landed on the handle of a hot
pan. Alex half turns from the sink with intention to minister, but
she waves him away, sucking hungrily on the finger. "But I have
a devil in my head about cooking," she says through the finger in
her mouth. "I'm trying to fuck up as much as I can, so he leaves
me alone."

Alex turns back to the sink in a welter of disagreeable thoughts.
He isn't accustomed to crass words from the girls he dates. Then
a new thought finds him once more: When Maya is not overly

declarative, she is overly self-deprecating. He doesn't intend to exploit this weakness, or even mention it, but it makes him feel less cornered.

"How did it start?" he says like a doctor filling out a chart.

"Maybe two years ago. Around the time you became an American. There was a festival on campus with local restaurants. All the chefs were wearing that white hat that French chefs wear. Every chef was a guy—except one. Her face was flushed to the roots of her hair. She had these hands—cut, burned, bruised. I just stared at them. They were beautiful. I felt like a twig next to her. If I saw her on the street, she would have struck me as a questionable woman. But there . . . She was magnificent. She was nice—she asked me if I cooked. I said not really—just dinner, you know, what my mother and grandmother taught me. Not, like, for people. And she said that if I was willing to spend one year practicing, she would come and eat at my house in one year."

Alex pauses, his hands around a patch of steel wool. "*That's* who's coming to dinner?"

"Not exactly," Maya says. "She can't make it, but she is sending a friend. The friend who buys into restaurants."

Alex whistles admiringly. "Not bad," he says. He can't resist adding: "Dima's missing quite the experience."

"Oh, he'll be back for the meal," she says. "He'll hold court. I cook, and he'll seduce with his talk."

"That doesn't annoy you?" Alex says cautiously, then berates himself—there is no cautious way to make a comment like that. He's overstepped, and tenses against Maya's comeback.

"Annoy me?" she looks up. "What, that my boyfriend knows how to talk?" Alex feels as if the word *boyfriend* has been flung at him like a rock. The compliment to Dima's charisma is a second rock. "Or that his best friend is helping me with the most important meal of my life while he's off playing hockey?" Again, the insolent smile is up on her face. It occurs to Alex that he is hopelessly literal. What law says that people say what they mean, that insolence means displeasure and politeness means fondness? It does in Alex; Alex feels as if his true intent is always inscribed on his face; it is why he strains so mightily to trap the surge of his feelings, why he never argues with Dima, why he goes along with Raisa's plans for his future. But perhaps others work differently. It strikes him that Maya has referred to him as Dima's best friend. That is news to Alex. He has learned and thought of so many new things in the hour he has spent with Maya. If that kind of person isn't deserving of his desire, who is?

"That's Dima," she answers herself. "You can't make a dog fly. He's wonderful. He's just Dima."

Until now, Alex has been torching himself trying to figure out how to finagle an invitation to remain through dinner. But after this comment, he wishes only to leave because all the trying in the world can't help Alex if Maya *does not mind Dima's flaws*. After Alex concludes his shift at the sink, the light outside growing dim even though the clock is only at four, he excuses himself even though Maya calls him crazy—he's not her charwoman; after everything he's done, he needs to stay for dinner, at least. *At least?* he thinks with a bitter hopefulness. No, he doesn't require charity. In fact, he is craving the cold sting of the outside air. He wants to slide his hands into his pockets and watch his breath unfurl out of his mouth as his cheeks turn the color of radishes. He wants to shriek like the parrot. This he knows how to do.

But he surprises himself again because—against his own wishes, in thrall to the movement of his hands, even as his dignity protests—he calls her the next day to find out how it went. And she surprises him with a delight at hearing his voice that he—even correcting for the fantasies that kept him awake, masturbating into his boxers while Eugene and Raisa slept on the other side of the hallway—can't write off as pure politeness. She owes him for helping; how can she make it up? No, no, he says unconvincingly. And then she says: "I want to see you, you idiot." He feels light-headed.

"But how did it go?" he says sleepily, inebriated with her. "I don't want to talk about it," she says. And that way it begins.

At first, not knowing how to square his desire with his guilt, Alex accommodates both: He proposes to cook dinner for his friend Dima and Dima's girlfriend Maya at his parents' house. You're going to do what? Dima says. Alex ruins everything, belatedly marveling at the obliterating sway of his infatuation: He thought he could impress Maya in a category at which she excels and he has not even attempted. They chew stringy rabbit as Alex ruminates on the spectacular way in which he has gratuitously kneecapped his aspirations. Dima makes fun but Maya neither makes fun nor pretends the meal is a success. She explains that everyone eats chicken instead of rabbit because rabbit is so lean; you can abandon a chicken in the oven for an hour, but a rabbit you have to bathe like an infant. Daydream for a minute, and you're dealing with tough meat. Alex does not tell her that he spent many moments at the stove daydreaming. Alex feels an alliance with Maya against Dima—an alliance of rabbit specialists, but he'll take what he can get. If you want, I'll show you another time, Maya says. He wants.

And so it goes until it has gone so far one has to pretend otherwise. Alex passes many nights mashing his pillow as he tosses and thinks about Dima. What was brazen then is timorous now. But somehow he holds on, powering blindly from he doesn't know what reserve. He alternates between avoiding Dima's phone calls and not letting Dima alone until Dima will allow himself to be treated to dinner (out, not with Alex at the stove), though when they are finally seated Alex is surly and distracted. Because Alex can't leave Maya alone, he can't leave Dima alone. His friend laughs—Alex has not wanted to see so much of him since they saw each other every day in junior high school.

In the mornings, Alex makes commitments; he will exert discipline and refrain from contacting Maya. Some days his resolve makes it all the way into evening. He's furious with himself; in college, he could make himself sit with schoolwork night after night, but that willpower has vanished. Maya doesn't help him because she doesn't say no. What was insolent then is solicitous now. Yes, she can come visit him for lunch at the investment office where he works. They go to a nearby park with sandwiches and a milk bottle that contains watermelon juice mixed with vodka, and push pins up and down a game board. Alex has always found board games asinine—until now. So this is how you fill the tyrannical hours: You play board games with the person you like (love?). This is what happens when Maya comes around—her presence kneads the unease inside him until it shapes into insight. His brain, formerly lake, turns to river.

He does not return to the office until three, four. He weathers the eyes of his supervisor, tastes spiked watermelon on his tongue, squints at his desktop. And where is Dima right now? he wants to ask Maya before they say good-bye at the park. He does not. He wants to kiss her. He does not. And even though she was first to confess some kind of interest—*I want to see you, you idiot*—she does not, either. In this department, Maya remains old-fashioned. In fact, she remains with Dima. If she is interested in Alex, why won't she break up with Dima? It follows that she's not really interested in Alex, merely drags him along for amusement—she's not solicitous, after all, but insolent like before, and cruel, too. He's drunk. Alex experiences hours-long bouts during which Maya is a subject of resentment, anger, derision. Then he calls her.

Alex and Maya are in Battery Park. Only three weeks remain until her return to Kiev, where the first flowers are coming in according to her impatient mother. Alex has volunteered to show Maya a corner of his city he himself does not know. It's May, the sailboats and weekend cruises are out on the rippling brown felt of the Hudson, yellow-beaked birds seen only in the coastal parts of the city wander about, the spring's last wind rustles the line of lindens flanking the water, and the season's progress is marked by the diminution of clothes on the wearers.

"This is New York," Maya sighs. She is participating in the diminution: a sleeveless dress, white with blue flowers, cinched together by a tan belt the width of a finger. It sits on her stork frame like a wall hanging. And yet, he desperately wishes to reach out and touch the sharp hip that sometimes comes through the fabric. His chest rattles: three weeks. Will they really leave each other without remarking on what's happened between them? Because something has happened, hasn't it? For Alex, life after college—adulthood—can be summed up as: knowing less every day. So if someone were to take him by the hand and gently explain that it was all some kind of misunderstanding, he would be surprised, but not very surprised. A part of him craves the humiliation. He will return to his corner—with clarity now, without illusions. Safe in having volunteered but not been called up.

Alex fears Maya. He wants her to leave Dima, but doesn't that mean she would leave him if someone else came along? Isn't the very thing that Alex loves about Maya—a year out of college, Alex was beginning to sink into a slumber he couldn't understand, though he knows it has to do with his parents, the life that awaits him, himself—the thing that is going to take her away from him when the next adventure appears? To be reassured that Maya consists not only of impulse but bedrock, mustn't she remain Dima's girlfriend? He recalls with jealousy the condolence he felt for her during their first encounter. In the cramped kitchen, agitated with cooking, cigarettes, and cold air, Maya would say something strange and Alex would pity her. (His parents, as always, his invisible audience: "Would you listen to her?") That reaction to Maya seems unimaginable now, like a language lost over the years. But the years have lasted only three months. His mind refuses to work itself into a pattern.

"You like it here," he says finally, trying to release his shoulders, trying to make himself stop.

"I miss my family," she says. "But once you've seen this, it's hard to long for Kiev."

"And what's this?"

"Energy. Movement. Possibility."

They wander in silence. Maya has taught Alex to love silence. Confronted by it, he had used to rush to say something. Now, he relishes silence as much as his pride at relishing silence.

"What happened that night?" Alex says. Maya has never brought up the dinner that took place the day that they met, Alex assumes because it was a failure; otherwise, would Maya be leaving? Alex has resisted his curiosity about the details, not wanting to embarrass her, and feeling proud of his self-control. Then he wonders if the reason all along was that he hasn't wanted to hear what a charmer Dima was at the table. And Maya would say so. Maya speaks as if she hasn't bothered to consider how the information might feel to the hearer. It's one of the things about her that Alex finds frightening. Alex says, "It's cold outside," and everyone Alex knows says: "Sure." Maya says: "No, it's warm." Why does he love this person? Does he *love* this person?

"The guy said he would invest if I slept with him," Maya says.

Alex stops in place.

"Take it easy, Alex," she says, biting her lip. "I'm joking." However, there is no play in her face. Slowly, his shoulders ease up, a look of tight-lipped embarrassment replacing his anger.

"I guess I'm grateful he came," Maya says. "His name was Truman—like the president. He drank the vodka and ate the food—he put away everything, the plates were empty. He talked nonstop. About this restaurant and that restaurant, and June—the woman chef. They'd had an affair. She was the only not-beautiful woman he'd slept with, because she was that good, meaning in the kitchen. He said these words at my table. No one else spoke except Dima. He and Dima, he and Dima—just shouting at each other in this happy, drunk way. At first, I was happy because I thought Dima was warming him up, but soon I realized they'd both completely forgotten why we were there. They kept pouring glasses for each other, but not for anyone else. The rest of us just sat there. I lost my appetite. The guy got so drunk we had to load him into a taxi. *I* had to—because Dima was like a block of stone on the sofa, drunk himself. I never heard from him again, Truman, I mean. I was too embarrassed to call June. I'm glad I didn't. This entire idea—I'm embarrassed to think of it. You're the only nice thing that came out of that day, Alex."

Now Alex is livid at himself for not asking about the dinner a month, two, three months ago. Maya's story makes him want to ask so many questions, issue so many apologies, direct toward himself so many chidings, that he makes the heroic decision to do none of it. He doesn't think, he acts. He is dizzy with fear because his hand is reaching out to touch Maya's hip. Because as it lands there, he feels under his fingers and the flimsy ply of her dress the outline of her underwear and how tightly it presses into her skin. And he imagines the pink grooves left on the skin. And he imagines the skin.

She doesn't recoil, and this restores some of his confidence. No matter what, he thinks, he will always be grateful to her for having elicited *this*. Even if she tells Dima, *this* can't be taken away. Whatever Alex was beginning to sink into before he met Maya doesn't matter because she's pulled him out. That's why he loves her. Yes, he loves her.

"I was wondering when you would finally . . ." She trails off.

"I am finally . . ." He repeats her words, because it is all he can do. She laughs. This laugh is the nicest thing ever to happen to him. The hip, the laugh, the sun—he feels ransomed. The day burns with a dull roar.

"I am leaving in three weeks," she says with the resignation that was one of the first things Alex noticed about her. He envies her weariness, the certainty even if the certainty is in disappointment, at the same time as he wishes to destroy it, to replace it with delight. He has seen Maya express irony, and cynicism, and humor, but never delight.

"I thought you would say something about Dima," he says.

"I am leaving in three weeks and something about Dima."

"You don't have to leave."

"Do your parents have friends in the visa section?"

"Then let's spend three weeks together."

"You are charming, Alex. And I like you. But I am not going to break Dima's heart for three weeks with you."

"Would Dima's heart break?" Alex says.

"You're right," she smiles. "But still."

He ignores the sting of the rejection. The sting of—brazen, truth-telling Maya, too mindful of Dima's feelings to hurt them. But what about Alex's?

"Dima is not a Jew," Alex says savagely.

She laughs and looks at the water. "It's true, I would like to marry a Jew. But Dima and I are not going to get married."

"But you and I can get married."

His statement is so foolish that he snorts out a terrified laugh. Maya, however, does not laugh in return. Her amusement is now anger. The muddy water sparkles like soda around them. Maya turns and strides away. In this one way—he is a citizen, she is not—the discrepancy in their power is so implacable that Alex's flaunting of it is heartless. The power of the powerful is tricky that way; truly, power is with the needy and meek. Unless Alex means it, of course. Does he mean it? Alex's head swells with the possibility that he means it. It is the first great achievement of his life—his and his own. He hurtles after Maya, imploring her to stop.

She stops. The corner of one eye fills with a tear, which makes him notice that she is wearing eyeliner. He has never noticed makeup on her; it's one of the things he's loved about her face without knowing it. Her face is not beautiful—he is proud of himself for not requiring beauty—but it does not need makeup. It is Maya's face—that is all that is necessary of it. But she has put on eyeliner because she was meeting him and she wanted to appear attractive to him; otherwise, why do women apply eyeliner? And as she pushes past him again, it is this detail—eyeliner!—that fills him with the recklessness to leap onto one of the benches lining the stone wall that borders the water. He has never done such a thing, and he will never do it again.

He has to find his balance because the planks are loose. It is quite a worn-out pedestal from which to make the announcement he is about to make, the bench's original paint flaking under his boat shoes. Alex shouts to the walkers of Battery Park that *he has just asked that girl to marry him.* At these words, Maya stops walking. *And she can't make up her mind. I want her to know what you think.* Maya spins around and regards Alex with an incredulity bordering on contempt.

The walkers have stopped. Explanatory whispers go around— that boy, that girl. The observers form a half dome now, encircling Maya and Alex at the stone wall that borders the Hudson. Maya Shulman is not too shy to break through and walk away, but she does not walk away. She stands and stares at Alex Rubin. She watches Alex leap off the bench and stride toward her. As he does, the members of the semicircle around them forget themselves; their mouths crinkle in wonder; in expectation, they rustle like the lindens about them. Alex walks up to Maya and places his hands on her back, touching surely now. The back of her dress is buttoned instead of zippered and his fingers graze Maya's skin. It is unfamiliar skin; it is warm from the sun; he feels a birthmark. He wants to get to know this skin very closely. Then he places his lips on Maya's. The low hum of the watchers erupts into shouts and applause; they have received the show they have stopped for. This is New York.

When Alex takes his lips from Maya's, she wears the same expression of scornful disbelief that she wore in Battery Park three months before. This time the dress she wears is organdy and tulle. The groom's mother bustles around the well-wishers and newlyweds trying to understand whether she feels relief or alarm, and casting worrying looks at the bride's mother, the only Shulman to cross the ocean because there was money enough for only one ticket and the Shulmans would not take Eugene's charity.

Maya, suddenly eligible to become an American citizen, looks at her mother, who wears a discouraging expression. It is Galina Shulman's first visit to America, but a week of wandering around Manhattan—she has mystified and insulted Raisa by spending her days walking around Manhattan instead of kibbitzing with Raisa at Camp Rubin in south Brooklyn—has made her understand that it is not everywhere that a woman answers an offer of marriage while thinking of more than what she feels for the man. No American has to marry because her country has walked off a cliff, as Maya must, must, *must* now, faced with this opportunity—this poisonous, diabolical opportunity. Diabolical because now how will Maya know whether she said yes to the man or the country? Several months more might have made it clearer, but they did not have several months more. Her visa said June 10, 1992. And she refused to take a medical job. That was her daughter.

If Alex had not come upstairs the day of the hockey game, Maya would have ridden out her remaining months in America with Dima Niskevich, who would have kissed her on June 10 and wished her the best. Then she would have returned to Ukraine and settled back in with her parents. Maya is doing the most practical thing Maya can do for herself. Only that, for the first time in Galina's life, the best thing for Maya has diverged from the best thing for Galina. This is what happens when you let your child leave home. Toward Alex, toward all the Rubins, Galina feels gratitude mixed with hatred. This, as much as her desire to get to know the city that will be her daughter's new home, accounts for why she leaves the Rubins' every morning to take the train to Manhattan. This makes Raisa only more solicitous, which sends Galina into the morning only more quickly.

Under the wedding canopy, Maya watches her mother's marble-faced stare from afar. She does not know her mother to fear, but her mother looks fearful, which makes Maya fearful in turn. For what both women know, but Alex does not, is that his wife—Alex constantly refers to Maya as his spouse even before they've been wed—will apply herself to this marriage with the constancy of an animal. Alex was wrong to imagine Maya as capricious and fickle. What Galina Shulman knows is that insubordination is only another kind of fidelity, and stays fastened as truly. And this is what she fears.

Maya turns back to Alex. Maya thought trying to cook Ukrainian food for Americans was unlikely, but *this*; this is something; the two of them together younger than a single one of their parents. She thinks: Alex, you are like a flower that grows on a barren ledge of rock face five thousand feet up. Down on the ground, where there is water and the elements are more kind, you don't thrive, you become disoriented. You grow where there is not supposed to be growth. You survive there. As the rabbi talks, she makes a prayer of her own—guiltily; to a God she has ignored until now. Let us be tenacious together. Let us be constant in a mutual way. Then she makes herself look once more at the rabbi, and mouths after him the authorized Hebrew words that sound like cries from a pack animal.

3

2012

From the blue queuing stripe of the bus platform, Maya looked back at her husband. Alex watched from the Corolla, as if she were leaving on a long trip for which she alone was eligible. You could come with me, her eyes said, but Alex remained. He did not see the sense in it; she would be asking him to betray himself.

Inside, her ticket extended to the driver, Maya surveyed the bleak collection of passengers. The 748 ran west from New York City into New Jersey and then north to the New York State line before retracing the route back to the city, a round-trip of three hours. Maya had never gone this way, only from Acrewood east toward New York. On weekends, the less mongoloid of the local Italians forced their bulges inside pleated slacks and went in for the theater matinees, each pair of bus seats a microzone of perfume and cologne. (Maya once had the transgressive thought that she could take up a lover in the city and have all the misted-up Joes and Franks on the bus to explain the hint of cologne on her skin.)

Acrewood was on the outer edge of the city's commuter ring; by now in its evening route west, the bus was nearly empty. The few visible faces were of unfamiliar ethnicity and peered at Maya with sleepy, malicious indifference. She was overcome by the rashness of her action, Raisa's prejudice against the darkness and her husband's dissent settling badly in her stomach. She would have been glad to see the Italians now, but at this hour the bus lines belonged to other kinds of riders. She felt the fright in her toes—they flexed inside the sweaty box of her flats—and she looked back at the driver imploringly.

"Will you give me the ticket?" he said. His fingers, in a driver's glove cut off at the knuckles, were on one end of it, hers on the other. She brought up an embarrassed smile and let go. There was something wrong with his other hand, tucked in his lap like a dead bird. Only one finger was a proper finger, the rest cauterized stumps. She wondered if this made him a reliable driver in the nighttime.

"This won't hurt a bit," he said into his ash-colored beard. It was neatly trimmed but had an old-fashioned style, a narrow strip down the jaws. He nodded toward the darkened seats, two weak lines of blue light illuminating the floor. "The drinks cart will be down in a moment. And then our award-winning cuisine."

The weekend buses between Acrewood and New York that Maya took to wander through the city had two kinds of drivers: For the first, transporting passengers between the greatest city on earth and its suburbs was an imposition on talents the driver was now unable to direct toward other endeavors. This sank the driver into a scowling depression; he—often she—declined to announce the stops, apologize for delays, engage the riders.

For the second type of driver, the cruise ship of the bus was on brief furlough from the debased preoccupations of the stationary world. It was time to fly. "Welcome on my bus, ladies and gentlemen," this type of driver said. "I want you to buckle up. I want you to keep your food in your purses and backpacks. I want you to close your eyes." Maya always listened. She closed her eyes and let the sun hit her eyelids through the wide square windows. "What's my name?" the driver said. "Who looked at my name tag? I will give the cost of the ticket back to the winner." Half a dozen shouts raced up the aisles, all wrong. "I want you to notice things, ladies and gentlemen," the driver said. "Open your eyes now. What do you see?" Now nearly everyone shouted, though Maya was too shy: They saw the guy seated in front of them; they saw the Acrewood Park & Ride; they saw the future (always one smart-ass per bus).

By then, the bus had touched off for New York City, and over the alternating rev and sigh of the engine and brakes, the driver, if Hispanic or Caribbean, told them how he had come to America (if he agreed to serve in Vietnam, he would be granted citizenship and allowed to bring his family over); and they listened respectfully. He told them about the wedding he had once had on his bus—the bride and groom had met on it (they asked him to chauffeur them on their honeymoon through the national parks, but the romantic imagination of the New Jersey state bus line ended here); and they laughed. He asked them which town near Acrewood George Washington had temporarily used as his headquarters; and they shouted guesses. "I don't want to tire you out, so last question," the driver would say. "Do you realize the brakes haven't been working since Clifton?" The passengers arrived at Port Authority slightly aroused, a sweat up on their spirits.

Invariably, somewhere around the Turnpike exit, the smart-ass would shout up, good-naturedly, How about you quit yakking and drive the goddamn bus? What this imbecile failed to understand was that he felt invited to make this stupid remark—and was rewarded with laughs—not because he was clever, but because his neighbors felt free to communicate with one another thanks to the yakking started up by the driver. The driver yakked, so they spoke. Creativity where none was required, generosity where none was required: The driver was advance notice of what you could expect on the streets of the city. As the skyline came into view, Maya's brain bristled with all the things *she* would say if she had to pilot the bus toward New York. And when the driver batted the imbecile away humorously—"If I stop yakking at my passengers, it'll be left for my wife, and she made her feelings on that clear a long time ago"—Maya swelled with satisfaction and pride. And then she wondered if the driver was telling the truth.

Frank Sarachillo—on entering the bus, Maya now always looked at the driver's name tag—was clearly this second type of driver, and Maya tried to shelter from the uneasy atmosphere of the bus in this fact. But tonight, she was a different kind of rider. As the bus abandoned familiar territory—for some reason, Maya couldn't imagine Max in any of the neighboring towns; he was farther; she felt it—Maya exercised the full extent of a passenger's privileges, yanking the yellow cord every time Frank announced a stop. When the bus came to a halt, she scrambled toward the tinted windows, startling the sleepers in her way, and searched for her son amid the wan light of the bus shelters, in whose depressing glare she was almost grateful not to discover him. The bus always drove off too quickly. In Ringwood, however, it remained by the shelter even after she had gotten a clear eyeful.

"Would the passenger who wants to get off everywhere come up to the front?" Frank said into his microphone.

"What gives, lady?" Frank said after Maya had shuffled up to the front, sleeping faces stirring resentfully. His face asked if his impression at the nice moment they'd shared at the beginning had to be revised because actually she was a lunatic.

"I'm sorry," she said, stone-faced. "There's . . . it's . . ." She felt tears start.

Frank's eyebrows, of the same gray bristly mix as his beard, slunk together. "All right, now," he said. "Take it easy." The night shift regularly put him in acquaintance with the glitches and flaws of human design, but Maya didn't seem crazy, only despondent. She nodded vacantly, grateful not to be dismissed so far from home, and turned back to her seat.

"Don't pull the cord anymore," he called to her. "I'll slow down at the stops. I'm supposed to, anyway." Maya nodded mirthlessly. At home, riding the bus had seemed zealous in the right way. Was her poor judgment a temporary function of her worry and grief, or were the worry and grief disclosing something about her true nature otherwise concealed by generally benign circumstances? She didn't know how to answer, did not want to.

Soon—Maya tried to keep up her vigilance, but the monotonous run of streetlights, churches, and trees lulled her—the land-

scape took on a different look. Neat lines of vinyl-sided homes gave
way to homes spaced farther apart, and set farther back from the
road, and then unpainted clapboard homes, and then homes that
looked like farmhouses, some with giant red stars on the front, and
then no homes at all, and then she was rolling through an inky-
green blackness without regular streetlights that could have meant
another country, even Ukraine. Around the next bend, forty kilo-
meters from Kiev, Uncle Misha's farm would appear. Maya would
disembark and commence cutting down sunflowers, binding every
dozen with bast and laying each bundle into the bed of Misha's
truck, resentfully driven by him to the open-air market in Kiev, a
city he avoided at all costs.

Only old people lived in the village, the young ones having run
away to the city—except for Misha, who ran from the city. The
family he left behind—his sister, Maya's mother; his parents, lucky
unlike so many to have survived the war—he placated by visiting
one weekend a year, during which he raised a glass to everyone's
birthdays and all the national holidays in one go. He was so tormented by the city's restlessness and pretensions that even his parents, who spent the other days of the year mourning his absence
(two million people Kiev was good enough for, just not Misha),
took pity and sent him away early.

Misha was unmarried. No one asked why, though it was generally
assumed that he would be able to tolerate the constant presence of
a woman no better than that of the capital city. That didn't make
sense to Maya, because while Misha did wander around in an ill
humor when he was in Kiev, muttering about plums and cabbage
and sunflowers through the cigarette in his mouth, it took only one
call of his name by his niece for the weather on his face to disperse.

With each visit, he seemed broader and shorter, as if the earth
was getting a stronger grip on him; he had the same embarrassing
mullet as his draft horse; only one's face, however, was commanded
by a nose in the shape of a pear. The other villagers called him

Mikol, the Ukrainian Orthodox version of Misha. This set his Jewish mother wailing. One day at the farm when Maya was visiting, Misha buried his hand in one of the furrows left by his tractor and stuck an oily lump of chocolate-black earth in her face. "You can eat this soil. If this soil says I am Mikol, what difference does it make?"

Maya had spent with him every summer from twelve to eighteen. "I hope you are satisfied." Maya's grandparents shook their heads at her mother. "She is turning into him. And now you are sending her away to America." And to think, when Maya had first been told she would be spending the summer with Misha, she felt guilty for an unknown error; was her mother trying to get rid of her? And what about their summertime rituals? The TV tower, the Viennese Café, the boxful of glasses they hurled against the brick wall of the garbage terminal, because you needed to hurl something now and then. To her own parents, Maya's mother solemnly acknowledged her dereliction, then sent Maya away all the same.

The Warwick Bus Terminal cut into Maya's recollection with a savage fluorescence. They were at the end of the line. She inhaled sharply. On the 8:37 to Warwick, you'll see passengers you don't see on the weekend matinee buses, and if you close your eyes, the unslacking roar of the engine will lull you into minutes-long vacancies during which no boy is missing. But you will not see your son.

Maya disembarked to look around. Frank followed, lighting a cigarette out of the good hand.

"How long does it wait here?" she said.

"You mean we're going back together as well?" he said.

She urged up a stiff smile; he was trying. They listened to the replacement passengers eating potato chips by the ticket counter, the crinkle of the small plastic bags the sole proving sound of humanity in the night. The terminal was a burp of blue light into the surrounding blackness.

"You want to tell me what's on your mind?" Frank said. He held the cigarettes out toward her. She couldn't remember the last time she had had one. Her first drag produced no special sensation; she remained there, in the parking lot with Frank.

"My son is lost," she said, toe-boxing the pavement. She drew on her cigarette as if it would give her her son. "We called the school. He rode this bus in the afternoon. That's all we know."

Frank looked relieved—about this he could do something. "I'll radio the dispatcher," he offered.

Maya nodded silently, afraid that if she spoke, she would be cut off by tears. "Please," she managed hoarsely.

"I have one," Frank said. "Seventeen. He's not missing, but it feels that way." He stubbed out his cigarette. "I'm sorry—that was flippant."

"He's somewhere around here," Maya said stubbornly. "He likes grassy places."

Frank nodded indulgently. Maya became aware of how shallowly optimistic her words sounded. She felt no especial chagrin, for she really felt what she claimed to feel. He was somewhere around here, near the end of the line, in countryside that looked more like Ukraine than New Jersey or New York.

She had not known that you could have such complete darkness somewhere in New York or New Jersey; she had never been anywhere else in America. Because of a vestibular imbalance aggravated by pressure changes, Maya was unable to fly, and this prevented her from going far quickly; Alex's work prevented them from going far slowly; as a result, she was the one waving good-bye as a taxi took Alex, Raisa, Eugene, and Max to the airport for the Rubins' annual all-inclusive week on the Riviera Maya.

Frank called out for her. The ash was hanging off her cigarette in a barrel. She smiled with deprecation and ground it underfoot. The Warwick Bus Terminal felt like a ship at the edge of the world: a strong wind and it would tip over. "What is it like here?" Maya said.

Frank shrugged and started on another cigarette. "It's a farm town. Up that way is a lake full of bald eagles. On holidays, the wait time between trips is more like two hours, so I drive up there if it's daylight. They've got an itty-bitty type of frog there, it's all over the place."

"You smoke too much," Maya said. "I work in a hospital."

"It would be my tenth if you were allowed to smoke on the bus," he said.

"I'm going to throw out the cigarette," she reported, as if she feared the darkness would take her.

"I am destroying my health, and also a litterer," Frank said, looking down at the butt he had tossed underfoot.

Maya walked to the edge of the terminal. From the well-lit spot where she had stood with Frank, the area beyond had seemed impenetrable, but away from the light it picked up a blue hem that softened the darkness. Maya stared at the crumpled butt in her hand, which sent up a distressed odor. On the other side of the roadway was an embankment that rose several feet above human height. It tilted at an angle that made it seem climbable; several cotoneasters spotted the bank. The roadway was freshly paved; Alex would have been pleased; Maya could not recall one vehicle passing in the time she and Frank had stood smoking, though, surely, some had. It wasn't the swallowing darkness she feared, but her own unreliability; her attention was off.

Maya felt Frank at her shoulder. "I am not sure do you want solitude or company," he said watchfully.

She conjured a weak smile that she hoped showed her gratitude. "I'm just killing time till—" He pointed at the bus. She nodded. She was standing farther from home than she had traveled in years, talking openly with a man she hadn't known two hours before. The order of things was like the thin spots of ice on a wintertime lake. You stepped badly and the cold gleam was around your ankles. This was what Raisa was trying to ward off. Usually, Maya waited out

Raisa's admonitions: superstitions and prejudice. But it occurred to her now that the woman had lived a life, too—had not always been a round ball at the feet of her husband and son.

"When Max was tiny," she said to Frank, "he disliked even to be taken out of the house. When the stroller appeared, he would bawl. My father-in-law said you have to break boys—the outdoors turns little boys into healthy adults. He decorates an office chair fifty hours a week, so I guess he would know. They were sitting out on the deck one time—Max was already a walker, my father-in-law was reading the newspaper—and a swarm of hornets came down over his head. I started screaming and ran for him—and was bitten. My father-in-law reached for him—and was bitten. But Max was not bitten.

"There were other times—we had to put a kind of harness around him so he wouldn't swim out too far in the lake. And every time, you ask yourself: Is that him being a child, or is that him being *my* child? And all the months that have gone by without you remembering, the count goes back to zero."

"I don't understand fully," Frank said apologetically.

"Max is adopted," she said, not looking at him.

"Oh," Frank bounced his head.

"No one knows," she said. "Not even Max. And I just said it to you."

"Oh," Frank said in a different way. "You ask yourself the same questions when you're biological," he said, wanting to help her.

"Yes, but you can answer them," she said.

"I guess so," he said. They stared at the darkened roadway and the bank beyond. "He'll turn up," Frank said with the resentment of someone forced into platitudes.

Maya felt a pain climb up her right arm and go off between her shoulder and collarbone. She was grateful for the sensation— her body at its own work, beyond hers. She wanted to use it. She dropped the butt into the trash can and set off across the roadway. A feeble call rose from Frank. She ignored it.

"Hey!" Frank called out. "Lady. I don't know your name!"

Her nails sank into the dried soil of the bank like a hide. She wanted something, anything, to occupy her hands, which for six hours had flitted between her mouth, her temples, her chest, as if she were restraining organs that wanted to leap out. Up above the lip of the bank, she imagined that her son awaited her in the shallows of some lake like the frog Frank watched on holiday trips. On her touch, the frog would transform into her son, as in the fairy tale. Her son turned into a frog when he left her, and now she would rescue him.

Frank cursed, chucked his cigarette, and set off after Maya, his girth preventing direct forward movement. Some of the awaiting passengers looked up. He looked ready to burst.

The bank shuddered slightly under her hands. She clutched roots and plants—the earth was less bare than it had looked from across the road—and prayed that they weren't poison ivy. The soil crumbled in her fingers like dry bread and lined her fingernails. She felt a sweat start in her groin.

She was surprised to discover herself fit enough to scamper up the bank without great difficulty; her body worked with resentful, creaking eagerness. She felt a deranged thrill. She was nearly up to the brim when Frank arrived at the bank. He stared at it uncomprehendingly.

"Lady," he whispered.

"It's Maya," she called back from her place.

"You're crazy!" he yelled. "What the hell are you going to do?" He affixed himself to the bank like a crab and clung to it, as if this effort alone was noteworthy, and now some mechanism should accelerate him up the incline. He cursed all mothers and began to lumber after Maya.

"Frank, you need to quit smoking," Maya breathed over her shoulder as she scaled the last of the bank, panting happily. Even in the grape-colored darkness, she saw the stains on her capris. There was loose soil between her toes.

"I don't leave the ground," he gasped. "I don't take elevators. I don't fly. I drive the bus and I go home."

"I don't fly either," she called.

There was nothing up above the lip, only a farm field flanked by telephone posts, wires clumping between them; it was divided into furrowed rows of what looked like lettuce and an unmowed segment that looked like pasture, though she saw no animals or fencing. Maya made the outline of a house on the far edge of the field, its windows glimmering like gold icons. It was definitely pasture— she smelled shit. The air was prickly with chill, and goose bumps went up on her skin. She breathed deeply of cow shit.

"Have you lost your fucking mind?" Frank said. He was bent over the top of the bank, wheezing dangerously.

She turned around—from the height of the embankment, the bus terminal was like a settlement on a lower flank of a mountain. She reached down and got a hand under both of Frank's armpits and pulled. He was heavy and her hands slid down his arms until she was within several inches of the maimed hand. Frank heaved into the sweet earth. She moved to close Frank's hands with her own and awaited the feel of the tormented flesh, but he pulled away at the last moment.

Frank coughed painfully. "I have a lunatic on my hands."

"I'm sorry," she said, her brief hilarity gone. "You didn't have to—" She stopped herself from speaking obtusely.

She slipped back to the ground, where Frank was. The smell of shit entered her nostrils more forcefully. She was sitting in the grass like a baby, one foot splayed under the other knee as if she had yet to learn where everything went. She pulled a clump of grass out of the soil with each hand. What kind of grass was it? Her son would know. She had walked ten miles with him to gather the many grasses of New Jersey for science class. He had rained the names on her—fescue, ryegrass, bluegrass, orchard grass, brome-grass, timothy, switchgrass, bluestem big and little, deertongue. They sounded like witch potions, and she felt slightly occult in their wanders through fields with no trails but ample signage against trespassing. "What kind of grass is it, son?" she said now to no one, released the clumps, and fell onto her back. The grass was itchy beneath her, and she tried not to move. A rash of stars disfigured the night sky above.

In the beginning, Max was so foreign to Maya that she regularly imagined slipping, knocking her head, and waking up with the delicious illusion that Max had come out of her. She came closer to this reckless action—that desk corner, this shelf—than anyone knew. Maya had gotten the one child in the universe who slept solidly through the night at twelve weeks. (Raisa rubbed a cognac-touched pinky across the boy's gums before bed for insurance.) And he had gotten the one mother who wished he would wake, bawl, drive her mad. She wanted to roll her eyes in the supermarket with the other young mothers (though her contemporaries were now on their second and even third children). She wanted to clasp her head because she couldn't remember the last time she had slept a full night, make jokes about how people in her condition shouldn't operate machinery or make important decisions. But Maya had received the blessing of remaining clear-minded through her son's flawless adjustment to her home. It was she who was failing to adjust to him. She felt like a nurse, not a mother, and even as such was only moderately needed.

She learned that babies processed breast milk faster than formula and therefore awoke more frequently from hunger, and actually spent an afternoon on the Internet researching surgery to stimulate artificial production of breast milk. She read the testimonies of early mothers like a draft dodger reading the weary but proud reminiscences of war heroes. Officially, it was awful, just awful, but when the milk finally let down, and all those hormones swarmed through the bloodstream—the young Internet mothers had not felt that kind of elevation since high school acid. And their breasts—it was just awful what it did to their breasts. They swelled like melons, like grapefruit, like coconuts, like pumpkins, like squash—the Internet mothers were georgic metaphorists. Maya wanted her breasts to swell, to be strained by their weight. She wanted to whine to Alex about their soreness. Apparently, she had adopted a child to remind herself of all the ways she wasn't a real woman.

Then six months arrived, it was time for more solid foods, and the breast milk predicament was concluded. Maya wondered if this, now, would mean intimacy and attachment; it meant inconceivable boredom. She actually longed to squeeze tits at the hospital. Eugene and Alex had insisted on prolonging Maya's permitted maternity leave, and she resented them for it. A howling emptiness from eight to six—she could not wait for Alex's stories of import battles with Customs—mitigated only by the appearance of Raisa around nine in the morning. Maya's social circle had somehow signed up a mute newborn and a logorrheic mother-in-law, and thrown out what few others it had. Maya imagined that she was slowly becoming Raisa. She was becoming the woman who bustles. She stared at the older woman and asked: What distinguishes me from this woman? We both live in this home, more or less; we both spend the day in the kitchen; we both watch Alex Rubin for signs of distress.

She tried to read books, but it was impossible to focus with Raisa addressing her at five-minute intervals. (The undeclared price for Raisa's helping was full-time interaction.) So Maya researched boredom. The Internet (Raisa was slightly fearful of the Internet and hesitated to disrupt Maya's work at it) recommended the Eastern solution, which was the opposite of the Russian solution. Go deeper into the boredom. Maya could hardly understand what that meant. She sat with her eyes closed and tried to "go deeper into the boredom." Invariably, she imagined boredom as a dreary, wet wine cellar and she just had to keep going deeper into it. Not much came of all this.

Did all adoptive mothers feel this punishment, to remain aloof from their children in some unnameable but undeniable way all because they had not birthed them? If so, how did they bear it? Did they close their eyes to this truth, or persuade themselves out of it? Or maybe this was Maya's affliction alone? Maya could not speak about what she felt to Alex or even Raisa. To the news that a woman who logged so many hours next to the child felt unclose with the child, the Rubins would only purse their foreheads and say: "But you're with Max all the time." Alex cooed to the child when he came home; Eugene shadow-boxed with the tiny bundle in the crib; and Raisa insisted at periodic intervals that Maya hand over the baby. But Raisa preferred to cook and scrub, and the men retreated as soon as they completed their routines. Even when the house was full, Maya was alone with Max.

Maya experienced this as part of the problem—she felt distance with Max because they felt distance with Max—until the afternoon of an otherwise usual weekday. Max was napping. Raisa was scrubbing. Staring into the refrigerator, Maya detected an unexisting need for milk and fresh greens. She only wanted out of the house—anywhere. She asked if Raisa would keep an ear out for Max's monitor and went off in the older Corolla they drove then—to the Russian grocery store she could manage to drive. She was holding two loaves of bread in the aisle. She could have been there for ten minutes or forty. Suddenly, she experienced a ravaging desire to be next to Max. She remained in place—she feared it would vanish when she moved. She needed to touch him, not the loaves. Finally, she dropped the bread to the floor, left her half-filled basket in the aisle, and ran out of the store, as if unsure would he be there when she reached home.

Storming into the house, she was out of breath, her hair half out of its ponytail. Maya pretended she was dying for the bathroom. But you didn't buy anything, Raisa asked her back. It was closed, Maya lied. Instead of the bathroom, Maya went for her son. As she looked at Max, sleeping, she imagined that he knew the truth—

about why she went, why she returned, why empty-handed. He was so solid and strong, her child, the unperturbable sleeper, that he could forgive a mother who found him foreign. And this brought her closer to him. Adoptive mothers seek out explanations that birth mothers do not. Maya's was: She and Max constituted a family of their own—a family within the larger family. They were together, alone.

The Rubins came around. The boy was unique—because the Rubins were unique, because they had crossed an ocean and set themselves up from zero on a new shore, and now they had multiple cars and multiple homes and an import business that might never take authoritative hold of Customs regulations but would cross the million-dollar mark in revenue each year all the same. Approaching Max with shyness and embarrassment, as they had when he was an infant, was a luxury of easier days, when they could afford to indulge their anxieties instead of the family's need for cohesion. The black halo that accompanied Max's arrival in their lives—he wasn't their blood—would never leave their cognizance, but they would save Max from its ever entering his. And this omission—was it not aided by the possibility that here was a recessive gift from the venturesome depths of the family gene pool? While the Rubins would admit to nothing other than delirious rage at the fair-haired Slavs who had made their lives so painful in the Soviet Union, the back springs of at least Eugene's mind purred with satisfaction at having such an unquestionable goy join their team. Next to the Rubins, Max was like a bleached sun crashing through a dark copse. Each of them made their adjustments.

Frank led Maya back to the bus like a grieving widow—the field sloped down to the road about a hundred feet from where they had climbed the bank. She felt his warped fingers at her elbow like a burning spot; the Russian superstition against touching deformity burned it a second time. Because of Maya Rubin, the 10:12 to New York City left with delay. The mounting passengers avoided her gaze from the front seat, where she had been deposited by Frank, dirty and disheveled, her hair sprung from its ponytail, her hair band sacrificed to the climb.

Raisa was right; the night proposed only loss-filled reflections, but what if, in fact, a loss had occurred? Wasn't the night the ideal setting just then? As the bus touched off, Maya said temporary farewell to her son. She slept the entire way home.

4

At Acrewood, Maya felt a palm on her shoulder. The bus was idling, the door open to a better-lit night. "It's Acrewood, isn't it?" Frank said. Drowsily, she roused herself. Her breath was sour and something was aching after being suspended awkwardly for an hour.

"You owe me a return ticket," Frank said. "And laundry services. And a new hip."

She embraced him. He laughed, embarrassed, but then eased into it. "You go ahead now," he said shyly from her collarbone.

"Stop smoking, Frank." She released him and took the stairs down to the ground. It was a day of exiting buses with hands empty. She heard the doors close behind her and felt the smeared pockets of her capris. With great belatedness, she discovered that she had taken nothing—not her bag, nor wallet, nor cell phone. Frank was disengaging the brake, the bus about to roll forward, when she spun around and banged on the glass of the door. Wearily, Frank opened the door.

"Let no one say the bus line is not a full-service operation," he sighed when she told him the reason. He extended a flip cell phone. As she dialed, he spoke an apology into the microphone.

Maya knew what would greet her on the other end of the line—she had sent no word for three hours, her cell phone ringing uselessly in her purse in the front hallway closet. She was rebuked like a schoolgirl, first by Alex, who threw down the phone, then by Eugene, whom she heard exclaiming in the background, and finally by Raisa, who picked up after Alex. Only then was she told that her son had been returned home just minutes after her bus had pulled away from the curb, whereupon Alex's cell phone rang with the jubilant news; whereupon Alex began dialing his wife, only to speak to his mother again once she traced the tinkle of Maya's cell phone to the front hallway closet.

"Raisa!" Maya broke in. "Is he all right?"

"In one piece, thank God," Raisa said. When she was relaying the news of Max's return, she was triumphant, but now a note of hesitation appeared in her voice.

"What is it? Maya said.

"Who does this, darling?" Raisa said. "Eugene said, 'The grandson we found, now we lost the mother.'"

"Raisa—"

"We were mindless with worry."

"You could have called the bus line," Maya said sharply. "Asked them to dispatch it to the bus that I took. It only takes a little imagination. But you would rather sit there mindless with worry."

Raisa, who had been starting to speak, fell silent. "I am not going to pay attention to what you just said because you are upset," she said. "And God knows where you've been."

"I've been looking for my son," Maya said. "Now tell me where he was."

"He was in a river!" Raisa said, as if Maya's willfulness were responsible. "They brought him here like Moses in the basket. Families that have nothing to do with ours keep bringing our boy to us."

"Watch your voice," Maya said.

"He's upstairs in the shower. Alex rushed him into a hot shower." A hot shower—the Rubin remedy for the humiliations of fate.

"What do you mean he was in a river?" Maya said.

"In a river," her mother-in-law repeated. "Facedown in a river. All right?"

"I don't understand," Maya said. "But he's fine. He's fine, isn't he? You said he was fine."

"They got him in time," Raisa said. "I can't make sense of it, honestly."

"That doesn't make any sense," Maya started to say, but Raisa cut her off, her own voice quavering—she did not make a custom of interrupting her daughter-in-law. "Just come home."

Maya saw Frank watching her. Meekly, he pointed at his watch. Maya hung up on Raisa and returned the phone.

"He's at home, just like you said," Maya said feebly.

Frank pressed the horn three times in celebration. Someone yelled up from the back. "I'm going to have a mutiny if I don't get going," Frank said. "You have a ride home?"

She did. Her husband was busy scrubbing down her son in the shower, and her mother-in-law refused to drive in the night, let alone after her daughter-in-law had been so rude. The chore was left to Eugene, and she and her father-in-law suffered a silent quarter-hour as he ferried her back to the house.

+

After an hour-long shower, Max stood downstairs and watched nervously as the adults shouted at each other. Finally he was remembered and stared at nervously in return. Then he was rushed up to bed. No one pressed him with new questions—the Rubins feared they would get answered. As Raisa hustled Max into pajamas upstairs, he stared at the spot outside his window where his tent had stood only that morning.

"Baba," he said nervously. "Can I sleep on the floor?"

"No, little boy," she said as she fought with a sleeve of his pajamas. Under her hands, Max felt as bony as a fish. She regarded him a little fearfully. "Good boys sleep in bed."

Max was left to stand by the wall while Raisa reapplied to the mattress the bedding that had been rolled up on the floor. She did not request Max's help, as if he could not be considered an ally, and he did not offer it. Occasionally, his grandmother looked up from the sheets to make sure her grandson was standing where she had left him. He looked the same: Floppy-haired and semi-translucent. As she worked, Raisa murmured optimistically at the sheets—now, Maksik would climb into a nice and clean bed, and he would dream of camels, and flying carpets, and tents, too, if he wanted, until he awoke the next morning and all the events of the previous day would dissipate like a dream, and probably his mother or father would make his favorite breakfast of farina with bits of turkey sausage, and if they didn't because they were upset with him (he could understand that, couldn't he), his grandmother would.

When Max was wedged into the billows of his blanket—his grandmother had folded its edge under his feet so that he was "in an envelope," just as she had done with Alex when he was a boy— Raisa sat down on the bed and studied her grandson. All Raisa's ministrations were powerless against his strange metabolism; the more she fed him, the skinnier he became. Even at home, Max looked as fragile and unprotected as a pencil, and he had decided to go wandering in the world and lie down in a river.

"Maksik, I am going to ask you a question," Raisa said. "And your only job is to answer me honestly. That's the only thing you have to do, because your grandmother loves you, and lies hurt your grandmother. Do you want to hurt your grandmother?"

Max shook his head.

"Exactly. People who love each other don't hurt each other. It's in the contract." She guffawed sadly at her joke. "Maksik, why did you run away? It's okay for you to tell me. If you don't want to tell your mama or papa, it's okay—as long as you tell me."

Max shrugged.

"When did you think of it? You planned it a long time ago?"

Max shrugged again.

"Max, you're not allowed to say 'I don't know.' Because if you don't know, who knows?"

Max's face was as expressionless as his blanket, which swam with stone-faced seagulls. Raisa could tell she was frightening him.

"I'll let you rest," she said. "But right after you promise to tell me tomorrow. Will you promise me that?"

Max nodded. His grandmother laid her wrinkled lips on the straight straw of his hair and let him be.

After Raisa had padded away on her bunioned feet, the landing in front of Max's room was quiet, only the floor beneath him gently reverberating with the sound of the adults in the kitchen.

"You could have waited until he was back to roll up the tent," Alex said.

"The boy is indulged," Eugene threatened.

Alex's resistance of his father was accompanied by glances at Maya that asked when she was going to pick up the rope of solidarity Alex was casting her despite her irresponsible disappearance. She chided herself for failing this gesture, for sloughing off onto her husband the chore of beating back his parents. She sat gloomily in the corner of the leather banquette by the kitchen table, Alex's cognac two fingers deep in a filigreed drinking glass. Raisa, not feeling bold enough to contradict Maya out loud, eyed her daughter-in-law's choice of seat—those who took the corner wouldn't get married. And Maya eyed her mother-in-law, asking silently why this was worth Raisa's attention when their child had spent the afternoon fifty miles away in a river. When Maya was already married.

Upon entering the house an hour before, Maya had clutched her son to her soiled blouse as if Max was being sent off somewhere, or perhaps she was. They were gently unsealed from each other by a team of Rubins—"Mayechka, he's just had a shower, look at your shirt." But now, showered and changed into sweatpants, the alcohol setting off a buzz at her temples, Maya felt an immobile sedation, not unlike the refrigerator that droned from the wall.

Alex rose and rummaged inside the pantry for an economy cylinder of canned peaches. The others watched him peel it open, envious he had a task. He ladled the contents into four bowls and set them out in front of the others. No one had had dinner. They watched him slurp away.

"These dry your tongue, like a persimmon," Alex said to his

father. "And the juice is viscous. We should go back. Those other we sold were like velvet."

His father shrugged. "And the price was like velvet."

"Can someone please tell me what happened," Maya cut in. "Please."

Eugene and Alex turned to her, remembering she was there. They exchanged looks. Even in her fog, she understood that the question of what to say to Maya had been discussed before her appearance.

"He left school on the bus," Alex said. He pushed away his bowl. "The town bus. The one you rode. Why he got off where he got off, obviously, the woman couldn't say. It's a farm. Her son came in for dinner and said there's a boy in the river. Her son's not all there— our Max knows how to pick them. He's got a scent for the insulted and injured. In any case, she runs down and there's our boy, sitting in her river. Facedown."

"Sitting?" Maya said.

"He says he was counting the pebbles," Alex said.

"What did she say?" Maya said.

"She said, 'I can't promise you your son wasn't trying to hurt himself.'"

Maya's chest filled with dismay.

"It's just the American obsession with insurance," Alex said.

"If she was obsessed with liability, she would've been sure," Maya said. "In the other direction."

"It's like George Washington," Alex said. "She's American, so she can't not tell the truth."

"Don't you want the truth?" Maya said.

Alex looked at his wife—now she would ask questions without an answer? Because he could do the same.

No one knew what to say, so they sat silently. Eugene moved around invisible crumbs on the table, his habit. Alex stared at his clasped fingers. Raisa eyed the sink of dishes with anticipation—it would provide her distraction when it was right to absent herself from the table. Finally, Maya set aside her glass, rose, and walked out of the kitchen, the Rubins following her warily with their eyes, as if now she, too, had become a flight risk, as if during her disappearance she had picked up some kind of microbe that rendered her foreign and incomprehensible. Maya took the stairs to the second floor. Gently, she pushed open Max's door, a triangle of light from the hall entering with her. Max was on the bed, a small hump rising and falling inside the cloud of the blanket.

Maya closed her fist over her mouth and sank softly to the carpet. Worried her son would wake up and see her, she made herself rise and came close to the bed, where she watched Max for a long minute. Hating herself for her lack of restraint, she rustled his arm. His eyes opened quickly, as if he had been awake behind their false curtain. He blinked twice.

"What's happening with you, my child?" she said.

"Am I in trouble?" he said.

"You had us worried," she said. "No, you're not." She took one of his hands between hers. "Are you okay?"

Max blinked, shimmied his lips, and nodded. She took a palm to his cheek. He felt cool, settled. She ran her hand carefully through his hair, wanting to feel its straight spokes under her fingers. The fingers felt hot, and the spokes would be cool. Her son's hair always occurred to her as an outbreak of pine needles, spiky and calm. She felt for the part, on the left side, that resisted every sweep in the other direction. Did Max's father have a part in his hair—this was always her next thought. He had nothing but stubble the time Maya had laid eyes on him. Max's hair reached his eyes—she was going to take him to the barber on Saturday, after Oliver—but she liked it this way. Then she wondered if she liked it because it made him look different from his father. His birth father. She tucked a strand behind an ear.

"Max, why did you do that?" she said. "Why would you go off without telling us?"

"I don't know," he said.

"You have to do better than that, Max. Please. You walked out from school with everyone else."

He nodded.

"And then? How did you end up on the other bus?"

"I walked to the stop. They take us past it when we go for recess. They have brochures with the time that it comes."

"But why, Max, why?" she pleaded.

"I don't know," he said. "I wanted to go away. I was sad."

"But why?" she yelped. She crouched by his bedside. "Why were you sad? Darling, tell me."

"I don't know," he said.

"Oh, Max," she said. "No. No."

"I'm sorry," Max said, and turned to the wall.

"There's one thing you have to tell me," Maya said. "You promise to tell me the truth? What were you looking for under the water?"

He turned to face his mother again. "I was counting the pebbles," he said.

"Why?" Maya said.

"They were pretty. They had different colors. Some of them looked like peas with eyes. Others were bigger—they were like the parents of the little ones. They were all there together."

"But you can't put your head in the water like that, Max. I know you're careful, but even when we're careful, things can go wrong. Do you hear me?"

"I tried to count them without putting my face in, but the water was moving too fast. I can hold air for more than a minute. Papa can tell you. You don't come with us to Mexico, you don't know. If you came with us, you would know."

"Papa comes with you and he's worried," Maya said.

"I don't know!" Max shouted. He buried his face inside his blanket and turned to face the wall once again.

Maya gave up her questioning. The headache that she had been, for hours, too upset to notice finally forced her to notice. She rustled Max's arm again, a soft something under the blanket. He looked back again and they gazed at each other. "Tell me what it was like," Maya said.

Max scratched his ear pensively like an old man, and his face loosened. "There was a boy there who was sick."

"Sick? In what way?"

"He said funny things. Ba-ba-baa."

"Did he scare you?"

"No. I liked him."

"Did you tell him that?"

"No. Should I have told him?"

"I bet he could tell. I bet he liked you, too. You're very likable. I'm sorry I woke you. I'm sorry I raised my voice just now."

"I wish I'd told him."

"Don't be upset that you didn't tell him. I think he knew. Very often, people know what you mean even if you don't say anything."

"Is Papa mad at me?"

"Papa doesn't know how to be mad at you. But if you want to do that again, you have to tell us. If you want, we can come with you. I will come with you, for sure. Maybe I'll like it, too. Can you promise me that?"

Max nodded. She wanted to believe him, but didn't. "If you're sad," she went on, "why not come to me? We'll do something together. We'll cook something fun. And if that doesn't work, we'll get the tent back out when Grandpa is gone. And we'll call Oliver, and have a slumber party. And when one of these things makes you not sad anymore, you tell me, and from then on we'll know how to fix it."

Max didn't say anything, just lay there contemplating her words.

"I'm sorry I woke you," she said.

"I don't mind. I'll fall asleep right away."

"Okay," she said. "Hey, I like your hair this long."

He started rubbing the heel of a palm in an eye. He kept going, and she forced away his hand. "Come on, you'll make it red," she said. But really it was because she was fearful that every strange gesture meant something strange.

"Can I ask something?" he said.

"Of course you can."

"You were the same age as me once, right?"

She laughed. "Yes, I was, baby. Yes."

"Were you like me?" he said.

She reached for his shoulder under the blanket. "I don't know," she said. "I don't remember a lot. My mother—your grandmother—you met her when you were tiny—we spent every day in the summer together. Do you know what we would do? We would go to the department store and buy a box of the cheapest glasses they had. Twenty glasses. Each one had a different fish stenciled on it. Then we dragged this box to the garbage terminal. All the garbage in the city went there. It smelled so bad out there. The men who worked there stopped to stare at us. They were not like regular men—if you worked at the garbage terminal, that meant you couldn't get a job somewhere else. But they weren't mean—just puzzled. They watched as we took the glasses out of the box one by one and threw them at the back wall of the building. They smashed into tiny little pieces."

Max giggled. "Why did you do that?"

"I don't know, honey. But it was fun. You shouldn't do it with any of our glasses, please. If you want to do it, please tell me—and we'll do it together. Because you're just eight years old. My mama wouldn't let me anywhere by myself for another four years. Do you understand? She would have been so upset if I went off on my own. We can do so much—but together. I like so much being with you. Don't you like it, too?"

Max thought, and, as if truly deciding, nodded.

"When we were done—ten glasses, each of us—my mama went and got a broom from one of the men. They laughed into their mustaches. She swept up the whole mess, put it in one of the trash bins, and we left. But when we came back the next year, she brought two boxes and she gave one to them."

Max seemed to be thinking about the story. She sat on the floor next to the bed, watching him.

"Did you ever run away?" Max said.

"No," she said. "But when I was twelve, my mama sent me to my uncle's for a summer. I really didn't want to go. I wanted to be with her."

"Did Papa ever run away?" Max said.

"Not exactly. He was playing in the sandbox with a friend once and two men came up to ask for directions to his school. And he volunteered to take them. He walked them all the way. He was lucky because Grandpa Eugene came outside just in time and asked his friend where Papa was. And his friend said. And Grandpa Eugene raced to the school. And he got there just in time."

"Just in time for what?"

"Just in time for nothing bad to have happened to your father. He was little and he wanted to be nice, but he made a bad decision. When you're little, even if you feel like doing something—even if it's nice—you have to tell your mama and papa. And then it's okay."

Max considered this information. Maya bent toward her son. "Can I ask you something now?"

He nodded and busied himself with an edge of the blanket, turning it this way and that.

"Were you scared today?" she said. "Was it ever scary?" What she wanted to ask was *Did you worry you wouldn't come back to us?* But she couldn't bring herself to ask that.

Max shrugged. "A little," he said finally.

They said I love you and touched nose tips—how they said good night. Maya watched Max close his eyes, as if to reassure herself that, indeed, she had not disrupted his sleep lastingly. She took the steps downstairs, where, upon her entry to the kitchen, the conversation stilled.

"How is he?" Alex said.

"He's okay now," Maya said thickly. "He needs to see a doctor."

"A doctor?" Alex said.

"He doesn't understand if there's something wrong—and why would he," she said. "There's a pediatric psychiatrist at the hospital. A wonderful man, Saltz. They know him around the country."

"And tell him what?" Alex said. "Our son runs off to sit in a river? Take him, take him. He'll tell you that Max suffers from psychotic episodes, multi-personality disorder, whatever you like. He'll put him on—I don't know what it's called, but you know what I'm talking about. Those pills. And then you'll see what fucked-up really means. Your child will never be the same."

"Sasha!" Raisa said. "If you want to use foul language, please wait till I leave."

You never leave, Maya nearly said, but silenced herself just in time. Alex held up a hand in apology.

"I'm afraid to leave things as they are," Maya said. "If not Saltz, we should take him to a psychologist."

"He can look in a crystal ball to see if Max will ever sleep in a regular bed again," Eugene said.

"You keep saying we got a bad deal, Eugene," Maya said. "Should we do something about it or not?" She got out the words, but her appetite for altercation had drifted away.

"So, you want ours to be the family with the boy with the"— Eugene twirled a finger into his temple in a Soviet gesture that meant: not all there.

"I spoke to him very directly," Raisa said. "I think things are going to be very different now."

"A psychologist?" Alex said. "And pay two hundred dollars for forty-five minutes? You're overreacting, Maya. Do you know that expression: 'There are no healthy people, only the undiagnosed'? You go to the doctor, the doctor will find something wrong with you. How else can they make a living?"

"What about Bender?" Raisa said. "Bender might see him for free."

"Bender in Whippany?" Eugene said, incredulous. "Our Bender?" He meant that Bender was Russian.

"You like to find problems in others' proposals," Alex said to his father, "but you have none of your own."

"Boys, please," Raisa pleaded.

"I am so tired," Maya said.

"Go to bed, darling," Raisa said magnanimously.

Maya obeyed. Sometimes, she was grateful for Raisa's mother-like agitation. She mounted the stairs once more, her thighs sore as if she had pedaled and pedaled somewhere, and sat down care-fully on the edge of the bed she shared with Alex. She watched the bedside telephone for a long time and finally lifted it, expecting it to feel unbearably dense in her hand. She listened to the dial tone long enough that it failed and the impatient beeping began. She clicked off and on and dialed Nina Benton, the woman on whose property Max had lowered his head inside a creek. The line rang and rang and she was about to give up when finally the receiver clicked and a distracted voice said hello. Maya checked the clock and felt guilty. It was a farm of some kind; surely they rose early. She apologized and quickly gave her name. The voice on the other end asked her to hold it, and then Maya heard threats about tooth-brushing, stories, and bedtime.

"I imagine the kind of night you're having," the voice came back, now more careful and allied.

"I'm sorry to bother you," Maya said.

"We're glad he's fine," she said. "It's the most important."

Maya asked for detail beyond what Alex had told her, but there was nothing.

"He said you have boys of your own," Maya said, deflated but not wishing to let go.

"Three," Nina Benton said.

"A handful," Maya said enviously.

"Handful because each is disabled."

"Oh," Maya said. "I'm sorry."

"Don't be," the voice said. "They're great boys."

Maya apologized again. Apparently, she had made her husband's view on handicaps also her own.

"I'm so scared," she blurted out. Then she apologized a third
time. "I'm sorry. I know you can't help me."

"Now listen to me," Nina Benton said. "I'm putting you off only
because I have to get these boys into bed. We break routine, and
all hell goes loose. But you can talk to me. You can call me tomorrow. You want to come here in the afternoon and have coffee, I'll
make time."

"Thank you," Maya whispered. "I can't drive." It sounded like
a disability of her own. She said another thanks and hung up. She
felt envy for the happy bedlam on the other end of the line. Still
wearing her clothes, she went down on the bed and collapsed into
a deep, hopeless slumber, the soft rumble of the others talking
below her. Her final thought was a thanks that the affliction she
felt made her want to sleep instead of unable to.

+

His mother having turned to the dishes in the sink and his father
to the newspaper that had gone untouched because of Max, Alex
left the kitchen and took the stairs toward his son's bedroom. The
door creaked slightly when he opened it, and he reminded himself again to oil the hinges. His son—Alex felt encouragement
and surprise—was in bed; Alex had kept his skepticism to himself
when Raisa had declared, on her return to the kitchen, that the
boy had been set up there. (She had paused shyly to give the others
a chance to admire her achievement; through the affection only a
grandmother could give she had managed to solve the problem.)

Max was six when he'd asked Alex to set up a tent for him to
sleep outside. Alex had just finished reading a bedtime story about
Arctic explorers; a satisfied silence had descended on the room,

Alex seated in an old armchair and his son interred in a pile of blankets. A lamp burned softly from Max's night table, the honeyed light casting the shadows that signal the decline of the day, a son ready to rest and a wife downstairs finishing the dishes before the adults make the last of the evening. Alex himself had nearly nodded off when Max said, with his customary directness, "Papa, would you build me a tent outside? I want to sleep there."

Alex felt buoyed by an affirmation of which his son couldn't be aware. Alex and Maya had argued about the language in which Max should receive his bedtime reading. English, said Maya; he was an American. Russian, said Alex; he would get plenty of America elsewhere. Alex and Maya's magnificent homeland could rot in hell, but a second language would only help Max in the future. Alex had won, partly because he did the bedtime reading, but the victory hadn't been satisfactory because the Russian-language books offered a somewhat selective view of history, in which the Arctic— and outer space, and medicine—were conquered exclusively by Russian and Soviet visionaries. But more, not less, Russian was necessary—Max, speaking Russian, had made an elementary mistake: He had said "build," not "set up," a tent.

"What?" Alex said. "You want to be like the explorers?"

Max shook his head no, the blond wind chimes swinging to and fro.

"When it gets warm," Alex said. "There's snow on the ground."

"If you wrap up, it's not cold," Max said, and turned away from the light.

Alex sat, turning over this remark, until he realized Max must have been recalling something one of the explorers had done. He rose, kissed his son good night, and went downstairs.

But his son had meant "build." Compliantly, Max had waited until that year's snow left the ground and was found one April Saturday in the Rubins' backyard, pulling a canvas drop cloth many times his size over a primitive contraption of acacia poles that he had scavenged in the suburban woods beyond the edge of their property. The drop cloth Max had scavenged from their neighbor Vincenzo, with whom the Rubins were adversarial due to Vincenzo's aggressive curtailment of the pygmy pines Alex had installed on the edge of his lot. To the boy, however, Vincenzo had lent the paint-spattered drop cloth with pleasure, imagining correctly that Max was freelancing and his dickhead father would erupt upon seeing his immaculate lawn staked with poles and a drop cloth with the drippings of ten years of house paint. Max had only had to fill out a chit that the old Italian, smelling of wine, thrust at the parents when they reluctantly came to inquire. Vincenzo fermented wine in a shed at the edge of his lot, and though he offered none to the Rubins, he shared with pleasure the swarming insects the process attracted; Maya was convinced Vincenzo was to blame for the hornets that had descended on Max on the deck when he was a toddler.

Alex would not remain indebted to Vincenzo; the canvas was stripped and the poles returned to the woods; his son would have a proper tent. Alex could not believe that something that could fit, folded, in the crook of his arm, could cost so much at the camping store on Route 23. The smaller they are, the more expensive they are, the salesman told him, and Alex felt that in these words was encapsulated the full difference between Russia and America. He presented it to his son like a keepsake from the dead ice of a northern expedition. Max nodded politely, as if this, too, would do, and raced to the backyard as Maya shouted after him to remember to say what when his father gave him a gift. Alex patted Maya on the shoulder munificently and strode toward the fervent unpacking taking place on a tender patch of grass he had so recently had the mowing service attend to. "This way, this way," he gently took the poles and fasteners from his son, but America had made great advances in tent making since Eugene and friends had set up filched army canvases on a birch-flanked clearing outside Minsk as little Alex observed, and Alex had to sheepishly give up the materials to his son, who had the contraption billowing in the crisp springtime wind in just minutes.

Now, as Alex surveyed his son from the threshold, he felt a strange cheerfulness. Now, Alex was needed for something much greater than building a tent. Maya's love for their son was complete but wishful, and blinded by wishfulness; patiently, Alex had kept his mouth closed so that Maya could have what she wanted. But now, his insight was needed. Alex's parents would have to receive their say, but he had no intention of allowing them anything other than that. He was Max's father.

He strode into the bedroom and ran his hand over Max's blanket. Max sat up, as if he would have to get dressed and go off somewhere. He put his shoulders forward and stared up at his father.

"I'm sorry I woke you," Alex said.

"What is it?" Max said nervously.

"Nothing," Alex said. "But now that your grandfather's put away the tent, how are we to talk man to man? But I have something to ask you."

Max blinked several times, chasing away sleep.

"Do you love your mama?" Alex said.

"Of course," Max said.

"When you go away like you did today, Maksik, you make your mama so upset. She cries. She won't eat."

"Why won't she eat?" Max said.

"How can you ask? Because she loves you. She's afraid you're not okay."

"But I got back okay."

"But what if something happened? You're lucky, that's true, I can see that. It's a great quality in life—maybe the greatest. But you need more than luck. You need this." Alex tapped Max's head lightly with his finger. "Do you understand what I mean?"

Max shook his head no.

"It doesn't matter," Alex said. "You can't do this anymore, son. Even if you want to, you can't. You have to stop yourself. You have to think of your mama—and of me, and of your grandparents, who love you—and you have to come straight home from school.

I am talking to you man to man about this. Do we have an agreement?"

Max didn't say anything, but when his father also didn't speak, he nodded.

"That's what I like to hear. You know, if Mama and I had a daughter, I would love her just as much as I love you. But I'm glad we have you."

Max blinked twice. "What about the tent?"

"No more tent, Max. Grown boys sleep in bed. Grown boys don't play around in the grass like animals. You're growing up."

Max slid back down under the blanket and turned to face the wall. His father apologized once more for waking him. He waited for Max to say it was okay. Instead Max said: "Did you run away when you were little?"

"Never," his father said.

"Ever?"

"Ever. Kids who don't care about their parents run away. Who think about themselves, and only themselves. I was not like that, and neither are you." Alex waited, then said again, "I'm sorry for waking you."

This time his son exonerated him, and he retreated. Flushed with a positive feeling that had been difficult to imagine downstairs—he felt it most often when he finally got some time to himself, or to speak to his son without his wife's interference—Alex shut the door to his son's bedroom and took the steps to his own, where he discovered his wife, fully clothed and lights burning, asleep on a pitiful edge of their bed, her mouth open in fantasy. Turning the light switches with care, he went into the bathroom, where he opened the faucet only a trickle and left the toilet unflushed. When he came out, he slid the house slippers from her feet, but otherwise left her in place. This left him a smaller portion of the bed than he usually used, but he fit himself around his wife. He kissed her hair, and realized she had been smoking. Maya, Maya, he sighed. Sometimes, he felt as if he had two children. Four children.

+

After their son vanished upstairs, Eugene and Raisa sat noiselessly at the dining room table. It was late, and they felt old. Eventually, Eugene, feeling the male's responsibility to act, stirred and gently took his wife by the soft meat under her elbow.

"Zhenya, I want to look at him one more time," Raisa said. Eugene shrugged to say of course—how could he refuse his wife. He cherished moments like these, which usually arrived as soon as his daughter-in-law—or his son; true, his son, too—left the room. Suddenly, the proper course of action was unmuddled, the language of the room clear and direct.

They climbed the stairs, Max's door opening for the third time since he had fallen asleep. He was wheezing softly. With satisfaction, Raisa noted that the boy remained where she'd left him. Then she remembered everything else and reclined her head against Eugene's shoulder, rolling it back and forth in dismay.

"Did you think, when you said you'd go ice-skating with me fifty years ago," Eugene said, "that we would be standing in America looking at our blond grandson after he spent the afternoon dunking himself in a river like a beaver?"

"I'm frightened, Eugene."

He touched her shoulder quietingly and strode into the bedroom. "Eugene!" Raisa hissed. "Let him be."

"I'm awake," Max said.

"He's awake," Eugene forgave himself, but in a whisper, because if Alex heard, Eugene would get an earful. "I want to talk to my grandson. When can I talk to my grandson without everyone else interrupting?"

Raisa threw her hands at the ceiling: "Should I leave you two alone?"

Eugene studied his wife's silhouette in the doorway. He perceived just how much Raisa had to restrain herself so as not to antagonize their son and his wife. He wished to give her some great freedom. In seventy years, had she not earned at least that? He said to her, mocking the sudden sincerity but also sincere: "I am no one without you."

Max watched them solemnly.

"What are you staring at, Columbus?" Eugene turned back to his grandson and lowered himself to the bed. A knee cracked, and Eugene wailed comically. He tickled Max's belly through the blanket. "How long are you going to sleep in pajamas, heh? Are you a grown-up or what? Grown-ups sleep in briefs and nothing else. Grown-ups make the room cold, so their lungs get bigger in the night. Do you understand? Who's going to have the biggest lungs in the world?"

"Me," Max obeyed.

"That's right. Now let's talk business." Eugene reached into the back pocket of his slacks and pulled out his wallet. "This, by the way," he said, pulling out a square photo with foxed edges, "is your grandmother fifty years ago. Heh? Look at that."

Max sat up and ran his fingers over the photo's ancient matting.

"She was the most beautiful girl in the world," Eugene said. He looked at the doorway. "And still is." Letting Max hold on to the photo, he reached back into the billfold and withdrew twenty dollars. "Now listen. Every week you don't do what you did today, you get one of these. You follow? You go back to sleeping in your bed and you stay there, you get two of these. Shake with me, because once you've shaken, it's a shame to go back on it. Give it here." Eugene stuck out a paw. Max placed his hand inside it.

"Do I need to teach you how to shake?" Eugene said.

"Eugene, leave him be," Raisa pleaded from the door.

"Woman, don't interrupt," Eugene said playfully. Max dropped his hand, giving up.

"Come on!" his grandfather badgered him, but then let it go, shaking his head. He reached under Max's bed and pulled out the board with the pouches of grass. He opened the one in the upper-left-hand corner and clawed out the wisps of dried grass.

Raisa approached and took them from his hand as Max watched apprehensively. Eugene rolled up the twenty and stuffed it into the pouch.

"Until every one of these is filled with a twenty, you can't touch the money, okay?" he said. "I see the money gone, I see the grass back, it's all over. You forfeit all the money, lose the game. Does a Rubin lose?"

"No," Max said.

"The only person I lose to is you," Eugene said. "Do we have a deal?"

"I am about to pull you away from him by the ears," Raisa complained.

"My commanding officer has ordered me to retreat," Eugene said to Max. "Okay?"

"Okay," Max said softly. He watched his grandparents go.

+

With no Rubins left to interfere with his sleep, Max sped down a creek astride a muskellunge pike, its scales sparkling under the water. Maneuvering around deadwood and stones, the fish split the creek with the speed of an arrow, the black buttons of its eyes occasionally sweeping up toward the riders. The other passenger was the odd boy from the house—he had circled his arms around Max's waist and dropped his head against Max's shoulder. He was burbling something—*bah, bah, bah*—but didn't seem to be afraid.

They moved quickly, passing bridges, silent woods, other homes, though each one looked like the white farmhouse from where Max's parents were called, set back from the road by two or three hundred feet. Children waved at them from the bridges, drivers peeked out of their windows. They had an escort of turkey vultures, circling overhead. Max's feet were pegged to the pike's flank, and it nosed through the water so neatly that only the rare drop reached his face, a cold pinprick of wet.

Bah-bah-bah. Max turned around and said to hold on, it

wouldn't be long now. He knew the place was coming, but when this stand of poplars ended, another began, and then a farmhouse, a swamp, a row of marshy fields, a thicket of electrical lines. It wouldn't come.

But then it did come. Max didn't have to tell the pike to slow down; it stopped and idled in place. To the unaided eye, there was little about this clearing to mark it apart from the many they'd passed, a plain field surrounded by hundred-foot trees, so tall they seemed to be talking about something up at the crowns. The roots were so thick the crowns didn't sway even when the wind gusted. Here and there wildflowers grew, winks of violet, yellow, and rose.

Max turned as far as he could inside the boy's hold. Then he put his own arms around him, and they held each other briefly. Then the boy, also knowing the moves, slid off Max, and plopped into the water. He stood up, drenched, and smiled an embarrassed, toothy smile, his eyes rolling back in their sockets. Max nodded. The boy turned away and slopped to the shore. Max called out that he would be back with the others. "Just remember, I have to take you back before morning." The boy turned around and spoke as if no impediment addled his mind: "I'll wait for you here."

5

2002

Alex and his parents had wanted children and grandchildren with the same mindless hunger with which they sat down to meals. None had prepared for the possibility that this may not be biologically possible. They believed that America was at fault; it wouldn't have happened like this back home. There—maybe it was the food, which had no preservatives; maybe the slow pace and absence of stress—everyone was fertile. America regarded adoption as a normal course, so American bodies adjusted to fit the culture's endorsement. This country all but authorized its citizens to go barren.

The Rubins' desire to become parents and grandparents was eclipsed only by their conviction that adopted children were second-class, by definition unwanted; and why would a child be unwanted? Because something was wrong. Maya was repelled by adoption no less than the Rubins; imagining it was like imagining marriage to someone one hoped one would figure out how to love. As Maya greeted the dubious outcomes married life had harbored for her—medical work, after all; all the ways in which the elder Rubins did not resemble her parents—childlessness had not even occurred to her, perhaps because she held to the same expectations about Russian fertility. She didn't know any infertile Russian couples. She knew very few people, Russian or otherwise, outside the Rubins, but the Russians among them were all fertile. Even Bender, the pulped, gray-faced psychologist in Whippany, and his snow-haired wife had a small Bender knocking around some college.

When Alex and Maya met, Maya was indifferent toward children. When she happened upon one, she spoke to him like an inattentive adult. In a woman like her, even displaced to America, the alarm should have beat sooner than in an American body—but it didn't. When children came up, she started clearing the table and made fun: Alex, should we have five? Or six? The elder Rubins loved making fun; it meant everyone was in a good mood. Maya also made a different kind of joke: "Running my cash register with one hand, turning over *grechanniki* with the other, and holding the little one with a third?" Like a sputtering engine, the Rubins' laughter caught in their throats. If Maya had to work all hours in a café, of course Raisa would look after the child. But—that idea had not gone out of Maya?

Had Maya wished childlessness on them? Now, no child possible, she had the time to open a café—a chain of cafés. That was the bitter irony for the Rubins. For Maya, the bitter irony was that now she could not. That obsession had belonged to another woman; every obsession withers if you just hold down the obsessive, she thought. She laughed at the way she had dramatized her youthful situation—could her fantasy, to cook in some café, have been any paltrier? Now, Maya would not know how to run a café if the keys were handed to her. That devil she had spoken to Alex about ten years before—he had abandoned her. Her devil giving up; the passage of time; the female clock; Moira at the hospital with her stories of Ricky and Anthony and the dean's list; also, the maternity ward was just a floor down from mammography—who knew why, but the desire for a café had been replaced by a desire for children. But the Rubins refused to consider adoption. It's not that they didn't love losing. There was a sweet surrender in it. But the loss had to be clean.

Because Maya was the interloper among them; because America had brought her to the Rubins; because she worked in medicine and occasionally expressed a contrasting opinion—the duty of persuading the Rubins to adopt fell to her, even as her own reluctance

remained. The amount of time that infertile couples spend on fertility treatments—luckily and unluckily, this was not necessary in
the case of the Rubins—Maya spent instead on persuading the
family out of its hostility to adoption. The Rubins would not even
rent a local apartment when they went to the Mexican coast—used
beds and sheets made them feel unhygienic and poor, even if a
hotel performed the same changeovers—and she wanted them to
take on a used human being? No. Heads shook. No, Mayechka,
no. And so the name Rubin will come to an end? she asked, hitting
them in a tender spot. It's already ended, Eugene sighed, and then
said that it was his and Raisa's fault; they should have had more
children. At which point Alex removed himself from the table, and
the dinner went on in a spectral silence.

Maya stopped making her case—the appealed-to must want
the appeal. Then, during one dinner, apropos of nothing, Raisa
mounted another attack on adoption. She conceded that it was a
fine and honorable thing to do, to give a homeless child a home
and all that, and perhaps she was not only backward but obsolete
to remain opposed, but she could not bring herself around. She
was too old, too set. Her sin, but not one she could overcome. It
was then that Maya understood that despite the show they had
been giving her, they would all sign on—but only if she took on the
responsibility. And so she said: "We're adopting." She was right:
They all shrugged, including Alex. They were good parents-in-law,
a good husband: They would give their beloved, capricious Maya
what she wanted. Everything they endured over the next two
years—nine months, morning sickness, and painful labor were a
favor from God by comparison—they endured for her.

They chose the adoption agency from the Yellow Pages, like
a tailor. Independent Adoption Services had retenanted a former
department store; the space, contrived to hold circular clothing
racks, rows of registers, and banks of mirrors, was overlarge and
overexposed for the more delicate task of finding new homes for
children, and every time Maya attempted to navigate its fluores-

cent cubicles and cream-colored hallways, she ended up at bathrooms for the handicapped. It wasn't until she strode the halls of
IAS that Maya understood what people meant by auras and mag-
netic fields. She felt like a dog responding to an unseen but undeniable scent. It was bad.

In the waiting area, portraits of successfully placed children and
their new parents, usually on the steps of the courthouse where
the transfer had been blessed by the law, faced off against childless
couples that aspired to migrate to the opposite wall. Maya, Alex,
and their sad compatriots studied the wall of success; the pregnant
women who came in, Maya observing them like the other party in
a car accident, studied the Mayas and Alexes. Maya was shocked
the first time she saw a pregnant woman walk in, then chastised
herself for her thickness; of course, the agency would serve both
sides. The effortlessly full-bellied women read the prospective-
parent profiles like personal ads, savoring a power that, by their
looks, they had rarely, if ever, enjoyed. She hated them because
they held the power, and she hated them because they were pregnant. Feeling a modest hysteria, Maya would snatch a palmful of
cookies from the center console that held the uneasy peace between the parents-already and the parents-they-wish and gnash
them mindlessly, hating herself as she did it. Generally, though,
she directed the anger that pooled in her throat at the agency staff,
which treated women who wanted to give up their children like
wounded angels, and people who wanted to turn their lives upside
down to make room for a foreign child like criminals until proven
otherwise. ("It's social engineering, only legal," Mishkin, the adoption supervisor, had noted. "You Russians should know something
about that.") If Mishkin had not accosted the Rubins one afternoon, trying on them the smattering of mangled Russian in his
possession—he had overheard them whispering—quite possibly
they would have remained childless. The slab-faced matron to
whom they had initially been assigned had been terrorizing them
into confessing their unpreparedness, unwillingness, doubt.

Slab-Face could have been forty or seventy. Did the Rubins own guns? Fire extinguishers? Were the outlets sealed? Her red pen hovered over a clipboard. Maya and Alex exchanged looks: Was she joking? Slab-Face barreled on: Where had they lived? Every state would need a background check. They hadn't crossed the river to live in New York, had they? Because New York was the worst.

The Rubins, she went on, would have to produce a self-advertisement like the ones in the waiting area. "Think of it like a newspaper personal," Slab-Face advised. "You want to go steady with the birth parents—what can you offer?" Spotting the Rubins' unease, she raised her chin: "Oh, yes. You have to."

"How did you . . . become involved with adoptions?" Alex mustered. He coughed lightly.

"I've got two little ones," Slab-Face whipped out a photograph of two bantam-sized brown children flanking her abundance as all three roared behind the seat rail of a roller coaster.

"It is possible to adopt at all ages?" Alex said, and Maya stared at him with mortification. "He means the children's ages," she rushed to add.

Perhaps Slab-Face would have been willing to forgo a personal verification of the Rubins' claims regarding firearms and ammunition, but comments like these, on steady supply from Alex, guaranteed otherwise. She arrived on a rainy afternoon wearing the same housedress in which they had found her at the office and proceeded to test the edges of their countertops, flick their stove burners, measure the height of their steps. The Rubins remained glumly seated at the kitchen table. They had refused to allow Eugene anywhere near the house during Slab-Face's inspection for fear he would insult her so gravely that he would sully their chances forever. Maya experienced a great gratitude to her husband for saying nothing about what she had dragged the pair of them into. Also for not mentioning the duration and cost of the adoption—a year and around twenty thousand dollars, "depending on what the birth parents want." "What do you mean, what the birth parents want?" Alex asked, thinking of Soviet bribes. "They'll tell you that at orientation," Slab-Face said, reluctantly marking Home Inspection Pass rather than Fail on the clipboard.

"Orientation?" Alex said.

The orientation, a statewide colloquy in an ocean-side town, was attended by nine couples and two solos, one female and one male, setting off in Alex's mind uneasy speculation about whether the solitary man's wife was merely ill, or here was a man taking on parenthood all by himself. Of the other eight couples, three were gay and two religious, the latter signified by pins that said "Building God's Army." The Rubins' eyes clung to the remaining heterosexual parents like floaters in a cold ocean.

Alex had never touched a gay man before, but now he was holding one's hand as the twenty participants formed a grieving circle to commemorate their failed fertility. Why were the gays grieving? They hadn't been failed by fertility, they had been failed by their dicks. He and Maya had been failed by fertility, and as the assembled strode and chanted, Alex absented himself by trying to guess which half of the other two normal couples (for that is the way Alex thought of them) was the sterile one. Was it the pale-face in glasses or his zebra-faced wife? Was it the ham-shouldered redhead with the pageboy, or her equally cavernous beau, wheezing like an asthmatic as they pounded the floor? Cupid loves every kind.

After lunch, which Alex and Maya had passed eyeing with envy the camaraderie starting between the other castaways, the group received a PowerPoint presentation on the various scams they could expect to encounter as parents-in-waiting. Financial Scams, one screen said. What other kind is there? Alex wondered. Emotional Scams, the next screen said. "Women will put up profiles claiming to look for adoption," the lecturer said. "They'll interview you, they'll spend hours with you on the phone. And in the end, there's no child. They're just lonely. Meanwhile, you've been riding the roller coaster."

The lecturer moved on, but Maya felt that a crucial piece of information was being left out, though she was too shy to raise her hand: How could a person protect himself from this kind of scam? Should she and her husband demand photos of a sloped belly as a precondition of talks? A signed certificate from the gynecologist? A meeting? Then she disobediently realized that she would not mind talking to this woman, the emotional scammer. She would prefer to know, of course, that there was no child, but this lonely, desperate charlatan struck her as someone with whom she could have a long talk, indeed.

That night, the Rubins were given homework: the profile that would hang on the IAS wall. Like the other applicants, they got a packet of samples and an instant camera, and were instructed to capture, between then and the next morning, three images that the rest of the group, playacting birth mothers and fathers, would cull for the one that made them say: I want to give my child to *these* people.

Alex and Maya had not filled out an application since writing colleges fifteen years before, and that was colleges; they were ap-plying for a human being this time. How could one begin to answer the question of why one deserved to become the parent of a child carried and birthed by another? It was like being asked who one was, and what one planned to do about it. Of course they were loving, and patient, and generous—why would they ask to adopt otherwise—but so was everyone else filling out these forms. One had to be oneself, but what if one's self was generic? In the seaside motel room rented with their orientation fees by the agency, Maya wondered what the other participants were writing. Alex didn't think they were writing—they were out on the town with each other. Bonding.

He was at the small table by the window, Maya curled up on the bed, which smelled of industrial laundry detergent. Daylight began to merge with dark outside. Should they emphasize their hard work as immigrants? Downplay their religion? Try to be funny?

Should they say they read books, or would that be looked upon with disfavor by mothers struggling with reduced circumstances? But they would want to donate their children to book-reading parents, wouldn't they? However, the Rubins didn't actually read books. With no forewarning, the assignment had brought on an existential self-examination they hadn't requested.

Alex proposed that they wander outside for some fresh air; it was the farthest he and Maya had gone together in a while. Maya felt soldered to the bedspread, its corners crowned with tasseled pads that looked like epaulettes. But seeing Alex awaiting her authorization, she swung forward, the bag of stones in her belly sliding into her feet. She watched herself throw water on her face, recinch her ponytail, consider and then decide against her bag. She felt like an apparition. How would that read on the adoption form? "Prospective mother occasionally feels a stonelike weight on the soul."

In the dying summer light, the humidity of the day mostly gone, jowled parents wandered in a lobster-skinned daze as their children set off sparklers and shouted. Next to them, Maya and Alex were overclothed, pale, monastic, disturbed. Weaving between the natives, they crossed the boardwalk to the beach, by now empty. Maya slipped off her shoes: the sand was grainy and cool. The ocean pounded rocks with a throttled boom, then wiped out on the shore with a hiss. Maya's blackness lifted slightly. She marveled morosely: the gray water was indifferent to her heartbreak, but was able to lift it. Alex was not, but couldn't. To her surprise, she didn't feel as frightened of the ocean's loud darkness as she expected.

She imagined a dolphin sailing out of the ocean and becoming their son. She had not thought of the child's gender in the two months since she and Alex had first driven to IAS. It was such an obvious thing to wonder about, in fact one of the few that could set an Infertile Parent to reverie. Perhaps because she didn't actually believe she would receive a child, son or daughter. With each step—the home inspection, the orientation, the brochure—the prospect of obtaining a child receded rather than neared, and she felt as if she were merely checking boxes so she could always say to herself that she had tried everything.

She pulled her blouse over her head, shivering quickly as a phantom wind whipped her chest. Alex called out her name questioningly; she ignored him. Her breasts, two miniature pears, felt oddly engorged, as if her imagining of motherhood had expanded them in preparation; for an unfamiliar moment, she experienced what a full-chested woman might feel like, her breasts straining at her bra. How many men had held them before Alex Rubin closed them in his grasp? Alex was a cupper, gentle and tentative; there had been pluckers, pullers, snappers, flickers, and mashers. One had emptied a full bottle of juice on her breasts before lapping it up with his tongue; some had emptied themselves. She remembered Anton, a metalhead, interrupting his vigil of sullenness to announce that they looked and tasted like marzipan. There were many. There could have been many more. Of them all, she had chosen Alex Rubin. Perhaps because he had started out tentative, apologetic, and shy; frankly, she was startled by these qualities. Had ceased to expect them from men. With her greater experience, she had given him the gift of his sexuality, and loved giving it. He bloomed in her hand, her mouth, her legs.

Her fingers met below her shoulder blades and flicked the latch of her bra, which brought forth another concerned question from Alex. The bra popped from her chest and slid down her arms until it plonked to the sand, a violet crab. Her khakis were next. To Alex's relief, her underwear stayed on, though his eyes remained nervously on the boardwalk; the burghers walking it would not look kindly on a striptease in front of their children, and the adoption authorities would not look kindly on an arrest for public exposure. ("We would make successful adoptive parents because we have known both sides of the law . . .") Was his wife having a nervous breakdown? In frazzled moments, Alex's instinct was to lay hands on his wife; her skin, cool and marmoreal, seemed to contain an unguent that interacted exclusively with the trouble he felt. But now she was the trouble, and so he stood, blinking, as she walked toward the water, her feet kicking up sand like a pair of hooves. His wife had nice legs that always asked for attention, even now. "I won't be long," she called. He leaned down and scooped up the bra, at least a slight gesture in the direction of order.

Now the ocean took Maya's breasts in its hands. Really, she could not remember the last time she'd swum, and without clothes. The water was soapy and warm, dreadfully gray if she lowered her head under the line, so she kept it above. With one hand, she pulled down her underwear; it floated up like a thread of spittle, then disappeared inside a whitecap. She lay back, stared at the pocked bowl of the sky, let the blackening water inside her.

Her shoulders flinched and she felt a furry cloud of warmth at her thighs. In her reverie, she had floated out, and off the arch of her back she could see Alex peering out worriedly on the tips of his toes. She raised her right hand, waved. Impatiently, he waved her back to the shore. Through the waves sloshing at her ears, she heard the long call: "Maaaa-ya." She flipped over and began to cover the distance to shore, her arms moving above the water in a downy fog. As she swam, she imagined a thread furling out of her into the ocean, a line she would reel in when their son arrived at their doorstep.

When she emerged from the water, Alex peeled off his T-shirt and held it out like a cape. As she wrapped herself in it, he fumbled to slide her sand-crusted feet into the loops of her khakis, as if she was incapacitated.

"We're going to have a child, Alex," Maya said, watching him work. She dropped the T-shirt and slid her hands into his hair.

"You need to lie down, Maya," Alex said, working below. He reminded her of her father, tying her shoelaces as she sang songs above his head and slapped at its bald pate.

"I was lying down," she said.

They walked back to the motel, Alex's shirtlessness blending unobjectionably with the promenade walkers. Alex supported

Maya at the arms, as if she had suffered some kind of attack. She enjoyed the feel of her husband's arms.

Alex laid Maya into bed and ordered her not to move until he returned with dinner. She watched him step outside and obeyed for some minutes, then sat up, stared at the questionnaire, and took a pencil in hand.

1. How do you give love?
A: To love is to lose. If you love someone, it means: "You winning means more than me winning."

2. How do you receive love?
A: I don't know.

3. How do you discipline?
A: I don't. I want to know why, and I ask, though sometimes there is no answer.

4. Describe a great personal disappointment.
A: I once wished to cook in a café.

In this way, she went down the list. When she arrived at the free essay, she wrote:

A child is a new expedition. The ocean refreshed by a new tributary. A child is strength—as three, we will be stronger than two. And a child is wisdom—he will teach us about ourselves as we will teach him. He will be the truth when we shy from it. Can it be, one day, that we will look on our inability to have children as a blessing, because it brought him into our lives? I don't know. The birth of a child is one of the greatest joys a human being can receive. When it's replaced by grief because it can't happen, the grief is as large as the joy was. (Was supposed to be.) But I will not say no. I will hope. In the meantime . . .

After finishing, Maya felt an enormous exhaustion—she could not even reread what she had written. She wondered if she had caught a chill in the ocean. She pulled the tasseled edges off the bed and climbed underneath. She would nap for a minute and wake up when Alex came in. She fell asleep quickly, only laughing once because she thought: What I wrote was so boring, it's put me to sleep!

She awoke she could not say how much later, though the lights of the room were still burning. She faced Alex's back—the room smelled of fried fish and potatoes. Alex heard her stir and swiveled in the chair. "I didn't want to wake you," he said. "There's fried haddock and French fries. Best I could find. Everything's fried here."

She inquired sleepily what he was doing.

"I want to read to you some of these answers," he said. "Do you want a cup of hot water? No lemon."

She held a palm to her forehead. "I'm fine," she said drowsily.

"Number one," he said. "How do you give love? One can express love through presents, a hug, or a vacation. How do you receive love? With open arms! How do you discipline? A child must know boundaries, but there will be no spanking in our home. Describe a great personal disappointment. We have lived a beautiful life. Our only disappointment is the one that brings us to this application."

Then he read the free essay. Alex kept several of Maya's phrases, for instance "the ocean refreshed by a new tributary," but otherwise he wrote about making a long journey to their present station (initially, he left the details vague, on the off chance the birth parents were of anti-immigrant cast), but now, having arrived in New Jersey, the Rubin appetite for wandering had been exhausted and the family wished to root in the soil like a tree. They wished to iterate and reiterate; they wished to put down generations, so in a hundred and fifty years, the great-grandchildren of their adopted son or daughter (in the name of increasing their chances, they could not very well leave Maya's careless assumption that it would be a boy) would feel as solidly American as the birth parents themselves. In this way, Alex betrayed the immigrant identity of the writers, but, he reasoned, the immigrant story was beloved by Americans, and, on second thought, there was no reason to hide it. Financially, the Rubins were finally ready for adoption ("you have to let them know the child won't starve," Alex explained to Maya). And even though the child's grandfather was standing by with a lengthy exercise list, that regimen would not begin for at least three months after adoption. "Funny doesn't hurt," Alex murmured behind his back. But Maya was asleep once again.

The next day, Alex's entry was unanimously voted #1 by the other participants. Alex, forgetting his resentment of them, smiled shyly. Maya wanted to take him by the shoulders and shake him—when he agreed to unshell himself, the world loved him. The agency presenter asked him to talk about his method. "This will be new information for my wife, too," Alex said. "The woman sleeps and the man works." He winked at her and the group rocked with laughter.

Alex withdrew a greasy newspaper. He had gone for takeout— fried fish. They came for a son, they left with a heart attack, ha-ha. Maya, still groggy after twelve hours of sleep, wondered who this wisecracking man was. Anyway, the fish was wrapped in a newspaper. Alex once more waved the oily copy of the *Asbury Park Press*. As he chewed on wet haddock, he glanced at the classified section. Slab-Face (though of course he didn't refer to her that way) had been right—the brochure should resemble a personal. Alex skimmed the entries until he found one that suited: a letter from a retiree who wished to fill the gloaming years with a companionable rest after a lifetime of drive. It wouldn't be all rest, though— the man had earned well, and the package included, in addition to the driver's considerable charms, a Mustang with a retractable roof. Alex cribbed Ride With Me's method: the subtle retranslation of unavoidable facts (the man was winding down) into virtue (the noble quietude of the gloaming years); the casual reference to considerable means (the Mustang); the humor ("in addition to the driver's considerable charms"). Alex was willing to bet the ad had been answered many times. "I hope we are just as successful," he summed up. One of the religious women burst into applause. "I'm sorry," she said, "I just want to hug you right now."

The picture Alex and Maya took that morning featured Alex grinning like a younger version of himself, his arm around Maya, the sleep hangover in her eyes masked by her pleasure in the pleasure her husband seemed to be taking, for the first time, in their shared endeavor. It was a triumphant photograph because carefree, a visitation by grace at its most needed, and it was selected as the Rubins' winning shot by the other participants without their needing to have taken another.

+

The morning's camaraderie still high on their faces, the Rubins were sat down for an exit interview by an Asian woman named Tran Caldwell. Instantly, they wondered if they had been given an immigrant because of their background. Then they wondered if they were given someone so young because they didn't rank highly with the agency. (Was this Slab-Face's subterfuge from afar?) Tran Caldwell had high, queenly cheekbones sprayed with a pollen of freckles, and the black sheets of hair that fell from her head glistened with a malevolent healthfulness. Elsewhere, she was as slight as a child—Maya, not a loomer, loomed over her. Maya, who had resolved that the agency employed only adoptive mothers, decided that Tran Caldwell had to adopt because her body was too small to hold a whole other being. Tran, however, was herself an adoptee. An alfalfa farmer from Missouri and his wife had taken her in after Da Nang—their son had been killed shortly before the Americans left. They were still out in Missouri, years past retirement, making war on weevils and armyworms. All this Tran offered by way of introduction.

"There was one last thing we wanted to speak to you about,"

she said. "It's the decision you make about open versus closed adoption." She allowed the words to settle. Alex was rattled by the transformation of this child-woman into yet another person intending to discuss children in a businesslike way. "Have you given any thought to the issue?"

"What issue?" he said.

"Whether the child will know he or she is adopted," Tran said. As Alex fought a distasteful expression, Tran said: "You don't have to discuss it with me. It's a private decision. But I wanted to tell you what it was like in my case—because I've been on both sides." She was gazing directly at Alex, as if—he felt—she intended to challenge him. His oracular flight in the brochure had led him to believe that a turnaround was in the offing for the Rubins, an atonement for Slab-Face and presenters who had rattled off facts about children as if they were reading to a hospitality conference. This expectation now stalled.

"It's natural to want no strings attached," Tran said. "There's that impression it's cleaner. Who wants competition from the birth parents?" Maya and Alex exchanged glances, this additional challenge never having occurred to them.

"But what children tend to do when they know they're adopted but they don't have clear answers is they make up the birth parents. They tell themselves stories in order to make sense of having been given away. They imagine they were given away involuntarily, which leads to suspicion of the adoptive parents. They say, 'My real parents really love me, and I am going to go live with them soon.' They run away. Or the opposite: 'My parents didn't love me, so they gave me up.' These are hard things for a little person to wrap their brain around."

"I thought you were supposed to say 'place' instead of 'give up,'" Alex said.

Tran closed her eyes and smiled. "All that stuff is silly, I think," she said.

"So the farmer—he told you?" Alex said.

Tran nodded. "I grew up knowing it."

"Excuse me," Alex said. "It's not exactly avoidable in your case."

"That's true," Tran smiled. Maya looked at Alex reproachfully.

"And you told your children?"

"Here," Tran said, reaching into her purse. She fished in a date book and pulled out a photo of three children bundled in neon-colored jackets on a playground shrouded in snow: two girls and one boy in various states of developmental anarchy—jug ears, mutinous teeth, shambolic hair. Maya marveled at the cycle: a Vietnamese woman had adopted three white children.

"They fit into your life." She replaced the photo, Maya watching it disappear with envy.

"So they feel like yours?" Maya said. "I'm sorry—maybe I'm not supposed to ask that."

"Even yours don't feel like yours half the time," she said. "At least that's what they tell me. As an adoptive parent, the question on your mind is: Is it me? Is this him being a kid or is this him being adopted? But we forget that birth parents usually deal with the same things—they just don't have the self-consciousness that makes them wonder these things. Also: You can ask whatever you want." She paused diplomatically. "Mr. and Mrs. Rubin. I am able to have children. But I wanted to adopt."

Alex snorted. High comfort these people supplied—now this person was waving around the fact that she was not afflicted by the same curse as the Rubins. "Excuse me," he said. "You're proposing we share custody with the birth parents?"

"Of course not," Tran said. "I don't want to say that involving birth parents is always a pleasure. Some don't stay in contact. Some lose touch when they move away, or break up, or start their own families."

"Some won't let you be," Maya added.

"Believe it or not, that happens more rarely," Tran said. "You work out terms. They're legally bound to obey them. I am saying only this, from experience: One day, your child will ask: 'Why am I tall?' 'Why is my hair like this?' And they want to know. You can't bullshit a child. Pardon my language."

"And so being told their mother and father are not their actual mother and father at age six is less shocking than a white lie about recessive genes?" Alex asked with the authority of a biologist.

"You tell them at age zero," Tran said. "You tell them at age one. You have pictures out. The birth parents visit. They grow up knowing it from the beginning. You have no idea the resilience of children."

"Then they'll be resilient about not knowing it," Alex said.

Tran pursed her lips and nodded, as if she'd asked for a donation and been declined.

"Wait, Alex," Maya said.

"Maya, we have a long ride home and work tomorrow," he said.

"I didn't want to upset you," Tran said. "So many of the counselors here lay out the facts and leave it at that. I've learned from mistakes. I wanted to share that with you. It was at my initiative that the orientation was revised to include this type of conversation."

"Every family makes its own rules," Alex closed the discussion.

+

The Rubins rode home without speaking, Alex banging the steering wheel with his thumb as if rock were on the radio and not classical.

"I can hear you boiling," he said finally. "It's a cult, they are."

"You were rude to her."

"I think it's rude to ask me to pay money for the pleasure of being told what to do with my own child. Do you ever think about it, Maya? They should be grateful to us, but instead they treat us like we did something wrong."

"You were rude to her because she was small. And Asian. A woman."

"Forget mammography, Maya. Open up a psychologist's office."

"You are always waiting for the world to recognize what a service you are performing for it."

He looked over incredulously. "Are you upset? Is your railroad mind chugging along? I am upset, too. Don't take it out on me."

Maya stared vacantly at New Jersey outside her window. Post-beach traffic was beginning to clot the highway, sedans overstuffed with children, umbrellas, and beach chairs. A truck honked at a convertible filled with beautiful girls.

"Do you think we live in a beautiful place, Alex?" she said.

"What?" Alex said.

"I think back to Kiev, and I realize: Kiev was ugly. It has its cathedrals and streets where you think you're in Paris. But, really, it's ugly. But I never noticed, you know. I didn't know it was ugly until I left. And all these people in the cars—they don't know that New Jersey is ugly."

"So why don't we pick up and move to Paris, Maya," Alex said. "What's with you? Where do you want to go?"

"Nowhere," she said after a silence. "So I guess we will put 'closed' on the form?"

"*It is kind to the child if he doesn't have to wonder who his birth parents were,*" Alex said, imitating Tran Caldwell. "You know what's kind to the child?" he said. "When he doesn't have to wonder who his birth parents are—exactly. When he lives as a happy child of parents who love him and does his schoolwork and goes to see friends and plays soccer with his dad."

"What if we get a six-year-old?"

"We're getting a *baby*. We're putting that down. I'm sorry—you made the big decision, you have to let me make some little decisions."

"It's true," Maya said mournfully. "Who needs a child after that experience? It's easier to get into the intelligence service. It could just be the four of us. Give your parents twenty years and they'll be just like children. What more do we need?"

"Also, I *like* New Jersey," he said.

"But we met in New York, Alex," Maya said.

"New York is for young people."

"We're thirty-two, Alex. Thirty-three. It's not old."

"That woman has three children already," he said. "You would like to bring up your child on New York prices? Should I commute from the city to my father's office? And which hospital is awaiting your mammography skills in Manhattan? What's gotten into you?"

What had gotten into her? Until now, she had imagined the arrival of a child in her life as an unconditional deliverance; the terror was of not persuading the agency people, and the full-bellied mothers, that she and Alex deserved to be parents. But what if the problems started only *after* the child arrived? Either because of the child, or how the child fit with her, or with Alex, or with the both of them, or a million other things. Light-headed, she had a macabre vision of putting up for adoption a child she'd just adopted. She felt crazy.

"Can I drive, Alex?" she said.

He looked at her helplessly. "What?" he said. "You don't know how."

"I need to learn," she said.

"Right now?" he said, indicating the baked gray ribbon of highway before them, vehicles from a dozen tollbooth lanes slip-streaming into three. She saw herself reflected in his eyes: petulant, unsteady, impulsive.

"I need to learn," she repeated, but now in a summing-up way, as a note to the future. She looked back at the road and imagined one of the other cars spinning into their flank, all the activity that would bring on, all the new issues that would now need decision, management, resolution. She and Alex wouldn't be hurt, of course, though the comfort of that certainty made her imagine the opposite—she saw her legs folded at an unnatural angle. In returning to the present moment and its unexceptional safety, she was flooded with relief. Imagining horror always helped her that way.

6

In the three days remaining before the weekend visit to Bender, the psychologist, each member of the Rubin family arrived at his own accommodations with the new situation. Eugene, having seen Max in bed, asked no questions about whether his grandson continued to spend his nights there. Raisa, wishing to hold on to her victory, did the same; she labored in the kitchen, grateful to be left alone. Maya allowed herself to be reassured that Max did not require a pediatric behavioral specialist, that Bender would do it. In the afternoons, instead of driving home from the hospital, she drove to the curb of Terhune Elementary and waited for her son: This far she could drive, and would have even if she couldn't. She had proposed to the other Rubins to ask the school to put Max on watch, but they had talked her out of it: Why did she want to mark their child as a misfit? The other children would find out. So the principal was told that Max had merely gone to a friend's without calling. The principal heard Maya out with indulgence: He had been level-headed while she panicked.

Alex maintained routine—if no one else would stay calm, he would. Only now he didn't know what to do with his afternoons—he noticed belatedly that he had become attached to his outdoor tent sessions with his son as a pleasurable burden: the men, alone, with the women and parents far away. Now forced to use his imagination to conjure an alternative, his mind rebelled—on principle, he did not like having to use his imagination; the need for it signified an inadequacy in the situation at hand, and he preferred to make peace with the inadequacy, to live without illusions. So he waited for his son to propose the alternative. His son did not, reverting to his afternoon duties at the side of his mother. Seeing them at the kitchen counter on his arrival from work, Alex went upstairs and turned on the television. Downstairs, they chopped and banged pots and stuffed napkins into crystal drinking glasses. Maya tried to consume her son's attention with greater tasks than before: one afternoon, he was finally elevated to knife work. Her left hand closed his over a fleecy clump of parsley; her right steadied his as he held a small chef's knife she had gone out to buy for his size. Obediently, Max's hand moved under hers.

Alex appeared in the kitchen and stared at them—their son could not be entrusted to return from school alone, but she was teaching him to be more deft with a knife? She gazed back at Alex—what was the worry if Max's behavior was normal, as he insisted? Alex shrugged and walked out to the living room. And yet, ultimately, their eyes separated without animosity; ultimately, their eyes said to each other: I don't know, I don't know, I don't know. This kinship rubbed the edge from their disagreement: the kind of understanding spouses rely on and regret in equal degree.

As a whole, the Rubins, until now of the opinion that psychology was for quadriplegics and nut jobs alone, relented: Fine, let him go see Bender if Maya wanted it so badly. Their derision for Bender's profession coexisted with a demand for its effectiveness; if their son and grandson had to succumb to the embarrassment, let him be healed rapidly, at the least. Any other outcome would confirm the other opinion, that it was all quackery. In this way, the Rubins forestalled the possibility of disappointment; each result would give them what they wanted.

Alex insisted on not telling Max about the impending visit to Bender lest he be needlessly frightened, but Max knew that some judgment awaited him; that is understood even by an eight-year-old. Eugene need not have refrained from asking about where his grandson was sleeping—Max continued to spend his nights in bed, though no one seemed to notice, save his mother, who seemed either unconcerned by the original behavior or unmollified by the fix. In fact, during one afternoon's battered whitefish, Maya knelt down, took Max by the forearms, and said: "You know, you can sleep on the floor. You don't have to sleep in the bed." So it did make a difference to her. That night, he returned to the floor. As a kind of insurance in case his grandfather came to complain, Max discarded his pajamas and slept in briefs like a grown-up so his lungs would get bigger in the night.

Maya operated in glazed preoccupation; there was so often, on her face, a gathering of lines that parted only, and only sometimes, when she and Max took up cooking together, to which Max submitted every afternoon for that reason. Even at his age, he understood the cooking as a specialized task performed by a particular caste, but he was too young to understand whether the caste was lowly or high.

Over the whitefish, he had turned up to her and said: "Would you still cook if you didn't have to feed us?"

She put down her knife and rubbed his shoulder. "But where would you be?"

"Like when we go to Mexico. Do you still make dinner?"

"No, I don't, sweetheart. Not really."

"So you do it for us."

"In a way."

"So what do you do when no one's around?"

"What, honey?" she bent down.

"When you're by yourself. What do you do?"

"I don't know, baby. I'm not alone that often. When you go away to Mexico, I miss you. I walk around the house. I don't do much of anything. Maybe it's not right and I should do more with myself. Why are you asking me?"

He said he was curious.

"Is that why you ran away, Max? Because you wanted to be alone?"

"No," he said. "I told you—I was sad."

"But why did that make you want to be alone—instead of with us?"

"I don't know," he said.

She let him be.

About Bender, Max had been told that his mother needed to see the psychologist—in the view of some, this was the truth—and could Max come along, because then they could go for bagels, his favorite; his mother had been wanting some, too. When the prescribed hour came, Max came down from his room only on the third summons. He looked pale and sleepy. His jeans hung on him like a laundry bag, and he hadn't even hitched them with a belt. Maya let it be, but Alex stared at his son distrustfully.

In the backseat—starting to do Bender's work before they reached Bender, Eugene again claimed that Max was spoiled by indulgence and insisted the boy be retired from the front—Max watched the leafing trees rush by even though Eugene had affixed a DVD player to the back of the passenger seat in consolation. Max had never shown an interest in movies. He had liked blocks, picture books with popping-up animals, little mallets, buttons, and knobs—he dragged it all around, liking the feel in his hands.

Next to Max in the backseat, like a squat, silent animal, rode a case of Turkish cherry jam, an enticement from Eugene to Bender. No Rubin had called a Bender in more than a year, and if memory served—and in such cases, at least on the aggrieved side, memory served dutifully—a Bender had been the last to issue a half-hearted invitation to socialize. So when Maya insisted that Max see a psychologist, Eugene agreed not because he thought the man could be useful—psychologists were charlatans, in his view—but because, disparage Bender or not, the ignored invitation had been eating at him. Eugene declined to be the one to call Bender, however, leaving diplomacy to Anatolian cherries.

"We're paying him," Alex had said when his father had proffered the tray, each bottle blown in the shape of a laughing pasha. "I can't believe he's charging us, but he is. This isn't necessary."

"It's the jam they serve with tea at the steam baths," Eugene said. "Bender can develop *positive associations* and charge you less."

Alex wanted to call no more than his father, but Bender was a Rubin-side friend—Bender's wife and Raisa had met at a grocery store years before and dragged the men into acquaintance. More importantly, Bender was the lesser of the evils Maya had dreamed up, the other being an American therapist. And so—even though Max was seeing a psychologist on his wife's restless urging; even though it was his mother who had drawn the first bridge to the Benders; even though it was Eugene who had insisted on ignoring Bender's last invite—somehow the privilege of calling Bender had fallen to Alex. He knew that Bender would respond to Alex's greeting with a long, satisfied silence. But it was even longer than Alex expected. Alex interrupted Bender's pleasure and tried to explain the issue in a brief, halting monologue, which Bender cut off to issue the magnanimity for which Alex had hoped. "I would be more than happy to see the boy," he had said in a narrowly professional tone. Then he clarified that it was uncustomary for him to answer the telephone—he had a receptionist; two in the morning, such was demand—and that Bella out front would take down the details. "We take cash and credit cards but no checks," Bender specified before instructing Alex to hold the line.

As chatty as her employer was clipped—given Max's name and age, Bella sighed and broke into a sedative patter—the receptionist caused Alex a mild palpitation when she named the cost of a forty-five-minute session (one hundred dollars). "It's twenty-five dollars less than the usual rate," she said. Sensing this wasn't enough, she added: "And a hundred and fifty less than a therapist in the city."

+

"What have *I* been up to?" Bender asked. Alex and Maya were seated in front of him, Max outside in reception. Alex had been considering the psychologist's office with hostility—a globe on a spindle; a foot-long replica of a sailboat replete with baby sailors;

for some reason, scales of justice—and had asked the question with an excessive and insincere enthusiasm. Bender joined his hands and shrugged: "I have written a book." He rose and extracted a slim volume from a wood-paneled bookshelf that held heavy blue tomes expressing the full range of mental disorder. Between them, the glossy white volume roosted insignificantly, though Bender had augmented its presence by stacking a dozen copies together. "You can keep it," he said, returning to his chair. "Maybe you'll learn something." They watched his thin fingers scrawl out a dedication on the front page.

In general, he had not aged. He did not look younger than his fifty-five or so, but not older, either. It occurred to Alex that it was this stranded age that made socializing difficult, for Bender and his wife (technically she was younger than Bender, but she looked like his mother, which always made Alex think of George H. W. and Barbara Bush, during whose tenure Alex and Maya had married) were older than Alex and Maya but younger than Eugene and Raisa. His own haleness Bender had once, on being faced with a less-than-salubrious table at the Rubins', attributed to being a gourmand. (That is what he said: "I am a gourmand," which Eugene sang out in mockery at least once a week.) Bender ate sushi three times a week and boiled greens most of the rest and did not long for any of the sinful indulgences Raisa had laid out. "You have a lucky metabolism," he had said to Eugene, "but cholesterol is cholesterol. You are thin thanks to genes. I am thin thanks to consciousness." "It turns out he's a nutritionist also," Eugene had said, flicking a slice of peppered fatback into his mouth.

"There you are," Bender said, extending the title. Maya and Alex both reached for it, which led to nervous laughter. *The Revelation of a Russian Psychotherapist on the American Land*, the cover said. It depicted, in one collapsed tableau, a kerchiefed woman in a peasant smock alighting from a ship hold with a dusty valise and a trembling smile; the Statue of Liberty, its face crossed with something other than joy on sighting this belted Madonna of steerage; and the Chrysler Building piercing the sky like a phallus. The book was self-published and written directly in English.

"We will read it very closely," Maya said.

"There is a section on the psychological lessons of Russian literature," Bender said. "I hope it meets with Raisa's approval." Raisa had been a literature instructor in the Soviet Union. Bender bent his head in tribute.

"They send their greetings," Maya rushed to add.

"How is Eugene?" Bender's face clouded over. "I'm grateful for the jam, but in honesty—too much sugar. There are sugarless jams—he should look into it."

"Since our time is so short," Alex broke in, "we would like to tell you the situation with Max." Alex looked at Maya, hoping she would continue.

Maya was about to start, but Bender cut her off. "I do not care what the parents think," he waved his hand. "I care what the child thinks. How about you switch places with the boy? Just wait outside. Bella can give you coffee, or there is a deli just a quarter mile down the road. Come back in"—he checked his watch—"thirty-five minutes." He looked up at Alex, who fought heat in his face.

"What are we supposed to tell him?" Alex said. "We thought you would discuss it with us. We said we are going to the doctor because his mother has an appointment."

"Oh, yes?" Bender smiled with pity. "Perhaps, indeed, we should begin with the parents. But when the stove is broken, you start with the stove. Then you can check the gas lines." He fell back in his chair to allow this observation to settle on the Rubins. "You are not professionals," he went on, "but you haven't helped with this deception. Now the boy will feel tricked." He shot his cuffs, gathered his hands into a steeple, and laid his elbows on the edge of his desk. "Let's work with what we've got. You made white black, let's not make it white all over again. I'll tell him that I've spoken to his mother, and now I'd like to speak to him, because maybe he can tell me something that'll help. Does he remember me?" Bender said.

"We speak about you all the time," Maya lied.

Maya dreaded explaining to Max that Bender wanted to speak to him, but even before the psychologist came bounding out after the Rubins, the boy put down the magazine in his hands and obediently slid off his chair, as if accepting a punishment.

The parents watched Bender's door close. Maya's heart tumbled. Was she doing damage? No, they had to try. What damage could a half hour with that man do? Bender, at least, seemed confident of improvement. And who knew? Her boy might walk out of the room changed; isn't that what psychologists specialized in? She was cornering herself with worry so she could remember that things might, after all, turn out more positively. She wondered if she rang an alarm merely to feel relief at its falseness.

Maya tried to occupy herself by flipping through Bender's book. Bender, who seemed disapproving of so much, turned out to also contain great enthusiasms, which he allowed to pour forth within the privacy of two covers. An immigrant at the not-very-old but no-longer-so-young age of thirtysomething, Bender had been driven by immigration and a motherly wife into a responsible vocation, setting, and lifestyle. But within burned a performer, a wit, an irregular mind. "Hello, my dear fellow Americans!" his preface began. "Russians have come! Being a psychologist I had paid attention to your American psychotherapy, of course. And so many thoughts and feelings came to my mind! Once a youthful poet from one good old Russian movie said: 'Happiness—it is when you are understood.' And I have a strong desire to share with you my thoughts and feelings. Reading textbooks is useful, but it is boring, I will tell you. But trying to help myself and other people to adapt to your country, I wrote my book, where the rules of psychology are expressed on the basis of the examples from life, literature, and art."

Maya flipped the pages to see if Bender had culled any lessons from family life, but despaired to see, after the dedication—a quote about trees and flowering out that Bender had scrawled in a Soviet person's unmistakable hand, at once florid and cramped—no such subject included in the table of contents:

I. What Does Classical Russian Literature Tell Us About American Psychotherapy?
II. Psychological Sketches from the Lives of Famous People
III. Meeting Interesting People
IV. Special Topics
    a. Cultural Shock
    b. Homosexuals

Desolately, Maya flipped back to the preface. There she was heartened to read Bender's observation that family issues did not receive a separate section because you couldn't get very far in *any* of the listed subjects without touching on family. "There is no life without family—just as there is no malady without family," Bender observed tartly. This set him off on a wistful recollection of Tolstoy's eternal maxim about unhappy families from *Anna Karenina*, an elegant transition to the first section. Maya flipped closed the book. What explained the universe's obsession with this novel? She had cracked its stiff cardboard spine at last in tenth grade with an excitement exceeding her first sexual congress (which had taken place not many months before). What followed described the sexual congress as well: confusion and then disappointment. Why would a woman like Karenina fall in love with a man like Vronsky? He was handsome, apparently, though Tolstoy did not make him transcendently so; other than that, it wasn't clear what he had in his favor. And Maya had heard the phrase "a woman like Karenina" many times before she wondered what was so special about Karenina herself, her endless mooning and splashing of hands. The whole setup felt provincial, long-winded, tiresome.

She looked at Alex, but he had closed his eyes and leaned his head against the wall. She opened the book once again. Here and there, Bender's discussion was leavened by lovely turns of phrase

of which she had not imagined the therapist capable. "The husband and wife are the long conversation," she saw on one page. On
another, he referred to immigration as the "cold shower of a new
life." In the celebrity section, which turned out to be a section on
celebrity scandals, Bender dispensed with Bill Clinton's indiscre-
tions in one sentence—"I did not vote for him"—before settling
into the subject that truly held him: the Kennedys. And it was here
that Maya began to glimpse the logic behind the approach Bender
was, quite possibly, employing on her son at that very moment.
For Bender, the Kennedy curse was nothing more mysterious than
a series of sons buckling under the obligation to live up to their
forefathers. "It often happens in families," Maya read with a chill,
"where children are passively and obediently doing what their parents want without their own understanding." To think, stamp-sized
JFK Jr. saluting his father's coffin with a stoic expression because
Jackie O had explained that *Kennedys don't cry!* "Perhaps it would
have been better if he had cried!" Bender shrieked uselessly into
the abyss of the young martyr's memory. "He even did not want
to take his last fatal flight," Bender insisted, pointing out that the
young Übermensch was an Untermensch pilot. "His *wife* wanted
that," the section's last line tolled like the bell of a graveyard. Maya
saw Bender shaking his head as he walked off the stage.

Was Max obeying his parents against his will? (And what did *his*
will want? to eat grass?) Maya was not heartened by this theory,
but she was lifted, at least, by the arrival of *some* theory. Until this
emergency circumstance, the Rubins—and now Maya counted
herself among them—had regarded psychology as the province
of lunatics and emotional diddlers, but in actuality it seemed full
of ideas, and relatively normal human beings trying to arrive at
answers to formidable questions. Maya felt a new fondness for
Bender. However, this impression was dispelled by the author's
presentation of another case study, involving a young man only a
handful of years older than Max—Sam. Sam's problem was that
he had not asked to be brought to America, but had been, at an

impressionable age, and the shocking unfamiliarity of what he encountered, coupled with his voicelessness in the matter, spurred him into a violent seesaw between quasi-autistic withdrawal into Russian books and music (increasingly dark) and bouts of rage and destruction of American property. Until he sat down for a talk with psychologist Bender.

"'It is we who came to the Americans, not them to us,' very carefully I was telling Sam," Bender relayed. He expanded his vista: "Pioneers of new lands did not have culture shock, because first of all, they were not passive! They were realizing clearly that they were going to another world. And they were acting: either attacking or being attacked. They felt themselves the seekers, not the victims of new circumstances." Bender relayed from his own history: "I remember how one of our first American friends liked to say: 'I have only one life, but you, two.' Both of them must be settled inside us, I told Sam, making us twice happier."

Was the doctor proposing the opposite of what he had suggested by JFK Jr.'s experience? The young Kennedy had been ruined by assimilating too much the circumstances he was brought into; Sam, on the other hand, had to dive into them in order to save himself. (Dive he did, "very carefully taking the first steps in his new life," according to Bender's humble postscript.) Or was Maya, due to her inexperience, failing to understand that there was no contradiction at all?

Dejected, Maya looked at Alex again, but he was still trying to pretend he was not there, his eyes closed and his arms crossed at his chest. Bella, who turned to face Maya every several minutes to propose the taking of coffee (upturned pinky, inquiring expression), was blissfully fixed on her computer screen. Maya felt vastly alone. She had the impression that outside the drawn shades of Bender's office existed a pure nothingness; she would open the front door of the converted ranch home and find beyond the aluminum-stamped steps a clean void. Inside, all resembled an ordinary doctor's office on Skyline Extension; out there, the opalescent deep. Maya coughed out a noise of self-ridicule, drawing a solicitous stare and a pinky from Bella.

Maya's stomach roiled. The void was also inside her. What a sentiment. Perhaps one did not even have to pay Bender; one could simply visit his reception room, whereupon the premises would confer a measure of enlightened unease. But then imagine what paying treatment might do, Maya thought, excitement returning to her; once again, she touched the hope that Max would emerge from Bender's office cured rather than baffled. Maya sensed that she had been short on such hope, and this was the reason a quarry was going off inside her stomach. That, and the parade of insights, or at least possibilities, that was besieging her. She felt slightly high.

At the end of Bender's opus, Maya found a *third* diagnosis of Max's condition, though initially she disliked drawing lessons from the section on homosexuality. Citing the stories of homosexuals such as—here Bender committed a slight Freudian slip of his own— "the world-renounced dancer gay Nureyev," Bender posited that rather than some kind of genetic destiny, homosexuality was either a rebellion against female liberation or a response to rejection. (Eleanor Roosevelt doted on her husband, but after he spurned her, what was she to do?) The next paragraph stopped Maya: "We must not forget that God created male Adam and female Eve. He did not create two gays or two lesbians. We are living in an open democratic society, not to tolerate any power over us. But we cannot say the same about power of the rules of Life!" In other words, genes are not a democracy. What had been written in JFK Jr.'s genes? In Sam's? In Max's? In her own? And was that what mattered, then, rather than resisting or welcoming circumstance? Maya wanted to ask Bender, though she felt the words would not form coherently if she spoke them out loud. She flipped to the end of the book. The back cover offered a glimpse of the author himself gazing solemnly into a mirror, the toll extracted by his emissions (their echo so disproportionate to their meager span of ninety-five pages) hooding his eyes—the greenhorn of the front cover transformed.

The door to Bender's office opened, cracking the dusty silence of the reception room. Max blinked twice and stepped out. Bender watched diagnostically from the doorway. Then he tapped his watch and summoned the parents inside with an impatient twirl of one hand. Maya went toward Max but he climbed back in his seat and rested his forearms on the arms of the chair, like a satisfied customer. He seemed less nervous.

"The boy has dreamed about pike," Bender announced to Maya and Alex when the door was closed behind them.

"He told you that?" Maya said resentfully.

Bender parted his hands wordlessly: a skilled professional gets the job done. "I made lemonade out of your ruse," he said. "I said his mother had been having bad dreams lately, and so I was wondering if it was a family-wide problem. That was when he told me about the pike."

"What about the pike?" Alex said.

"I'm afraid I must protect client confidentiality," Bender declared.

"What is the point of all this then?" Alex said. Maya laid a palm on his wrist.

"To heal your son?" Bender said. "I have two observations to share with you. You can call one good news, one bad news. Which would you like first?"

Maya and Alex glanced at each other.

"The pike," Bender went on without waiting, "is, essentially, the Russian national fish. It's present here in America, but in nothing like the volume back home. Surely your father took you fishing for pike, Alex."

"I was quite young when we left," Alex said.

"There are entire communities in Siberia that would not survive without it. You can attribute a portion of Russia's control of that vast region to the presence of pike. They have so much pike the dogs eat pike in Siberia.

"In any case, what I'm saying is that the boy is making good progress in the direction of his—his—his"—here, Bender's smooth monologue stumbled and his brows rode together. Bender's desire to obliterate his visitors with the power of his diagnosis had foundered on the uneasy etiquette of discussing adoption. No one among the Rubins' acquaintances officially knew, though all understood. The psychologist took in a long breath and composed himself. "In the direction of his adopted culture," he finished calmly.

Maya and Alex exchanged glances once more. They were prepared to celebrate, and they were prepared to despair, but they realized they didn't understand which reaction Bender's revelation was supposed to elicit.

"Which culture is the adopted culture?" Maya tried to clarify.

"That's the good news," Bender ignored her. "The bad news is that the pike is easily the most murderous freshwater fish in the world. They call pike 'waterwolves,' did you know that? Their teeth are like needles. When they come upon prey, they contract like a mamba and then lunge. I'm not talking about bluegills either. They will eat muskrats, duck, other fish their own size. They swim around with tails hanging out of their mouths—they can't quite get down the victim. They build no nests and give no care to their young. Baby pike eat other baby pike to survive."

"How do you know all this?" Alex said incredulously.

Bender flared his nose. He was caught between the desire to perpetuate his visitors' impression of his work as a recondite craft and an equal compulsion to show them his research skills. The latter had the advantage of schooling his guests. He rose, plundered two shelves, and deposited two tomes on the edge of his desk: a book on the interpretation of dreams, and the *Encyclopedia Britannica* volume for Otter–Rethimnon.

"Elementary, my friends," Bender folded his arms.

"But what does it all mean?" Maya inquired hesitantly.

"He is making the transition to his adopted culture," Bender said, now getting out the sensitive words without difficulty. "Alas, it is not an untroubled transition."

"But he's eight," Alex said. "It's been eight years."

"Until we are adolescents, and even beyond," Bender said, staring off into the window, where the sun suffused the parking lot, "every day is a new world. Add to that having to get used to a whole other culture." Bender tried on a poetic summation: "For him, it's a new world squared."

"So what do you propose?" Alex said.

"You should be glad you came to see me," Bender said. "An American therapist wouldn't answer that question for thirty sessions. Milk your teat a bit first." He caught himself. "Forgive my language, Maya." Then he realized that his phrasing had also reminded his patients of their infertility. He ground his teeth.

"The boy is a boy," Bender said secretively. "He's growing. And childhood is a mystery." Alex was prepared to receive these words as a confirmation of his view that there was nothing especially wrong with Max, and that everyone around him loved to panic. But then Bender swerved away. "Clearly, the boy is acting out some kind of fantasy," Bender said. "So: Guide his fantasy. Take charge of his fantasy."

Maya did not understand. Did Bender want her to run away with her son? But how? Max had not alerted her of his disappearance.

"You are wondering how," Bender read her mind. "I'll tell you how. Select him a new name. Let him choose it. Also, acquire him an animal. Again, let him say which. His choices—they will say things."

But what if he chooses a snake? Maya thought. Or a rhinoceros, for God's sake. Maya deplored the way certain specialists—dentists, mechanics, accountants, apparently psychologists also—gave out results without explaining how they had arrived at them.

"That is, of course," Bender said, "if Eugene will tolerate an animal on his carpets. In six months, come back, if you wish. Though"—Bender leaned forward conspiratorially—"I think you won't need to come back."

"That's it?" Maya asked feebly. "A new name and an animal?"

"Once more," Bender said wearily, "most therapists will take ten months—and ten months of billing—to tell you that. But I am a healer. My goal is to heal, not supervise monologues while I plan a vacation." He folded his lips modestly and opened his right hand. Maya and Alex turned around to see where he was pointing. But Bender was merely showing the Rubins the door—time was up.

In the reception room, their son, having surrendered to Bella's ministrations, was gnawing on a candy bar. Maya was perplexed—Max was customarily indifferent to sweets, the one child in the world. Perhaps it was easier to overcome his disinterest in candy than to fend off the receptionist's siege. Bender followed Maya and Alex out of his office. "I asked Max what he thinks of his mother's condition," he announced to everyone. Bella looked up from the computer and Max stopped chewing. "He believes his family suffers from an overly relaxed attitude toward returning friends' phone calls." Bender giggled. With that, he spun on his heel and ran inside his office before the Rubins had a chance to respond. Maya had forgotten all about the questions she had meant to ask the psychologist.

+

The drive back home was less fraying than the drive out. The roads out multiplied, multiplied, multiplied until the great green signs above the roadway forced a driver to choose between six lanes and four highways; the roads back fed and funneled until there was only the single drive leading down to the Rubins. It was not a grand house. But they were marking their twentieth year inside it. Nothing of particular distinction had happened inside it: the occasional barbecue, a snowstorm. Longevity helps where singularity fails.

Maya and Alex had had to fight no one for the town house. It was a strange construction—no basement, a ground floor with an open design, and a cluster of bedrooms off a tight landing upstairs. It was unfitting for a standard Acrewood family, which needed a formal dining room and a basement for toys. No, the Rubins didn't have any children. No, they didn't know when they would. Alex attempted to explain that it wasn't a practical home—it would make resale challenging—but Maya had pleaded with him. The architecture made her feel open, unboxed. They had Filipinos, always smiling, next door, an old Italian who made his own wine on the other side, and up the drive a retiree now devoted full time to enforcing development code, such as when Alex was alerted by the management office that he had painted their garage door the wrong shade of off-white. They all lived in standard Acrewood homes, and Maya loved when the plum-colored darkness swallowed them up.

Inside, the clutter Maya had tried to keep away was eventually introduced anyway by the inability of the elder Rubins to refrain from buying things for their children. Within Eugene and Raisa, the immigrant desire to see how much of a day could pass without the spending of money collided with the American unease at seeing the sun sink without having parted with so much as a cent. The elder Rubins resolved this conflict by refusing themselves the luxuries that they then bought for the children. In this way, every windowsill in Maya's dining and living rooms came to be decorated by items like a set of martini glasses filled with plastic gin bobbing with plastic maraschino cherries and olives. While cleaning one weekend, Maya reached out a finger and dragged one of them off the sill by the stem. She watched it bang to the floor without breaking. Dismayed, she picked it up and put it back on the sill. There were eleven more.

"Maxie?" Maya called out to the backseat. "Have you ever wanted a different name?"

Alex shook his head at the wheel.

"Where do names come from?" Max said. The seat belt back there looked too large on him, as if it wouldn't protect him in an accident. He was flanked by the same tray of Turkish confections, minus the one bottle Bender had kept out of politeness. Maya and Alex would have to hide the tray in the garage and empty it down pasha by pasha.

"Mamas and papas give names to their babies," Alex said. "When they're born," he added carefully.

"Why did you call me Max?" Max said.

Maya wondered if this line of questioning meant that Bender was on to something. "Did Bender say something, honey?" Maya said. "I mean, Dr. Bender?"

"You take Maya—your mama," Alex said. "And you take Alex—me. And you add them together. What do you get?" He inclined his heads toward the backseat. No answer came.

"You take the first two letters of your mama's name, and the last letter of mine, and what do you get?" Alex repeated.

"Max," Max acquiesced.

"See?"

"I like it," said Max.

"He likes it," Alex repeated.

"But that's not what Grandma and Grandpa did with you," Max said. "Eugene. And Raisa." He thought about it.

"Sometimes you get named after someone your parents want to remember," his father said. "I had a grandfather named Alex. He died before I was born. They called me Alex to honor him."

"What's honor?"

"You'll learn all about it when you grow up," Alex said. "Don't crowd your head."

"Honor is respect," Maya said. "It's when you like someone very much." She turned back to her son. He seemed less upset than when they had left. She allowed herself to be supported by this.

"If you like another name better than Max, you can tell us," she said. She weathered a look from Alex. "For instance, when I was little, I wanted to be called Zoya. Do you want to call me Zoya once in a while instead of Mama?"

Max shook his head.

"Okay—what if I call you Maximilian?"

"No."

"What if I call you Sam?"

"Noooo," Max whined.

Alex kept his eyes on the windshield—she could try if she wanted. He savored his success with Max and did not want to be sullied by Maya's failure. Maya fidgeted in the front seat. Her seat belt was suffocating her. She hated seat belts. She had been told at the hospital that in some countries motorists could purchase T-shirts emblazoned with a diagonal black stripe, to fool traffic policemen.

"What about Tim?" she said to her son.

"What is wrong with you?" Alex hissed.

Maya saw the beginning of tears on Max's face. Because she had gone too far? Because Alex had raised his voice? They did not allow themselves to argue in front of Max. Alex's eyes bored into the side of her face. "Watch the road," she said in defeat. She asked him to pull over, knowing he didn't like to—he didn't wish to be in the breakdown lane unless he was really in breakdown—and climbed into the backseat next to Max, where she covered him with kisses. She cradled her son against the flat board of her chest and rocked him until he quieted down. Alex chauffeured silently the rest of the way.

When they returned to the house, Alex shut himself in the garage, as if he had been the one whom Maya had unfairly attacked. Maya, no nerve to take on a large meal, diced fresh vegetables for a salad. She was so absentminded that after she had chopped cucumbers, carrots, and a handful of roasted red peppers, she started hacking the knife through a mound of corn kernels. She let the knife fall to the board, drew a wrist across her forehead, and closed her eyes. She was interrupted by the porch door sliding open to reveal Eugene and Raisa hefted with grocery bags. "So, are the inner demons cured?" Eugene yelled. As if Alex had been waiting for the appearance of referees, the garage door burst open.

"Who's got the inner demons?" he battered his wife. "Tim, she calls him." He lowered his voice. "Why don't you tell him his mother's name, too? Sit him down and tell him the whole story." He raised it again: "Meanwhile, that genius wants him to change his name and purchase an animal." He held up a palm, fastidious and insulted; the fingers were tight with each other as if he was swearing on a sacred book. "No more quackery. I went along with this, but: enough."

"I told you," Eugene said happily.

"But Bender was your idea," Maya said to her husband. "I wanted to take him to an American psychologist."

"Was taking him to a psychologist my idea?" Alex said. "Psychologists are for mentally ill people." Alex mimed a paraplegic. "Max is fine. I've talked with him. We understood each other. He's perfectly normal."

"Except for this one thing," Maya said. "Which puts his life in danger."

Alex cast Maya a contemptuous look. "You keep taking him to Bender and the like, they'll find what you want and ten other things. Anything to keep the checks coming."

"Someone's always cheating you, Alex," Maya said.

"For me, this is the end of the conversation." Alex's look furiously offered to repay further silence with silence. Eugene and Raisa swiveled their heads between them.

"Bender made several points in his book—" Maya began.

"The end!" Alex bellowed. He did not allow himself to raise his voice at his wife often.

Maya gave up and returned to the vegetables. Alex returned to the garage. Eugene unloaded the grocery bags around Maya, whistling an old tune. Raisa admonished him—it was bad luck to whistle inside.

7

2004

Adopting a child, it turned out, was nearly as difficult as conceiving one. Mishkin, the new adoption supervisor, had laughed when the aspiring parents had gently inquired whether a Jewish child might be available. "A Jewish child?" he'd said. "A unicorn comes online more often than Jewish." Even though the Rubins were participating in the last American pastime that allowed for open discrimination—they could ask for Jewish; the birth parents could ask for non-Jewish—realistically, their choice was between a Catholic, familiarly dark-haired but unfamiliarly Hispanic, and a Protestant, familiarly Caucasian but unfamiliarly blond. Asian Americans seemed to fall into the same category as Jews, though there were plenty of Asian children from Asia. There were African American children, of course, and these were—no way around it—less expensive, but the Rubins could perform only one radical departure from the familiar at a time.

Periodically Mishkin called to haggle: raise the acceptable age; expand the list of eligible birth countries; change the adoption from "closed" to "open"—no one did "closed" anymore. Several times Maya came close to buckling, but then Alex spoke to the supervisor in such a way that Mishkin never needled again. Maya was at once grateful and angry. Grateful to be looked after, angry that Alex had disciplined the man who, Maya felt, held the keys to the kingdom. And, in fact, Mishkin, who was on speakerphone, had signed off with: "You want the impossible. You want an American newborn in five minutes or less, without a relationship with the birth parents."

"What, Mr. Mishkin, you work on commission?" Alex had re-plied. The line went dead.

Three generations before, Mishkin's own ancestors had made the passage from Old World to new, and the soft spot—not to say unreasonable patience—that Mishkin confessed to feeling for the Rubins he explained on account of this heritage. In fact, the Rubins had stirred in him such a fury of curiosity and nostalgia that he decided to embark on a self-discovery tour in the archives of both the Mishkin family and Ellis Island. It was because Mish-kin had overheard the Rubins whispering in what he thought was Russian at IAS that he had inquired, and volunteered to take over the file from Slab-Face.

This was a strange custom of American Jews: They assaulted recent émigrés from the former Pale with biographical thumb-nails meant to produce . . . what exactly? Maya would listen po-litely before finally, timidly, asking if the Rubins' profile had had any bites. It had not, Mishkin conceded, which filled Maya with a brutal sense of rejection, as if not only genetics but even other humanity had deemed the Rubins unworthy of parenthood.

"Ask him if he knows Mishkin is the name of Dostoevsky's idiot," Eugene remarked after yet another Mishkin monologue about pat-rimony, casting a meaningful look at his wife, the former teacher of literature. Eugene, like his son, considered Mishkin tainted by the whole idea of adoption and refused to deal with him, leaving it to Maya, though the adoption supervisor's cavalier style and self-absorbed prologues enabled Eugene to pretend that he disliked Mishkin on Maya's behalf.

"Dostoevsky's idiot is an idealistic figure," Raisa reminded her husband.

And then, with no ceremony—"it only takes one," Mishkin had warned them, "like love"—the wait was suddenly over. A young couple in Montana had chosen them to receive their newborn. Maya felt rewarded, or placated. Like an addict slipping back under the spell, she had cooked prodigious amounts of food during their months of waiting for news, pressing it on the senior Rubins, Moira and the others at the hospital, the trashman, the electric-meter man, the lawn guys, the lifeguard at the Sylvan Gate pool. Periodically, Alex would wander into the kitchen, purse his lips at the bedlam, extract the cognac from the cupboard, and tiptoe out carefully. "The maternal instinct is kicking in," Eugene observed sourly. She had pressed her kitchen, the only blandishment in her arsenal, so fervidly on the universe that God had broken down, relented, agreed to send her a child if only she'd quit. However: Montana?

"The child must be sick in some way," Maya had said to Mishkin when he'd told her, late one afternoon. She was just back from the hospital.

"No!" Mishkin yelled. "Not at all. You must not think in that old-world way, Mrs. Rubin."

"So what is the reason?" she said, trying to ignore Mishkin's insult. She tried to sound skeptical. How odd that a child could be announced like the win in a contest. But wasn't that the way with normal mothers? One day they woke up and, eureka: pregnant. It was in what followed that the pathways diverged. A normal mother had nine months to get used to the result; Maya could have her child right away. She stopped herself: She was missing crucial information being transmitted by Mishkin. In the chaos of her mind, he appeared to her as a spoonbill, the huge mouth moving endlessly.

"We don't know the reason, Mrs. Rubin," he was saying. "We don't ask. But the child is healthy. Which isn't always the case, you are right. But it is here. Full medical checkup, full family history, verified and reverified."

"He is just born?" she said.

"Just about."

"So why don't they want him?" Maya said.

"Do *you* want him, Mrs. Rubin? Let's not lose our eyes on the prize here. They chose you, Mrs. Rubin. They want you."

Maya tried to ignore the warming flush of the affirmation.

"Why us?" she insisted. She tried to keep up the skepticism that Alex would have channeled were he home. (Had the adoption supervisor purposefully called when he knew he would get the gullible Rubin?)

"I don't know. Because you're far. They want the baby to go far."

"Far from where?"

"Montana, like I told you."

"What's wrong with Montana?" Maya said. "Where is it?"

"Again, I don't know. I mean, I know where Montana is. I don't know what's wrong with it. Nothing's wrong with it. It's beautiful."

"It can't be more beautiful than New Jersey," Maya said savagely, and, defeated by the mysteriousness of her ill will, sank into a chair.

"I don't have a dog in this fight except you getting a kid, Mrs. Rubin," Mishkin said. "Can I ask you a question because this, actually, we didn't discuss. Did you hope for a boy or a girl?"

"I don't know," Maya said. "A boy?"

"Okay," he said. *"Okay.* It's a boy."

In the kitchen that evening, Maya and Alex sat and stared at each other. Montana? Well, they had demanded an American child; this, too, was part of America. They had imagined Chicago, Florida, even Texas. But Montana? Maya had almost asked Mishkin if English was spoken there, then lamented her idiocy.

On the phone, she had declared that she would refuse the adoption until she spoke to the parents. With satisfaction, the adoption supervisor reminded her that she and her husband had insisted on closed. Photos would come via the agency, the medical work-over, too. But no information about the parents. At a certain point, the Rubins would have to fly to Montana and take up residence in a hotel room while the state verified their identity and dotted the *i*'s with New Jersey. Then the child was theirs.

The pictures arrived with an equally perturbing lack of significance; she was looking at a newborn with sleepy eyes and a wary expression. He looked like a big cake. Why was this her child?

Desperately, she studied the margins of the photographs instead of the child at their center. Who were the parents? How did they live? Were there baby wipes in Montana? How did they hold the feet when they wiped him? Did he get diarrhea? How much diarrhea was okay before getting concerned? It was the parents she wished to possess. By being denied to her, they became what she most wanted to know. She and Alex signed the papers.

A week after, the late-evening phone call came—too late for it to mean anything good. Alex was on the La-Z-Boy clicking through channels, and Maya was making a soup to last their lunches the rest of the week. Wooden spoon fishing for cabbage leaves, she called out to Alex, but he had fallen asleep. She hustled over to the cordless and jammed the receiver under her ear. Her stomach lurched. Mishkin wouldn't call so late unless there was terrible news, unless it could not wait till the following morning, unless it was all off.

"Mrs. Rubin," he said. "You sitting down?" For a moment, Maya wondered if Mishkin was going to make her sit down at nine thirty P.M. just so he could tell her: The adoption was off. Or: The ancestral Mishkins had grown plums.

"So, look, Mrs. Rubin," Mishkin said. "Adoptions are volatile. Emotions are high. It doesn't mean—a person's unstable. It drives people to act . . . in ways they wouldn't otherwise act. In yourself—I think you've seen that."

"Excuse me?" Maya said. The choppy way in which Mishkin spoke made Maya suspicious, as if he was titrating information whose badness, should it come in a torrent, would become obvious.

"Never mind that," Mishkin said. "My point is, Laurel's a firecracker. She's eighteen, but she comes on with a force twice of that. A hole in my ear every time that we talk. You two are made for each other. You ought to meet."

"We can't," Maya reminded him.

"Well, that's just it," Mishkin said.

"What, Mishkin, what!" Maya demanded. In her condition,

she had forgotten to filter his name through the sieve of diplomacy and referred to him by the shorthand used by the Rubins. But Mishkin was silent, a hesitation unbecoming the cataract of Gabriel Mishkin. Whereas a moment before Maya was angry, now she was frightened.

"Now don't *you* go cuckoo on me about this, all right?" the adoption supervisor finally said. "I've been in this business getting on twenty years and I've never seen it myself. But it's high emotion, like I said. Makes people do funny things. The mother is a wild one. Not that—not that—please don't think she's irresponsible. You can tell these are responsible, well-thinking young people because they've chosen you to adopt their boy. That's how you know."

"Please explain right now," Maya said, stifling a wave of murderous anger.

"Laurel and Tim," Mishkin said. "They want to deliver the child."

"What do you mean 'deliver'?" Maya said.

"You know—like takeout." Mishkin giggled.

Maya wanted to tell Mishkin that he could be far more pious toward the vocation he had selected, but she didn't dare. She felt she depended on this man's goodwill, even as she detested both him and that fact. She didn't say anything, for if she spoke, she would speak an insult.

"They want to bring the child, Mrs. Rubin. Hand him over to you. And I know it doesn't sound like it, but this is a positive development. It saves you from—if you'd gone to pick up the child, you'd have to sit in a Montana hotel room for three weeks while the states talked to each other. Otherwise, it's kidnapping. But if the parents bring him to you?" Mishkin produced a whistling noise meant to indicate *problem solved.*

Maya remained silent.

"Mrs. Rubin, the child is a blessing," Mishkin said. "Healthy and beautiful. The only thing holding you back now is all of a sudden you're wondering what you got yourself into. I know the feeling.

But you're not like your husband—I say this with all due respect. You have the drive. Leap forward, Mrs. Rubin. I know this is unconventional. But if you get past the wrapping, it's actually a very good thing. I know you always think I am trying to push you. I have nothing to sell here except the fulfillment of what you told me you wanted. This is what I'll never understand about you folks, no matter how much time you spend in the country. You fight like no one fights for the things that you want. And then they arrive, and you push against them like children. Why is this, Mrs. Rubin? I guess it has to wait until the next generation. Well, I am giving you the next generation. Please take it."

Maya was speechless. She was within rights to censure him, but he knew that before he spoke, and since he had, anyway, she would not. A long silence ruled the telephone.

"But we are not supposed to know each other," Maya said, enforcing a rule she hadn't made.

"Yes, it's not standard," he said. "But there's a lot of leeway built in. You know their first names already—you won't know their last. You'll see what they look like, of course, but they live two thousand miles away, you don't know what town. Unless you go looking for them, I doubt it makes a difference in practice."

"They're not the only ones I am thinking about," Maya said, defensive of her husband. "They will know where we live. What about that? The point of a closed adoption is it's closed. This way, they can drop down on us whenever they wish! That's not right. My husband will disagree. No, Mr. Mishkin, this won't work."

"Mrs. Rubin, you can say no. Tell me no, and we will go back to the original plan. Don't worry about it."

"Will the mother become upset because I said no?" Maya said. "Can she change her mind?"

"I have no idea, Mrs. Rubin. I have a hard time with Laurel even when I'm not guessing what's in her mind. But the papers have been signed—that makes it a lot more difficult for her to change it. Mrs. Rubin—this girl is intent on finding her boy a new home. They're eighteen—they can't raise a child. They're Christian, they don't do abortions. They're giving him up. They're too young. You wanted to find out about the parents; you did, I know, even if your husband and your parents-in-law didn't. So here they are. Here's your chance."

"She told you that?" Maya said hungrily. "She told you that was the reason? Too young?"

"No," Mishkin said. "They do not have to explain."

"Why," Maya said helplessly. "Why. That is the most important thing. The very most important thing. It is the only thing they have to explain."

"I don't want to stray into psychological territory, but in life we must occasionally make peace with the fact that we simply won't know. That is their right, not to say. However, if you allow them to come to you, you can ask them."

Maya did not answer. On the other end, Mishkin took a deep breath. The conversation had become intimate. She hated him less.

"You can have this child tomorrow, Mrs. Rubin." Mishkin said. "That is it at its plainest. Do you want to have this child tomorrow?"

"Tomorrow?" Maya said.

"You're wondering why I'm phoning so late in the night," Mishkin dared. "For which I'm sorry, by the way." His tone was grave, and on hearing it, Maya discovered, with petrification, that she preferred the old, unserious Mishkin. "They're harvesting right now, or something: I don't really get it. They've only got the weekend, they need to get back . . ."

"What is it?" Maya yelled, waking up Alex, who looked up reproachfully from the La-Z-Boy.

"They're halfway to you already," Mishkin said. "Now, don't get upset, Mrs. Rubin, I just found out myself. I told you she's impulsive. I tried to explain they had to get your okay, and, look, they're not going to show up on your driveway, they don't even know what town in New Jersey yet. But if you can live with this, Mrs. Rubin—"

The soup bubbled over, hissed the flames, stained the burner, slithered down the face of the oven until it disfigured the kitchen tile. Alex sprang from the recliner intending to halt the absurd progress events had made while he had allowed himself to drift off—he could not let down his guard even for thirty minutes on the backside of the day. But, seeing the wild look in his wife's eyes, he had his first apprehension of the fact that within twenty-four hours he might be holding his son.

+

It was nearly dusk when the headlights of Laurel and Tim's coffee-and-milk Datsun swept across the Rubins' living room. The previous evening, Alex had been made to extract the ancient United States driving atlas the Rubins had been given by the resettlement agency when they'd arrived in America. It still held together—Alex rarely opened it. The cover depicted a dark-skinned man in jeans and Native American headdress hopping around a campfire, an Alaskan iceberg, tall buildings in New York, and a curvaceous brown river.

If they were from Montana, and they were halfway to the Rubins at ten o'clock on Friday evening, when would they reach Acrewood, New Jersey? Maya was returned to the algebra classes of her youth: If Comrade So-and-So's train starts at Point A at eleven o'clock . . . "Maya, don't be silly," Alex said. "Do they stop for the night or do they keep driving? How long do they sleep? It's not possible to answer. Don't panic. When they come, they come." But his voice carried a tremulous note—as superiorly acquainted with America as Alex was, he was alarmed at the prospect of two people from Montana in his home. Three people.

She pushed the atlas at him and asked him to try. He pulled out a notepad and worked at it, finally announcing that Laurel and Tim would be in Acrewood at around seven P.M. the following day, depending.

"So I have to make dinner."

"You don't *have to* make dinner."

"You want to welcome these people with an empty table?" she said. She sank into a chair and covered her eyes. "This is absurd, every step of it."

He laid his palms on her shoulders. "Maya, look at me," he said. She did, because usually he didn't produce effort of this kind. "We've been reading books for a year. We have enough diapers for our child to shit himself until college. This is what you wanted. Your son is coming."

She began to whimper into her fist.

"Now this makes no sense," Alex said.

"I made you do it," she said.

"Did you?" he said. He stared at his hands on her shoulders. "It's a dramatic experience, Maya, so it's natural you would feel upset now. But it doesn't mean you're upset. You're happy." Maya rolled her head into her husband's shoulder, and he pawed at it.

Maya did cook, if only out of anxiety; the dining table was filled with highlights of the Ukrainian kitchen: peppers marinated in buckwheat honey, lemon, and garlic; cabbage salad; and, for good luck, the *grechanniki* that Maya had made all those years before. The table also featured a Mishkin, who, for one, was glad Maya had cooked. When no one was looking, he thieved a disk from the plate of *grechanniki*, encountering the same problem Alex had all those years ago: It wasn't possible to have just one. But he couldn't have another—the Datsun bounced onto the driveway. The dense woodland of gray hair that crowned Mishkin's heavy-jawed face doubled handily as a napkin for his oil-stained fingers—in her nervousness, Maya had forgot to lay out actual napkins. Mishkin looked like he was rubbing anxiety out of his scalp, which neatly aligned him with the Rubins. "Here come the cowboys," Alex said mournfully. Gathered at the living room window, the Rubins could not see into the vehicle, though they believed they could be seen. For a moment, no one emerged.

"Must we open their doors and invite them in?" Alex said.

The two young people who eventually stepped out of the vehicle were shocking in their youthfulness. They were Maya's age
when she had come to America—was that how young she had
looked then? The young woman, Laurel, wore a superfluously
pleated yellow sundress under a turquoise blouse with buttons.
She crouched before the passenger's-side mirror, which showed
her that her hair was unpresentable, and called out in a sharp,
hoarse voice to her boyfriend to wait while she fixed. Tim, coming
around the car, paused. He had a limp in his right leg and wore a
baseball cap. Maya knew his eyes were blue without seeing them.

He looked like the Slavic boys who had used to ask out Maya.
She was adopting a non-Jewish child: this arrived with visceral
clarity at the moment Maya saw Tim's eyes on the other side of her
doorstep. He swept off his baseball cap, revealing a blond buzz cut
of a type Maya had seen on military men, and ears that stood out
slightly. He had a plain face—he had a nose, and eyes, and ears,
but they did not cohere into anything especially memorable—and
weariness in his eyes, but otherwise you couldn't tell, or smell, that
he had been driving for two and a half days.

"Ms. Maya, Mr. Alex," he said, nodding shyly and extending his
hand; he didn't know their last names. "You must be Mr. Mishkin,"
he called out behind them, and she knew that was the first Jewish
surname he had spoken in his life.

"Bad luck to shake across the divider," Alex said, pointing at the
threshold. "Come in, you're tired."

Behind Tim stood Laurel. It must have been due to the radical
emptiness of the territory they inhabited that such a plain-looking
boy could seduce a girl of such prettiness. In this, maybe Montana was like the Soviet Union after the war—any man would do,
twenty million having been lost.

She wore no makeup; the white around each pellucid green
iris burned with redness. Her hair was blond like Tim's, the color
of starved grass. She had finger-combed it, and it splayed every-

where; it fell from a central part like two messy sheets. The sundress, which bore a pattern of monkeys on unicycles, looked like a child's outfit, and was even poorer on close inspection. Maya enviously eyed the two full breasts; was she feeding the child? Under the sleeve of the dress, she saw the sash of an ACE bandage; Laurel was restraining the breasts, to discourage milk.

On the small landing behind them was a car seat with a small bundle in it. The boy was asleep, unmindful of the adults. There was a small gym bag next to him, too small to contain a person's whole life. Tim turned back and picked up the seat. Maya and Alex stared at him, dumbfounded, and even Mishkin was overcome by a deferential silence. "Where should I put him?" Tim asked his wife.

"Give him to the parents," Laurel said coldly, and stepped inside. Tim followed. From one of her pockets, she withdrew folded pieces of looseleaf: "Been writing through ten states," she said to Maya. "Sleep, formula—it's all in there. There's some extra in the bag. You mind emptying it so we can have the bag?"

Tim, as the male biological parent, extended the bundle in his arms to the male adopting parent. The male adopting parent would have preferred his wife to receive the newborn, but hesitated to appear less than authoritative before the profoundly American male before him. The tiny, affectless creature continued to sleep, the slightly upturned nose sniffing the air. His little tongue was shimmied between his lips, like a cat's. The skin—it was newer than anything Maya had seen. That was the only word for it: *new.* She thought: How could someone part from this creature? What kind of person did you have to be? The little person jerked in his sleep, the shoulders shrugging invisibly, and she felt her last, unspeakable terror give way: He was living and breathing; he really existed.

"He was cranky all afternoon," Laurel said. She spoke with the steadiness of someone ten years older—it unnerved Maya. Is that what childbearing did to an eighteen-year-old? She wanted Laurel to be as nervous as she was. "I got him to go down just a little while ago. Let him sleep a little bit longer?" This catalog of domestic rituals and observations covered Maya with jealousy.

"It's safe to drive a tiny baby all that way?" Alex said skeptically.

Of this liability, Maya had not even thought. There were so many, all of them unfamiliar, that this one had not even occurred to her. She wanted to give her husband a restraining look, but she was grateful for the question. Alex noticed things that she didn't—by leaving unnoticed the many things that she couldn't ignore. He allowed those to slide off him, leaving attention for those that mattered.

"It's seven weeks," Laurel said. "Their necks are ready by then. That's why we waited to come here till now. We started the paperwork only once he came out, but we found you a good while before he was born." Together, Maya and Alex looked at Mishkin behind them, but he only shook his head—he didn't know that Laurel and Tim had been planning to drive. Maya didn't know whether she should resent Laurel. She looked at Alex—his eyebrows were crossed with suspicion.

"Why did you pick us?" he said.

"Alex," Maya said. "Let them come in, look around."

"If they've graced us with a visit, they can tell us," Alex said in a way that left clear that no one would be coming in or looking around until the question was answered.

"It was one thing the most," Laurel said. "It was what you wrote about putting your roots down here for a long time. Here in New Jersey."

Hearing his work praised, Alex softened. "And all the other things that go without saying," Laurel went on. "You're good people. Stable, and nice home. You have money. You know what's a baby."

Alex looked at Maya, asking with his face what he should do with the child.

"Please come in, won't you?" she said to Laurel and Tim.

The guests moved down the hallway. The young man favored his right leg. In the presence of such foreign characters, the spread Maya had spent all of Saturday preparing suddenly appeared unacceptably foreign itself. With forced casualness, she took her guests through the dishes. They nodded politely.

"We really shouldn't," Tim said. "We've got a lot of driving ahead. They only gave us so much time at work."

"But you'll stay the night," Maya said. "We have extra bedrooms. We want you to see the house."

"And what is work?" Alex said, hoping to distract the guests from agreeing. He unburdened himself of the car seat on the tiled floor and quickly checked Maya to see if he shouldn't have.

"Laurel's at the front desk at the Ramada," Timothy said. "And me—" He wanted to fidget with his cap but it was long off his head. He rasped his buzz cut with a nail.

"He does rodeo," Laurel said.

"That's with the bulls," Alex said. "And that's a living?"

Tim shrugged. Alex sensed that he was wearing a mask of discomfort for Laurel's sake. "You have one out here too, once a year," Tim said. "At Madison Square Garden. More of a show."

"We haven't been to that," Alex said.

"But we will," Maya reassured Tim. "We will go this year, absolutely."

"No, you won't," Laurel said. From a pocket hiding among the pleats of her dress, she withdrew a crumpled pack of cigarettes and a lighter. The other four stared at her.

"I didn't start it till after," she said, reading the togetherness of Maya's brows. Also Mishkin's—finally, Maya and Mishkin were concerned in the same way.

"Because we were told the child was healthy," Alex said. Maya, who had been exhaling after Laurel's comment, froze after Alex's.

"The child is healthy," Tim said curtly. His face unclenched, regretting his sharpness. "This process been stressful on Laurel."

"Hooray, Tim, for your heart is twenty-twenty now," she said.

"No one smokes in the house," Alex observed.

"I'm sure it's *fine*," Maya said, staring at her husband. She wished to reward Laurel for starting to smoke only after the birth of her—their? her Maya's? her Laurel's?—son.

"I'll go outside," Laurel said.

"I'll join you," Maya said.

"You don't smoke," Alex reminded her.

"I can stand with our guest," she said.

Outside, a cobalt darkness had got hold of the evening. Maya loved this hour. The last light had crept out of the sky, but the full blackness had yet to take over.

"If you move around the corner with me," Maya said to Laurel, "I'll have one with you."

They smoked in silence. Laurel folded one arm under the other.

"I'm sorry we did this," Laurel said at last. "I want you to know I am."

Maya looked at her with surprise. She had been thinking of herself as the one in error, and only now wondered why. "I'm glad you're here," she said. "My husband and I don't have the same views."

"Why his way, then?"

"His need is greater," Maya said.

"I needed to see it for myself," Laurel said. "You can understand that, can't you?"

Maya nodded eagerly. "Of course I can." She pulled on her cigarette without desire. "Are you married?" she said. "The forms didn't say." She added hastily: "It doesn't matter to me."

"We fight like married people, don't we?" Laurel said. She seemed to enjoy the thought.

Maya watched Laurel out of the side of her eyes. This little body had brought forth a child. From where? It must have retracted immediately to its original shape: that was the meaning of youth. Maya surveyed with jealousy the pears of Laurel's breasts, the slight knob of the nose. This body had brought forth a child. As hers never would.

Laurel was going to chuck the butt into the grass, then remembered where she was and crushed it against the heel of her boot. She dropped it into a pocket of her dress. It had many pockets.

"It'll smell," Maya said, watching Laurel light another. "Here, we'll put it in the garbage. Oh, I must be so irritating, talking like your mother. You are half my age, but already a mother yourself."

"Just because we're here," Laurel said, "you don't have to worry about us trying to interfere with you. I just needed to see it." Youthfully, she added: "I promise you."

Maya felt relief—on Alex's behalf. She thought that if ever she had been unfaithful to Alex, he would have wanted her to keep it a secret. And she would not have been able to.

"Some things you should know," Laurel said. "I haven't been breast-feeding him even though this milk wants to come out of me like the Yellowstone. And we haven't named him even though a nameless baby is a pretty Friday-the-thirteenth kind of thing." She dragged on her cigarette hungrily, then looked around her. "I'm just going to sit down in the grass here for one minute."

Before Maya could object or offer a blanket, Laurel was sitting on the grass, her boots one under the other and the pleated sundress flared over her thighs. Maya had an impolite desire to touch her skin. Even in the near-bituminous darkness, she saw it was thick like rubber, just manufactured. Maya was hardly an old maid herself, thirty-four, in America that was just starting out, but Laurel was like a former version of herself come to shame her for waiting so long. Most girls in Kiev were mothers by twenty-one. Instead of a child, Maya had given birth to a new life in America. It was twelve years old now, and she was ready for another. She wanted for it a sibling.

"This grass is soft like hand cream," Laurel said. "It's luscious."

"My husband . . ." Maya started, and trailed off. She found herself without the energy to remark on the lawn now. It was a special concern of Alex's. He worried over it to the point of detriment. She had read that fallen leaves ought to remain—their decomposition fed the soil. But those leaves were in Home Depot bags before they hit the ground. For this, Alex had massive energy. Once, he had hauled himself out of bed with a fever because the leaves were choking his grass and had to get cleared. He was contemplating cutting down the large oak that was responsible until Maya reminded him it would probably lower the home's resale value.

Forgetting her earlier mindfulness, Laurel stubbed her cigarette into the grass. Then she lay down. Maya looked worriedly toward the house and the yellow light falling from the kitchen, which turned a small square of space outside the sliding doors indigo. What were those three discussing? She needed to get back inside.

"Come down here, won't you?" Laurel said.

Maya looked down, flummoxed.

"Just get down here next to me," Laurel said.

Maya's jeans were dark—the grass stain would not show. "Where should I—" she started, and then just came down. The grass was cool under her hair.

"You're shit for stars," Laurel said, looking up.

"There's more where you are?" Maya said.

"It's way open," Laurel said. "You have to drive a couple of miles to see as many homes as I can see from right here. It's like a giant board. And if you do anything too sudden-like, you'll fall off. Here, hold my hand so we don't fall off the board." Nervously, Maya allowed her hand to be fished for in the dark. If Alex saw her now. Laurel had work hands. Was she lying about the Ramada to seem more respectable? They lay listening to cicadas.

"I don't like to fly, either," Maya said, trying to ingratiate herself. "Actually, I can't. It sends me into convulsions. I came to America on a boat, like they did a hundred years ago."

"Oh, I'd like to try flying," Laurel said.

Maya's cheeks colored. She was grateful for the darkness. Laurel and Tim drove not because Laurel couldn't fly—they didn't have the money for it.

Maya lifted herself partway and looked over at Laurel. "I'm sorry for asking this," she said. "Please." No response came from Laurel, but also no objection. "Please tell me he's healthy."

Laurel looked over at Maya. "You've seen the medical history."

"Please."

"He's the healthiest boy you'll ever lay eyes on."

Maya wanted to embrace Laurel down there on grass—then reproached herself; she was always too ready to believe. But then she darkened and said: "Why us, Laurel?"

Laurel stared back up at the sky. "I don't have to tell you he's an accident baby. Tim's eighteen years old, and he makes six thousand dollars a year riding bulls. And you saw the way that he walks. So I don't know if I'll have a husband in a wheelchair in five years. Like half of them end up in wheelchairs, making the best of it. Making the best of it—I hate those words. Being heroes about ending up in a wheelchair. Why can't he make the best of what he's got now— instead of waiting to make the best when he's got so much less? But he wants less, so I gave him less. I ain't letting him raise a child this way. Not with me, if that's what he does with his life. My own fault for getting my days wrong. But Tim and I, we have to be together. Him I can't let go of. Him"—she nodded toward the house, meaning the baby—"I can."

"But how?" Maya said, Laurel's words so unbelievable that she smiled in astonishment.

"I'm going to find out. He'll be with good people. You're good people, I can see it. Earn real money. And don't ride bulls for a living."

Maya wanted to tell Laurel that she was making a mistake. But if she happened to persuade her? She said with incredulity: "He won't quit? He'd rather give up the baby?"

"It's complicated," Laurel said. "In the meantime, decisions need to get made. I made it." She laughed coarsely. "My need was greater."

"But if that's all it is—if it's just his rodeo—" Maya sputtered out.

"Make him stop? Why don't you persuade your husband to change the adoption to open?"

"But that's different! Alex would never—a child!"

"You don't know the first thing about rodeo, so you think it's not important," Laurel said.

"No. Yes. Of course," Maya hurried to appease her. She went back down on the grass. She got relief out of it; propping herself up required a keeping together of something that was allowed to dissolve when prostrate. "We are like castaways on an island here," she said. "Only there's been no accident."

"I guess that's why I wanted it," Laurel said.

After a moment, Maya said: "If our form didn't say 'closed,' would you have agreed to an open adoption?"

"I don't know that," Laurel said. "What's done is done. We didn't specify either way. I care he's far, and with good people. It's probably better this way." Laurel stood up and ran her hands down her thighs and back, but Alex's grass was so severely maintained that none of it had detached onto her dress. "Come on. It's time that he met you."

But Maya wished to keep talking to Laurel. The new information made things less understandable, not more. There was so much more to talk about—enough to justify them remaining known to each other. After a moment, Maya rose, heavier than she had gone down.

Inside, Alex was speaking to Tim with an animation that surprised Maya while Mishkin busied himself on the other side of the dinner table. "We thought you ran away together," the adoption supervisor said on sighting the women, his mouth full of *grechanniki*. "You're a genius at the stove, Maya."

"You'll raise him in the Jewish faith, won't you," Tim said, his idea of a tension-defusing subject change. He looked around the kitchen, as if he expected it to broadcast some signal of Jewishness. The boy continued to sleep in the car seat like a grocery bag that still needed unpacking.

"They might, being Jews," Laurel said.

"We never met someone of the Jewish faith," Tim said. "We read about it."

"We don't drink the blood of Christian babies," Alex said in a failed effort at humor.

Tim regarded him with mortification.

"We are not very Jewish," Maya rushed in. "The Soviet Union was an atheist country. That's how we grew up."

"We're both fairly devout," Tim observed. He looked over at his wife. Alex frowned. Maya wished desperately to change the subject. Tim helped by asking for the bathroom. He was over six feet and had to pull his chair far from the table before his legs could swing out. He limped away.

"What happened to the leg?" Alex asked Laurel, of whom he was slightly afraid. Laurel only grunted luridly.

"Maybe you want some time with him," Alex said, motioning to the car seat.

"We just had forty-two hours together," Laurel said. "The long good-bye."

When Tim returned, the four of them stood awkwardly over the small bundle, the clock clicking from the wall, Mishkin retreated into the corner, from tact or a fearfulness of his own. Laurel broke the silence. She ran her fingers through the gold sheets of her hair and tucked them behind her ears.

"Ma'am," she said, stepping toward Maya. Maya's blood ran cold from the formal greeting. "This is your child. You're the mother. You will raise him as you see fit. But I want to ask you for one thing. This is why we drove two thousand miles. I wanted to look you in the eyes and ask you. Please don't let my baby do rodeo."

She looked at Alex, at Tim, at Maya, at her boy, hers for only the rest of this minute. Then she spun around and walked out of their lives. She hadn't touched her son once since walking inside. And Maya understood that she had been seduced outside, apologized to and reassured and made to look at stars and hold hands, in order to become an ally—someone of whom this request could be made, and who would, through the years, honor it.

8

"I moved to the United States to refine my understanding of bureaucracy," Eugene said sourly. The other Rubins buttered and chewed: Saturday breakfast. Eugene had cleaned his plate and was scratching it with the tines of his fork. "Except you can't bribe anyone here—the government must be allowed to do a poor job without interference." He deposited the fork on his plate with a monk's carefulness—if he allowed disorder into his gestures, he might put the fork through somebody's eye. He was upset because many pallets of New Zealand honey had been held up at Port Newark over a classification error. He had taken the table through the difference between C4 and C3 sugars. "Ten thousand dollars," he said bitterly.

"Please don't count money that hasn't come in yet," Raisa said. "It's bad luck."

"I'm sure it's a misunderstanding," Maya said hesitantly. "If the labels list the right number, they'll have to—"

Eugene gave her a pitying look.

"You know better," Maya whispered, nodding.

Eugene burped and said "Oi." He wiped his mouth and looked at Maya. "A compliment to the cook. And no butter, unless you're not telling the truth. With butter, everyone's a chef."

Maya smiled vanishingly at him.

Eugene turned to Alex and nodded at the backyard. "Those pines look like they've had their balls cut off. Pardon my language," he added, making a face at Max. Then, to Alex: "Your neighbor is showing you his affection?"

"It's deer," Alex said irritably. Three weeks later, the argument with his wife was still with him. He had tried to dispel it with a stumpy centerpiece of hydrangea, spray roses, and carnations, which wilted amiably on the table, but it made no difference to either of them. He had done it without meaning it.

"Tie soap bars to the branches," Eugene said. "I've seen people do it."

"New Year's all year long," his son observed. "With Irish Spring instead of tree ornaments."

"You have to use Ivory," Eugene said. "Irish Spring isn't nasty enough."

"I do your wash with Ivory," Raisa remarked defensively.

Mechanically, Eugene sniffed the collar of his shirt.

"There's a spray now," Alex said. "I just haven't had time." He looked at Max, who was trying to saw down the top of a cereal box with a butter knife. Alex looked back at his father. "Do you know what I found on my stoop a week ago? A ceramic deer half the size of this table. Guess who."

"You should have put it back on his doorstep, the bastard. Sorry, Max."

"No, I took it into the garage, smashed it to pieces, and lobbed them over the fence one by one."

"If one of them landed on his face, he could sue you," Eugene said. "The first lesson of revenge is you leave no marks."

"Can we change the subject to something more pleasant?" Maya said.

Eugene shrugged and looked at the newspaper. "There's nothing pleasant in here."

"Then put it away, sweetheart," Raisa said. "Speak to the table."

Eugene obediently folded the paper and looked at Alex. "Let's shoot one of these deer and leave that on his doorstep."

Alex held up a pleading hand. "I'll get the spray this weekend."

"I'll get it," Maya volunteered.

The men turned to her.

"I have errands," Maya said. "Max will come help. Right, Max? You just have to write it down, Alex, what to get."

"Maya . . ." he said. He was unprepared to contend with generosity. "You won't get the right one."

"There's only one way to learn," she said.

"Your wife is offering to do it so you can sit at home and relax," Eugene said. "What's wrong with you?"

Alex conceded. "It's called DeerSanta." He nodded. "Thank you."

Raisa cleared the table while the men dispersed. Maya sat staring out the window, pretending she still had coffee to finish. It was time to switch the flower water, though the petals were molding and puckering beyond help.

"You're going to hurt yourself, honey," Maya said to her son, still serrating away at the cereal box. "Want to come for some errands?" She leaned toward him. "You'll have the front seat."

Max kept sawing, as if he hadn't heard her. "Honey," she said again. He put down his knife, slid out from under the table, and went into the hallway to find his sneakers.

For three weeks, Max had been quiet. Maya had spent them on the Internet, researching dissociative episodes. They were a kind of sleepwalking—the individual was functional and alert, but obeying a different mental channel. The descriptions terrified her. Her mind pictured a dissociative affliction as an invisible gas, a cellular sickness. Bumps, scrapes, bruises, and pimples: She could get all those out. Cutaneous infections unnerved Alex—he would worry pimples, moping until they went away— but she had a medical specialist's equanimity toward innocuous things. Things Alex could not see, he dismissed, whereas they were what terrified Maya.

When she wasn't at work or in front of the computer, Maya shadowed Max. She was clandestine not only from him, but her husband, who seemed intent on regarding continuing panic as a personal treason. Maya found an unspoken ally in Raisa. School having ended, Maya canceled her son's morning camp, saying she wanted him to spend more time with his grandmother. "Anything?" Maya would inquire fearfully of Raisa upon walking in after work. "Nothing, daughter, stop your worry!" Raisa would exclaim from the floor, where she was demolishing Max at cards. For the welfare of her loved ones, Raisa would give away not only the chocolate in her mouth, but the tongue that was working it—with the exception of cards. A great, unsparing beast emerged when Raisa Rubin took cards in her hands; even an eight-year-old got no mercy. Maya wished to believe her mother-in-law and could not. She slept poorly.

Saltz, the pediatric psychiatrist, Maya did not dare contact—because she did not want to antagonize Alex, or because she didn't want to hear what he might tell her? Then she was seized by an alternative idea. Was it crazy? Maybe it was imaginative more than crazy. If she were found out, for some reason she felt she would have less to answer for than if she had contacted Saltz. Saltz was a betrayal. But Madam Stella—Madam Stella was just Maya being Maya. The Rubins would understand—they avoided the corners of tables, the stepping over of each other's legs, the unfurling of umbrellas indoors.

Maya had her own reason. She had been five, playing in the kitchen doorway as her mother swept the floor. Her mother yowled: There was a mouse behind the radiator. Startled by the broom, the mouse scurried out, ran chaotically in several directions, and vanished again. Maya shrieked and began stomping her feet. She tore off her underwear and T-shirt and stood naked, shivering and screaming. Her mother dropped the broom and rushed to embrace her. By that evening, they were on their way to—Tamara? Fatima? a Gypsy name—the two hexed clothing items in a grocery bag her mother held between the tips of two fingers.

The healer, who was young, tall, and heavily boned, looked nothing like the old, gaunt Gypsy women at the market, and her home looked exactly like the Shulmans': doors of frosted glass, a wall unit, and the wallpaper with bicyclists by a lake. She even wore what her own mother wore, a tracksuit, the soft protuberance of a belly distending the elastic. Her oval face, dark except for slightly eerie eyes of sea green, was beautiful, but the way a horse is beautiful. Maya wondered if *she* had a Maya. How could she heal someone else's daughter if she did not have one of her own?

It was only later, on the walk home, that Maya realized that the woman had not touched her. At first, Maya felt discouraged by this, as if there was something so wrong with her that the woman could not risk catching it. But the terror that Maya experienced that afternoon was no longer causing the same misery in her stomach. And all it had taken was—the woman had extracted Maya's T-shirt and underwear from the grocery bag (she touched them without fright), whispered to them softly, as if Maya and her mother were not in the room, then rubbed both with water from a long-necked glass bottle, then smiled generously and returned the items, though Maya knew her mother would throw them out just in case. When would they need to return? Maya's mother asked. They wouldn't, the woman shook her head kindly, and Maya desperately wished for her to have a girl sometime soon.

Now, in the car, worry fingered Maya's chest: The drive to Madam Stella's would take her and Max slightly beyond town, and—for two exits—down a highway she had never driven before. A second worry: How would she explain their destination to Max? They were receding farther and farther from the hardware store. Max pointed this out, but without alarm; it had taken her some time to understand that Max didn't need to get his way, only declare his position. She said she would get it on the way back. He shrugged and didn't ask on the way back from where.

New emergencies—a sick child, a deceived husband—humble the old; Maya managed the highway without trouble. She had found the gate of the botanical gardens on whose grounds Madam Stella had somehow acquired property without having to stop and ask for elaboration on the instructions the Madam had given her over the phone. But the gate was closed and the two guards assigned to it inspected the Corolla with doubt. It was a private gardens bequeathed to the township by a chemist who had participated in the discovery of antihistamines—so the plaque mounted on the gate said. It was closed on Saturdays. Maya consulted the paper crumpled in the ashtray—Saturday 12:00—but this did nothing to sway the guard in her window. He had a scar by his left eye and she did not want to contradict him.

They heard rustling up ahead. A dark gray mastiff was hurtling down to the gate. Behind him waddled the Madam, because if not the Madam, who would be wearing a sun-colored sari hemmed with coins in the middle of a private botanical garden? "Down, down," she waved at the gate, unclear if she meant the mastiff or the guards. Both obeyed, the animal unraveling into a dung-colored slick by the gate and the guards rolling open the bars.

"I was lovers with the son," the Madam breathed into Maya's window after the gate had closed behind the Corolla. Maya smelled cigarettes, lipstick, mint. She looked over at Max—he did not need to hear such confessions—but his eyes were fixed on the mastiff. Madam Stella had colored outside the lines with her lipstick; her eyelashes clumped together when she blinked so that for the briefest moment she seemed at risk of falling asleep. "Follow me," she said, and jangled up the drive.

"Where are we going?" Max said as his mother inched after the Madam.

"It's a game," Maya said, trying to sound excited.

Two hundred feet later, they arrived at a two-story pastel-yellow home with two entrances that Madam Stella shared with a workman's family, their rent reduced but hers subsidized in full in perpetuity thanks to her seduction of the chemist's son. The faint yellow, which recalled an overmilky omelet, was the color of the grand residences and palaces lining the embankment of the Neva in St. Petersburg, the wan yellow of aristocracy, and Maya was transported for a vanishing moment back to the Soviet Union, even though she had never been to St. Petersburg. Those palaces were property of the international imagination.

"I don't know why you didn't call . . . at the beginning," Madam

Stella said into Maya's shoulder. The Madam lit a cigarette and blew a column of smoke at the gravel. Maya eyed the cigarette enviously, but was afraid to ask. "I offer the full suite of services," the older woman said. "From the cradle to the grave. Infertility, difficult pregnancy, difficult birth, post-partum depression. Some people have me on retainer—they come once a week, just in case. Families stay with me for generations." The Madam gargled out a phlegmy laugh. "That sounds as if I've been around since the war with Napoleon."

Maya glanced nervously at her watch. She knew Alex would be checking the clock soon, her cell phone going off. She had brought it this time, had no cover.

"Guess my age," Madam Stella said.

"Fifty-five?" Maya said, underestimating by twenty years in the name of politeness and a discount at the end of the hour.

Madam Stella whistled. "Try seventy-three."

"We're here for a game, okay?" Maya whispered though Max was out of earshot. "He doesn't know."

"There are demons in his head," Madam Stella said. "We are going to very nicely, very politely, ask them to leave. Do you have any demons in your head, Mayechka?"

Maya was briefly startled by this intimate address, used only by her mother and Raisa.

"If it's a game, everyone plays," Madam Stella said.

Like a well-painted face that parts to reveal ruined teeth, the smooth, eggshellish exterior of the building gave way to a rotten, sagging staircase that creaked under the four climbers as they summited to a garret of the kind Maya had always imagined inhabited by a Dostoevsky consumptive. If the street was in St. Petersburg, the garret was in a lightless village deep in the Carpathians, next to which even her uncle's Misha's modest countryside home was vast. Maya was stunned to discover herself more correct in this than she wished: Madam Stella had them gaze through a window—the mastiff got its plate-sized paws on the windowsill—that revealed a patch of ground sealed by a cellar door. Everything that Madam Stella pickled and cured in the autumn was down there, covered in the summer months by enormous blocks of ice that the workman changed out weekly for a small fee. Madam Stella had had her residence disconnected from the electricity line, and held money only when she received payment or transferred several bills to the workman. Everything that she ate and brewed, she foraged in the botanical garden; she hardly ate meat, and for dairy she bartered.

"With whom?" Maya asked, looking anxiously around the premises: two rooms, the first of which doubled as a kitchen, bedroom, and entryway.

"With the people who have it," Madam Stella cheerfully informed her. "Sit."

Where? The twin bed, despite summer, was loaded with horsehair blankets and two enormous square pillows. The dining table held a log of butter the size of a loaf of bread on a triangular cutting board; a bottle of spirits that would have reached Maya's waist; and a huge clump of tiny, yellow-tipped field flowers that resembled the frizzy hair of a giantess; but no chairs. There was a sour smell in the air that Maya traced to a bread yeasting in a large industrial sink. Her son was poking his nail into it. Maya hissed at him. He scurried back to her side, where she grasped his hand and stood like a wax figure, trying not to touch anything. She felt an attack of remorse; her decision had seemed inspired when she had seen the classified in the Russian newspaper, now reckless and rash.

On one wall hung a clumsy painting of an older woman, a black band of mourning in the corner. Above it, a display of herbs was mounted on a board of cherry-red wood, clump after clump socked into aluminum cones, a handwritten legend beneath: eucalyptus, valerian root, coltsfoot, mint, bur marigold, stinging nettle, cranberry leaves, melissa, motherwort, cabbage. The other walls were decorated with farm implements, for decoration or use who could say: a scythe; clamps with a human-height handle for extracting hot pots from a furnace; ancient, rusty mandolins; not one but two pitchforks.

Madam Stella, who was rummaging in a pantry next to the bed, noticed and said: "All of that's from the garden." Her hand emerged wrapped around a jar. She set it down next to the butter. "Young man, I require your help," she said. Reluctantly, Maya let go of Max's hand and he followed the Madam into the next room, from where they returned with three backless stools, Max's lips pursed as he fought to keep his above ground. Madam Stella carried two while her dying cigarette bounced between her lips, the smoke wreathing the room.

"I live like this because I want to," Madam Stella replied smokily to Maya's bewildered expression. Max bounced onto his chair in exhaustion, his palms on his knees like a worker, resting. "I made ninety-four thousand dollars last year."

Maya laughed nervously. Even a witch had to brandish her salary if she was a Soviet witch.

"Now, who wants to begin," Madam Stella said, unscrewing the jar. The room was filled with a sharp smell that made Maya sneeze. She knew the mixture was slimy and gray without seeing it, perhaps because the odor was of the swamp, of seaweed.

"How about you, honey?" Maya said to her son. Max sat on his little stool with concentration, as if he needed to gather strength for the next task.

Madam Stella made a *ts-ts-ts* noise with her tongue. "Don't you know that ladies go first?" she said to Maya. Finally disposing of the cigarette that had expired in her mouth, ash tumbling to the floor, she lowered herself heavily to the second of the three stools, which miraculously sustained her, and gallantly directed Maya to the third.

"This way to the gallows?" Maya said, again laughing anxiously.

"Sit, darling, sit," Madam Stella said impatiently. Though the Madam was endowed with supernatural curative powers, she did not have supernatural levels of patience. "Your son needs to see how the game is played."

Maya sat down. Immediately, she was assailed by a fantastic weariness. She wished the chair had a back. When the jar of gray slime appeared at her nose, she was surprised to discover that it was neither slime nor gray, but a harder, less viscous black substance that smelled like freshly paved highway, as if it had altered its scent on its journey from table to nose. Perhaps *she* had altered in sitting down. She tried to shake off foolish thoughts—she was so tired. If she planned to help her son, she had to be alert—she had to figure out how to sleep a full night.

Maya peered into the jar, then at Madam Stella, wondering whether the treatment was contraindicated if you weren't the one with the problem. She remembered Soviet people who had been helped by a healer but had then taken to this doctoring with indiscriminate zeal, developing new ailments or diminishing the efficacy of earlier treatments. But Maya felt she could not bring this up without reinviting Madam Stella's impatience and closed her eyes. Soon, she felt two fingers at her temples, each smudged with the gray substance, abrasive as a cat's tongue. She smelled nicotine and knew Madam Stella's face was just inches from hers, her voice reaching Maya as if muffled in cotton, the scent of cigarettes mixed with lipstick and breathing.

"Everything's resting," the voice was saying. Against Maya's temples, the tar was like a salt scrub, and Madam Stella's fingers—again Maya was reminded of a cat, for Madam Stella's fingertips were as soft as the pads of a paw, only the sharp edge of her fingernails occasionally nicking Maya's hair. "Everything's resting," Madam Stella intoned. The veins under Maya's temples eased into a washed-out slumber—she saw a road whose markings had been wiped out by a long rain—and the bone under her eyebrows pillowed into soft clay. Maya wanted to open her eyes and check on Max, was he finding this strange or frightening, and she would in just a moment, a moment.

The fingers at her temples worked in repeating circles so that she could imagine them whorling new channels into her brain.

The words intoned by Madam Stella were blurring into meaning-less sound. Maya shuddered. Her embarrassment at being min-istered to had vanished. She was so disarmed, so satisfied by the touch, that she actually felt wetness between her legs. She wasn't sure when it had started, like looking up to realize the window is slicked up with rain.

Maya remained distantly aware that she was visible to her son, but she couldn't resist the recollection coming upon her, as if she was being walked into water and was willing to drown. *Maya slaps Alex's belly, as flat as her own. "Hey now," he says sleepily. "It's your cooking. Don't cook so richly . . ." "I'll move it," she says, sliding her hand down to his penis. He shudders slightly. She squeezes it like an udder. "Ow, Maya . . ." She squeezes harder. He grows hard in her hand, like a balloon filling. "Take mercy . . ." he says. "Think of our children." She moves down over him. "No, up here . . ." he says unpersuasively. She holds him in her mouth, feels him fill out. He breathes deeply and mutters something. His hands come up on her forearms and he drives her up toward him. Alex is stronger than she is and can make her go where he wants. She wants that. He brings her lips to his and mashes them with his own. Then he notches her up by another foot so that his tongue is on her breasts. She feels the cool, slick trail of his tongue around her nipples. "Revolutions around the track . . ." she says. "Rubin is after the gold . . ." He yanks her up again. She slams into the headboard. "Ow, ow . . ." They dissolve in laughter. "But don't stop . . ." "When they bury me," he says, "the stone will say, 'He loved belly buttons above all . . .'" "This belly," she corrects him. "He loved this belly," he repeats obediently. She continues moving above him—his mouth is on the fleece between her legs. "I am going to tell you a secret," he whispers, lifting his mouth away. "The girls I've been with are all bare, but I prefer it this way." "Put your mouth back on me," she says. Her thighs are next, her knees, her shins, her toes. He plucks each toe with his lips. "You can't take them," she says. Finally, he lowers her onto himself, his legs underneath her. They rock back and forth. She buries her nose in his hair, then hiccups. They giggle. They talk about something—shelves? They slide up and down a little to make it easier to come—they try to synchronize. As they get closer, they fall away from each other, though they try halfheartedly to hold on. She feels him hit the walls of her like a warm rain. She twitches painfully in an attack of her own. They remain inside each other as Alex goes soft. "You first," she says. "You first," he says. "I'm not moving," they say at the same time. They laugh.*

Maya's underwear was soaked, and she felt a cool bracelet of cum exit and trace a half-moon around her leg. She was being led somewhere—in life, not the dream. Maya felt her arms and legs meet a rough surface, as if she was being laid across the back of an animal. She swam, an anchor on each leg. She sank and sank, and though she was aware she could make a reach for the surface, she did not. She went where she was being summoned, down, down, down.

She dreamed. Her family was at the dinner table with guests, though they weren't familiar to Maya. She eyed the group from her post behind the cooking island. Where was Alex? Not at the dinner table. Maya checked again—he was not there. As he was not in the bathroom, nor away on some trip. In addition to Eugene, Raisa, and Max, the table held three men and two women. But which man was her husband? She recognized none. How could she be married to a man she couldn't identify? And why did Eugene and Raisa—Eugene was orating with a glass of wine in his hand—find this so untroubling?

Maya winced awake. The room was blurry and she tasted sourness. The mastiff was folded into an impressively compact circle at her feet on the horsehair bed. On the other side of the closed slats of the window, it was still daytime. Her eyes adjusted to discover her son tippy-toed on one of the stools as he rearranged the weeds that lined the cherry-red board. Maya called out for him sharply.

"But it's mixed up," Max said. "This is bur marigold, not colts-foot." He added defensively: "I waited till she left."

Maya brought her hands up to her temples and flinched. They felt raw, as if they had been rubbed with sandpaper. She closed her eyes. What time was it? She swept away the sheet that covered her and leaped out of bed. The mastiff opened its eyes. An interrogation of her son revealed that Madam Stella had gone to use the workman's toilet. Maya paced the room, but the door would not yield the healer. Finally, Maya counted out five twenties, wedged them under the cutting board that held the loaf-log of butter, demonically keeping its shape despite the close heat of the room, and commanded her son to follow her out, which he did, obediently unhanding the clumps in his fist.

Creaking down the stairs, Max's hand in hers, Maya called to Madam Stella, but no answer came, and she did not wish to embarrass the older woman by banging on the door of the toilet. She yelled that she had left the money under the butter and hurried out.

She drove above the speed limit; she compensated by inquiring of Max three times whether he was wearing his seat belt. The sex Maya had remembered was twenty years old, back when Maya was still teaching Alex. Thinking of those young people was like thinking of other people entirely. The two of them had turned out to be physically matched in a way that could be explained only by luck—sometimes it went your way, too. She treated this fact as a vindication of the reckless decision she had made in marrying Alex—why weren't things allowed to work out? Alex was not initially an adventurer in bed—the first time she mumbled arduous words into his cheek ("I want to feel it in my chest, in my throat"), his hard-on drooped, and he remonstrated with her to watch a porno film if that's what she wanted. But he learned, even as he disliked being a student. He was solid, thick-skinned, the fleshly block of him above her like a good fact, and their unflagging desire was as responsible as anything else for moving them through the years. But over time it had cleaved from the rest of their story: an organ driving at full throttle while so much else tripped, sank, got turned around on itself. And since Max's trouble began, they had not touched each other at all. Their disinterest seemed as mutual as their erstwhile desire; they did not discuss it, simply heeded the feeling, a bitter harmony. She glanced at the car clock: 5:47. They had left just after two. She pressed the pedal.

She berated herself. Unlike her outing on the bus, which risked sacrificing only the mother, she had now disappeared with the most precious cargo of the Rubins' lives. And instead of paying attention to the road, she was examining the clotted shallows of her psyche. A gruesome word floated up. You are a cunt, Maya, she mouthed silently at the wheel.

Maya turned to Max. "So Madam Stella played the game with me . . ." She trailed off, hoping Max would fill in the rest, but he only nodded. "Did anything strange happen?" she said.

"You made noises," Max said.

Maya ran a hand through her hair. It felt reedy and damp, as if she really had just emerged from a tangle of sheets.

"What kind of noises?" she said.

"Like it hurt you somewhere," Max said. "But Madam Stella said you were fine."

Maya nodded, the corners of her eyes filling with tears. She felt a great desire to close her eyes.

"Max, my darling," she said. "Did Madam Stella play the game with you?"

"We didn't have time," he said. "She said we would after you woke up. Let you sleep."

Maya nodded dolefully and scratched Max's hair with a failing smile on her lips. "We will definitely go another time," she said.

Again the gruesome word floated up.

By the time Maya was traversing the final artery between the Corolla and home, she was exceeding the speed limit less out of guilt than an anguished desire to reestablish the contours of her life as she knew them before she'd set off. Much as a lump in the breast felt at nine A.M. makes small pain of the toast burned at eight thirty, Maya recalled the uneasy home in which she lived prior to her trip to Madam Stella's as a redoubt of solidarity next to the fury she was sure was awaiting her now. As her car pulled into the driveway, she resolved to act nonchalant but solicitous when she entered the house. No one would hear argument from Maya tonight. Then she realized she had forgotten the deer repellent.

Perhaps it is when we are at our most vulnerable that life throws us a line (though not until then). When Maya stepped into the house, clutching Max's hand for comradeship, her mind trying to measure the distance from the truth she was willing to travel in her explanation and how Max would comment, Maya was accosted by an Alex bewildered not by her tardiness or the absence of deer repellent in her hands but by the unannounced appearance of Bender and wife on their doorstep an hour before. If Alex had once been aware of how long she and Max had been absent, now he was aware only of Time Before Bender and Time After. Raisa was off on a walk around the lake—who walked around the lake for hours; well, Eugene had been on her about her weight—and it was left to the men to entertain these sudden visitors with what sense they could make of the dozen Tupperwares in the refrigerator.

If asked, only a moment before, to rate her enthusiasm for a repeat sighting of Bender, Maya would have thought twice. But now her affection nearly toppled him, also his stout, white-haired wife. Bender repeated his story—he and wife had been in Acrewood for a matinee at the community theater and had decided to drop by and ask about Max. Bender blinked, his wet eyes the color of steel wool, as if awaiting a judgment on his claim. But by then Maya was too busy rummaging in the fridge in order to supplement the pathetic table the men had set up: cold cuts, matzoh-like crackers, and a jar of roasted peppers. For life's emergencies, some men carried condoms, Band-Aids, umbrellas. Eugene Rubin carried a jar of roasted peppers.

As Maya popped open lids and spooned out self-made hummus,

Mediterranean chicken, and lemony salad, she understood that Bender's story was an unskillful lie. The Rubins' visit had given Bender cover for a return visit of his own, and with it a potential resuscitation of the acquaintanceship that had fallen moribund as a result of . . . what? As Eugene and his son, on a typical night, took their customary post-dinner positions in front of the living room television, the son slumping asleep long before the father, who remained alert late into the evening, staring blankly at news program after news program, Maya often wondered how this pastime acquitted itself in superiority to a cup of tea with a human being, even if that human being was Bender, even if Bender was in mortal combat with Eugene for who could exhibit the greater indifference.

In Kiev, the Shulmans' living room had up to half a dozen extra bodies if it was a weekday, more on the weekend, usually neighbors (this is how Maya's mother came by so much of her material), two in the corner slinging bile at the president of the tenant council, two others fixed on a soap opera, a solitary soul smoking wistfully out of the kitchen window while sipping from a thimble of balsam. It was not an astrophysics symposium, in fact the television dominated here as well, but at least it served as an invitation to others. And unlike Eugene—who sneered at the false sophistication of Bender and held up, as a contrast, the purity of his own—those who stopped at the Shulmans' Kiev apartment for balsam and tea did not consider themselves with special regard, in part because they were professional gossips and knew it, and partly because all their lives had low ceilings courtesy of the state in which they had the misfortune to live. And so there was nothing to brag about, was there, might as well enjoy a thimble of balsam with the neighbor. The Low Ceiling made ambition impossible, so not one of those heads was riveted by the next day's work docket, and that was the only way Maya could explain Eugene's preferences—the American economy gave you an excuse not to see people. You were unavailable until retirement; until then, it was one long dark night in the embrace of

Profit, the eternally undersexed mistress. While Eugene watched
TV, he worked over in his head bills of lading, sales numbers, the
new van driver—not something you could do with a Bender in front
of you. However, now, one hip propping open the fridge door, she
was seized by another interpretation. It filled her with pity instead of
the usual bafflement. Did Eugene and Alex avoid acquaintances to
avoid the possibility of a careless word alerting Max he was adopted?
Perhaps they themselves did not understand it.

She made herself stop. Was there nothing that would keep her
from drifting away? What crisis was urgent enough? It would have
taken nothing for her to crash the Corolla on the ride home. Now,
she was blessed to have arrived safely, and she was standing and
thinking about . . . what? Why did her plans get away from her?
With the visit to Stella, she had meant only to help Max. As, now,
she meant only to make things easier for the bodies in the living
room. Why couldn't she keep to her plans? She felt afflicted alongside her son; she did not recognize herself. Alex always panicked
when the fridge door remained open for too long, wasting electricity, and with a guilty tremor she knocked it closed—she intended to cause no provocation tonight—though everyone was in
the living room.

Maya would expertly steer the Benders through several plates
and then out the door, earning the gratitude of Alex and Eugene;
the problem of her disappearance would be buried in the relief
that would follow the Benders' departure. Maya had failed to get
Madam Stella to lay hands on Max, but several weeks had now
passed without Max acting strangely, and so perhaps her husband
was right, and the thing to do was to leave the boy alone, to let
him grow out of it. He had, after all, come out of his bizarre adventure unscathed. Perhaps he was protected. Maybe her son
was charmed in some way. If she couldn't be, then maybe he was.
Abruptly, Maya was filled with a light-headed optimism. She took
four plates, two in her fingers and two balanced across her forearms, as she had seen waitresses do at the Acrewood Diner, and,

feeling a frisson of otherness (she was a waitress in some diner), stepped into the living room.

It was only now that she realized that she'd heard no sound from it for some time. If Maya had been less preoccupied by her thoughts and looked in to check why the Rubin/Bender quartet was so quiet, she would have seen much sooner what they were seeing. They were all four standing in a hushed pall at the sliding door to the backyard—Bender *femme* was actually shaking her head slightly in a kind of pained wonder. Alex was rigid with disbelief, Eugene impassive, and Bender had slid his hands professorially into the pockets of his striped trousers, as if the vision before them would require not a little professional insight.

What they were witnessing was the resolution of Alex's problem with deer damage—sans deer repellent. Its ingredients surrounded their son in a clearing beyond the lawn, where the pines began: a carton of eggs from the refrigerator in the garage, a small bucket filled with water, a spray bottle, a second bucket, empty. The five of them watched him extract an egg, crack it on the rim of the water bucket, and seesaw the two halves until the yolk and albumen were separated from the chalaza. The former went into the water bucket, the latter into the other.

But it wasn't this ritual, strange though it was due to the cabalistic overtones of the odd, raw ingredients—for a moment, Maya tensed at the thought that Max had been cursed in a new way at Madam Stella's—that held their attention. It was the fact that around Max milled a convention of bucks, does, and fawns, who always bolted as soon as Alex heaved open the yard door in fury. Maya counted, stricken: There were nine. They were chewing the twigs around Max's feet. Though Max had yet to utilize the mixture he was preparing, the teeth of none were clamped around the pines. Occasionally, the visitors rubbed their white-spotted flanks against Max's side, like housebroken cats. Except for the fawns, all were bigger than Max, and when they sidled past him, they bumped his small body so that it looked as if he might fall over.

Maya reached for the handle of the sliding door. But another hand—she was too startled to check whose, but it was an unfamiliar hand, and later she thought it must have been Bender—held her forearm. They watched Max bumped hard by a fat buck, stupidity in its eyes. It was the color of dead leaves save for two white circles around the eyes and a patch below its mouth; it looked like it was wearing a mask. Max put down the water bucket—which, perhaps out of sensitivity toward his father, he was trying to pour into the sprayer without spilling onto the lawn—and turned toward the buck, its antlers like two gnarled, splayed hands. Then he laid his palm on the velvet-looking spot between the antlers. They stood like that for a minute, the deer's eyes shielded by Max's palm. Finally, the buck tucked its hooves under the muscled flank of its belly and dropped to the ground.

Bender's hands fell out of his pockets. Though he had solved the Kennedy curse, he had never witnessed anything comparable.

Maya felt—she felt rather than saw it—a body break from the group by the door. It broke forward, it heaved open the sliding door with a melancholy sigh, it lunged ahead only to discover the screen door blocking its way, it uttered a curse that had never been heard in the house, it ripped open the screen door, and burst onto the deck. Only then, from the back, did Maya see that her husband was rushing out after their child. She mouthed a weak no—mouthed it weakly and without any intention to be heard.

Seeing Alex, the buck with the masklike face sprang from its seat, an antler grazing Max on the side of his head. Max yelped and clutched his temple with both hands; the Rubins and Benders did not need perfect vision to see the blood spurting down his little fingers. Maya shrieked. The fawns and does became agitated and began to flee, trampling the ground. Max, down on one knee, went down on his butt, and then he was prostrate. As they stalked away, the animals trampled him. He tried to roll up like a snail to protect himself from the stampede.

+

Alex was shouting for her to get Max in the car. Max was sobbing in short, agitated bursts. Kissing him up and down his face, Maya managed to pry his hand from his temple. Alex barked Maya's name again. The elder Rubins and the Benders stood fixed in place, terrified. After she wiped his temple with a damp cloth, Max wincing and wriggling and his sobs turning to squeals, Maya saw a puffy pink welt, but no broken skin. But where had the blood come from? She soaked a gauze pad in peroxide and then tied a strip of gauze around his head so it would remain in place. He looked like a war wounded. Max whined, too tight. "Shhh, my love, shhh," she whispered into his ear, and allowed the two of them to be swept toward the car.

In the emergency room was the usual collection of young men with heads in their hands, blood on their T-shirts, and hastily wrapped bandages marking the injury, and mothers with whimpering children. It was the latter group that frightened Maya more—partly because it was mothers and children, and partly because you couldn't tell what was wrong.

In the car, Maya had got Moira from the hospital—Moira was off on the weekends, but she had a friend in the emergency room. The Rubins were quietly seen as soon as they entered, though it was not apparent whom to thank. However, the doctor they were given looked no older than twenty and spoke wearily from behind owlish glasses. Maya wanted to insist on someone more alert, but settled on apprising him that she was an employee of the hospital, though this did not alter his manner. The blood was not Max's. "It's summer, they're in velvet," he said. "It's soft tissue. One scratch, and it flows. You're lucky. If it was fall, your son might have been really hurt. Disinfectant twice a day, and he's going to be fine." He squatted before Max, who wouldn't let go of his father's hand. "You got yourself a fright," the doctor said to him. "Usually, someone's walking out onto the deck, and they'll startle a buck. Is that what happened?" Alex rushed to say yes before his wife had a chance to answer truthfully.

Maya spent the night next to Max in his bed. She didn't sleep, though he did. She resisted her craving to check the wound. Because it was night—because the chorus of Rubins had quieted, because she was sleeping in a different bed with a different body beside her, because sometimes she did drift closer to sleep— several times she believed for more than a moment that it had all been imagined. The remainder of the time, she marked the slowness with which time passes when one is watching the clock. It was 2:17, and an hour later, it was 2:23. Was she responsible? Had the visit to Madam Stella hexed Max instead of unhexed him? But everything had been fine until Alex intervened. And yet, what had been fine—her son playing with deer? She didn't know what to do because she didn't know what to regard as the problem.

At six, she had the impression that the sun would not rise. It was not dread that she felt, more a general impression that incrementally—imperceptible in the passage of days—her life had tilted from its center, like a ship listing. This was the new level. After seeing her son surrounded by more deer than he had ever had friends, it was not difficult to imagine the sun no longer rising with the same regularity. When it did, at half past six, it did so rudely, all at once. A blast of gray light cut through the night, and then it was everywhere.

Belatedly, she heard the sounds of coffee downstairs. It was too early for Alex—he took advantage of being one of the principals at work by arriving at nine. Maya's work started earlier, and Max was sometimes out the door for school before his father had woken. Maya eased herself out of Max's grip and tiptoed downstairs. Alex was at the kitchen table—in a bathrobe and leather slippers, a cup of black coffee steaming in front of him. He drank it milky and sweet but there was no milk or sugar in front of him. He didn't seem particularly interested in the coffee—he just fingered the handle and stared at the cup.

"You're up," she observed.

He nodded distractedly. She leaned against the doorjamb and crossed her arms.

"Sit at the table," he offered.

Maya didn't have the energy to pull out the chair and merely wedged herself into the thin space between its back and the table. She felt thin—scooped away. She had eaten badly in the previous weeks, and her body showed the change quickly. Until now, she had not noticed it, really. The only thing she was aware of was how unaware she felt. And this despite trying so hard to pay attention. Trying to notice every little thing.

There were papers in Alex's hands. He was fingering the handle of the coffee cup only because his other hand was tracing the lines on the pages before him. One never saw papers in Alex's hands. The paperwork was Maya's domain. Alex handled the lawn, the fireplace, the doors when they needed oiling. Maya handled the bills and the coupons and Max's permission slips and everyone's medical records, and invitations from the local synagogue. There was a basket in the corner of the kitchen counter that said MAYA; all paper items requiring attention went there. But now Alex had papers in front of him. He was up an hour before his usual time, red-eyed and strange, with papers in front of him. All at once, she knew it was Max's adoption paperwork. She knew it before she saw the agency's logo on the stationery.

"Why do you have that out?" she said cautiously. The folder's location was not a secret for the adults, but it was buried in the back of a file drawer in Alex's home office so that Max would never stumble across it. Maya had the berserk thought that Alex wanted to give Max back. No. Even she knew that was insane.

"One page," he said.

She looked at him quizzically.

"When they give you a human being, they give you one page of medical history."

"I don't understand what you're driving at."

"One page?" he said. "That's all you needed to know? Look at this." He waved the paper. "'History of heart disease—none.' No further detail. Did anyone bother to do more than ask? In this country, it's assumed that the other person is telling the truth unless you can prove otherwise." A look of—not perplexity, but grief—came over Alex. "Why?" he asked simply.

"You should have gotten involved," she said coldly. "Save me from mistakes."

"Give you the paperwork," he said, "and I wasn't involved. Take the paperwork away from you, and I'm cutting you back. How should I behave? Explain it to me. Give me a list of instructions."

"There are privacy laws, Alex. That's why it's so thin. But the hospital said everything was fine. And Laurel said so, too. Why was he such an easy infant? He's been with us for eight years. It can't have anything to do with his background."

"Privacy?" Alex said incredulously. "I must respect their privacy after they've decided to surrender their child? What about my privacy?"

"Yours was respected in turn. You insisted on a closed adoption and got it."

"Oh, it was very closed," he said. "So closed that I had the pleasure of the birth parents in my living room. I'm too soft, Maya—because I didn't like growing up under my father. But as I become older—I hate to say it, this is the thing that children hate to admit, but I won't lie to save myself the embarrassment of having been wrong—I see he was right. To know where *I* live, those people were allowed. For what reason? She needed to see with her own eyes it was far from Montana? Look at a goddamn map. But when *I've* got a question? And for a slightly more significant reason than I want to see where they live, such as my son consorts with wild animals? No—the privacy of the birth parents must be respected.

You know what the issue is? We're too nice, Maya. Too decent. Too fearful. Still the immigrants, thirty-five years later. Still asking permission."

"Alex," she said quietly. "First of all, please lower your voice. Secondly, you're not making sense. You wanted the adoption to be closed."

"I'm not asking to become their friends. I want a thorough medical history. Down to the Indians, or whoever the hell spawned these people. 'Don't let my child do rodeo,' she said. What does it mean? Don't let him be like his father? But who is his father? And children are sometimes like their fathers whether they live with them or not. It's called genes. This is why I was against adoption, Maya. Because you get genes that belong to somebody else. We didn't ask enough questions. The most important thing in our lives, and our eyes were closed by wishfulness. We wanted too badly for it to work out."

"You mean my eyes were closed by wishfulness," she said. "*I* wanted it to work out."

"I am saying 'we.' I am trying to be charitable. To hold us both responsible."

"But that's only what you are *saying*."

"It's impossible with you."

"Alex, yesterday, it was you—it was only because you ran out that he got hurt!" She did not want to say it, had promised herself in the night to keep her mouth closed. He was only trying to help.

Alex's eyes were weary and threatening. "Perhaps you should say thank you that I saved him from worse? Because you were standing at the door like a theatergoer."

She buried her face in her hands.

He looked at her with spiteful merriment. "This is what you wanted," he said. "You wanted to have a relationship with the parents. I was against it, yes. But changing circumstances revise facts." He was not stubborn; he would happily acknowledge a badly made move. Alex leaned gloatingly against the back of his chair. "Tomorrow, I will call the adoption agency and demand their information. And I will threaten to sue if they decline."

Maya took her fingers from her eyes. "Alex? Let's go there."

Alex's forehead puckered. "Where?"

"To Montana. Just like they came here."

Alex closed and opened his eyes. "Why would we do that?"

"To meet them. To spend some time with them."

"I'll consider us blessed if we can wrest their phone number from the agency," Alex said. "There's no reason to go there."

"Yes, there is. I *understand* why they came here. It upset us, but I understand it."

"So, go," he said, aware of his cruelty, as she did not fly, could not drive far by herself. "You want to go—go."

"I want Max to see it, too. If he can't know where he's from"—she lowered her voice—"at least let him see it."

"He's eight—it will mean nothing to him."

"You left Minsk at eight. It meant nothing to you?"

"Yes, but I knew why I was leaving where I was leaving," Alex said. "And going where I was going."

"Shouldn't our son, too?" she said, again in a decreased tone. This is the way she spoke nowadays: up, down, up, down.

"Please let's not have this conversation again," he said.

"What if that's why he's acting out?" Maya said. "He senses a lie."

"Who's superstitious now?" he said.

"We were told by the adoption people—when they're confused, sometimes they run away."

"He thought he was going to find his mother under that river? He was born to a pike? Come on, Maya."

"Okay, *I* want to see it," she said. "Isn't that good enough? I want to see it. I want to see"—she lowered her voice—"where Max was born. And I can't take myself. Laurel got to see where we live, I want to see where she lives."

"*Lived,*" Alex said. "They're gone. They took that money and ran. If you don't know that, you're a fool."

"Then that's what I want to see," Maya said.

They heard Max descending the stairs and fell silent. He appeared in the doorway to the kitchen. He had gone back to pajamas—he didn't like sleeping in briefs. "Are you fighting?" he said. He had never asked such a thing.

"Because sometimes, Mama and Papa—" Maya started to say, but Alex was speaking over her.

"Because Mama wants to make you pancakes and I want to make you eggs," Alex said. "Tell us who wins."

Max blinked twice, and stared at them.

"Who wins, Maxie?" his father said again.

+

For the second night in a row, Maya did not sleep. In the night, the back of Alex's hand fell onto her belly. She was about to remove it, but changed her mind; she enjoyed its weight, as dense as a small animal. Her awareness of it made sleep impossible, but sleep was impossible without it, too. She lay in bed and felt the grooves of Alex's skin with her white belly. His fingers trembled slightly in sleep, the cold gold of the wedding band touching her skin now and then. Other than that, it was his smooth, unworried skin on her own. She resolved that, come morning, she would approach her husband in a new way. Despite different reasons, each had come to desire the same thing: to find Laurel and Tim. They should work together, find their way back to each other, step in tandem. Maya filled with the enthusiasm of a new mission. She required only an objective; that given, she would be set free from the resolutionless murk that ate away at her spirit. In the morning, Alex found her lying as open-eyed as she had six hours before. "Maya," he shook his head, tenderness in his reproach. "You need to sleep. Need to." The creases of her eyes watered. With her eyes, she tried to say to him everything that she had felt in the night. Did he understand her? He must have, because he said: "I'm calling—today."

9

"Rubins," Gabe Mishkin said, astonished, from the other side of the screen door. "Boy, baby boy," Mishkin said. "A little thing, but you didn't pick him up. They showed up at your damn house." Mishkin's face opened in recollection. "That was one of the all-time doozies."

Maya also could not believe she was standing across from the adoption supervisor. Alex's call to IAS had given them the news that Mishkin had retired. The woman who replaced him wore a tunic marked by gamboling nautical objects and, in her ears, two turquoise crosses—it was to this that Maya attributed their diffi-culty understanding each other. No matter what Maya said—and eventually even Alex spoke up, embarrassment settling on the room after the new case worker mistook a back scratch for a reach for his wallet, that is, a forthcoming bribe—the woman returned her fingernail to the bolded text in the upper-right-hand corner of their file: CLOSED ADOPTION. Eventually, she let out a long, besieged breath and walked to the doorway to ask her secretary for a Form to Request Contact. That was when Maya's hand reached for the pen-holder on the woman's desk and swept it onto the carpeted floor. Maya apologized loudly and knelt to collect the scattered pencils and clips, but not before taking a long look at the file that remained open on the desk. She got a bit of luck—her eyes landed on an address. But luck rarely comes pure—it was the address not of the birth parents but the forwarding for Gabriel Mishkin, retired.

Mishkin had bellied out with new weight and his facial hair had taken after the woods surrounding his home: three days of messy, pebble-gray growth on his cheeks, and the stymied coiffure that he had sported as a savior of unwanted children was now out past his ears, though it managed to look elegantly disheveled instead of abandoned. Belatedly, Maya remembered that it wasn't only Mishkin who was eight years older, and wondered what thoughts about her and Alex's appearance passed through his mind.

"You're on my porch," Mishkin noted, burying his reading glasses in the copse of his hair. His other hand held a book, a wedged finger marking his spot. The three of them listened to a fluting call from the woods. An answer came, a series of taps. "At least I called you with a warning," Mishkin said. He smiled without opening his mouth.

"Mr. Mishkin," Maya said. She had practiced the simple line with Alex on their way up the Thruway, a sour fog blanketing the starting gold and red of the trees. They had decided that it would be more persuasive coming from Maya. "We need your help."

"They gave you my forwarding?" Mishkin said, startled.

"Not exactly," Maya said.

"I see," he said. "I'm not being very hospitable." He unlatched and swung open the screen door. Maya thrust at him a box of cellophaned chocolates.

"By the look on your face, I better take this," he said.

The home had two stories, the chimney of a rust-edged woodstove rising through a clumsily hacked opening in the ceiling. Upstairs, Mishkin must have slept. Downstairs, he was deep in written work of some kind. The oval dining room table was covered with notebooks and books in plastic library covers. An aluminum can of turkey chili nested among the hardbacks, a spoon planted in its muck like a flag. On the kitchen counter, a dozen similar cans waited around. No woman would permit this, Maya thought. Was the adoption supervisor, who had filled out so many families, unmarried himself?

"It's a bachelor lifestyle," Mishkin said, watching Maya's gaze wheel across his possessions. "You're supposed to heat it up. Won't you sit?" He indicated a torn leather sectional that spanned two of the walls in the living room. Maya and Alex fell into it like a final resting place, their knees higher than their waists. It would be impossible to make a formidable argument from this position, Maya thought, and tried to wedge herself out, unsuccessfully. "What can I offer you?" Mishkin said.

"Coffee?" Alex said.

"Actually, something stronger for me," Maya said, "if that's not impolite."

Mishkin bowed his head admiringly. "That's the very opposite of impolite, Mrs. Rubin," he said. "The very opposite." He retreated to the kitchen, where the Rubins heard the kettle filling with water and the rattling of cupboards.

"You remembered us right away," Maya called out to him.

"Do you know how many families and children I helped bring together?" Mishkin called back. "Guess."

"Twenty-five?" Maya yelled.

"Ha!" Mishkin cried. They heard the dull seat of a bottle land on the tile of the cooking counter, then fumbling with glasses. "Try a hundred and fifty, Mrs. Rubin." Glasses were fondled and they heard ice cracking. "I bet you're wondering what are all those things on the dining room table. I'm writing my memoirs. And I guess it's some kind of serendipity—do you know what serendipity means?—to have you show up on my doorstep, because if you think about it"— Mishkin leaned out of the kitchen doorway—"it started with you. Those family explorations I started in earnest after we dealt with each other." He returned to the kitchen and yelled again. "I took retirement early. I went to Belarus. Poland! My great-grandfather's village is the size of your palm. And look, look—" Mishkin stepped out of the kitchen and directed the Rubins to gaze through the living room window at a small construction on the edge of the backyard painted the burnt-red of the house. It was flanked by a hammock and a portable shower. "A sauna!" Mishkin said. "Just like they had in the old country. But you folks know all about it."

He returned with a cuffed tray bearing a weak cup of coffee for Alex and two glasses with amber-colored liquid for Maya and himself. Unlike the coffee, the drinks were made expertly, and Maya extended her glass toward Mishkin. She did not want alcohol at two P.M. on a Sunday but she needed Mishkin off guard. However, just as she extended, Mishkin emptied his glass in one tumble. They shared an awkward laugh. "Looks like I'll have to get another," he said, though he remained in his chair, as if he needed Maya's approval. Maya took a greedy gulp and stared at Alex. He looked displeased, perhaps because he had ended up with coffee when he could have used amber-colored liquid of his own. He cleared his throat.

"I am actually from Belarus, not Russia," Alex said. "I don't know if I ever clarified that."

"Aha!" Mishkin said.

"Many things connect us," Alex offered feebly, trying to help.

"They sure do," Gabe Mishkin said, and rose. "I'll freshen you up," he said to Maya.

"I still have some—" Maya said.

"Don't be silly," Gabe Mishkin said. "Bottoms up."

Maya obeyed, the liquid scorching her tongue, and handed Mishkin her glass. He was back in a minute with refills, his glass iceless. Maya racked her brain for other ways to set Mishkin rhapsodizing on the ancestral subject, but nothing came. She exchanged glances with Alex. He closed and opened his eyes at her. She wanted to extract the necessary information from Mishkin also so that she and Alex could continue on the mutual course they'd so recently found.

"All this time . . ." Maya said now to Mishkin. She would start open-endedly and leave it to the adoption supervisor pick up the thread.

"How's the boy?" Mishkin said. "It's like the secret service, the adoption agency. After you retire, you're not entitled to ask. I am putting that in the book. The adoption system in this country needs a reform. I'm laying out—"

"That's actually why we're here," Maya interrupted. "We need to find the parents."

She cursed herself. The drink that she had intended to weaken Mishkin had instead weakened her. This was not the way to bring it up! She had worked out the plan in the car with Alex: charming stories about the boy to arouse Mishkin's sympathy; a reassertion of what a blessing Mishkin had helped bring into their lives; a laugh about that crazy visit by the birth parents. But that was it, you see, Maya would say casually, the parents had known something, the mother had made that odd comment before leaving . . .

It was too late now. Mishkin's wooded face, which had relaxed since their greeting, became dark with anticipation. Maya wanted to take some kind of gardening shear to it, to set free the man underneath.

"The boy is wild," Maya said, giving up.

"The boy is savage," Alex added.

"Excuse me?" Mishkin said.

"He runs away—"

"All the time," Alex said, animated.

"They find him—"

"Sitting in a river," Alex finished.

"He eats grass," Maya declared; if such a detail was not going to get Mishkin's attention, she didn't know what would.

"Are you joking?" Mishkin said.

"We need to find the parents," Alex said, taking over. "They know something. The young man, Tim, he was limping—you remember. And the strange thing the mother said before leaving. About rodeo. I'm not sure that was the truth. We just want the truth, so we can help our boy. We don't want from them anything else. Or the agency—if something was missed, something was missed, let us find out about it now." Maya was aware that Alex had tried to speak carefully, cautiously—he was trying to use her language because he was aware that his was antagonistic. "We're not going to sue," Alex attempted to be reassuring, but the very invocation of legal matters had the opposite effect.

"Mr. Rubin," Mishkin said as he tried to sit up in his rocking chair. "How long ago did this—" He stopped himself. "I don't know where to begin." He fell back into his chair and rocked silently. "I don't see what it has to do with the birth parents."

"We want to have one conversation," Alex said. "Is that so much to ask?"

"You want to converse with the parents?" Mishkin said. "If I remember correctly, Mr. Rubin, you were pretty firm about a closed adoption."

Maya held out her glass toward Mishkin. If he had another as well, perhaps it would make him more charitable. But when he returned a moment later, he held only her glass, refilled.

"Mr. Rubin, you know you can have the agency send them a letter," he said.

"No!" Alex said. "No more agency."

"The agency called the number they have," Maya lied, glancing at Alex. "Someone else answered. They don't live there anymore."

"So what can I do?" Mishkin said, defending his chest with his hands.

"You can tell us the town," Maya said.

"Mrs. Rubin, those kids can be in Shanghai by now."

"If so," Alex said, "someone in town would know."

"Mr. Rubin, this isn't the Soviet Union. People are free to move about with no warning to anyone. Those kids could have spent a year in Montana on the way from California to God knows where."

"She said 'rodeo,'" Maya said. "There's no rodeo in Shanghai. There is rodeo in Montana. I looked it up. It's only the town, Mr. Mishkin!"

Mishkin looked over at Alex in a plea for help. Emotion was keeping Alex's wife from seeing the full network of dead ends:

Yes, those were the places for rodeo, but the young man might no longer be *in* rodeo . . .

"Mrs. Rubin, when you leave the adoption agency, they take away your clearance, so to speak," Mishkin said. "But they keep the gag order. I don't have any of the files. I signed an agreement."

"Oh, yes?" Maya said. "Are you writing your memoirs from memory?"

Mishkin tsked unhappily.

"You brought together one hundred fifty families," Maya said. "You remember that we didn't get Max from the hospital. But you don't remember the town they're from."

"I don't," Mishkin said unpersuasively.

"So it was all right for them to come into our house, but we can't return the favor," Alex said.

"I understand that was a departure from"—Mishkin searched for the words—"the norm. But things like that happen at the eleventh hour. In retrospect, there may have been a better way to do things, sure. But you have to make the call in the moment. You want to say I made a mistake, go ahead."

"Make another one," Alex said.

"Mr. Rubin, two wrongs don't make a right."

"Yes, Mr. Mishkin," Maya said. "Please explain to us how things are done in America."

A resentful silence settled on the room. Maya clutched her temples, which pounded with the animus of the whiskey. She swung her legs into the small space between her and her husband. Mishkin's eyes grew wide; now, Maya Rubin was prostrate on his sectional.

He cleared his throat. "Are you all right, Mrs. Rubin?"

"We will leave," she said hoarsely from the couch. "I just need fifteen minutes without noise until this migraine goes away. I am a terrible sufferer of migraines."

"Mrs. Rubin!" Mishkin exclaimed. "Making you feel this way is the last thing in the world . . ." He trailed away. They sat silently for a minute, until Mishkin was no longer able to bear the tableau of agonized wife and stone-faced husband.

"How about going upstairs, Mrs. Rubin?" he said. "There's a guest room there."

Maya moaned in distress, her palm on her forehead. Mishkin consulted Alex again, but Alex was looking past all of them, out at the woods.

Mishkin rose. "I'm going to give you some time," he said. "I have to chop some wood for the sauna."

Maya turned to face Mishkin. "Please don't," she said. "The chopping will make it worse."

"Of course," Mishkin said. "That was foolish of me. Sorry."

"No, it was kind of you," Maya said. "If I can be alone without noise, it should go away quickly. Will you take a walk with my husband?" She looked fleetingly at Alex, and, catching his eyes, wished to believe that he understood her intentions—or simply that she had some, and needed his help. They had had many moments of misunderstanding, of dissent—weren't they due for one of silent concert? "Show Alex the homes here," she went on. "We've been talking about a country place to please Max. If he wants to eat grass, let him at least eat grass where the air is clear. Come back in a half hour, and I will be back to normal."

"Mrs. Rubin," Mishkin said. "Please don't take this the wrong way. But all the paperwork related to my time at the agency is under lock and key."

She turned to face him again, wincing from the effort. "Mr. Mishkin, my son seems to have been birthed by a wolf. I came to you to plead for a clue, and you said no. Don't add insult to what I am feeling. I need a half hour without noise. Every minute that we talk extends the recovery time." She searched out his eyes. "And now forgive *me* for being rude, Mr. Mishkin, but I am a Jewish mother. When was the last time you went outside?"

Maya looked up at her husband. Alex rose, hoping that would

stir Mishkin. "Go, please," she said, in a voice choked by imminent tears. That did it. Confronted by the possibility of imminent tears, the men hustled into the hallway. Then the door shut behind them. Maya counted out a minute and swung her feet to the floor.

No, she was not going to look for agency paperwork. And she didn't have time to clean as she would have liked. As she passed the crowded dining room table on her way to the kitchen, she saw the cover page of Mishkin's opus: *Memoirs: An Attempt at Living.*

The cupboards held a rich array of amber liquids but little in the way of potential ingredients. A dusty bag of dried-out apricots, two baby trays of honey of the kind they gave out at the diner, a bag of turnipy potatoes, and a dozen cans of chili. The fridge offered a half-opened container of bacon and a decent clump of carrots, but that's all. Maya closed her eyes and thought, the clock on the wall moving with twice the usual speed. She needed a little fortune. With eyes closed, she imagined her mother at the stove, her grandmother. But it was Uncle Misha who saved her. He had started a patch of sweet potatoes the summer before Maya flew to America, and when the first plums came in in late June, he set out two dozen on a screen under a cheesecloth and two bricks. A week later, he tore some carrots out of the garden Maya had started, and of all this—sweet potatoes, sun-dried plums, carrots—made tzimmes.

Maya didn't have sweet potatoes, but there was a box of white sugar in the cupboard. She ran the kitchen faucet until scalding; in the meantime, she cubed the potatoes to the smallest size that would cook quickly without dissolving in boiling water. She worked on assumptions. Carrots—there was no time to peel them. The apricots were like wood under her knife, so she threw them in a bowl of hot water along with a tablespoon of sugar. Mishkin had once possessed cinnamon sticks; conveniently, they had crumbled into a cinnamon dust far more useful to her. She flavored with desperation.

When Gabriel Mishkin and Alex Rubin returned from their constitutional—evidently, they had found something to discuss, because the door opened to a sentence in progress, spoken by Alex, no less—a rectangular baking dish steamed from a corner of the dining room table where, Maya felt, she was causing the least disturbance to Mishkin's research.

"What in God's name is that—" Mishkin started to say from the hallway as the men removed their shoes. Indeed, the home was afloat with the perfume of butter, carrots, honey, and sugar. The sight of the baking dish spitting up steam toward the ceiling stopped his sentence.

"If you are going to write about the old country, you should know how they ate," Maya said.

"Tzimmes," the adoption supervisor said, his voice perturbed with wonder. "My *grandmother* made tzimmes. I haven't had tzimmes in five hundred years. How in the world . . ."

Maya looked over at Alex with pride. He was marveling—his wife could make tzimmes out of water and sticks. "The carrots are a little burnt because I had the highest heat going," she issued the cook's obligatory self-deprecation. "I wanted to finish it before you returned."

Mishkin sniffed the tzimmes and looked back at her, shaking his head in disbelief.

"It helps with the migraines," Maya said unconvincingly.

"Should we set up plates?" Mishkin said.

"No," Maya answered quickly. "No, we have intruded on you long enough."

Mishkin didn't argue, but Maya made no move toward the foyer. Alex looked from Mishkin to his wife, squared off across the expanse of the dining room. Behind Mishkin, the tzimmes continued to send up cloudfuls of steam. Then the right understanding dawned on the adoption supervisor.

"Mrs. Rubin . . ." Mishkin said.

"Do you want me to beg?" Maya said. "I will beg."

"Mrs. Rubin, there are rules!"

"Rules such as in a closed adoption, the birth parents are not permitted to just . . . just . . . show up in our home?" Alex joined in.

"You gave permission, Mr. Rubin. Mrs. Rubin did."

"We were very eager to give permission, yes," Alex said. "Almost as eager as you to let her lie down on your couch. Did you have much say in the matter?"

"Mrs. Rubin," the adoption supervisor said, wheeling toward Maya. "I am not a psychologist, but you did me no favors. You—"

"Stop calling me Mrs. Rubin!" she shrieked. A terrible silence descended again on the house, which, until just an hour before, had heard too little noise rather than too much. Maya gulped back a sob and covered her mouth. She was tired, very tired. A strand of hair had tumbled out of her ponytail and now hung in front of her eyes like a bramble missed by the gardener.

"I am so tired of you, Gabriel Mishkin," Maya said finally, so quietly that the denounced man himself leaned forward to hear better. "You are condescending. Like all you American Jews. You are going to write a memoir about the Old World? What do you know about the Old World? You're an American, a complete and hopeless American. I miss Ukraine. In Ukraine, I could give you a thousand hryvnia and you would tell me what I want to know. So easy."

"That isn't the way things are done in America, Mrs. Rubin," Mishkin said softly, forced to issue the correction but wishing to inflict minimal damage by it. "The birth parents have rights, too." He was whispering.

"You mean the birth parents who refused this child?" Alex said. "Their rights are the rights you are so concerned about protecting? Not the mother who is standing in front of you because she is trying to do a good thing for her son? I hope they put your picture up on the wall where the saints are. Gabriel Mishkin, he never broke." He laughed in an ugly way.

Maya sank into the chair next to the tzimmes. It had finished steaming and was beginning to cake around the edges. She was grateful to Alex for standing up for her.

"It's time for us to go," Alex said.

Maya rose and dried her eyes with the tips of her fingers. But she remained in place.

"It's time for us to go," Alex said again, and now stepped toward his wife, his hand held out.

Maya wedged out of the glass baking dish the spoon she had lodged there and dug out a yellow-orange mound of tzimmes. She puckered her lips and blew slightly. Then she swallowed the spoonful with the hungerlessness of a sick person, the spoon clinking a tooth.

"It's good," she said. "Very good." She returned the spoon to the dish, took her husband's hand, and, without looking at Gabriel Mishkin, stepped out of his home.

"That's how they are," Alex said as he piloted the Corolla down the switchbacks of Mishkin's mountain. "He won't save his drowning mother if it means stealing an oar. You decided to cook the tzimmes because you thought it would melt his heart?"

"Let it go, Alex," she said as she stared blankly through the windshield. It was an unusually cold day for early October, December sending out an early invitation. "Let him eat some tzimmes. He hasn't had a hot meal in I don't know how long." She ran her thumbs to her temples and pressed. She really did have a headache. They wouldn't be home for two hours.

"I hope he chokes on that tzimmes," Alex said. "You cooked for him after he let those people into our home."

"*We* let them into our home," Maya said.

Alex slammed on the brakes and Maya nearly rode into the dash as they came to a squealing stop at a curve in the road. Maya had yelled out, but he hadn't been going fast enough for her to be hurt. They sat without speaking while Alex opened and closed his hands on the steering wheel, his jawbone tight. "Maya, how many times can I ask you to wear your seat belt?" His voice carried the extra resentment of someone responsible for the situation.

"What is it?" she said, breathing hard. "What did you see?"

"I didn't see anything," he said. "I saw them pulling into our driveway. We were watching them from the window."

"So?" she said weakly. She was on the verge of tears.

"So I remembered their license plate," Alex said. "I saw the license plate as they pulled up on the driveway. Rodeo. RodeoMT1. Or maybe Rodeo1MT. But it said 'rodeo.'"

And with this recollection, Alex Rubin restored to himself and his wife all the hope and faith that had been sapped by their talk with Gabe Mishkin. That's what Alex did. He noticed things it would never occur to her to notice. Yes, he was quiet and mulish, but that's because he was busy observing. Noticing. For instance, he had noticed that Mishkin wasn't going to help them about an hour before she did. And had kept silent so she could unspool her act, the actress.

Maya yelped, threw her arms around Alex, and began to cover his cheek with kisses. He smiled and tried to fight her off: "Maya . . . Maya . . ." First, she wouldn't listen to him, was full of childish wishes, of which he was the chaperone and chauffeur, but then she wouldn't let him alone, again like an impetuous child. It wasn't until a hatchback nearly met them head-on around the blind spot of the curve, the other driver setting off a squeal of her own tires, that Maya let go of Alex's neck. As the two cars gingerly passed each other at a distance of inches, the middle-aged woman at the other wheel regarded the Rubins with hatred. However, the middle-aged woman in the passenger seat of the Rubins' car was clapping with joy.

+

That night, without design, they slept touching hands. They had shut their lamps at the same time, a rarity, and lay in the dark on their backs, not moving. They were thinking the same thing—the license-plate variations had been given to Eugene, who had a friend at the DMV. Eugene asked mockingly who was going to give him fifty dollars for the task—on-the-side statewide checks were twenty, national fifty. Eugene was reminded that he was the first to propose that the birth parents were responsible. Maya wondered if Eugene's exasperated attacks were a way of covering fright, not something he could betray in front of Raisa. Or was she simply imagining fright in everyone as a way of getting a hold of her own.

Maya and Alex lay next to each other and listened to the other's breathing. Maya felt enclosed by the moment, as if she and Alex were down in a bowl while the world went on above. Her fingers reached for his forearm before she froze, fearing the touch would interrupt their stillness. But he allowed his arm to be covered, and then to be scratched lightly with her fingernails. She scratched in rows, up and down, until the motion ceased to register. Though her nails were not long, she was scoring his skin. He didn't stop her. Eventually, her hand opened and slid down to cover his, palm down on the bed. In this way, they fell asleep. In the morning, Alex's forearm had four raised welts. At breakfast, he rolled up his sleeve and shook his head.

As they waited for the DMV information, the Rubins performed the tasks that were required of them, but without vitality. Something had broken under the weight of the mystery in their lives. In the preceding months, they had busied themselves with the dark pleasure of addressing a problem. The Rubins loved problems— the state of mild emergency they brought on, the wagon-circling they demanded, the temporary marginalization of other, less tractable problems they suddenly authorized. It was delicious to swarm upon a new problem with a thousand solutions—the solutions really were legion, as each of them insisted on a different approach, a happy babel—to batter it with the considerable persistence, ingenuity, and force of this team of survivors and prosperers. The problem of Alex's depressive performance at the investment bank had been resolved by new employment under his father; Maya's shock at the amount of time the elder Rubins logged in her home was addressed by the transfer of some of her kitchen duties to Raisa; and Maya's failure to become pregnant was solved by the arrival of Max in their lives. The Rubins loved problems. They had been born under a dark star; they had been abused by circumstance. But they persevered and survived.

But this time, they faced more than a problem. The familiar rituals of their days, the inability of someone driving by to distinguish Maya and Alex's home from another Sylvan Gate town house: all this concealed the despair that had been settling on them since the evening with the deer. (That was the colorless designation by which the event came to be known: the evening with the deer.) A problem had finally spurred the Rubins to unanimity—in helplessness. Even Eugene seemed bereft of his usual enthusiasm. Over the previous three months their horizons had narrowed to a single point, and from this place optimism had gradually departed. On some day, the Rubins had begun to talk of almost nothing other than Max's "difficulty." As recently as a week before—before Gabriel Mishkin; before the Rubins took the law into their own hands by bribing a friend at the DMV; before, in other words, the matter gained a new kind of reality by involving forces beyond the family—it would have seemed perfectly sensible for, say, Raisa to propose some new remedy. However, her proposing the same now—no, the other Rubins would not have ridiculed her; exasperation and disagreement about the best solution was a luxury of more hopeful days. No, they would have simply stared in baffled silence, or nodded desultorily to avoid disrespecting her effort.

Dinner was nearly wordless, the adults trading responsibility for the small talk that would keep Max from sensing that something was off. They were relieved if he finished first and retreated upstairs; then they could be silent. Sometimes, they tried—

"He used to be so cheerful."

"Well behaved is different from cheerful. You're rewriting the facts."

—but it refused to take. They trailed off because there was no way to speak about Max without conceding that they didn't know their child and grandchild as they wished to, and that admission no one wished to make.

Max wandered the house sullenly, occasionally lifting his fingers to the side of his head and wincing theatrically. His wound had frightened him. Maya wondered if she was watching her son come to resemble his father—his adoptive father, who was as sensitive to illness as he was suspicious of doctors. At least this made her face fill with a bereaved amusement.

And then the information they didn't want came from Eugene's friend at the DMV. There were seventy-three license plates registered to Montana addresses with variations on the word *rodeo*. But there was only one plate that also featured the number *one* and the state's abbreviation. However, the listing carried an address—2207 New Missouri Trail South, Adelaide, Montana—but no phone number. The Rubins called Information—no associated phone number. Who did not have a phone number in 2012? The printout looked too big for the miserly information it contained.

"So, let's go there," Maya said.

"Maya," Alex said wearily. "Not again."

The table sat in silence, as if admitting that its authority had been exceeded.

"You're going to stop now?" Maya said. She rose and retreated to the kitchen counter, her fingers clutching her hair.

"Maya," he said sharply. "It's one thing to make a phone call. We're not going to—to—Montana." He let out an amazed chuckle. "We can write them a letter." He opened his hands, offering a compromise, though it was clear he was giving up on this approach.

"A letter they'll forward to the adoption agency," Maya said. "There's probably a law that says we can be sued for violating the agreement without their permission. Who knows what the penalty for that is. No, we have to get in front of them, Alex. I have to get in front of Laurel. I know I can speak to her. I just need to find her."

"So let's hire a private investigator," Alex said. "He'll look and see if they're there. Then maybe I can fly by myself."

"And I?" Maya said. "Do I deserve to see where my child was born? Does he?"

"Voices," Raisa said. "Please. He's upstairs."

"We discussed this," Alex answered his wife. "The parents is what we need."

"What if they want him back?" Raisa said in a conciliatory tone. "Let's say you find them. Have you considered that?"

"They can't," Alex said. "Legally, he's no longer theirs."

"And what, the law is everything?" Eugene piped in. "So they can't have him back, but they can make our lives difficult. Eight years have passed, they're living their quiet, dead lives out there wherever they are, and suddenly you call, stir things up, give them something to do. Just the excitement they need. Think about it. Think about Max finding out. Think about a difficult situation becoming difficult in a new way."

"What do *you* propose, Papa?" Maya said, exploiting the endearment; she referred to Eugene paternally rarely. Eugene's shoulders slumped in a new way and he looked out toward the backyard, simmering in the blue haze of dusk.

Maya watched Alex. She was being forced to surrender the solidarity she had felt from her husband in Gabe Mishkin's home; it had been tactical, not strategic. Their aims had overlapped, but in the manner of allies who share an enemy rather than a purpose. Her chest filled with helplessness. She imagined water in her lungs, frothing and burbling as she tried to breathe; she felt waterlogged with misery. She wondered if, secretly, her husband wished to go, but merely feared responsibility for another error and needed her to insist on it—then dismissed the possibility as another fantasy of alliance.

"Alex, it can't hurt for him to see it," she said without energy. "If nothing else, he has a right to. He has a right to know where he was born."

"But he won't *know* he was born there," Alex said. "Because we aren't going to tell him."

"*Voices*," Raisa hissed.

Alex's eyes narrowed at his wife. "You've been wanting to leave New Jersey for twenty years. It's like a prison to you. You want to live somewhere else, go live somewhere else."

"I want to live somewhere else with my family," Maya said.

Eugene and Raisa sat like two Buddhas; they wished they had not been around for this part of the argument. You can't unhear what you've heard.

After a long silence, Maya sat down again. Again, she wedged herself in without sliding the chair out from the table. Again, she spoke as if her parents-in-law weren't there.

"Yes, I do want to know what it's like out there," she said quietly. "Twenty-five years in America—thirty-five for you—and to never have gone farther than Florida and Chicago. Aren't you curious? Aren't you dying of curiosity? Okay, we won't tell Max—but you and I know. Don't you want to see it the same way that Laurel wanted to see this?"

"I see you've been reading Bender's book," Alex said. His face was tight with embarrassment—to have been spoken to that way in front of his parents. "Okay," he said with withering softness. He rose from his seat, walked to the stairs, and called for Max. They heard the door of a bedroom open upstairs. "Maxie?" his father called again. "Come down, please, okay?"

"What are you doing?" Maya said.

"'You want,' 'I want,'" Alex mimicked as they listened to Max descend the carpeted stairs. "Let's ask him directly."

"Ask him what?" Max said, blinking twice and surveying the adults in the kitchen. He reached up and touched the side of his head gingerly. One of his Indian masks from Mexico was around his neck on its string. It was the one with the snakes coiling out of the red mouth.

"Max, why are you wearing that mask?" his mother said.

"I was playing," he said.

"He wants to go to Mexico, not Montana," his father said. "Re-

member, Maxie? Turtle stakeouts after dark? We'll take pictures
this year."

"You can't, it startles the babies," Max said. He slipped the mask
off his head and winced again when it grazed his temple.

"Max, honey, stop that," Maya said sharply. "It's long healed."

Max's hand fell from his head as if he'd touched a flame with his
finger. Alex eyed his wife with the satisfaction of a winner before
the contest has started.

"Max?" Alex said. "Mama wants to ask you something." He
nodded at his wife.

Startled, Maya cleared her throat. She tried to collect herself.
"Maxie?" she said hoarsely.

Max raised his eyebrows.

"How would you like to go on vacation? Me, you, and Papa?
Mama's always staying behind because of the airplane, but mama
wants to go somewhere with you. We'll drive there. A road trip."

"Uh-huh," Max said. He looked up and blinked twice. Every
time he did that, Maya had the same thought: He didn't get that
from us. And then she fought it. "But where?" he said.

"Montana," Maya said. Eugene and Raisa stiffened, as if the
word alone would reveal to Max everything that had been so dil-
igently kept from him. "Do you know where that is?" Maya went
on. "It's beautiful. More stars than you'll see here. And very different kinds of grass, too. Many more kinds, I think. We'll be gone for
my birthday. We can celebrate it out there. Isn't that fun?"

"It's Mama's birthday soon!" Raisa clapped, remembering it.
She was eager to remind everyone that the future harbored good
things as well.

"But what about school?" Max said to his mother.

"You'll *miss* school," Maya said. "How would you like that?" Alex
looked at her—an unfair move. But it wasn't—Max liked school.

"For how long?" Max said suspiciously.

"We'll decide together," Maya said. "If we like it there, we'll
stay longer. If not, we'll come back."

"If we like it, we'll stay there longer?" Alex interfered. He was done leaving the conversation to his wife. He looked at his son. "Do you want to go, Max?" he said. "We won't go if you don't want to."

Maya shot him a betrayed look. "School can wait," she jumped in. "Did you know that your father missed the first two months of third grade because he was busy making his way to America?" She looked up at Alex, who confirmed resentfully.

Max shrugged heavily, a little Eugene. (Why did Max demonstrate only distinctions from Maya but resemblances of the other Rubins?) "But that wasn't vacation," the boy said, pleasing his father. For someone who wished to commune with the wild, her son could be annoyingly pedantic, Maya thought. And from whom had he inherited this blessing?

"And this is," Maya said quietly. "The three of us are going."

Alex slapped the table: See? She was conscienceless, his wife. Without the answers she wanted, she would force the child.

But then Max touched his ears with his shoulders. "Okay," he said. "Let's go." Some internal switch, mysterious to the Rubins, had been touched and the cloud of skepticism was gone from his face. The adults peered at him, not sure what to make of his acquiescence.

Maya walked to her son and embraced him. He let her. When Maya and Alex had fought as young people, Maya had her arms around Alex's shoulders before the argument was over. Alex would cast her off: He wasn't a robot to switch from anger to affection like that. But Max was different. Perhaps there was a trace of her in her son after all.

+

In the manner of a larger organism unable, to its own surprise, to fend off the negligible parasite that has beset it, the Rubins gave in to Montana, though, as the days passed, it became clear that they would go only if Maya took charge of the arrangements. Alex wandered in an itchy moroseness. Raisa banged around the kitchen, trying to memorize things and clucking her tongue in despair. She asked if Maya had all her recipes in one place.

"I'm not dying, Mama," Maya said. "We'll be back." She half believed this herself. Her unease created the impression of illness; her ears roared and there was a constant sweat on her forehead.

"What are we going to do here without you," Raisa said, shaking her head.

"I'm sure you'll survive," Maya said. "You might even enjoy it."

"Maybe we should come with you," Raisa said, her voice loading with excitement. "All together, you know?"

Maya blanched. "No," she said. She had blurted it out before she could soften it.

Raisa stared at her, wide-eyed. "Of course," she said after a moment. "What was I thinking? You children need to go off on your own."

It was Eugene who opened up to Montana the most, perhaps because he was certain not to be going. He became promiscuous in his advertisements of the voyage, if not the reason for it. The cashier at the Russian grocery heard about it, as well as the line of customers; so did the honey wholesaler; even Bender was called. Answering the half-curious, half-skeptical inquiries he aroused, Eugene only shrugged: More than three decades had passed in America; wasn't it time the Rubins found out what it actually looked like? Immigrants like Bender hid out in their American port of arrival, but the Rubins did not fear change, exploration, discovery. Livingstone, Amundsen, Rubins. (On their way, the children could stop to see Eugene's brother Karl and his wife Dora in Chicago, thereby relieving Eugene of his guilt for failing to do the same in more than a decade.) Because Eugene could only hint at his true meaning—the junior echelon of his family was about to embark on an honorable, romantic, spiritual action; and what has yours been up to?—his listeners enjoyed the possibility of not having grasped it and sent him off with tight-lipped good wishes.

Maya spent her evenings with the Internet and the road atlas. She read that Montana was the fourth-largest state, and New Jersey the fourth-smallest. Twenty New Jerseys could fit inside a single Montana. The latter felt to her like a giant, poorly known animal that would leave New Jersey bloody and pulped. She read the road atlas like a student of English reciting the dictionary. Rudyard, Rocky Boy, Roscoe. They had a Harlem as well. "Zortman, Landusky," she said feebly to the evening lamp, naming a pair of towns that huddled together astride a vast emptiness. The Jewish-like surnames gave her comfort.

How did one plan for a trip of this kind? When she tried to imagine the out there that waited for them, her heart beat quickly and her palms moistened. The vision would not even resolve into discrete dangers, just a black mass of badness and trial. Only fools make unrequired journeys, Raisa had quoted a proverb. They could scrap the trip. Max hadn't shown the enthusiasm on which she had counted. By canceling, Maya would receive a boost with the Rubins. She could show Max pictures of Montana on the computer. She could find a book about the animals of the West.

But Maya had been telling Alex the truth—she wanted Max to see where he was from, even if he would never find out that he was. She couldn't say why she thought this would help—but it was what Laurel was after when she drove two thousand miles. Laurel needed to see for herself where Max was going. Maybe it gave her some kind of rest.

Maya rummaged in the rolltop desk in the home office and withdrew a note pad. On the first line of a fresh page, she wrote, DANGERS. Below, she wrote:

1. snowstorms
2. rainstorms
3. hailstorms
4. bad brakes
5. snakes

6. getting robbed
7. one of us getting hurt
8. all of us getting hurt
9. running out of water
10. running out of gas
11. poisonous berries
12. poisonous plants
13. losing our bags
14. losing money
15. losing each other

Outside, the enormous oak creaked with the weight of the wind. Back and forth it went, like a badly oiled swing. It was the sound of loneliness, a malevolent mystery to which the answer was you and you alone. Upstairs, Alex was snoring lightly, his mouth ajar. The wind kicked up, rustling leaves, and a branch scratched at the siding of the house as if asking for shelter.

If they went, it would have to be now. If it was in the fifties here, it would be in the thirties there; that much Maya knew. In the morning, she would pack warm clothing. She would buy lanterns, thermoses, warmer socks. She would place herself in the hands of the clerk at the camping store. She would flirt and get a discount. She would take Eugene's Escape without asking.

She shut the light and lay down on the living room couch. She dreamed of a field of snow. Her house—it was not the house she shared with Alex, but she knew it as hers, a smallish log cabin with a yellow sconce outside the door—was off its foundation and sliding through the snow like a sled.

II

West

10

Maya whimpered and awoke. Her head was cantilevered over the shoulder of the passenger seat of the Escape, a ball of pain at the base. Fearfully, she angled it back. The pain was less blinding than shaming—a promise, good for days, to remind her of her careless-ness. For careless behavior, you paid.

She looked around unpleasantly—why had she passed the night in the car? The Escape, boxy as a slow animal, tilted off the sloping berm of the road, the blacktop steaming with mist, which, along with the golden light it was suffusing, indicated early morning, though sedans and pickup trucks passed regularly. Had the Escape broken down? They had barely started. Maya allowed herself to relish the tantalizing possibility of this failure: They could turn around with honor.

She squinted against the light on the passenger side. The berm ran off into a stubbled field that dead-ended, it was difficult to tell in the morning glare how far, in the foothills of humpbacked brown elevation. On the other side of an electric fence, fat white cows marked the field like an irregular crop. Oblong white birds popped around the cows, leaping for worms in the turned-over earth. The cows were folded down in heavy-thighed, spinsterly repose, studying the creatures that had washed up at the edge of their kingdom. Maya felt observed. The mindless vacancy at-tributed to cows could be seen also as mindless concentration. Before Maya's eyes adjusted to the light, she had a mirage of the brown stone humps behind the animals rapidly rearranging them-selves before slumping once again into stillness.

She turned, fresh pain blossoming in her neck. Max was supine across the backseat, his mouth open in slumber, a small blanket tossed about his feet. Several feet off the berm, his ankles covered by grass, Alex was smoking. Maya squinted: Alex was not a smoker. Carefully, expecting it to deliver fresh pain, she pulled on the door handle. The door began to ding, as if responding to an emergency.

The bitter, piney astringency of the air, flecked with something metallic as well as the universal scent of cow shit, walloped her so that she reached out for the frame of the car. She had an after-image of the road: The drivers were wearing jackets. One face in particular loomed retroactively, which genetics or weather or excessive inebriation had scoured with a supreme network of cross-hatching channels. That face had beamed out its last smile when Maya could walk under a table.

The door dinging, catastrophically urgent, stirred Alex. Maya tried to close the door far enough for the cursed sound to cease but not so hard that she would rouse Max. Alex stiffened as she hobbled toward him.

"It smells like somebody's poking your heart with a needle," she said, folding her arms around her chest for warmth, but it was a satisfying coldness, clean and riveting.

"Fall is coming," he said philosophically.

"You kept going," she said.

"I wasn't tired," he said unpersuasively.

"Under cover of night, you covered as much ground as you could to get this over with sooner."

He didn't look up at her, instead working at something in the grass with his foot. Alex had found that, as he became older, people were more willing to take him at his word. He interpreted this as evidence of an increasing substantiveness, a coherence into someone possessed by ideas and opinions that raised no doubts among others. At the office, his father dealt with him as an equal partner, deferring to his views on Turkish versus Georgian *kashkaval*, and the secretary rushed to address his requests with the slight fearfulness and apology that indicated respect. At home, his mother and

father stated their opinions, the former cautiously and the latter in-
sistently, but the decisions were Alex's. Only his wife strayed from
this pattern. Not always, and when she didn't, he thought of her
reserve and cooperation as another benediction of aging, wisdom,
maturity. But then the other Maya would come. He wondered if all
these things worked differently for women.

They had left Chicago the previous morning after three days
of house arrest by Eugene's older brother Karl and his wife, Dora.
Each day, they awoke in a cramped corner bedroom with a low
ceiling, were herded into the also low-slung living room—the
house, like the woman who ran it, was short and wide, one endless
floor-through—and were incarcerated there as one meal turned
into another, the holes in conversation filled by the crystal carafe
in Karl's hand and aphorisms he had clipped from the Russian
newspaper. Dora occasionally appeared to switch serving plates
and immediately vanished back to the kitchen—she seemed un-
starved for Karl's insights—except for a period on Saturday afternoon when she left the house altogether (Alex and Maya gazed at
her departing frame longingly) and came back with half a dozen
silk shirts for Max and Alex from Marshall's. Maya wondered why
she had been passed over, but eventually decided it was a compliment of sorts—unlike the men, who would wear a burlap sack if it
buttoned easily, women could not presume on each other's behalf.

Maya did not think of her own home as particularly American-
ized, but next to Karl and Dora the Rubins were indigenous. In
these fifteen hundred square feet of America, the Soviet Union
lived on, long after it had exhaled its final breath elsewhere, a
hallucinatory enclave where linoleum covered the floor and the
wallpaper sagged with a Persian rug. What nation was this? Every
evening, Maya and Alex staggered back to their bedroom, bloated
on carp and Karl's wisdom. It bred a beleaguered solidarity between them that had now been destroyed by Alex's reckless action.

"We were supposed to see places," Maya said.

"We are supposed to see the *parents*," Alex said. The cigarette smoldered in his fingers. Maya, her back to the keening strain of motors from the road, felt that each passing driver was studying the foreign couple off on the shoulder. Studied from both sides, by cowlike humans, and humanlike cows.

"We were supposed to observe Max," Maya said.

"He's not a pelican, Maya, to be studied in his native habitat," Alex said. "Fall is coming. Do you know what happens when fall comes to these places? It doesn't. There's a fart of summer and then it's winter for nine months. Our winters back home look like a sprinkle of snow next to it. So let's get there."

"But I wanted you to ask me before you did it," Maya said.

"Where exactly do you plan to deposit him while we go meet these people? You're going to find a babysitter in that town?"

"I don't know, Alex. We'll figure it out."

He shrugged and flicked the cigarette into the grass. It was a reckless trip—three voyagers into the gloom, on the doorstep of winter.

"Why are you smoking?" she said.

"Why are *you* smoking?" he said, and nodded at the car where, indeed, the glove compartment held a pack of Parliament 100's that Maya had impulsively bought along with the other things.

She tightened her shawl. She craved coffee. Hot, lip-scalding coffee. Terrible coffee, weak and plain, a pale perimeter rimming the blackness. Maya had glimpsed enough movies to know this was the kind of coffee they drank out here. She wanted some.

She stared at the humpbacked brown bestiary in the distance. The earth looked tired. Someone had spent it. Little tufts of green shrub rose here and there, like the indecisive patches on Alex's chest. Like Rubins—erstwhile of the same square mile in Minsk— dispersed across the broad back of America: Eugene's brother in Chicago; Eugene's second cousin in Omaha; Raisa's second cousin in Denver; someone, Maya could never remember who, in San Francisco. It turned out, given the chance, they all preferred to live far away from one another.

However, the land spread voluptuously, disdainful of restrictions, and this lifted her. The openness was heedless, spoiled, uneconomizing. It sprang something in her chest, got out of her a clutching deep exhalation, transmitted a clarifying signal to the haze in her head. The white oblong birds watched the cows, the cows watched her, she watched the brown ridgeline, and the brown ridgeline watched everything. She liked being in the relay.

"Don't you want to know where we are?" Alex said.

"No," she said. It came out resentfully, a petty revenge—she was not asked where to go, and so she would not ask where they'd gone—but she didn't mean it that way. On the cusp of inquiring, she decided not to inquire. She enjoyed not knowing. She even enjoyed not knowing why she enjoyed not knowing. There was a weightlessness to it—her husband had unwittingly kidnapped her from the designated and mapped. How could anyone try to reach her if she didn't know where she could be reached? She watched his face struggle with the senselessness of her answer.

"Maya, what is all this for?" he said. "It's a fool's errand."

She shrugged and pulled again on the shawl, setting off a shudder of pain from her neck to her fingertips. "I thought . . ." she started, but trailed off.

"Let's just hope nothing bad happens," Alex said.

She needed a cup of coffee, an ibuprofen for her neck, a cigarette. "We need to find a campground," she said.

"A campground?"

"I want to camp with my son. You said cold is coming: Better to do it sooner."

"I don't understand," Alex said, spreading his arms.

"Your preference is to spend the night in a vehicle," she said. "I also would like to not sleep in a bed."

"Maya, I don't want to sleep in a tent."

"I didn't want to sleep in a car, but you didn't ask. You can rent a hotel room. Max and I will sleep in a tent."

"What is it you expect to find out?" Alex raised his voice. "You think he'll sit up in the middle of the night and confess to you the secret of his being? We had a tent in the backyard."

She looked past Alex's shoulder. If she spoke, she would say something that would scatter the last of the goodwill stored up in Chicago. The morning fog was dissipating, setting loose a golden light streaked with pink. The brown humps had turned blue. If she kinked her head—fresh stab of pain—they looked like the shoulders of a beheaded colossus, buried below the rib cage, and the stony wrinkles that ran up and down the rock were his strain at trying to lift himself from the earth. Dumpy clouds hopped above the shoulders like little white horses.

Why did the hills in the distance becalm her with their mute, maintaining consistency, but the same quality in her husband made her unhappy? Was the vision in the distance especially majestic, or was she especially impatient?

"Maya," he called to her, a peacemaking note in his voice.

Her head was sideways in an inspection of hills. *Once upon a time there was a woman who left her husband and married a mountain. The blue giant's headless torso, inspired by her love, wrenched its fingers from the ground and pulled at a wick in her belly until it had unfurled her like a scarf and the ground was covered with the eiderdown of an unraveled Maya. Nine months later, the woman gave birth to a tree. There it grows in the shade of the blue giant's shoulders, watered by snowmelt and the brine of her tears. What the freshwater enlivens, her saltwater destroys.*

There. Not only her mother could tell stories. Her mother found fairy tales annoying, however: the ticking grandfather clock, the house on stilts, the talking wolf. Her stories of their Kiev neighbors were about real people suffering real lives. Why the gloom of a fairy tale when you could have the desperation next door? That was fine, Maya thought: Fairy tales would be the daughter's department. She touched her temples. Being out of New Jersey was having a strange effect on her. Her imagination was working, but not the remainder of her. Belatedly, she looked up at her husband. She said she was fine.

They heard Max climbing out of the car. He stood shading his eyes against the light, which, having vanquished the fog, had turned severe. Alex walked to his wife and placed a hand on her shoulder to reassure his son that mama and papa were not fighting, but it looked as if he was either leaning on Maya or keeping her in place.

"Max, honey, we're going to camp tonight," Maya said excitedly and walked toward her son, letting Alex's hand drop from her shoulder.

"I need to go number one," Max said unhappily.

"Max, what do those hills look like? Sleeping rhinos or a brown headless giant?"

"I need to go number one," Max insisted, knocking his knees. He was blinking furiously. She walked over and embraced him, inhaling the sleep in his hair. He stomped his feet impatiently. She took his hand and pulled him toward a stand of trees by the fence. "There isn't a bathroom?" Max said, pulling away.

"Maya," Alex called out in reproof.

"Honey, you'll be fine," Maya implored Max. "Don't be fussy. There's nowhere else to go. Just quick in the bushes."

The pair of them took the decline down to the trees. What kind of trees? Trees. Maya pointed Max toward a thick trunk good for concealment and faced back toward the road. They all heard the burp and whoop of a police cruiser at the same time. As it pulled up behind the Escape, the siren went off but the lights continued to rotate and flash, menacing in their silence. Max turned back to his mother and now she shook her head. Maya felt Alex's furious gaze and avoided it. She felt a sweat on her spine. She remained in place, as if any movement could be misinterpreted, and took Max's hand.

The policeman took time climbing out. They watched him through the windshield of the cruiser, recording their license plate and murmuring into his radio as if they were fugitives. Maya had a panicked urge to laugh. Their first morning! She imagined the incredulous silence on the other end of the line when she called Eugene and Raisa from the local jail. Her neck ached incredibly. She remembered Max and rustled his hair. He stared at the police car inscrutably.

The policeman looked as if every grain of superfluity had been swept from him: His pale cheeks had been so closely shaved that they burned like mirrors in the cold sun. He covered the distance between his cruiser and the transgressors, Alex left in the margins, and greeted Maya, but her tongue had gone dry, so she only nodded.

"Your vehicle?" he said. "Welcome to South Dakota."

"Will we be arrested?" Maya said.

"Arrested?" the cop said.

"It's our first time," Maya said in self-defense. "I'm sorry. We were driving all night—"

"They let you relieve yourself on the side of the road in New Jersey?"

He had a young man's voice, and Maya realized she was probably older than him. She shook her head mournfully.

"We like our land urine-free, too," he said. Alex, until now rooted in place, called out for permission to approach. The cop shrugged; it was a free country. Alex stepped carefully toward them.

"I'm sorry," Maya croaked out. "It was a mistake. I'm very sorry."

The cop watched her with curiosity. "I'm not going to arrest you," he said, as if the trouble would be greater for him.

Maya was covered with gratitude, and felt on the verge of tears.

"But I will give you a ride to the diner," he said. "It's just up the road."

"But there will be a ticket," Maya said, wanting to offer up a lack of illusions.

"There will be a *warning*," the cop said. "And a ride in my cruiser. Let's go. Your husband can follow in your vehicle."

Down the field, the white birds leaped and plunged. The birds dove for buried worms not only when the cows chewed the grass, but when they shat it out, the birds' feathers turning oily and brown.

Alex watched with astonishment as Maya walked her son to the police cruiser. They climbed in behind a mesh-wire panel. The patrolman leaned out the front window and ordered Alex to follow. Alex nodded energetically and ran toward the Escape. The cop turned toward the backseat. "You all right?" he asked Maya. He looked at Max: "You ever been in a squad car?"

Max shook his head. He was taking in his surroundings like a cat—alert but unsure what to think of things.

"It's going to be your first and last time. Unless you decide to sit where I'm sitting. We've got a deal?"

Max nodded. Adults were constantly striking deals with him.

A quarter mile up the road, the Badlands Diner sent gray plumes of wood-scented smoke out of a scuffed, dented chimney. The cruiser pulled up by the large windows, and Maya had the fresh experience of being watched by two dozen diners as she and her son idled in the backseat of a police cruiser.

The cop looked back at Max. "Keep your mother out of trouble," he said. To Maya, he said: "Do you know where you're going?"

Maya nodded feebly. "Thank you," she managed.

"Enjoy your stay," he said.

"I don't like New Jersey," Maya blurted out in conciliation.

"I don't blame you," the cop said. "Though, to be fair, haven't been myself."

Maya nodded, as if accepting a reprimand, and opened the back door. The diners at the window stared. She climbed out, dragging Max behind her. "Thank you," she said once again into the cavern of the car. The cop raised a finger to his temple. The last thing Maya saw before heading in was her husband's glare from the wheel of the Escape, which he had parked sufficiently far from the cruiser to avoid obvious association with the woman getting out of it. He looked as if he wished the South Dakota law had addressed this case differently.

Inside the diner, a fireplace was roaring and the short-order bell was clacking over and over—Maya had expected, in the wilderness, soul-chilling, funereal quiet, but her morning clamored with bedlam. Every scalloped red banquette was taken. A clothesline strung with fans of pleated red-and-blue bunting wavered lightly above the seating. There must have been rooms upstairs because the ceiling heaved with footsteps and scurrying. Children? Animals? Children fleeing from animals? Maya almost learned the answer— some cataclysm befell the feeble flooring, sending a skein of white dust onto the hostess stand. Maya quickly swept it off with her hand.

A mincing son at her side, she was ignored by two waitresses, gliding around each other with the resentful familiarity of people who have spent long hours in the same kitchen. Maya instantly feared both of them. "Well, they're salting everything at the tables, Charlie," one of them said to the sweaty face peering out of the short-order window. Her hair was pinned up in a businesslike pile, as if in the morning she gave you pancakes and in the afternoon she loaned you at the bank. "My job is to tell you," she said to the sweating face. "What you do with it, that's your job."

A man at the counter was watching Maya; the manager? Maya tried to avoid his eyes, which bored into her with a glinting amusement—she did not feel up to another correction. The stains of paint on his jeans and his wrists, and his shoulder-torn sweater, would have made her think he was poor—Maya thought everyone in the American West would be poor—but the sweater was thickly woven, and his knife and fork were poised above his eggs with a strange delicateness, as if he was shy to cut in. A book was open next to his plate.

"Sit down, if you're looking to order," he said to Maya. "They don't know what to do with you if you're standing."

Maya colored, feeling the interloper's familiar cluelessness. It, not Alex, was her true life's companion. Just when she began to get free of the feeling, she mispronounced a word or failed to apprehend some invisible rule, and lived the next days like a guest, a cherry pit of self-reproach in her stomach. How was one to know these things? The hostess podium said: "Please wait to be seated."

"My son just needs to go to the bathroom," she said timidly. Because she was trying hard to pronounce the words without an accent, she sounded to herself like someone who'd arrived yesterday. But the man only smiled in that American way, at once vacuous and reassuring, out of grayish-green eyes. With the tip of his butter knife, he indicated an alcove at the end of the counter.

"You can just go?" Maya said. "It isn't only for customers?" Now, Maya was intent on scrupulously observing laws both written and unwritten. She would be the Badlands Diner's most desirable customer. She would cause no further provocation this morning.

He plucked an inverted cup from a long tray with two handles shaped like buffalo skulls and set it to the right of him. "There," he said. "You're a customer."

Maya knelt before Max. "It's just that way, honey."

"Come with me," Max whispered.

"I can't go with you. Girls can't go into the bathroom with boys."

"You have to wait just one minute," the man said. "The Furies are in there right now."

The bathroom lock cracked open and two teenage girls tumbled out. Giggling, they made their way down the counter. It was plain that they were sisters from their heavy legs and soft, swimming cheekbones, but their laughter rang out differently—one hid it in her chin and the other, a year or two older, sang it out. They were Laurel's age when she delivered her son, if not older. But they were children, just children. But Laurel, in her home, had felt like a woman. The laws for each person are different. Maya saw the girls' father in the strict cut of their mouths, the eyes glowing gray-green and mossy like his. They were like the same words in two slightly different languages. On the father's face she saw a reticent satisfaction. Seated, the older one tried to steal an egg from his plate. She got the yolk, which dripped all over the counter, setting off a fresh round of laughter. He tried to get a corner of her shirt to wipe it, and she yelled. The waitress with the bank haircut laid down a pile of napkins on the counter without looking at anyone and went into the main room with a coffeepot.

Maya watched with the helplessness of someone behind glass; she was watching others live out their lives, the rituals familiar but incomprehensible. Max squirmed, and, smiling weakly at the man, she led her son down the length of the counter. "I'm right here," she said, kneeling in front of him. Max took the knob of the door, looked back at his mother resentfully, and disappeared inside.

She craved coffee. Her head felt attached to the rest of her only by the stem of pain that rose from its base. Of course she could have taken Max into the bathroom; she had abandoned her son for coffee. Not knowing where else to go, she sat at the counter, by the cup waiting for her. The man squinted at her. He had a pleasantly shaped face that headed toward but missed handsomeness. The long, narrow nose flared out slightly on one side; the lips were thin; and his skin showed age. But it missed well. The features added up to make a coarse but appealing American face. She liked its Americanness, a different kind of Americanness than what she was used to. The face studied her with a slight sneer—the upper lip was up slightly—or maybe it was amusement again. The inspection was not unfriendly, something forest-like to the eyes, lush and somnolent. Melancholy—or maybe Maya was hoping; she felt a monopoly on despair while the rest of the world celebrated. He was not young—Maya liked this as well, because she felt disheveled and old. Up close, his eyes were grayer than green, baleful not playful.

"They're nice girls," she said, and nodded toward them. They were staring at the screen of a cell phone.

She remembered she had not brushed her teeth. Was wearing

yesterday's clothes. Bedding down in the bucket seat of a Ford Escape had sprung half her ponytail loose, and several strands hung in front of her eyes. Her usual instincts were asleep. With frantic casualness, she tried to feed her hair back into the ponytail. And then she was out of steam even for this simple mission, her hair falling over her shoulders. Her fingers worked the unemployed hair band.

The man studied the short-order window. In her sleepiness, she was touched by the intensity with which he gazed at it—he was looking for something to say. Of course the waitresses would have found her at the podium—he had wanted her to sit at the counter.

Finally, he turned to Maya and said, "In this book"—he indicated it with the tip of his knife; the spine said *21st Century Parenting*—"they talk about how when a ewe lambs, it's *mystified* by what's come out of it. It wants nothing to do with that baby mess. She'll sniff the lamb and head butt it down in the straw. But after a time, they're inseparable. If the lamb dies, the ewe won't take another. You have to skin the dead guy and sit that new pelt on some unmothered lamb, and smear the pelt with the dead liver. And little by little, the mother will agree to be fooled."

Maya laughed—loudly, lavishly. She understood nothing except the keenness with which the speaker had spoken. He was older—at his temples, his hair, which came high off his forehead before falling past his ears, was flecked with gray—but he was not the only one at the counter with gray hair. She was ready to forget this about herself as readily as her occasional accent. There was no end to the things that needed forgetting. She saw the look of dismay on his face and beseeched him with her hands.

"I'm sorry—I wasn't laughing at what you said."

"I'm just blurting away," he said. "I've had too much coffee, and you none."

"Is it that bad?" Maya said, touching her hair.

"No . . ." he started, and she also held up her hands—they stared at each other in an awkward silence, then both laughed lightly, then looked away, then looked back at each other, and finally, he drove a hand at her.

"Marion Hostetler," he said. Again, she saw the beads of paint on his wrist. She wanted to scrape them off, like crumbs off a tablecloth. She took his hand. How quickly a trip revised what seemed normal; she was shaking another man's hand in a diner. But this is what Americans did; they just started talking to each other, a nation with the oafish amiability of the slightly touched.

"I slept in the car," Maya said, trying to explain her appearance. It made her sound homeless.

"I've got no excuse," he said. "I go on sometimes. Isn't that so, girls?"

"Daddy, we love you," the older one said. When she wasn't laughing, she had a deep, reasonable voice.

"Only since you and Mom split," the younger one replied to her father. Maya wondered if she was hearing a reprimand. Or he was. Behind the soft lips of youth, sharp teeth.

"Which left you with a calico cat with one eye and limited opportunity to *express your mind*," the older one said. "You don't have an *outlet*."

"Well, the university is certainly doing its job," Marion said mournfully. "Alma and Celia," he wagged his finger between the girls for Maya.

"That's 'soul' in Spanish and German, the two sides of the family," Alma, the younger one, said. She was still smiling, but Maya saw that she was worried about her father.

"Let's flag you some coffee," Marion Hostetler said.

"I should check on Max," Maya said, glancing at the bathroom door, but remained on her stool. She looked longingly at a coffeepot crinkling on a hotplate by the short-order window. Marion had been right about the waitresses; Maya's glance sent some kind of homing signal off in the one with the bank hairstyle, and she filled a cup for Maya and returned the pot to the hot plate without setting eyes on either the cup or the pot. It looked just like the coffee of Maya's imagination, more brown than black.

Maya took a sip. It was revolting, but she made herself drink again. Marion looked inquiringly at the bathroom. "He's my only," Maya said. The English words felt good in her mouth—she had used them before, many times, but she liked the way they sounded now, here. "No sons?" Maya asked the man—Marion.

"Brothers," Marion said. "Three of them. My mother pulled hard for a girl in my place—there were three boys already. She thought that if she settled on Mary, God would have to be a real SOB not to give her a girl. And out came I. Calling me Marion, that was revenge. Only she missed the Lord and got me instead. She refused to have any more kids after that. Stopped believing in God, too. But then I got only daughters. When she was dying, my mother said, 'You get what you want, but not what you were planning.' I tried to put it on her gravestone. No such luck."

"Why?" Maya said.

"Rick. Rick is the car-dealership brother. He had them engrave a heart on the stone, and inside it, 'Mother.' Jesse did it—he's a stonemason. And accessory. Jesse's the second. One night I'll have too much to drink and go in there and deface the thing. What can you make out of 'Mother'? Other."

"This coffee is disgusting," Maya said.

"Come on, you don't want any of that," Marion said. He pulled a thermos from a pocket of his coat and poured some into a new cup from the tray. "The other middle brother made out the best. He farms coffee beans on a shady hill in Guatemala. Now you know every one of us."

Maya smiled weakly. She felt soldered to her seat, by her fatigue and his talking. Working herself loose from the heavy fingers of both, she made herself slip off the stool—it was like another woman doing it, her legs were like stone—and laid her palm into the door of the bathroom.

"It turned into number two!" Max shouted from within. They all laughed at the counter, the girls looking up from the cell phone. Maya laughed, too, enjoying the moment—then wondered if they were embarrassing Max. When the man, Marion, laughed, the balefulness went from his eyes.

Maya returned to the counter. The diner clamored around them with the universal sound of forks on plates, water pouring into glasses, a laugh from one of the booths. Was it the surrounding emptiness that explained the unfamiliarly convivial feeling of the restaurant despite its godforsaken appearance—a huddling amity, exiles roped together on a crevasse at the edge of the world? She inhaled the thick aroma of the coffee; just the fog of it was tantalizing: leaves, a wood, autumn.

Marion waved his hands. "It isn't hot anymore."

"I walked away for a second," Maya said, rolling her eyes.

"Hot," Marion said. He took her cup for himself, and poured her a new one.

Maya sipped at the coffee. It brought her closer to sleep but loosened the strain in her neck. On the other side of their father, Alma and Celia stared rhapsodically at a cell phone. They were as square-shouldered as their father was lean. She imagined their mother in some kind of heavy robe that hid the ample folds of her figure.

"Max is adopted," Maya said. She bolted upright. Her heart started pounding, lifting her fatigue. She looked over her shoulder: Max was still in the bathroom. She clenched her jaw to try to get some focus into her face. She was really letting herself get away from herself.

"Sometimes, I think they're adopted," Marion said, bending his head toward his daughters.

"You're having breakfast with your daughters, I would say that's a triumph," Maya said diplomatically, wishing to return the conversation to comprehensible ground.

"They're having breakfast with their cell phone," he said. "I'm having breakfast with you."

The bathroom door swung open, and Max stepped out. How especially frail he looked in the fierce light pouring in from the large windows. The light was all but coming through him. She set her coffee down on the counter.

"Finish your coffee," Marion said. "We'll get some juice for— Max."

"We're . . ."—momentarily Maya struggled with the tense— "we're being waited for."

Marion nodded. "I see."

"Mama?" Max said.

"Just a second, honey," she said. "This man will tell us about a campground where we can stay tonight." She tried to sound casual, but her ears were still ringing with the unnecessary disclosure she had made a moment before. She should have rushed out of the diner—Marion didn't know that Max didn't know and could say something carelessly. She tried to collect herself—for the tenth time in ten minutes. She turned to Marion. "I don't know where we are," she said. She felt the fright she had given herself in her body: Her tiny breasts swelled; her belly felt soft; her heart was beating.

Marion moved his eyes from Max to his mother, and considered her with that balefulness. "In a diner outside Badlands National Park. If you want to camp, there's just one place. You go down 240 until it splits off. You'll have gone past the park. But you stay on the road—it's just 377 then. You can't miss it."

She thanked him and stood. She stood longer than she needed to. "Will you tell your brother how good a coffee he makes?"

"Enjoy this magnificent country," Marion said.

+

Alex was on the phone. She could tell from across the road that he was speaking with his parents because he was speaking with extra volume. Was he reporting to them what had happened? "Already, Maya has acquainted herself with the law," she imagined him saying. Her temples were aflame. She clutched Max's hand so hard that he squirmed. She didn't trust herself, crossing the road.

Alex paced the shoulder, as if he was in their living room. He could not sit and speak on the telephone at the same time. How tiny he looked splashed against the ridgeline, like an insect parading down its broad brown windshield. Only a little larger than the oblong white birds, which continued to leap as if they never lost hunger. The ridgeline looked as if it had grown in the warming rays of the sun, a sun-shower mushroom of rimrock and scree.

The sun was burning strongly and the stinging chill of early morning had gone. Maya knelt before Max and yanked off his jacket. The zipper wouldn't give and she was too violent with it. The sun felt good on her face, and she lost a moment staring up at the sky, her eyes squinting at the light, Max's jacket half off.

"What do you see, Mama?" he said.

"I bet you're hungry," she said. "We should have gotten you something inside." She wondered whether she could go back in. She could leave both of them in the Escape while she went in to get takeout.

"Who was that man?" Max said.

Maya hesitated. "He was the coffee man. He comes to the diners to give them their coffee."

"When will I be allowed to drink coffee?"

"When you go to college."

"I don't want to go to college."

"Oh, yeah?" she rustled his hair. "What do you know about it? Go say hello to your grandmother and grandfather."

He turned to walk toward his father, but she held him. "Hold on. I'm sorry. That wasn't the coffee man."

"Who was it?"

"Did you get scared in the police car?"

Max shook his head.

"I'm sorry. I made a bad decision. Sometimes I do that. I'm sorry. Okay?"

"It's fine," Max said. "I wasn't scared. Who was that man?"

Maya laughed sorrowfully. "That was a new friend. Like Oliver is for you. Do you miss Oliver?"

"He borrowed three books."

"Is he the kind of person who returns the things that you loan him?"

"I don't know," Max shrugged. "I've never done it before."

"Why did you agree this time?"

"I thought I would miss him."

Maya bit her lip. "You're a very good friend to him. And he to you."

"How do you know if someone is a good friend?" Max said.

"A friend is if you feel good about them in your soul."

"What's a soul?" Max said.

Maya laughed and nearly let a tear fall. She took his ears in her hands and rubbed them like wishbones. "A soul is that part of you . . . It's that part of you where you're the most honest about yourself. It's always the truth in your soul. Does that make sense?"

"Am I honest?"

"You're more honest than anyone I know."

She let him go. She circled the SUV until she was out of Max and Alex's sight, slipped to the ground, and leaned against its sturdy black frame. She stared up at the blinding light until it started tears again. Here were reasons for a trip far from home in a big car: The sun was strong enough to set off tears in her eyes, the Escape large enough to conceal her as they fell to the ground.

11

The Rubins drove past Badlands National Park/Pennington County Campground even though the sign advertising it was large and clear—too clear against the burnt-gray nothingness that it fronted. They drove past in a unanimous wish—so rare for them unanimity these days; perhaps they wished to savor it—for the campground to turn out to be some place other than the fenced-off patch of hard ground to which they reluctantly returned. The hard-baked pan of the plot was rejected even by plants. They gazed longingly at a rickety-looking motel off on a ridge—it seemed grand. The campground fence was strung with warnings against rattlesnakes, exhortations to conserve water, regulations regarding campfires, the opening and closing hours of a little shed on the edge of the lot that said OFFICE. How could a place of so few amenities require so many regulations? The Americans were regulated even when practicing wildness. In Kiev, Maya and her schoolmates had crept into the Alexeyevsky Theater at night because the city did not bother to keep it locked. They acted out their favorite film scenes on stage and drank moonshine in the aisles. They always deposited a bottle with the old watchman so that he would be amiably distracted. They did clean up when they were done—they weren't savages.

On exiting the Escape, Maya was buoyed a little by the dry, sweet, grassy air. Where was the grass? She could see only puckered gray stone—she thought of small elephants. The day was enjoying its best heat at this elevation at this time of year; Maya turned her face up and closed her eyes, letting the light wind whip her hair. Now it carried the sound of rustling grass, and again she looked around, as if she had heard speech in an empty room. Perhaps neither humbleness of imagination nor low funds were responsible for the bare facilities; perhaps they were meant to accentuate the views that lay open in every direction. The terrain looked like a cardiogram—the stone was beating healthy and sound. She remembered her husband and son; they were off to the side of the small dirt parking lot, waiting for her. She called out to Alex to set up the tent while she and Max registered. "Which one?" Alex said, pointing at the numbered campsites. "Any one," she said and, after Max joined her, went into the office.

Something had expired and then expired again in the low-ceilinged front room of the shed. Behind the wood partition, a red-faced man in a check shirt and suspenders was clutching a telephone and listening loudly to the senselessness on the other end of the line. Maya had been enlarged by the landscape, he by elk sausage in gravy: mother and child could fit inside of him twice. A moth the size of Maya's fist banged around a desk lamp, on despite the blasted severity of the light outside. Other insects had tattered the lampshade into a rag that barely held on to the harp.

"Well, Carla, your piss don't smell like gingersnaps, either," he yelled and slammed down the phone. Its tinnitic echo rang through the stale air of the office. Maya smelled gasoline, dried meat, wet straw. The attendant flexed a pair of porcine ears. A nameplate identified him as Wilfred Shade. "How can I help you?" he sighed. He held up a palm the size of Maya's head. "I'm sorry, little fellow. Pardon my language."

"Is piss the same as pee?" Max said.

The adults smiled. "We're not laughing at you, honey," Maya said. "Come here."

"There's two ways of saying things," Wilfred Shade said. "After you walk out of here, you could say: 'Mr. Shade, he was big.' Or: 'Mr. Shade's fat.' What would you say?"

Max looked up at his mother. "We would call Mr. Shade big, honey," Maya said.

"Your mom is nice, see," Wilfred said. He pushed a paper at Maya. "Fill this out." He retreated into the back office, but a moment later, his big head emerged. "You want an Oreo, either of you?" he said.

"Here is the one boy in the world who doesn't like sweets," Maya said.

"You and I part ways there," Wilfred said, and disappeared. Then his head popped out again. "I've got graham crackers. Dieter's delight."

Maya smiled wanly and thanked him, and now the attendant vanished for good.

"Max?" Maya looked down at her son. "Are you all right? You haven't said much. Did something upset you?"

"Why did you cry?"

"When?"

"You went around the car and cried."

"No, no. I had something in my eye. And then the sun here is so strong. I started tearing up. But I'm fine, honey—fine. Look at me—I'm laughing."

"Why did we come here?" he said.

"We're on vacation, sweetheart. You've never really been on vacation with your mama."

"If we're on vacation, why are you crying?"

Maya heard the television go on in the back office. Through the doorway, Wilfred was breathing heavily into a half-bitten Oreo. Was he trying to give her privacy? But she did not care about being overheard. As if feeling her stare on him, Wilfred turned back to look at her. "What I do," he said, "is I bite and then count. To twenty-five, and sometimes to fifty, if I can manage it. This way I eat five instead of the whole pack."

"You look great," Maya said.

"Ho-ho-ho," Wilfred said, and turned back to the television.

Maya crouched in front of her son. "Do you know what, Maxie? It's okay to cry sometimes. Good, actually. We've got laughs inside us, but cries, too. And they both have to come out. Sometimes, they come out at the wrong moments. They don't listen like that."

"It's strange to miss school."

"I have the one son who doesn't like Oreos but likes school."

Max shrugged and puffed out his mouth.

"I love this about you," she said. "Do you know that? I do. I don't want you to be any other way."

"I believe you." Max nodded.

"We're going to see how Papa is doing with the tent, and then we'll go take a walk. It's beautiful here, don't you think?"

Max shrugged.

"You don't think so? Aren't you excited you'll have a tent to sleep in again? I made Papa do it so you would be happy."

"The ground is hard," he said. "It's softer at home on the lawn."

"Just give it a shot—please. I've been looking forward to being away with you for so long. Just me, you, and Papa. We love Grandma and Grandpa, but just us three this one time."

"Okay," Max said. "I will."

Maya and Max returned outdoors to find husband and father lost in the embrace of a giant tent that billowed in the strong wind like the sail of a boat. No sooner would Alex slide a stake through one side of the piping than the opposite would shoot out into the next camping plot over, where, luckily, there was no one to impale. Maya and Max walked over. Alex asked why Maya had bought a tent when they already had one, Max's. If it was a purchase in error, why couldn't it, at least, be a good one? She had bought not a tent but a barracks for a small army. The same army was needed to mount it. Alex's monologue was halted by the arrival of a strong gust of wind. The bottom edge of the tent furled up, Alex lost his footing, and Maya and Max were soon gazing on him plastered across the hardpan, arms and legs splayed. It was only the weight of Alex's fallen self that kept the tent from flying off with the wind.

Max moved off toward a post with a coil of rope tied around it. One decorated the edge of every campsite—it was the border.

Max unwound the rope, looping one end over the post and the other through an opening at the crown of the tent. This gave the operation the traction it needed. Maya and Alex watched their son move around the tent, staking poles into the hardpan, which, now shimmied properly, held the poles with unvarying force. Finally, it was impossible to continue without Alex giving up his position, and he crawled off the tent. Muttering, he walked off to wash his hands. Indeed, Maya had made an error—the tent was much too big for three. But it was beautiful, too, warlike and protective at once, a dryland ship awaiting assignment.

+

"Call me Rose, call me Ranger Rose, call me Ranger Holliver. But don't call me 'lady,' don't call me 'yo,' and no 'hey there's, okay? Mom Holliver did not sit with a name-omen book for three days for no reason." The retirees filling out the noon natural-ist walk chuckled. Maya gripped Max's hand. Alex had insisted they go alone. He would spend time with the map, designing the shortest route to Adelaide, Montana. Maya felt a wave of futility. On a weekday in late October, when the adult world was at work, she was in an arid moonscape with a child and ten old people in the downswing of their lives. She felt at once undeservedly idle and frantic to no purpose.

   "Late-season groups are my favorite," Rose Holliver said. "This is the time to see it." Her chest was shapeless in a many-pocketed worsted forest-green shirt, her belly hemmed in by coarse gray slacks with black piping. The strap from her broad-brimmed gray hat accentuated the downy ampleness of her chin, the cinch making Maya think of horses and bits. Where did Rose Holliver come upon love in this emptiness? Or was there a man who joined her in the modest trailer they shared in a residential development nearby after his own day working at something for the national park? They fried hamburgers, on special nights they had merlot from the store. They had a half collie that had appeared one day and had been seduced into staying by leftover hamburger bits. In the evenings they watched the same television shows that Alex and Eugene watched, and they even paid a fee to the neighborhood association for electricity and water. Was their life so different? What difference did location make if they got along and liked the same things—she fried; he washed up after they finished. Maya had come ready to find savages, desperate characters, the poor, but there was no savagery. It was nice between Rose and (Trent? Charlie?), it was close, the shaggy collie watching the two lovers until they stopped and had a laugh over the dog's watching. They didn't smoke after sex. They didn't have children, and probably wouldn't. (Whereas Maya was forty-two but looked thirty-two, Rose looked forty-two but was thirty-two: she was the fertile one.) They had the pup. They called him Anna. Like Santa Anna, not like a girl.

Rose was giving out information about the Badlands: It looked like hopeless rock, but two-thirds was actually grass prairie. Maya was gratified by the information: It answered her earlier question. "You could run a herd of cattle on here if you wanted," Rose said. Maya pulsed Max's hand. They were on a mile-long boardwalk that led from the visitor center to an overlook down on a hundred-mile ridge of striated stone that ran all the way into Nebraska. Nebraska! To Maya, the word was as exotic as Neptune, and yet Maya stood within sight of it. Actually faced, it seemed unfamiliar and ordinary all at once.

Max looked up at Maya. "Grass, Max," Maya said, and nodded encouragingly. But he gave no reaction.

Rose was counting on her fingers, the thumbs male in their thickness: "Some of the last wildflowers you'll see before we get this freeze in the next couple of days: prickly pear, prairie cone-flower, needle and thread, sideoats grama . . ."

After the dim glass cases of the visitor center, the wood-etched signage around the park, and the shit-brown bathroom stalls that followed their progress down the boardwalk, the names of the grasses were beautiful. Sideoats grama sounded like a Negro jazz act. Maya wanted to know who got to name them. Even though the seniors were regularly interrupting the lecture, calling out "Ranger Holliver?" with happy compliance, Maya was too shy to raise her hand. Max might know, she thought, but he was refusing to become involved.

Rose was on to the animal life. Two small birds, black knobby heads and torsos like white eggs, were bouncing on the upper rail of the fence separating the visitors from the wilderness. "Little tuxedoes they've got on," Rose said. The birds had a hot-turquoise cummerbund on each flank—nature's bid for grace and surprise amid the universe's black-and-white plodding. "Who can tell me who these little guys are?" Rose said. "Your prize is a refund on your tour ticket." The retirees grumbled with laughter—the tour was free. Maya knelt in front of Max: "Max, honey, do you know what kind of bird that is?" Someone said butcher-bird. No, a fly-catcher. "It's just a magpie," he whispered. Maya leaped to her feet. "We know!" she exclaimed. The retirees swiveled and gazed admiringly down on the young mother with the fair-haired boy. "Now this apple *did* fall far from the tree," a tall man with watery eyes said. Chuckles murmured through the group. "I'd give a dollar to be your age, young naturalist. The bottom dollar."

Maya, stung by the first comment, was placated by the second. "Tell them, honey," Maya said, looking down at Max. But her son stepped a half foot behind her and dropped her hand. Rose and the retirees waited. "Max," Maya hissed. "Magpie." He turned and faced away from the group. Maya colored. She looked back at the seniors and swallowed. "We're shy today," she said apologetically, wondering if her accent was coming through. What had seemed unimpeachable emerging from Max's mouth felt like an embar-rassing guess from her own. "Magpie?"

"You got it," Rose said. The gallery went up in cheers. "Some-times the simple answer's the right one, folks, that was the lesson on that one," Rose said, and the retirees banged their walking sticks on the boardwalk in agreement as they touched off again, play in the boards after a summer's use.

Maya knelt again and took Max by the shoulders. "Max, what's going on? Are you warm? Cold?" She touched his forehead.

"Where's Papa?" he said.

"Papa's with the map. Do you want to go back? I can try to get him on the cell phone."

"When we go on vacation, we go to the beach. This isn't vacation."

"When your dad and grandma and grandpa go on vacation, you go to the beach," Maya said. "I like different places to go on vacation. When you grow up, you can choose your own. Don't you like it?" She motioned toward the outcroppings of striped sandstone before them, now looking like a horse's head, now a marzipan cookie, now a hand clasping a cane. How rapidly the otherworldly magnificence of the sight ceased to seem otherworldly. But it remained magnificent. Maya wondered how such a barren, howling emptiness could fail to fill a watcher with fright; she felt light-headed, though not exactly with fright. Not barren, either—Rose Holliver's mission was to make the group understand that the stony hills teemed with life. You just had to know how to see. Maya marveled at the rookie pleasure she'd taken in the nondescript elevation they'd seen in the morning, an immigrant marveling at the bounty of the corner grocery when the supermarket awaited. She thought to make a game of divining the shapes of the buttes, but her son did not look interested.

"Do you want to stop?" she said.

He shrugged.

"Just give it a chance," Maya said. "For me."

They banged the planks in pursuit of the seniors. Maya told herself to calm down. She heard Alex—she was frantic, and doing her best to make sure her son was, too. In the harsh clarity of the surroundings, she saw herself harshly and clearly: She spent her days waiting for ill news of her son, and had now set to demanding it. Her fright was so pervasive that it was no longer exceptional; its absence was exceptional. But she had not felt its absence since the day he ran off to the creek. Was she turning into a hypochondriac like a good Rubin? They lived in expectation of danger and setback, even walked accordingly, a slight stoop in deference to the axe that would swing. She hated herself for always trying to hold the Rubins responsible.

After Max had vanished in June, Maya gave twenty nights to racking dreams involving a gang of small, malevolent boys peering into the glass on either side of the front door of the house— urinating on the doorframe, banging on the glass, sticking their tongues out, though never attempting to enter. Sometimes, in the dream, she confronted them—so large was her fury that once she leaped from the second story down to the foyer, a drop of ten feet. This scattered them from the window, but her sleep remained fitful. When it worked, she dreamed of the boys. The only way to stop the dream was to wake up, but then she was up at three thirty, four, a wreck at the hospital, misplacing plates and X-raying the wrong breast.

She wanted to stop fearing. Did that mean that she had wanted the trip for herself, as Alex had said? No, she had wanted to give Max the gift of native feeling, for Maya was on intimate terms with its absence, knew its constant sensation of slight poisoning, of living in error. It was sprung on Maya right at Soviet customs. "Anything to declare, little sister?" a barbarous face in a uniform sneered at her. Only carefree thoughts and a sense of belonging.

So what if the larger box of this gift to Max contained, like a nesting doll, the smaller box of a gift for herself? Some gift: She would feel twice as odd in Montana as she did in New Jersey, all so her boy, so ill at ease in New Jersey, might feel at home. She was increasing their alienation from one unit apiece to two for Maya and zero for Max. So that when Rose Holliver asked what kind of bird that was, Maya expected, as if she was dealing with a mechanical spring rather than a boy's brain, that Max, bright with an unfamiliar ease, would answer. How simple she was; how hopelessly rigid her thinking. On a switch, he would become new? She really thought so—and it was her husband who had to correct her, in the grass earlier that morning. How much patience, after all, Alex had for her. She despised herself—in addition to fear, she lived according to a constant diminution of wits.

Maya stared off at the magpies, black specks wheeling against the sandstone, a burning gold shading to bone-white in the glare of the sun. In her years at university, Maya could not pass a bird without demanding its name from the person next to her. This bird, that type of arch, those curlicues on the railing. She wanted to know the proper names for things; the prospect of filling these vacancies was ravenously satisfying. Anton the metalhead, Jeremiah the black Buddhist, her exotically named roommates Soraya and then Philomene and then Soraya again—had laughed at their peculiar lover and friend. They did not know what those things were called, and they did not care.

Maya watched the shaking backsides of the seniors before her. They knew what things were called. Even if they had gotten this one answer wrong, they knew. The only thing they did not know was what it was like not to know.

+

It was in the campground's sclerotic showers, tauntingly situated within sight of the Ridgeline Motel, which, undoubtedly, offered doors on its showers, that Maya felt the full measure of that singular despair reserved for travelers and travelers alone. It is the despair of losing home and all that is familiar, a despair whose known temporariness allays none of the feeling. The bed, with its uncustomary sighs and creaks, is as welcoming as a cold hand in the gloom, no matter how tiring the journey; the view, even if of spellbinding peaks, is an affront; the smells of the street are the smells of people who make themselves at home in a different way. The whole world is a language the traveler does not speak. The soul, blind to reason, is bereaved. The soul—the part of the self where one is most honest, as Maya Rubin explained to her son—is *bereaved*; the life that's been taken from it is its own. By undertaking the trip, the soul has engaged in a lie, and, therefore, for the trip's duration, died off.

All this is doubly so for the immigrant, who does not realize the tenuousness of his hold on the originally adopted home until he has cavalierly relinquished it in the service of . . . what? Scrubbing herself with an animal's urgency under a lukewarm trickle from a showerhead speckled with rust, Maya was forced to ask herself the question Alex had been asking, if only she would listen: Why were they here? Rather, why *here*, in this awful dusty campground rimmed by signs about rattlesnakes? She tried to persuade herself that this was simply that American obsession with indemnification; who would build a campground in a spot beloved by rattlesnakes?

Maya was frantic for pleasure. She turned toward the wall, ran her fingers toward her crotch, and rubbed with desperation, the water cascading off her shoulders and sluicing between her breasts. Despite the avidness with which she worked, her orgasm was as far away as New Jersey. She tried to think of Alex, but it didn't work.

She thought of the man from the diner, Marion. Maya, the weaver of fairy tales, altered the morning's events: Outside they had decided that they wanted takeout breakfast; Maya returned to the diner, placed the order, decided she needed the bathroom herself. Marion said he would show her where, she said she knew, but he slipped off his stool and followed her anyway. Their eyes locked in a strange way. He followed her inside. The bathroom was cramped—eating places always saved money on bathrooms.

"What now?" she said.

"You have to go to the bathroom," he said, nodding at the toilet.

She hiked up her sundress, the one with the mother-of-pearl buttons running down the front, pulled her underwear down to her ankles, and lowered herself onto the seat. Maya's heart was beating fast in the shower, and also on the toilet seat, so it took her some time. When a stream finally hit the toilet water, Marion leaned down and kissed her mouth as one of his hands reached underneath her. The yellow water hit his fingers; he held them there. As it slowed to a trickle, he closed his hand over her and held her this way while they kissed.

Then he lifted her by the arms, turned her around, and led her palms to the rough paint of the wall. He kissed the back of her neck and undid the front buttons from behind her back, his fingers still wet. She took one hand off the wall and fished for him, but he knocked it back. Soon the dress was unbuttoned and on the floor around her feet. She felt him sliding inside from behind. She was tight and he moved slowly, opening her, until she felt him fully inside of her—she felt his waist pressed to her ass. She scratched the wall with her nails. She asked to look at him.

He ignored her at first but then turned her to face him and lifted her slightly until she was wedged in the tiny alcove that had been hacked for the sink. It had been hacked for her—her torso fit with an inch on each side. She held the faucets for support. Kiss me, she said, and this time he listened. Her hands moved to his face. He entered and withdrew slowly as they kissed, the sharpness of the initial encounter changed into something gentler and pensive.

It was then, near the moment of crisis, that an ominous clang went through the shower pipes imprisoned behind the wall and the trickle turned arctic, eliciting a yelp from Maya and forcing her to finish sooner than she wanted. She shuddered once and stepped out. In the parcel of space the cursed architect had sectioned off for a dressing room, two women were silently toweling themselves. She inspected them for detection, or solidarity, or both. They offered neither. They rubbed their tired, bloated bodies with inanimate rhythm, exercised by a million showers, tilting their hips, arching their asses, kinking their shoulders, lost in private illusion. They could not offer Maya even the camaraderie of fellow shipwrecks. But Maya had the wealth of her secret, still sending warmth down her legs, which trembled slightly. It helped where the temperature of the shower had not.

The South Dakota climate had changed its mind once again. In the blue-colored dusk rising from beyond the motel, the temperature was falling. Maya, her hair wet and the cold of the water still on her, shivered back to their campsite. Despite being outside rather than inside in such weather, her hair incautiously wet (Raisa, if present, would be moaning in terror), and the impending sleep on hard ground, she tried to remember the elation she had occasionally felt during the day. Alex and Max were mincing uneasily by the tent.

"It's freezing," Maya said quickly. "Let's get inside there."

"Max seems to think there's a rattlesnake in the tent," Alex said.

"A what?" Maya said, stepping back. "Max, honey. What? You saw a rattlesnake?"

"Not exactly," Alex said. "We left the tent flap unzipped when we all went to shower. He's saying—he's convinced—well, he's right here. What took you so long, Maya?"

"A snake went in there while we showered," Max declared. He stared at the tent with—not fright, but a kind of chagrin.

Maya exchanged glances with Alex, ignoring his question. "Have you looked inside?" she said. Alex shook his head. Maya's heart was jumping, but she tried to conceal it. "We have to go to the office," she said. "I'm sure they deal with this all the time."

"I'm afraid," Max said.

"But you're not afraid," Maya said, and crouched before her son in her bathrobe. She took him by the shoulders. "Right? You're not afraid?" The boy wriggled out of her hold and encircled his father's leg with his hands.

"Alex?" Maya said.

"You want *me* to look in there?" he said.

Maya slumped onto the bench of the picnic table; they were nailed to each other. "*First-time visitors to Badlands National Park frozen in the night while rattlesnake sleeps, warm, in their tent. The trip had been the mother's idea.*" She thought of what Raisa—better yet, the outdoorsman Eugene—would say about how quickly they had arrived at an emergency. She felt as if she had wished the rattlesnake into existence by thinking of it in the shower; in her mind, she heard Alex saying to their son, "Mama won't rest until everything's upside down." She wrapped her robe more closely and stared, despondent, at Alex and Max.

To her the light had been clarifying, to them barbarous. The sweep of the land was menacing to them, imperial to her. The abrupt departure of the morning's cold had felt to Maya like the thaw of a steam bath in winter, to Alex and Max like a diabolical snap from freezing to burning. Even now, as a rattlesnake slithered across the floor of their tent, the indigo night settled on her with an aching crispness. It was beautiful here—epically, rinsingly beautiful. Her humpbacked hills (in the end, she preferred their modest spread even to the glorious sightings of the afternoon), squatted somewhere in the darkness, awaiting reunion with her at daylight. Maya breathed the wood smoke of campfires, the campsite's inhabitants like a caravan of pilgrims bedding down for the night. Could something felt so cleanly and deeply be felt incorrectly? She felt far not only from her husband, but son.

Alex went to call his parents; Maya went to the office. She reached a hand out for Max. He watched her warily. "You can come with, or you can wait for me here," she said without energy. "I'll be back with Mr. Wilfred. He'll fix it."

Max gave her his hand. Silently, they walked up to the shed. They heard the shouting inside before they walked in. Maya stood outside on the small deck with her son, wanting to give Wilfred privacy. But then she grew cold and pushed open the door; she could hear every word anyway.

He was pacing the small slot behind the reception counter. He stepped like a top-heavy animal—his shoulders shook with each step. She wanted to embrace him. He stopped striding and gazed at the mother and son from the morning. "I have to go, Carla," he said, his shoulders sagging. "There's customers." A strangled squawk came through the phone. Wilfred's eyes flashed and he shouted "Up yours!" before slamming down the telephone. He withdrew it and slammed it again. He withdrew it a second time and was about to shout into the receiver once more—then remembered the line was dead. He lowered the phone weakly.

"You have every right to give this campground a low rating," he said, and fell into his swivel chair.

"We're very happy here," Maya said. "But there's a rattlesnake in our tent." She tried to sound steady.

Wilfred looked up, alert. The day insisted on trying him. "You sure?" he said. "Not really the time for them anymore."

Maya looked down at Max. "We haven't seen it," she said. "But we think so, yes."

"Fine," Wilfred said. "Fine." He dipped below the partition and popped up with a two-gauge shotgun, even this item a plaything in the logs of his fingers.

Maya moved back. "Is that necessary?" she said.

He looked at her like a surgeon second-guessed by his patient; instinctively, she rechecked his nameplate—this abrupt escalation put her in mind of police reports, and she was on probation in that department already. "I'm not gonna shoot *you*," he said. His eyebrows, long free from the tyranny of regular grooming, moved up.

"Have you owned it long?" Maya pleaded toward Wilfred Shade's rump as she and Max bounded behind him on the weakly lit path back to the campsite; it was fully dark now. She meant the campground, but he could have answered for the shotgun. She cared about neither—she was hoping to distract him, separate out in his mind what was Carla and what was the rattlesnake. The shotgun rocked in Wilfred's hand like a baby. The crisis of five minutes before, which involved only a rattlesnake and no shotgun, seemed desirable by comparison.

"It was an accident that the campground was placed where the rattlesnakes come?" she pressed, hearing no answer. To this, too, she received no reply. She lost her politeness. "My son is scared," she blustered at Wilfred's back. To this, too, Wilfred said nothing, but paused and waited for the two of them to catch up, a gesture.

When they reached the campsite, Alex surprised Maya by nodding solemnly at the shotgun and taking several steps back. Though, due to work, Alex despised bureaucracy, he admired all displays of authority. Acrewood's relative affluence and isolation meant that its police was forced to channel most of its energy into traffic stops; Acrewood Police came at a pulled-over speeder guns drawn. The regional liberals were appalled but Alex applauded. His admiration passed the ultimate test when he was pulled over for going forty-seven miles in a forty-five zone. He nearly put his wrists together in ecstasy. He even paid the ticket enthusiastically, the rare time Maya saw Alex part calmly with money parting with which could have been avoided.

"Stand back, all," Wilfred Shade said.

"I really don't think—" Maya started to say, clutching Max's hand and moving him behind her leg.

"Hold it, hold it," a voice came from the shadows. She knew the voice. Its owner was vaulting through the shadows like a bear, little bits of gravel shooting out from his feet. Maya's brain was wet moss in the morning; of course, there was more than one campground; he had sent her to the one that was his also; he and the girls were on a camping trip. A smile escaped Maya's lips. She killed it.

"Wilfred," Marion said, stooping to regain his breath. He gave Maya a quick look, the darkness giving them cover.

"Rattlesnake," Wilfred said. His voice was less strident: Marion seemed to demand a greater solicitude.

"Wait now," Marion said, holding up one hand tenderly as if reasoning with an assailant. He had the other down on his thigh, breathing heavily.

"It's Mama's friend from the diner," Max said honestly.

Maya looked over at Alex and registered the change on his face even though it was too dark to actually see it. She knew the expression: His forehead rode up; his brows furred; his eyes squinted. Confronted with unwelcome information, Alex declined to certify it as such, preferring to plead incomprehension.

"Carla?" Marion said. Maya watched Wilfred's shoulders slump in the shadows.

"One of these days," Wilfred said, and brought the shotgun down to his side. He exhaled painfully. His drive gone, he scraped the gravel of the footpath. "I left my flashlight, Marion," he said.

Marion dug in his jeans. Wilfred turned to Maya. "One of these days I'm gonna *leave* her," he clarified. "I *might* shoot her, and then this conversation is going to show up in court. So I am clarifying for the record: I meant *leave* her."

Marion shone a pocket light, and Wilfred swept aside the tent's entry panel with the shotgun.

"Run it around in there, Marion, for Christ's sake," Wilfred said. "This your first tent rattler?"

"I am ignoring the way you are speaking to me on account of your domestic distress," Marion said.

"A man with a shotgun is the most forgiven man in the world," Wilfred said. He looked up at Maya. "Empty as the day you bought it. The boy saw it go in?"

"Not exactly," Maya said.

"Good to be vigilant," Wilfred said magnanimously. If nothing else, this ate up the final twenty minutes of his shift. He would have spent them pacing the tiny shed and biting his nails.

"You've been saying that for twenty years about Carla," Marion said. "Do it already. You look like a fool."

"I need a mercy killing," Wilfred said. He bounced his heavy round head. "Who wants this sack of lard, Marion? I am holding on for dear life, and you cast it away." Wilfred tamped the hardpan with the butt of the shotgun, setting off in Maya the momentary fear that after all that, the gun would go off by accident. Wilfred seemed indifferent to the rest of his audience, Alex, Maya, and Max turning their heads between him and Marion. "People laugh at you, you know," Wilfred said. "I would laugh at you, too, if I didn't know you my whole life."

"Who else do I need besides Willy Shade in my corner?" Marion grinned abusively. His features were obscured by shadow, but there was a low-shouldered stoop to his posture that again made Maya think of leaves and the forest. He carried it with him.

Looking like a defeated baby, Willy Shade waved away his friend and slowly started up the drive. It had a slight incline, harder to take on the way back. Marion was left with the Rubins. The four of them stood in the gathering cold watching Wilfred labor up the path. He gave them a gift; it took him forever. "I didn't say anything to Mama and Papa about the rattlesnake," Alex broke the silence, reminding the intruder of what he was intruding on. He held the flap of the tent open for Max. His son moved hesitantly. "Don't worry, son, I'll go first," Alex said and disappeared from view, Max following. Their sudden aloneness unacceptable, the two friends from the diner said good night to each other, loudly enough for Maya's husband to hear.

12

On her back, staring at the vanishing peak of the tent, Maya's rib cage felt corseted. She switched to her stomach; the corset switched with her. Careful to avoid noise, she sat up, but there was no way to get support in a tent without right angles. Who chose to sleep on the ground in gathering cold? Well, she did. She expelled a mirthless laugh into the frostbitten air of the tent. On either side of her, Alex and Max slept without suspicion, Max's knees at his chest. She felt a vague irritation with her son, and a less vague irritation with herself for feeling it. She looked over at her husband and felt sympathy for him, laid out on the cold ground of a campsite in the middle of nowhere.

She tried to lie down on the thin nylon of the tent, but every pebble on earth was congregated under her. Jeremiah the black Buddhist had tried to teach her that nothing was unwelcome. He ate only macrobiotic foods, which meant that she rarely had the pleasure of feeding him, but he was smarter than anyone she had met. She had loved his name—so epic, so biblical. And the transgression of dating a black, something that would have started a long silence on the other end of the line in Kiev. So she tried very hard to understand him—to understand how nothing could be unwelcome. How would Jeremiah welcome these pebbles? Was she supposed to try to imagine the pebbles as smooth as her mattress at home, or give in in some way to their discomfort? She felt dense and laughed at herself, at the pebbles (like small animals listening to her madness), at the insane line of her thought. Shivering, she climbed out of her blanket and, wanting to do an undebatable good, positioned it around Max.

She wanted to go outside but was terrified of what she would find there. She sat in place, the time blurred by the soft gallop of her thoughts and the steady, shallow report of her breathing. Through a mesh panel in the tent flap, she could see a complete darkness save for the firelight of the cold stars, the only way to tell up. They seemed to hang by invisible thread. She shuddered at their raw cosmic terror: how resplendently indifferent they looked, how implacable. But was placation required? A star asked for nothing. Her rib cage loosed slightly before seizing again. She snorted at her absurd meditations. She wondered whether some subtly toxic element in the atmosphere was actually affecting her thinking. The altitude hadn't bothered her as much in the afternoon—maybe she was deteriorating. *Patient suffers from euphoria mixed with despair. Cardinal manifestation: mild hysteria followed by disorientation. Refers primarily in the chest. Restrain.*

She ordered herself to declare, at least, what it was that frightened her on the other side of the flap. Was there a congress of rattlesnakes at the foot of her tent? A boar hooving the dust in anticipation of sinking a tusk into her flank? No, she couldn't say what exactly she feared in the vacated blackness. Did she fear the vacated blackness? She thought of Uncle Misha. Misha would not be afraid. He would be out under the heavenly firelight, pulling shyly on his rolled cigarette, stamping one foot against the other and back. It startled her to remember that Uncle Misha was alive—declining, her mother said, but alive and cursing away offers of help. He was as remote as the firelight in the sky, Uncle Misha—how could Maya have allowed that to transpire? *Her* uncle Misha. Was it simply the ocean between them, or had she abandoned them all? Why? Did she want America so badly; the Rubins? Was there any reason she couldn't have both—that was the sole advantage of Ukraine becoming a free country, she could. Or was her tether to the Rubins so frail that it risked breaking with every departure?

The Rubins rarely asked about her family, though they never expressed negative feelings. Her adopted family was not at fault, even as she loved to hold it responsible. For some reason, Maya had decided that the old family could only come at the expense of the new—and allowed it to drift away in ways easily justified by the distance and time. She still spoke to her mother once a week, but it had been years since she had returned to Kiev, and years since Galina had come to New Jersey to visit her grandson, whose adoption she had greeted with more equanimity than the Rubins. Maya felt a sinking regret. The parched moonscape outside was a solace by comparison: to the regret it added butterflies, as if she were a teenager about to be kissed. It was easier to fear than regret. Fear held out the possibility of being unwarranted, regret meant it was too late. She envied the barrenness outdoors; it struck her now as streamlined purpose rather than desolation. She wished to be equally whittled, to carry not one extra grain.

She flung herself through the flap in the tent. In her boldness, she had forgotten that the flap was zipped—it had been virtually duct-taped by Alex against the encroachment of further intruders, reptilian or human—and she nearly sank the entire contraption. But Alex and Max continued to snooze. With a compensatory guiltiness, Maya unzipped the flap an inch at a time.

Outside awaited a brilliant cold. The corset around her rib cage was replaced by a knife blade. No, something blunter: a dull stone wedged where no stone should go. The hospital had rid her of hypochondria, but the hospital was in New Jersey, and if someone told her that health issues worked differently here—at three thousand feet, zero population, and walls of Oligocene rock—she wouldn't have argued.

The air drizzled her arms with invisible needles. Was that not a symptom of strokes? She lifted her hands imploringly—there was only so much she could be asked to lose her mind about. If she needed to be felled by a heart attack, two days shy of forty-three, amid this splendor and squalor, so be it. If health issues worked differently here, accountability could work differently also. As in: she abdicated it.

She gulped the air—an unfamiliar taste—and sent it back out in swirling white gusts, the silence roaring in her ears like a hard wind. It was more than a person could take in all at once: the black mirror of the sky shaking with stars, the charging air, the din of the silence. Maya's head swam, a black rose unfurling under her forehead, but she didn't want to return to the tent. The raw air was doing work on her dread. It had been working through her since well before sleep—since she had watched the sun sink behind the warped landscape like a mother driving away. The fear was greater inside the tent than outside, the thing finally faced. She was surprised to discover the darkness less complete out here: the dull fluorescent green of an overhead lamp pointing the way to the bathrooms cut into the icy black gleam. She squinted into the darkness, wondering if it would reveal the shape of a man, but there was nothing. Belatedly, it occurred to her that a camper other than Marion might be out for fresh air. Her thinking was holed in critical ways that would not have eluded her attention at home. It was an exhausting, hopeless feeling.

She sank to the ground, crossing her legs under her knees, and closed her eyes. It was hard to do for more than a second—the dread closed in once again. She popped them open. A graveyard stillness, just the handful of tents scattered across the campground, squatters on the infertile plain of an alien planet. But she tried once more, for a second longer. Then again, for a second more still. Her eyes were becoming used to the darkness, which was changing to a bruised violet. After her next try, she saw the orange point of a cigarette hanging in the murk like a miniature fruit. She made out Marion's faint outline by a picnic table twenty feet away. Her heart leaped, and she lifted a weak hand. It really was as if she had conjured him.

He wore a heavy plaid shirt that looked warm, properly warm for the weather. A gust of wind cuffed her shoulders; she wished she had brought her shawl, but she couldn't return now. He waved at her and moved from his place. They walked toward each other until they met at two old juniper stumps that belonged to no tent. Even now, probably years after being sawed down, they gave off a faint hint of cedar.

They said hello and stood shyly by the stumps until Marion pointed at them with the tip of his cigarette and they sat. They watched the rock beyond the edge of the campground, the cigarette's orange point circling the air like a moth. He said nothing, only moved the cigarette in a line from his mouth to his side and then back. After a minute, it fell to the ground, where his boot ground it.

"I don't think I've spent so much time outside in my life," Maya said. "I have a headache," she added cautiously, wanting to know was there something to worry about, but unwilling to tempt truly bad news by revealing the extent of her discomfort.

"Oxygen headache," Marion said. "I couldn't wait to get back here when we'd go see Clarissa's family out east."

She was stung to have been offered his wife's name so cavalierly. Well, Marion had got the picture when she had told him she and Max weren't alone. Again, she saw that he was older. A good ten years older than her; in his early fifties.

"You speak about it as if she left you," Maya said. "But Alma said you left."

He nodded appreciatively. "Most people take a while to recall which one is Alma and which one is Celia. They don't help—they wear nearly the same thing. They're only a year apart. I think they're shoring each other up."

"It was difficult for them," Maya ventured.

He shrugged—with uncertainty, not indifference. "They seemed fine. They approved. At least Alma did. Because they know something's wrong before you do. It took a while to understand there was more going on. Little things, like Celia's pig was so hot last summer, but Celia didn't see it. I had to tell her to hose her down. And she just said, 'Oh.'" Marion saw Maya's face and smiled. "She's in the animal husbandry program at the school. She was going to be a rancher. Maybe not the first female ranch head in Fall River County, but close to it. At six years old, she would have had a hose on that pig in a second."

"She changed her mind?" Maya said.

"She's up in the air, she says," Marion said. "That's what she says, 'up in the air.' It makes me think of her as a kid, I'm throwing her up in the air, and she's squealing. But this is a different 'up in the air.' I wonder if I did that. If I messed with my kid's certainty."

"Have you spoken about it?"

"She doesn't want to. They're quiet, the girls, actually—I know you wouldn't think so. Celia more so. Because they heard their mother and me splashing it out year after year and now they are going to keep it zipped at all costs? Some other reason they themselves don't know? And if they don't know, I'm supposed to know because I'm the parent? The books don't say anything, and I don't have the spleen to go see a therapist." He kicked the heels of his boots against the ground one by one, the hardpan giving out a dull echo.

"Maybe I want to go just to get my exoneration," he said. "'It wasn't you, Mr. Hostetler. Your daughters are not going to spend their lives closed up because they don't want to turn out self-indulgent like Daddy.' There's a fellow in Spearfish they say is a miracle worker. Retiree from New York. The East Coast gets them when they're young and unproven, and we get them when they've been stocking professional wisdom for fifty years. I'd say you have the losing end of the bargain."

"I used to think psychologists worked with mentally sick people," Maya said. "But then we went to someone to help Max, and even though he didn't help Max—even though he proved Alex's point, I guess—for some reason I became more open to it."

"What's wrong with Max?" Marion said.

She traced her own shapes on the hardpan. She liked hearing

him say her son's name; it came out differently. Unable to sleep in heavy shoes despite being outside, she was wearing flats on heavy wool socks. She was really going for elegance every chance that she got.

"I am filled with nervous energy," she said. "I can't focus. I feel like I'm going to make a mistake. Actually, I felt that long before coming here. In truth, I feel safer here. I should be more afraid, and then I realize I'm not." She looked over at him. "I sound crazy, I know."

"I don't mind it," he said.

"It's different for you because you've been here many times. You've been here many times, haven't you?"

He nodded.

"There's more than one campground, isn't there?"

"Guilty," he said.

She laughed sharply into the night. "I don't mind it."

They sat silently for some time. "I'll tell you about my son," she said, "and you tell me about Wilfred and Carla."

"Look at you," he said. "You're shivering. Take my shirt. There's some hot tea in this thermos. With whiskey in it." He spread his shirt over her shoulders—she smelled woodsmoke and a faint hint of dried sweat, but the dried sweat of activity rather than inactivity—unscrewed the cap of his thermos and poured. Maya inhaled something like grass bleached by the sun. "There's some lemon balm over there," he said, pointing. "Strained through the nicest sock that I've got. Nicest *clean* sock." The seat of the thermos unscrewed to make a second cup, and he filled it with tea for himself. "A thermos for making friends," he said.

"Is that what we are?" she said.

They drank silently. She liked the way that he sipped his, first worrying the liquid with his lips, then slurping it loudly, his brows gathered. It was a child's way of doing something, unself-conscious and very serious all at once.

"Max is wild," she said.

He looked over at her. "He looked normal to me," he said.

"Here he's normal," she said. "I would say I cured him by bringing him back to where he was born, but I doubt that's true. I don't know what it is; I'm at the end of my understanding. At home, he's wild. He runs away. Turns blue sitting in rivers. Eats grass. And then goes back to being a normal boy. Who can't tell you a word about why he did what he did."

"You don't think it's a phase?"

"That's what my husband says."

"I guess all men are alike."

"Is that what Clarissa said?" Maya thought that she could corner the woman by speaking her name out loud, but the opposite happened. It killed the possibility that she was a marginal person in Marion's life. "'Don't let my baby do rodeo,' his mother said when she gave him to me," Maya said. "What does that mean? I'd never heard of rodeo. I looked it up. You have to stay on the bull for eight seconds. But why?"

Marion smiled. "You have to think as a person from here, not there. What is there to do around here? The world looks everywhere but here. There's money in rodeo. Glory. Your heart beats fast for a change."

"You don't seem like that."

He shrugged.

Maya took Marion's new cigarette out of his mouth and stuck it in her own. She took a long drag. "His dad—his original dad, I mean . . . I really don't know what words to use." She took her head in her hands. "Max doesn't know he's adopted—we call them 'cowboys' when Max is around, when the 'cowboys' brought the 'little fish' . . ."

"Easy now," he said, and put a hand on her shoulder.

"Tell me about something else," she said. "Tell me about Clarissa."

Marion made a little noise of recollection. "Clarissa," he said, and beat the thermos with his fingers. "It got to be we had nothing to say to each other. At first, we couldn't get enough words in, always interrupting each other—'Let me finish, let me finish.' And then, little by little, it went to we had nothing to say. There's a surreal aspect to when you realize that's happening. Like swimming in a fishbowl. You're moving, but slowly, you're tired, and everything looks a little dead."

"But why, Marion?" Maya said. "I don't understand why."

He kinked out the tips of his boots and laid his hands on his knees. "You're talking like her now. That's all the why there is. I wish I had more—it would certainly make people understand better. She kept rising in her workplace. They started flying her here and there. She liked it—she wasn't planning on it, but she liked it. Taking meetings in Washington, D.C., and the like. Getting a tour of the Capitol— she's a lobbyist for the cattlemen. At first it just seemed like less time to talk—if the time was there, it'd be fine. But then we started to get a kick out of different things. And if you want to know the truth, we stopped going to bed in the same way. She got perfunctory with it—so much so I started thinking were all these business trips just a name for a man, holed up somewhere like Chicago; she was always flying through Chicago. One night I went for her credit card bills— and I stopped myself. I didn't want to live that way. We talked. She said there was no one. I told her my problem—again. Again, she said we would fix it; she'd gotten real good at listening to problems and promising fixes. And again nothing changed. And I left. Staying together despite all that seemed like the wrong thing to do. Just the principle of it. I want my daughters to live by principle. Of course, Clarissa thinks there was a woman. She calls up and says, 'How's the whore?' But there wasn't—that's not it at all. People like principle on a man, but not too much."

"And on a woman?" Maya said.

"A woman lives a life of contradictions wrapped inside paradoxes wrapped inside a big candy wrapper."

"You took vows," Maya said. "You made promises."

"I thought about that," he said, giving her a hard look. "But kids are smart. They got the smell of a wolf. Alma said, 'High time, Daddy.' I gained respect with them."

"When people say I did it for the children, they usually mean staying."

He gave her another hard look, and for a second she could see what he looked like in an argument. "My mood changed and stayed changed," he said. "For ten years it stayed that way before I let myself go. I waited until the girls were in college. For ten years I waited."

"I'm sorry," she said, wrapping herself up. "I shouldn't be allowed to speak. Everything coming out of my mouth is wrong."

"No, I'm grateful," Marion said. "Most people don't ask anything. They've got answers without needing to ask me the questions."

"How long ago was it?" Maya said.

"A very long year. There's been five years in this year. That part I underestimated. Even after ten years alone in a marriage, it's still nothing like a year alone, period."

"You've been leading a monk's existence?"

"I didn't say that."

"The waitress at the diner," she said.

Marion chuckled. "Just fooling around," he said.

"What are you looking for?" Maya said. "Can it really be better than what you had with your wife?"

He didn't answer. Maya watched him with the hanging desperation of someone who wanted one. Feeling her gaze, he turned to her.

"I want to talk like Clarissa and I used to talk. To roll around like we used to roll around. I want to be an old man and have that. I made my wager maybe I can find it again. I wasn't going to be one of those people who looks while keeping one foot safely inside the house. No, that's not true—you think I didn't look with one eye those ten years? I looked. I'm no saint. But then I thought—it won't come while you're in this. You've got to go all the way."

Maya nodded. "I am emotional, and my husband is stoic," she said, as if to give him company in his history of divergence. "We live in a house in the suburbs. The only thing about our lives that isn't a cliché is our son, who eats grass."

"And who is that, speaking now?" he said.

"Clarissa," she said, and they laughed. The tea-whiskey was making things easier; there was padding around what she was feeling. Momentarily, she did not actually feel the despair she was describing. Because she was speaking to this man? She might feel the despair again soon, but until then she was out on a bail whose guarantor was neither clear nor important. Jeremiah the black Buddhist was always telling her to live in the moment. She never understood him—in what other moment was it possible to live? She understood a little now, however. She wondered fiercely after Jeremiah. In her recollection, he remained twenty, but he was also forty-two now, and where? She wished for news of him, for he knew her even before Alex did. In her heart, she sent him a powerful wish for well-being. Jeremiah, Dima, Anton, Soraya—where were they? Why had she allowed all these people to vanish?

She drank off the remainder of the tea, still warm in her fingers, and watered the hardpan with the last drops. Somewhere out there, her mountain was resting. Was it a mountain? Was there a more accurate term? A bluff, a butte, a ridge? She felt the old desperation for the right names. Out here, one had to learn English all over again. Earlier in the day, Maya had tried to hold on to the words Ranger Holliver had called out. Washes, canyons, mesas, eskers, and fells: she gave up. It had used to make her feel unsafe, this encirclement by the unknown—but known to everyone else. It had occurred to her on the naturalist walk that this sense of endangerment was discretionary. If one does not know things, one also does not know one can be harmed by them.

Couldn't she invent her own name for the mountain? Just as Laurel and Tim were "the cowboys." Only that was a lie. How to be truthful about the mountain? Because a mountain was always truthful, she felt. The mountain did not make mistakes. (She remembered Uncle Misha: "A snowflake never falls in the wrong place.") It would never work, her union with the bluff-butte-ridge-mountain. She resented its unapproachable splendor.

"I wanted to open a café once," she said for no reason. "Café Gogol. Isn't it something to open a café named after someone you haven't read?" Somewhere far away, an animal howled at the night. She made a slight noise and recoiled.

"Just a coyote," he said. "Mile away."

"It feels like a short mile," she said.

He smiled. "Don't think about it. Keep telling me about the café."

"I wanted it to have a library. I would be strict—you would have to read the book there. But you could pay with books. One day a week, for example, you would not be allowed to pay with money, only books. And I would be the cook. At the diner today, I looked at the man in the cooking window, with sweat and grease on his face, and I imagined myself in his position. In this small town, forgotten by everyone, everything."

"I'm sure it looks like the desert to you," Marion said. "But I wouldn't be surprised if a million people come here each year. Man who owns that diner's a millionaire. I'd pay money to see you take him on to put in a library, though."

"I never thought it could be cold in the desert," Maya said.

"Oh, sure," he said. "I clean my brain here."

They sat on their stumps, looking ahead. The silence was split by an occasional call, something that sounded like loneliness to Maya and to the caller probably like a basic self-affirmation. Her first night on Misha's farm, Maya was awoken by a donkey shrieking like a sheep caught in barbed wire. She rushed to wake up her uncle. "Oh, little daughter, he's just checking himself," Misha said, smiling sleepily. By the end of the summer, the call had merged with the other sounds of the night. Now, the howl having receded, there was full silence, not even cicadas, the usual custodians of the darknesses Maya had known.

"You're trying to find the parents, aren't you," Marion broke the silence.

"I've spent eight years thinking about it," she said. She told him the town. "Sometimes, I think it isn't an actual place, Montana. It exists but not in the way other places exist."

"Are you nervous?" he said.

"I envy Alex," she said. "He thinks this is a mistake. Today, I think it's a mistake, tomorrow I think it's not a mistake." She felt the ground with her fingers. "It's my birthday in two days. But I want to fast-forward to the day after. Isn't that sad?"

He shrugged. "I don't care about my birthday. You can't assign good things." He slapped his knees as if this was a concluding statement and he was about to rise, but he stayed put and a little nerve seemed to go out of him. He shook his thermos. "My flawless feel says there are two capfuls of this whiskey-tea left. Let's finish, and then I'll show you something. A birthday present." He pointed into the gloom.

"You want to go—there?" she said.

"It's not bad."

"Are you sure? I'll need to hold your arm."

"I won't object."

After finishing the tea, they walked past the edge of the campground, the hardpan murmuring under their feet, Maya's head filling with rattlesnakes. Every step resolved amicably was a small deliverance—she got sixty a minute. But you couldn't feel those attacks of relief—safe, safe, safe—without striding around darkness where rattlesnakes roamed.

"They don't really come out at night," Marion said, guessing her thoughts. They weren't hard to guess: She was stepping through the gloom like a horse, her legs kicking out before cautiously meeting the ground. "They like sunshine. Just like you."

The campground was far behind now, though Marion walked

steadily without the aid of a flashlight. She asked if he still had it, and he shone it in front of her. "But it only makes it darker, in a way," he said. She nodded and he flicked it off.

In the darkness, Maya felt uneasy down to her bowels. She made herself think of an evening at Uncle Misha's. Her uncle had not brought her to the farm to stand in the crystalline sun, finally revealed after nine months of winter, and admire fresh soil. She was given a spade and pickaxe and sent to ruffle up plots for corn, squash, and beans in the garden Misha had decided to get going. By two P.M., the sun, looking to make up for time lost in winter, had reached the spot in the sky from which it could shine most directly on Maya's pigtails, and she felt that her stomach would tear in half if she lifted the pickaxe once more. But she refused to reveal herself as unequal to the task, buried her face in a trough Misha had just refilled with icy well water for the pigs, and went back at it. At the dinner table, as Misha stuffed behind his cheeks bread smeared with sour cream and sunflower oil, he glowered at his niece pridefully. The niece fell asleep at the dinner table.

The night that Misha had asked Maya to go out to the garden and snip off some zucchini for his farmhouse stir-fry—eggplant, old bread crusts, blistered tomatoes—was well into the summer. (She observed with pride the copper of her skin, dried out by the sun; her forearms, which, she imagined, showed new lines and veins; only her breasts refused to grow.) The garden had lost its mind. The leaves of the squash, pitted by some infestation Misha had explained but Maya had forgotten, hung about like giant elephant ears; the squashes themselves trampled underfoot like Buddhas; the cucumbers and zucchinis swung at every step like—well, it was impolite to say what she gathered they resembled; and the tomato vines had wrapped themselves around every fencepost or slithered down the loam like reptiles. Snakes lived in the garden, and gophers, and rabbits. The entire animal world approved of the garden she'd made.

It was dusk when she walked into the garden for Misha's dinner zucchini, violet bands of light on the horizon, the grass exhaling after being released by the sun. Pushing aside the cratered squash leaves, which regathered above her, she felt as if she was disappearing into an unfriendly wood; she imagined the pest that had riddled the leaves crawling around her ankles and snakes coiling around her feet. She got hopelessly tangled, but when she tried to free herself, she found an even denser clump, and then something pricked her skin. She screamed and tried to fight her way out of the patch, trampling the harvest. Stalks banged her shins, sandpapery leaves rubbed her thighs, thorns pecked her cheeks. She fought with the thicket until she ran out and collided with Misha, who had come running out of the house.

"What is it, *dochen'ka*?" he huffed out. His smoking made him short of breath. "What is it?"

She could not bring herself to say; she was too embarrassed. She only pointed at the garden.

"Are the boys stealing?"

Her face was so dusty that her tears left gray marks on Misha's white dinner shirt. Fifteen years later, she would look into the mirror after an argument with Alex, her tears streaking her mascara, and think back to crying through dirt onto Misha's shoulder. Maya forced herself to pull away—she hadn't come this far for Misha to see her crying. "It's nothing, Uncle Misha," she said. "I'll prune tomorrow."

He took her shoulders and they watched the violet light, now with pink threads. "It's different every time," he said. "One season, half the seeds don't make it, and it's three feet between every plant. Another summer, every goddamn seed sprouts and it's like a train terminal in there, everyone pushing and shoving. You're good luck, *dochen'ka*: everything you sowed came up. Come, let's look."

She hesitated for a moment but followed him. He held her hand as they walked back into the garden. She flushed with embarrassment—it was the same old garden. But she became frightened again when Misha led her to the spot where the squash leaves clumped the hardest; inside his, her hand became clammy.

"You made this garden, little one," he said, letting go of her hand. "Every single thing here was grown by your hand. It won't hurt you." With that Misha lowered himself in his dinner shirt to the dusty topsoil, turned gray by the daily violence of the sun, and marveled again because the tomato vines ran so thick there really was no place for a man to lie down in his own garden. Maya had to lie down in the next row, though Misha said twice, "I'm right here, I'm right here." And they lay like that, the fear receding from her chest, until Misha said he wished he could remember if he had turned off the gas, and she giggled. But he had remembered his *horilka*—the flask was always in his back pocket, dinner wear or not—and he let Maya have a sip, which melted the sky into a star-spangled fleece, and at first blunted but then sharpened her hunger.

"Here," Marion said, stopping.

"Here but not there?" she smirked nervously, trying to lighten the quivering darkness. Now the leaden smear of the bathroom light seemed very desirable. The range of audible calls by un-known creatures was vaster and clearer here, and she practiced her vocabulary: yowls, hoots, shrieks, howls, and yelps. She thought she heard the earth tamped by hooves and nearly bit her tongue before clutching Marion's sleeve. "They really want nothing to do with you," he promised her. "You're too big for them." "Except rat-tlesnakes," she reminded him. She could feel her heart aiming out from her chest. "Not at night, right, right," she reminded herself. She hung off him like a branch.

"You are standing on the Pierre Hostetler and Marion Hostetler Time Capsule," Marion said. "Which this year turns . . ." He thought about it. "Thirty-five years old. It's a grown-up."

Maya stamped her feet in the cold. "Your daughter said Spanish and German. Pierre sounds French."

"The Hostetlers are fond of sticks in the eye. German villagers circa 1930 were not overly fond of children born out of wedlock. So my grandmother gave my father a French name. They got out before Hitler took over. That's what they said, but if you ask me, they left because she was alone and he was a bastard.

"My dad was off-season. I don't think he'd ever gone east, so he didn't know what it was to be crowded. You swim in the tank you were given—even Rapid City was like one giant hive of insanity as far as he was concerned. He'd scoop me up and we'd come here. It was always me he took, not the other boys, which made me feel pretty good, as you can imagine. I didn't understand it then, but he needed to be quit of my mother for three days. Even my mother was one person too many. Why'd he have four sons then? But he couldn't very well take off by himself—what decent man is allowed to do that? I was the cover. Don't take it the wrong way: he loved me. Once you figure out what's happening, you think, Did he take me not because he loved me but because out of the four boys, I was the easiest dupe? But he loved spending time with me. He just needed to be quit of my mother.

"It got so that I knew most of this around here with my eyes closed. But we never camped. We always stayed in a motel. He always got two rooms, always at opposite ends of the motel. Didn't understand that either until many years later—or I understood it the way a child understands, which is to say that part of you that Freud knows all about. And I guess it's because I understood it that one time that I said, 'Dad, I want to camp this time.' And he said yes, of course we would. And we got out here and he said we have to do this time capsule. It was about this time of year, cold getting on colder like now, not many people to get in the way—would you believe fat Willy was already here then, skulking around?—and my dad dug this damn hole like he had a body to bury. *Here*, he said. 'You put in here what you want to get rid of. You want to be quit of it, you put it in here. You got a bad habit, you put it in here. And you don't have to tell your dad about it either. Just put it in here. Like a birthday wish.' Except with a birthday wish, you wish to get something, and this was all about getting rid.

"He made a show of putting his cigarettes in there. But they were a stand-in for: did he put my mother in there, or did he put all those other women in there? No answer to that, but I bet on the latter. He hated himself for these trips. On the way back it would always be, *Well, son, don't be mad, but we may not go again for a while.*

"I smoked too, only he didn't know it. He would hang me by the collar if he knew, even if he did it himself. But I wanted so bad to be with him in that moment, to say *I got faults too, look at me*— and so I took out my pack and threw it in there, too. He looked up at me, but didn't say a word. And then pushed all that hard federally managed ground we had violated back into place. Two packs of cigarettes and a whole bunch of other invisible God knows what.

"So that's the deal here. I'm going to leave you here for a minute. I don't have a shovel but just picture it, it's right under you. Something you want to get rid of. That's my happy birthday to you." He searched out her eyes. "You think it's hokey?" he said.

"You're still smoking."

"Be the better version of me I never managed."

"That's for your daughters. It's too late for me." She wrapped herself more tightly. "What if it isn't something I want to get rid of? What if it's something I want? Will it still work then?"

"It takes all comers."

"Don't walk away, please," she said. "I'm too scared to stand here by myself."

"I won't step away if you say so."

"Just another minute, stay. It gets colder and colder?"

"People camp here through the winter. Some people seek out wildness at all costs. And God blessed you with your own supply."

"Did your mother know?"

"I loved my mother. She never asked me, never put me on the spot like that. I don't know what all they discussed with each other.

But there was one time when she came out of the kitchen as my father was packing the car, and said, 'Marion ain't going with you this time.' Said she needed help in the basement and whatnot. She didn't ask—she said. He looked up at her for a while—I remember that look. And then he nodded just the tiniest bit and went back to packing, not a word. I stayed back."

"Okay, don't go far."

"Ten steps."

"I won't see you."

"But you'll know I'm here. In a minute I'll come back to get you."

Marion was eaten up by the darkness with his first step. Maya breathed a long, settling breath, in and out. Then another. At some point, the ache in her rib cage had gone. If she breathed in and out thirty times, each breath a little acquittal, Marion would return. She only had to hold out thirty times.

It was so clean up there, in the whistling emptiness where the rock peaked. She was able to imagine it effortlessly, the way a room stays lit in the mind for a moment after the light goes off, the way she knew Alex's face without needing to look. During the afternoon, she had felt rock that was as rough as sandpaper; and as knobby but lustrous as glass; rock that crumbled in her hands; and rock that looked as if a jackhammer could not take it, let alone time. What a jackhammer could not do, water could, however, over a million years.

Maya didn't know in what direction she faced, so she may very well have been giving her rump to her sunk giant, but it was intention that counted. He was watching her even when she wasn't looking. Could he really allow her to come to harm? She doubted it, and even experienced a flash of arrogance—there was nothing to fear out here, not under his gaze. She was a protected woman, a tended and prized woman.

She looked at the hole in the ground—or where she thought it must be; really, she could see nothing—where Pierre and Marion

Hostetler had deposited things they no longer wanted, and asked forgiveness for having allowed her family to dispose of something they had no right to take away from their son. Then she asked the universe if it had enough mercy for her, despite all her errors, to grant her a second sighting. Grant Marion Hostetler a second love, and grant her a second sighting of Laurel and Tim. She tried to conjure them the way she had conjured Marion out of this sorcerous earth.

Marion's voice was at her side. "Ready or more time? I didn't want you to think I had vanished."

"I knew you wouldn't vanish," she said. "I didn't worry about it for a moment."

They walked back to the campground slowly—now she wanted the way to be longer. By the time they returned, the subfusc prologue of the morning was pushing up the black sky with impatience.

13

After a turbulent night—turbulent for one—the Rubins awoke to a scouring beauty. The sun, risen before them, sent down blasts of light. The warmth called up from the ground a powerful mist tinted gold and rose and even, if you squinted in a particular way, aquamarine. Alex stood with his hand sleeved above his eyes, marveling. Maya stared at him, feeling a parent's vindication and a wife's penitence.

"The air smells like someone's cleaning you out with a brush." Alex smiled hesitantly. He had coffee grounds out and set to fiddling with the portable burner that Maya had bought along with the tent, even whistling as he did so, occasionally calling out to Max for implements. Maya watched Marion climb out of his tent and pat himself down for a cigarette. He looked in her direction, stopped moving, gave a shy wave.

When Alex had woken, Max had woken, so Maya had no hope of continuing to sleep, though she had climbed into her sleeping bag only two hours before. An electric hum sounded between her eyes—two nights of bad sleep. They did experiments on this type of subject. How many days did it take to reach full-blown madness? Perceptions registered, but to form impressions about them she had to coax forward something that did not wish to be coaxed.

Little by little, the inhabitants of the stranded encampment crawled out of their tents, stretched away the kinks of the night, rubbed their eyes, and looked enviously at the energetic settler who had already started his coffee. Maya gazed on them, too, as fellow survivors who had made it through the defenselessness of the night. She fished Marion's thermos from the folds of her sleep-

ing bag. She had slept with it between her legs, an obscene gesture, but its heat, after he refilled it with hot water, had bloomed
through her hips and thighs and sent her to sleep.

Alex watched as she filled it with coffee, then three spoonfuls
of the sugar that he had had Max hunt down in their luggage.
Maya stirred endlessly, fixated on the spoon. Closing the thermos,
she walked over to Max and laid a kiss on his hair. Max wriggled
out—he was busy setting up breakfast: bread, butter, and jam,
surrounded by utensils, napkins, and plates. Did he relish this reduced simulation of breakfast at home?

Feeling Alex's eyes on her back, she walked off toward Marion's tent. Marion tried to hide the happy surprise in his face. The
fingers he closed around the thermos were crab-colored from the
cold. She wanted to wrap hers around them.

Before she could warn him, Marion unscrewed the cap of the
thermos and took a long swig. He shut his eyes in pain. "Sweet
mother of God. Your husband knows how to boil water."

She laughed, a bird's snort of a laugh, swift and sudden. "The
girls are still sleeping?" she said.

"First to fall, last to rise. It's called youth. It's all right—they've
got five hours to drive back to school. In this regard, they went
after their daddy—they like the road."

"Is there a choice?" Maya meant the vastness around them, the
gray line of 377 cutting submissively through it.

"I guess not," he said. He looked past her shoulder, and his eyes
lost their mirth. "Breakfast is getting cold for you," he said.

She wanted to stand in front of him like this and talk more, a lot
more, about anything. It was so small, this want, and she couldn't
have it. She felt Alex's eyes on her. He was making oatmeal, his activity drawing fresh glances of envy from the slow-moving camp-
ers, most of whom were only starting on coffee. The oatmeal's
creamy aroma invaded the clean, hard air of the campground with
the smell of their kitchen at home, of all the kitchens of her life.
Oatmeal was made in America—she had seen an enormous pot

bubbling at the diner the previous morning and with her amateur cook's nose gave it ten minutes before it started to burn—but to Maya it remained a Russian smell, the smell of early mornings and starched school uniforms and the dinged kitchen in Kiev with its fanlight window out of which her mother smoked her first cigarette of the day while Maya put away the buttery, raisin-flecked porridge that scalded the roof of her tongue. "Slower, darling, slower," her mother would say distractedly from the window—she was busy devouring her own satisfaction.

"On three, we'll walk away from each other," Marion said. She had to shield her eyes from the sun to look at him. "A Western, but pacifist."

"Sometimes I don't know what you're saying."

"Will you be careful?" he said. "There's weather on its way where you're going. It doesn't snow here the way it snows back home for you. It'll put a foot down in an hour. Beautiful, but if you're looking from your house and there's a fireplace on."

"It snowed from September to April where I grew up," Maya said.

"Were you at seven thousand feet and did you drive through it?"

She dipped her head to say she understood. It was hard to imagine snow with the sun blazing the way that it was.

"Three," he said. But she remained in place. Concealed from Alex by her back, she fit a hand around his and held it. "Three," she said. Then she let go, turned, and replaced the expression on her face with another for her husband and son.

Alex watched her return. He and Max were seated on the same side of the picnic table, breakfasts started in front of them. "Everything all right?" Alex asked in his indirect way. She stared at him in disbelief. Did he prefer not to know? Was his desire for oblivion so strong? He had been more reproving the previous night.

"I had to give back his thermos," Maya said, sitting down. She waited for Alex to ask how she'd come by it, but he didn't. She began to scrape butter on toast. They sat in an uneasy silence, neither Alex nor Max touching their food, Max waiting for some kind of signal from his father. "Let's eat, Maksik," Alex said.

They chewed without looking up at each other. Now Maya filled with guilt; she was ruining the first flicker of enthusiasm from Alex and Max. Maya felt eyes at her back again, only now Marion's. Then the singsong of his daughters, tent poles collapsing with a hollow ring, the tent scratching the ground as they folded it.

"Our plan is the same?" Alex said.

Maya looked at him questioningly.

"I am asking, we are continuing west?" he said.

"Why are you asking?" Maya said. "You don't have to ask, you can answer as well."

Alex breathed heavily and went back to his toast. A moment later, he gave up and threw it down, half-eaten, on the porcelain plate. The Escape had lumbered a set from New Jersey.

+

The Montana state line came and went without any of the ceremony that Maya expected on crossing into the fabled Montana. The word had worked a furrow in her mind until its overuse had rendered it free of association altogether, just a gurgitation of the Rubins' astonishment, sorrow, confusion. Montana, Montana, Montana. Marion, Marion, Marion. Three, three, three.

She made Alex stop and reverse so they could pose for a timed photo of the state sign for Eugene and Raisa. The sign, its blue uncannily matched to the head-beating blue of the sky, was in the shape of the state. The circle at its heart divided, inversely, into snow-capped peaks rising above a lemony sun. But the sky was so general in every direction over the prairie they had been crossing, which was so flat it looked pressed with an iron, that she would not have been surprised to see the sun rolling along the fields rather than up in the heavens. When she piled out of the car, she nearly tipped over. Maya would mail the photo to Mishkin. *Choke on it, Mishkin,* she would write on the back.

Alex grumbled about reversing, but there wasn't a vehicle in either direction; there had not been one in some time. They had trouble with the photograph. Their surroundings functioned on an abnormal scale. You could get the Rubins and nothing else, or you could get the landscape with the Rubins as specks. The Rubins gave up on the landscape and got little more than the sign, the result looking like they could be anywhere, only that the sign did say Montana.

The landscape ahead blurred and shimmered, so that now and again Maya balanced her gaze on the undemanding gray with which the Escape was upholstered. She lowered the window and the wind rushed in like surf haranguing a beach; she watched it swirling the endless umber wheat on either side of the car. There were sharp calls from ploverlike birds up above: dee-dee-dee, dee-dee-dee. They were tapping out a message to her, only she couldn't decipher it. She thought of Marion. His recession with each mile felt inaccurate, false.

Once in a while, cutting the bleak sameness, a two- or even three-story home rose from the prairie, lifting Maya's spirits: other people. The care with which the plot was maintained, the emerald lawn a rebuke to the bleached land all around—it was as tended as a lot in New Jersey—reassured her. She would look away, and, upon looking back, greet the home's reappearance with a grateful surprise. She didn't see any people. She watched mournfully as the sparse settlements disappeared past her shoulder. She craned to catch the last of them, willing some inhabitant to venture outside before the house dropped out of view.

About once per five of these homes appeared the loser in whatever game of survival was being played out here: a derelict home, the roof caved in, the windows broken, every shape that was once at right angles now off-center. The survival rate was 80 percent. She wondered why people lived in such barrenness. It made them frightening to her. She wanted to know the reason. It would be less frightening then.

The roadside was suddenly full of commemorative crosses twined with plastic flowers. One dead, two dead, then so many dead she couldn't count all of them in the short time the Escape took to sail past. They had entered an Indian reservation. There were no walls or fences on it—perhaps because you could not fence this land adequately. She strained her eyes for evidence of the distinct kind of living that went on here, but nothing had changed from before: the dominion of wheat. What were a dozen Indians doing on this road all at once when she hadn't seen a dozen drivers all day? Getting killed. The crosses grew out of the road's meager shoulder like cattails. If you weren't wheat and you wanted to grow here, you had to be a death-marking cross.

The state line had given her twenty minutes of distracting activity, backing up, photos, rechecking of Max's seat belt, all wonderful. But now there was no escaping the landscape. The mountains had gone, correcting her expectation that there was no flat land in the West. She understood why the sky seemed so sovereign—nothing cleaved it. For some reason, peaks had been less frightening to her than all this flat nothing. First shock, and then pancaked by nothingness: It was not unlike adoptive mothering, the American West. The sun burned the prairie with summertime force; it was impossible to imagine the weather of which Marion had warned, though she enjoyed thinking of its threat because it was a reminder of him. All at once, she hated Montana, flat, featureless, and demonic, and wished instead for South Dakota, which felt familiar and settled, and also had Marion in it. If the rest of Montana was like this, she would understand very well why Laurel and Tim would have wanted to save their son from it. She tried, and failed, to keep her mind off Marion. She chewed on the cud of his name. She imagined living with him in one of the homes they passed. What did they do in those homes that remained standing and pretty, what correct choices had they made? And what had those who'd lived in the other homes done wrong?

She flicked on the radio, but there was only static. She turned the dial with infinitesimal slowness, but still nothing. She was dizzy. She turned to Alex and asked him to pull over so she could pee.

"Where?" he said.

She raised her hands in exasperation—up and down this prairie all of China could pee. "There." She pointed to an unpaved turn-off, the roadway raised above the lip of a field. Beneath the slope, she could be private. Alex slowed down. "Not too far," she admonished him as they turned off the main road. The side road was badly rutted; a rainstorm would have sunk anything but a tractor with balloon tires. A sign from the Montana Department of Agriculture said it was a winter wheat field, experimental because a seed specimen from North Dakota had been grafted with one from Montana. Maya had paid for the experiment with her taxes. Alex unlocked the doors.

Maya scrambled down the slight incline like an animal without adequate prehensility. She had not been brought up by this landscape and had not evolved the necessary adaptations. She did not have to pee. Assured she was out of view, she lay down on the itchy young wheat and closed her eyes, trying to steady herself. With a welling of guilt, Maya wished that no Alex and Max awaited her on the brow of the hill. She would hold out her thumb—didn't people do that here—and get a ride back to the Badlands. Then she remembered that Marion would be long gone. Well, it didn't have to be so in her mind. She saw why her mother liked to tell stories.

For steadiness, she spread her arms. A little better. She closed her eyes and counted, one, two, three, three, three, and carefully opened them. All was still rolling. She shut them again. She ran her arms up and down through the wheat, nausea in her stomach. Flecks of wheat stubbled her arms, making her itch. From far away, Marion asked her to get calm. Again, she opened her eyes. This time, there was a little more steadiness. Close, open, close, open, until her heart was beating less badly.

She made quite a sight rising above the slope, winter wheat

clinging to her hair, sweater, and cheeks. Alex and Max, a window per man, eyed her with worried antipathy.

They had been playing tic-tac-toe. Alex was careful to lose.

"Are you all right, Mama?" Max said cautiously.

From the front seat, she made herself pull his ear. "Of course, Mama's all right," she said. She wanted them gone. But there was nowhere here to go away from each other. Here, where there was more space to disappear than anywhere she had known—a mother with a felonious heart could ask for no better place than the prairie of eastern Montana—you huddled together, your protections against the surroundings already so meager.

"I'd like to drive," Maya said.

Alex went from impatience flecked with concern to his look of straining to comprehend. He expected her to read in it all the skepticism he wished to communicate without having to state it explicitly in front of their son. But she would not grant him that favor of intimates. Alex clucked his tongue. "You don't know how to drive on the highway," he pointed out.

"Precisely," she said with false reasonableness. "If I did, you wouldn't have had to come and chauffeur your wife up and down the moon."

"Maya," he said chidingly. Not with Max in the car, the rest of him said.

"Where would I learn if not here?" Maya said, and pointed to the road, straight and empty, though the lanes seemed narrower than back home.

"Now, you want to learn?" Alex said.

"Now," Maya said.

"What if we see a policeman?" he dug into her. "We're on a short leash and you don't have a license."

"I don't know," she said.

Alex checked the rearview window. "Maxie," he said, turning around. "You're going to be all right back there?"

"I want to drive, too," Max said, blinking twice.

"I will drive for a little bit, and then you will go in my lap," Maya said before her husband could answer. "And we'll learn together. How does that sound?"

Before Max could reply, Maya opened her door, commencing the car's dinging. As Alex and Maya passed each other at the hood, he looked at her but she did not look at him.

Montana Rte. 212 was actually an inferior place to learn driving—the straight line of the road required negotiation of no four-way intersections, parking restrictions, K-turns, or merging. (Alex had insisted on taking the interstate from the Badlands, which would have spat them out near Billings, only two hours from Adelaide—he imagined an evening visit with Laurel and Tim, and an early start back the following morning; though this was more driving than he wished to do in a year, he would have been happy to strain himself if the strain was aimed eastward—but Maya had asked for the local road.) Montana 212 required little outside Drive, with occasional sharp deployment of the brakes though they were going no more than forty. Alex harassed Maya from the passenger seat, his feet tapping his mat as if he were the one at the wheel. He leaned forward as if riding out stomach pain. He couldn't understand why a job had to be performed poorly when there was someone around to perform it the right way. Maya relished his discomfort.

"Uh-oh," she said.

"Uh-oh," Max copied from the backseat.

There was a battered sedan pushing up from behind. The way to find other cars was to go forty on the highway and they would find you. The sedan, a sickly green Taurus, gained on them quickly.

"Alex, what do I do?" Maya said.

"It's okay," Alex said. "It's okay."

"Uh-oh!" Max shouted.

"Should I stop? Should I slow down? Does he want to pass?"

"Maya, how can I know?" Alex said. "Just stay steady. Don't

slow down. Don't do anything. If you're too slow for him, he'll do what he has to."

"And what is that?" she asked, but Alex was silent. He was full of recommendations when no emergency presented itself, but now he sat wordlessly.

She grasped the wheel with two hands as the Taurus loomed.

"Uh-oh!" Max shouted. There was a note of madness in his voice.

"Max!" his father howled.

"It's getting into the oncoming lane!" Maya shouted.

"He's going around you," Alex said.

"What do I do?"

"Don't do anything," Alex said. "Do *not* do anything, Maya. Let him do it."

The Taurus blew by on the left with such force that Maya shrieked and yanked the steering wheel hard to the right. The Escape demonstrated itself to be unexpectedly lithe and followed her command too obediently. However, Maya managed to turn the wheel again, righting them before the car reached the edge of the road. In the second before she managed the correction, she heard Alex shouting her name with something like hatred. He was not lunging toward her, or the wheel, or their son; he was shouting her name with hatred at the top of his voice.

Alex did not wait for the shock to subside before he yelled for her to pull over, pull over, pull over. They were hardly stopped before he flung open the passenger door. As they crossed at the hood, now she sought him out but he ignored her chastised, re-lieved look. There was such enmity in Alex's eyes that he was too embarrassed to look at his wife. Maya felt the dour satisfaction of the more generous side. Then she wondered if she had asked to drive only because Alex did not know how to teach and she knew it would breach the anger that he was keeping in such magnificent, magnanimous check.

+

An hour outside Adelaide, the earth started climbing. First, there were hills, patchy and tentative, then, all of a sudden, mountains upon mountains. Maya eyed them with gratitude; she willed them to keep rising. Even Max stirred at their sight, leaning into his window. Emerald firs rose off the flanks in neat rows like heads in a choir, the cottonwoods among them so gold they looked like bullion bars. The Escape was soaked by a shower that arrived from nowhere and disappeared just as instantly. Max shrieked when the first heavy drops stunned the roof. They were pounded on for ten minutes, Alex clutching the wheel and straining to see. Then it was over and clear, an argument settled. The sky came back with a histrionic palette of yellows and pinks.

And then, with no warning, Adelaide was growing around them, the windshield suddenly full of tackle shops, muffler specialists, diners. The road had been so lulling that they had taken several lights before Maya remembered why they were here. Laurel and Tim could be eating in that diner. Max might lay eyes on his birth parents as a conscious being for the first time in his life. Maya had reassured Alex that they would visit the cowboys alone, and that if Laurel and Tim became demanding, they would be told Max had not come on the trip. But what if Laurel and Tim were not patiently awaiting the Rubins at 2207 New Missouri Trail South? What if they were living, breathing beings walking around town? Would they recognize their son? Would they stir recognition in Max?

"Town of bars, town of churches," the laconic legend underneath the Welcome to Adelaide sign said; no other comment appeared, not even the date of settlement, save for the words "Adelaide, Australia 8830km (crow only)," sided by a kangaroo silhouette. Some inner flag raised by the symbolism of their arrival, Alex pulled over on the gravelly shoulder. Traffic had been picking up steadily; they were at the edge of a veritable metropolis. They felt the accomplishment of having made it to some other side.

Maya put her hand on Alex's forearm. "Let's go to the hotel first. Please."

Alex looked ahead, both hands on the wheel. He had been hoping to go directly to Laurel and Tim's, but they couldn't very well show up with Max. Setting off his blinker, he pulled back out on the road.

A series of mountain ridges loomed behind the town, each paler than the previous, like the paint lightening with each swipe of a brush. At every intersection, an unobstructed view ran to the foothills, Maya craning to get the particulars—it looked like they simply began, with as little ceremony as the town itself, at the edge of the last backyard—before Alex sped on and another brick building briefly covered the view. The kangaroo stared at them from the galvanized roof of a gas station, the medical clinic, and even the park in front of city hall, as if the other Adelaide had equal claim to the place.

There was only one lodging in Adelaide, the Dundee, a four-story brick box with mullioned windows. Trying to get inside with their bags, Maya, Alex, and Max were halted by the exit of a procession of elderly tourists. These were hauling commemorative take from the gift shop: a silver-plated replica of a revolver; a poster with close-ups of bullet holes; a phlegmatic-looking piebald brown cow that came alive with pinging bullets when you violated its udders. The caravan crossed traffic in a humming, neat single file to a massive coach slumped on the other side of the road.

"Germans," the woman at check-in said. Her nameplate said: "Wilma Gund, Boss." "They love this stuff." She pointed at the wall behind her. Obediently, Maya and Alex studied the massive brass plaque hanging there. An old film director, his name unknown to Maya, had stayed in the penthouse. He had shot a dozen holes in the copper-plate ceiling before relocating his muse and finishing a screenplay in one booze-powered night. Visitors were invited to come view the bullet holes, which remained unmended; for a premium, they could stay in the suite itself on the understanding that in the afternoon it would have to be surrendered to walk-throughs. In a wall of photographs next to the plaque, Wilma Gund embraced one or another artistic personage, all unknown to Maya. In fact, it had become something of a pilgrimage spot for blocked writers, poets, playwrights, and screenwriters.

Alex nodded at the burgundy stairing, each carpeted step popped to reveal honeycombed netting, and asked if the entire hotel was being kept in its ancient condition in tribute to the director's experience.

"You don't like marble staircases?" Wilma Gund said icily. "We did add the Wi-Fi for your convenience."

There being no elevator, Alex heaved their suitcases up the stairs with grim déjà vu: Europeans also liked elevatorless buildings with narrow, vertiginous stairs, and it was up steps just like these that Eugene had hauled the family's five suitcases in Vienna, the first place the Rubins had reached after leaving the Soviet Union, as little Alex got tangled in his legs trying to help.

This was why the Germans flocked here—they were drawn by amenities that had been contrived specifically in the name of inconvenience. Alex loved America, or what of it he knew, though, being satisfied with what he knew, he had no great need to search out more: the obscenely large coffees, the oversized couches, the one million little appurtenances that came with the blender and anticipated every blading and liquefying and pureeing maneuver he might desire to take up. Unlike most Russian husbands—and unlike most husbands, period, though this was less noted than it should be, he felt—Alex loved going to department stores with Maya; while she bought clothes or what the house needed, he held court with the salespeople in the housewares and home-appliance departments. Only the most hardworking country in the world could come up with conveniences like the ones offered by the shiny objects on the shelves. No country worked harder for you, and if it was motivated to do so by the prospect of claiming your dollars, so be it. This is something Maya did not understand about Alex. Did she think him cheap? He wasn't cheap. He paid, paid happily—but only for the things that deserved it. Maya paid indiscriminately. Maya paid out of feeling.

In case Maya had been wondering whether Max preferred campsites to hotel rooms, her son's romp across the beds of Room 31 answered her. He leaped around and shouted. Flying from one bed to another, he delivered a kick into Alex's spine. Alex clutched his back in agony.

"Max?" Maya said. "You're dusty from the road. I want you to go to the bathroom and wash up." Max climbed off the bed, embraced his father, and bounded off.

Alex watched the bathroom door close. Rapidly healed, he let go of his back.

"Can't we just get on with it?" he said. "We're here to find the two of them—so let's find them."

"Why didn't you speak up, Alex?" she said. She battered the hair at her temples. "When I asked you to drive to the hotel. Order me around, Alex. But order me by speaking, not by not speaking. You are like a general who doesn't fight, only waits for conditions to kill the other soldiers one by one."

"I am trying to respect you," he said.

"Alex," she clasped her hands in front of her face. "Please. Please save me from your respect. Please stop respecting me."

He swung his hands at the ceiling and looked away.

She flopped down on the bed, kicked off her flats, and massaged her toes. "It's my birthday tomorrow," she said. "You want to hunt them down tonight, get some answer as if it's a folder they forgot to give us, and spend my birthday racing across America so I can have the pleasure of cooking a meal for everyone."

"Birthdays are meant to be spent at home," he said.

"This is his home," she said.

Alex stood, grasping his back once again. "In case you haven't noticed, he's been nothing but frightened for the past forty-eight hours. He wants to go home. Which is in New Jersey."

"He seems better now," she said feebly.

"Better than what? Better than frightened and miserable?"

"He hasn't done anything dangerous while we've been out here."

"We've been out here for two days."

"So," she said. "Let's give him some time. We can't tell anything yet. We'll go home and he'll go right back to what he was doing before."

"Maya!" he shouted at the ceiling—the floor of the film suite. To Alex, it was an especially offensive version of a nightmare: to pay extra for a hotel room so as to have the pleasure of a hundred Germans trooping through in the afternoon. "How will we know something's changed?"

"I don't know," she said. "But we'll know. We will get some kind of signal. We'll know."

"He wants to go home, there's your signal," Alex said. "For anyone actually paying attention to him, it's quite obvious. For anyone actually paying attention to him instead of herself."

She slapped him. Alex smiled in astonishment. "You forgot to call me a whore," she said. She swept their suitcase from the ottoman next to the bed, imagining a dramatic spill of its contents out onto the floor, but it only thudded on the carpet. She stalked toward the door.

"Where are you going?" he demanded.

"To fix it, Alex," she said. "As always, I am going to fix it."

+

Maya returned thirty minutes later. Alex was seated where she had left him. Max had emerged from the bathroom and was unpacking the clothes that Maya had punted to the floor. Had he heard their argument? Alex's face broadcast so many accusations at Maya that it was impossible to discern whether this was one of them.

She knelt in front of her son. "Max, darling—are you hungry? If you could have anything, what would it be?" As soon as she uttered the words, she paled because she thought Max would say: "I want to go home." But Max, who seemed grateful to come to a standstill, cocked his head in a funny way and said, "Anything?"

She laughed without joy. "Well, you know—within reason."

"What is reason?" he said.

"Oh, it's too many things, honey," she said. "Not now."

"Fine, ginger ale," he said.

"That's easy," she said.

"Easier than reason?" he said, knowing he was being funny.

"Max, do you know the way you help Mama chop vegetables in the kitchen?"

"Sure. I'm good at it."

"You're very good at it. The lady downstairs who checked us in? There's a restaurant on the other side of the hotel. But one of her cooks didn't come in. And she's got a hundred potatoes that need peeling. You will be paid in ginger ale."

"What is this?" Alex stirred.

"Mama and Papa have to go somewhere for an hour," Maya said. "And when you're finished with your one hundredth potato, we will come pick you up."

"Are you leaving me?" Max said, the humor gone from his face.

"Leaving you?" Maya exclaimed. "For about one hour, silly goose." She wrapped him in her arms and rolled with him on the bed, her face pressed into his cardigan. He looked so grown-up in that cardigan—like a grandfather in a boy's body. "Why don't we go downstairs and I'll show you what I mean. You don't like it, we'll figure out something else."

Max didn't answer—he seemed placated.

"Max, wait for us in the hallway outside?" Alex said. "We have to lock up."

Max looked between them, rolled off the bed, and walked out of the room.

"What are you doing?" Alex said after the door closed.

"You want to go and get it done with, so let's go. We can't take him with us."

"Where were you?" he demanded.

"I went to the supermarket and bought five bags of potatoes. And then I gave fifty dollars to Wilma. And all of a sudden she developed a need for a hundred peeled potatoes, in exchange for watching an eight-year-old boy. Free potato with everyone's steak for dinner tonight."

"You're going to leave Max with a woman who had to be bribed," he said. "A woman we met an hour ago." Alex was right, but in Maya's mind, Wilma's avarice was mitigated by her attachment to a kitchen. She would save on old carpeting, but she would not let a boy come to harm. Kitchen code. "Why not just leave him in the room?" Alex said.

"Because then he would not be distracted. Then he would be worried and sad. Then he would want to escape. As would I."

"Then I'll stay with him, and you go."

"I can't drive, remember?" she taunted him. She taunted again: "Want to go by yourself?"

They took the steps down in a file. By the time they reached the restaurant, Max had forgotten about being left behind and bounded into the kitchen, the air thick with the aroma of browning meat and herb-scented steam rising from a pot larger than him. A man in a spattered apron with tattoos up and down his arms reached down for a low-five from his apprentice, which the apprentice supplied. Max walked through the kitchen like a cat—like someone who had been in a kitchen before. Maya was proud of him.

"I got you a bucket to sit on," Wilma Gund appeared in the kitchen. "You mind sitting on a bucket?" Max shook his head no. "I've got a large Canadian party, so I've got to shoo. You'll tell Derek here how things go?" Max got the joke, smiled.

"He looks like a street urchin," Alex said to Maya.

"Eugene and Raisa don't have to know," Maya said. "Max, honey, we're going. We'll be back in an hour." Max shouted bye.

"An hour," Alex said when they had bundled into the Escape. The antique clock attached to the Valley First National Bank said six o'clock. He watched one of the arms slide: 6:01. Both nothing and too much had happened already on this day, and it was still light outside. The Rubins were in Adelaide, Montana. He was about to call on Max's birth parents. In mere days, he had traveled definitively away from life as he knew it. How little it took to unravel things, compared to what it had taken to make them cohere. It was masochistic, this behavior—because voluntary. Yes, he had remembered the license plate. He could have pretended he hadn't, though he had called it out before he could think to suppress it. Either way, he could not—he was not in the habit of hiding things from his wife. But he regretted being here. He regretted it—that was the only word for it. He was filled with the foreboding that accompanies gratuitous risk. And wondered in mystification at the person in the passenger seat.

14

The stunted emptiness of eastern Montana had been so demand-ing—it was a negative demand; the demand was for stillness, to bear it—that, in some way, Maya's confidence that they would make it through was not final. When she had seen Adelaide rise from the road as abruptly as the shower that shook them a half hour outside town, she blinked twice, just like her son, wanting full con-firmation. Now the Rubins were reciprocating the unannounced visitation of the other side eight years before, only, incredibly, even more unannounced. Maya had tried other ways. They didn't have a phone. Who didn't have a phone in the twenty-first century?

Alex turned on the ignition and the car came to humming, obe-dient life. It was colder here than in the prairie, also later in the day, and he switched on the heat. Despite the drop in tempera-ture, the sky was clear, stingingly clear.

"What if they're not there?" Alex said. Maya looked over at him and saw that he was holding down half a dozen unanswered ques-tions. If they're not there, do we wait for them? Leave a note? But what if the note spooks them? But we can't very well stake out the place, can we? And then what if they're not there in a more permanent way? That is, if the whole thing is an error and there is no Laurel and Tim at 2207 New Missouri Trail South? Or no 2207 New Missouri Trail South? And what if they say they want to meet Max? Or they can't tell us why he behaves the way that he does? Or that they don't remember saying not to let their child do rodeo?

"I don't know, Alex," she whispered.

"Can we go home tomorrow?"

"It's my birthday tomorrow."

"You want to spend it here?" he said.

"Better than in the car, driving all day."

"We are so far from home," he sighed. "We are on the other side of the continent. I wish we could fly home."

She wished to tell him to take Max and fly home—and leave her behind. "Okay, we'll leave tomorrow," she said, so quietly that Alex gave her his straining look. "Let's drive. Max is a genius at peeling potatoes. He's probably halfway done."

The GPS said nine miles from Adelaide proper to New Missouri Trail South. The first bit of sunset, pink as a dog's ears, was creeping into the sky; the Rubins would return the favor of a visit at dinnertime. As they slicked along the new tar of U.S. 89, Maya stared at the mountains blurring in an unbroken line outside her window. At first, they were so vast and eye-filling that Maya could not manage to do anything but stare senselessly or look away to the dashboard, so reassuringly minor and *there*. But now, some invisible thing having happened inside her—she was checking into the hotel, arguing with Alex, buying potatoes, but somewhere offstage some wheel was turning without her awareness—she wanted to look at the mountains. The mountains were large enough to blot out Laurel and Tim, and even Alex and Max. She had nine whole miles to spend on them—fifteen minutes according to the especially careful way Alex drove here, even though there were few cars compared to New Jersey. She, a non-driver inept at measuring distances between vehicles, was always grateful for his care at the wheel, but she was especially grateful now. When she was young, by some miracle awoken fifteen minutes before the alarm, they appeared endless from the vantage point of a matted head on the pillow. For fifteen minutes, the world was hers. They lasted forever. She wanted the same now.

The mountains looked indistinguishable, one wrinkled silver pyramid after the next. She wondered if someone raised on them could tell them apart. Surely they could, though by now the ubiquitous peaks would have become invisible, the way the homes on Sylvan Gate Drive were invisible to Maya, though she could say with a moment's readiness who lived where if only somebody asked. But nobody asked.

Compared to these peaks, the Badlands were scratches in the ground, turned-up earth. But despite her certainty that she would vanish without trace if she dared venture into these mountains— how did one venture *into* the mountains, as people said? they looked like sheer walls of stone—she could not persuade herself that they were a hostile force. It was so clean up there.

Maya had sooner expected to find Max's biological parents than to encounter the reaction that she had got from her son to the place he was born: nothing. Max became animated when the Rubins came closest to the rituals of home: oatmeal at the campground, the hotel room, the potatoes. But when she looked at the mountains, it made her believe that some kind of solution was possible to the impasse Max and his family had come into, life before which Maya recalled with difficulty, as if the situation compressed their first eight years together and pitilessly expanded the previous six months. The smallness she felt next to the mountains was the smallness of a young person, a ward, not the smallness of insignificance.

Her next thought was: One day, and perhaps soon, her mother would die. And so would she, and Alex. Even Max. She held these facts placidly; she felt collected and ready. Until it happened, however, she wanted very badly to go at something in a way she had never gone at it before. But what? She could not say. She clucked her tongue. She began flight down so many paths she had not traveled before, and then: dead end.

"Alex, darling, would you pull over?" she said. "Just for a minute."

"You wanted to get there," he said, but she knew he would indulge her because she had used the endearment.

Alex clicked the blinker and with a protracted glide came to a halt. Out of town, the roadway had become provisional once again—a bright dotted line bisected the middle, but the lanes were barely wide enough for an SUV and were not marked at the edge of the road, sloping into patchy grass and loose rock below, as if this was as far as the road makers could push out because the landscape couldn't wait to take over. She knew why Alex disliked pulling over. It drew attention, signified extraordinary circumstances, the machine of their lives in sudden, panicked disarray. He disliked disarray, therefore lived with certainty that it waited at all turns. Or perhaps not: Perhaps he was able to shut his mind of its possibility until Maya forced him into contact with it.

In the few minutes since they'd left the hotel, the temperature had lost ten degrees. She dug in the backseat until she found the blanket Max had used to cover himself two nights before—was it only two nights? The night that preceded her meeting with Marion felt as if it had occurred weeks before, and Marion himself dipped in and out of reality, though she had only to think of lemon balm or cedar or fat Wilfred Shade. Already, those things were taking on the sheen of lost history, foreign experience, nostalgia. For years, she would have the privilege of nostalgia about something she'd savored for twenty-four hours.

Outside, shivering slightly, she leaned against the warm, ticking vehicle and gazed out before her. She breathed deeply—her shortness of breath had gone at some point. The air rushed in with a cold sharp scoring sting, already cold enough that what she breathed out was visible, ghostly and white. She was trying to take in the enormity grandstanding before her; she wanted something that she could take with her. Or were a mountain's powers unborrowable, lost unless one lived within constant sight of it, some kind of refill occurring with every morning's first gaze? She laughed at herself. She was the local lunatic. She was the one at whom people would point.

The wind picked up and tugged away the edge of the blanket. She would have let it fly off but that would have brought Alex out of the car to point out the obvious. She felt the slightly hysterical wish to undress, shiver with the wind, rash all over with goose bumps. She wanted to be skinned like a hide, reduced to parts, cut open to the hot glowing center. Or was the soothing blankness she was experiencing the blankness of barrenness, her hot glowing center glowing with nothing? She was forty-two. Forty-three. It was too late, in any case.

She climbed back into the vehicle. Alex said there were tears in her eyes. She snorted. Alex would not ask why she was crying, but also could not go on without alerting her that she was—something that needed her attention, like a spill on the floor. She had always thought that, in a moment like this, this was because he wasn't interested in the real story. But perhaps it was because he didn't know how to speak about it, and the observation was as far as he knew how to go.

+

Was the sight of an '80s-model coffee-and-milk Datsun with the license plate MTRODEO1 in the yard of 2207 New Missouri Trail South Maya's reward for all her difficult thoughts? All these years, the Datsun had chuffed along somewhere out there. Well, here. It was mounted on a rough-hewn wooden platform, the way you saw sometimes at the car dealership, an unnatural situation for a car, like an animal trapped in a tree. Clearly, it wasn't being used any longer.

Seeing it, Maya grabbed Alex's wrist and he squeezed back as he could from the wheel. The long driveway off a rutted side road off 89 gave onto an old country farmhouse with a gouge in one of the walls, as if the place had been bombed, though the garden had a neat fence and the driveway looked freshly graveled. Two dogs stormed out of the house, a runt leaping and barking hysterically and a lean, triangle-headed hound that observed the scene with brambled indifference. Then they gave up and gnawed on pebbles of gravel. The screen door slammed open: a short man with a full belly. He rattled a soda can filled with coins and the dogs trotted back inside, the small one fitting neatly under the legs of the large. They had known each other for some time.

Alex and Maya exchanged looks and stepped out of the vehicle. They were surveyed by the man at the door, his mouth working. It was working them over. He had a copper-colored face as round as a melon, the left eye turned unnaturally in its orbit, the lid half-shut over the eye. Around the mouth was a pelt of goatee neatly clipped and gone white. The blasted eye squinted at them. He looked like a giant bird, grounded.

"Mnyah," he said to no one in particular.

Alex stepped ahead of Maya. "Excuse me," he said. "We're looking for Laurel and Tim. There's no phone. We tried to call."

The man whistled. "Who's asking?"

"We only want to talk to them," Alex said.

"Please," Maya said. "It's a family emergency. Are they inside?"

"You're their family?" the man said. The good eye rolled up and down.

"We are, in a way," Maya said.

"We are the parents of the child they gave up," Alex said. Maya eyed him with gratitude.

The man whistled again. "And they gave you this as their forwarding?"

"It was a closed adoption," Maya said. "It was the best we could find. We know this isn't right—but we came anyway."

The good eye flickered, and he swiveled to regard them with it. "Why?"

"But you know them," Maya insisted. She half turned toward the old Datsun. "That's their car. That's the car in which—" She broke off. "It was registered here. Without a phone number. We would have called."

"I see," the man said. "Come in—I'm interrogating you at the door."

He vanished inside the house. Maya and Alex looked helplessly at each other. Maya stepped forward and held the screen door for Alex. He shivered in the cold air and followed her.

The house had a Mediterranean feeling, with stone walls and earthenware jugs peering from decorative shelves. The dogs were laid out in the middle of the hallway, snout to snout. Maya and Alex stopped, afraid of rousing them.

"Step over," the man said from the doorway to the kitchen. "They're novelty junkies, they don't care about you now." Maya and Alex hurdled over the dogs, who answered with low simpering moans. The man waddled back into the hallway—one of his legs was as good as his eye. "Harris Sprague," he extended a hand. Maya shook it, Alex shook it.

"It's a beautiful home," Maya said, trying to placate him.

Harry flicked on the lights and said "Mnyah." He was an author. The Harris Sprague oeuvre stared at them from bookshelves running the length of the hallway. There were so many titles, and then each had as many translations. They were reading him in Bulgaria and Norway and even China—if that was Mandarin and not some other fantastical tongue. An entire hallway filled with books by the same man saying the same things in different languages—it was dizzying. The dead eye evaluated their impressions.

Maya expectorated a sound that she hoped sounded like marvel. She raked her mind for something to say. "What do you write about?" she said finally.

"And what do you do?" Harry Sprague said with a whimper. His breathing was labored, like a smoker's. The silences were kept festive by the loud rise and fall of his breathing.

"Mammograms," Maya said.

"And what do you mammogram about?" he said, a naughty smile on his face.

Maya felt shame at her mistake, but it was distant and muffled.

"That's Dreamer," Harry nodded at the larger dog. "Named for a writing teacher I had. He said, 'You're a dreamer, Harry, if you

think this'll be published.' So I'd send him every one of my books
with a big middle finger for an inscription. Then he died on me.
We're all going. When I got him, Dreamer ran faster than a horse.
He's a lurcher. He could tear the soul out of a deer."

Harry twitched, the dead eye rolling toward the kitchen. "Get
out of the hallway and come in here," he said. "Sangu would put
me in the corner if she were at home; I'm not being hospitable."
The Rubins were instructed to sit at a wide-planked kitchen table.
They were surrounded by two walls of glass cabinets behind which
sat mounds of elaborately painted china. "There's no one for linens
and service sets like Sangu," Harry said. "No British woman is devoted to service sets like an Indian woman. I'm a savage to her. She
thinks I brought her to Mars." On the long wooden table, Harry
deposited an unlabeled bottle of red wine. "Mnyah," he said. "She's
out for poker. Harry's on parole."

He poured thick red wine, dark as paint, into three tumblers.
"Sangu has a cell phone," Harry said. "Two cell phones. She's
phoned up. But the house is phone-free. You need me, you send me
a fax." He pointed to the hallway, and for a moment Maya thought
she would be ordered to get out of her seat and lay eyes on Harry
Sprague's fax machine. Maya heard the metronomic beep of a machine ready to receive news of Harry Sprague having sold in Hindi
and Finnish. That's why there wasn't a phone. Harry Sprague was
rich enough not to have one.

The author lifted his glass. His good eye crinkled. "So what is it
you want with them?"

Maya stared out the window, where the day was moving reso-
lutely toward darkness. "Our son misbehaves," she said. "Maybe
they would know why. He was normal," she rushed to add, as if
persuading an authority. "It's only recently that he . . ." She cursed
herself—she was making no sense.

The author regarded her. "This calls for something stronger,"
he said. He opened a new cupboard and peered at a crowd of bottles. "I've got admirers placed around the drinking capitals of the

world. There's a young fellow in Burgundy who sends me a case every time I write a book. He's half the reason I write. Where are you from?"

"New Jersey," Maya said.

"Oh," Harry said.

"Russia," Maya elaborated.

"I knew a pair of Russian legs once," Harry said. He stopped and looked over his shoulder in mischief. "We'll drink vodka, then."

Alex looked at his wife and cut in: "Could you tell us what you know? Please. We drove a very long way."

Harry turned back from the bottles and they saw his face lose its play. "I'm yakking, but it's not really a celebratory situation, is it," he said. He put thimbles in front of Maya and Alex, but Alex held up his hand; he was driving. Maya, however, downed hers and slid her glass forward for more. Harry flashed her an approving look.

"About ten years ago, the young people you're talking about got some kind of a windfall," Harry said, pouring. "Well, I guess you were the windfall. They got the money to buy something better than the shit can outside. I bought it from them. From the junkyard."

"But why?" Alex said.

"My dad's old car. It must have been one of their dads that he sold it to, I don't know which one. I got a call one day from Hoyt at the junkyard. He said, 'You ain't gonna believe what rolled in here today.' Hoyt will remember a car from thirty years ago."

"I don't understand," Maya said.

"I don't know where they are," Harry said. "I never even laid eyes on 'em. I can ask for you. My friend's still there. He'll die there. But I think he said they went off in a big way. I hope I'm remembering that wrong. They got their fancy new car and drove the hell away."

Maya and Alex stared at him dumbly. The sounds of a house at rest rushed into the silence: a ticking clock, the dogs readjusting their flanks, branches swinging outside. Maya placed her hand on Alex's forearm, a silent plea not to look at her.

Alex exhaled painfully and his shoulders slumped. He braided his hands and looked at his thumbs. "I don't understand this kind of person," he said finally. "To give up a child." His disinterest in brandishing his triumph frightened Maya; she wished for the old Alex, the brandishing Alex. Alex looked at Harry, but in defeat, without aggrievement. "We couldn't have children," Alex said. "They could, and gave him up."

"But then you wouldn't have gotten the boy," Harry said, trying to correct his earlier levity.

"I wanted us to come here because I thought he would see where he was born and something would happen," Maya said. "But nothing's happened. Max wants to go home." She looked over at Alex—she had meant the concession for him.

"So that's something," Harry said.

"By accident," Alex said.

"It still counts," Harry said. "Sangu's first husband died of leukemia. At forty. He was a doctor, a handsome Indian man, certainly more handsome than the one-eyed wonder she ended up with. His loss was my gain. We lived with him for the first three years of our marriage. It was Sangu, Harry, and Amar. I wondered during those years about this special humiliation I had earned, to share a bed with a dead man. Sangu wailed into the night. I said, 'Why did you marry me?' And she would say things like, 'Because you asked.' Or: 'Because I love you.' I would ask how it was possible to love two men at once, and she would look at me like a wolf, like no one who had to ask that question deserved an answer. So I shut up—not my favorite setting. I shot a real wolf around that time. I was breaking the law but I felt anger inside me. As I aimed at him, I was aiming at Sangu. I got him down with one shot and then I raced home because I was convinced that she would be dead in the kitchen. But she was alive, reading, wearing those big glasses of hers. I covered her with kisses. And I waited. And now I am the luckiest man in the world."

Alex nodded. "We should go," he said. "It's an hour, Maya. He'll be waiting."

Maya looked up at Harry. "Can I ask you for something?"

"You can't have the car," Harry said. "That car's been sold for the last time."

"I don't want the car," Maya said. "I want to sit inside it. For five minutes."

"Knock yourself out," Harry said. "It's open. Hasn't had gas since 2005. If you see a five-foot-one Indian lady in a Prius pull up, just say Harry's inside, polishing china."

They rose heavily, Maya unsteady after two drinks.

"Look," Harry said. "I'm sorry."

Outside, the passenger door of the Datsun gave way with an anguished squeal. Maya's heart decelerated—for a moment, she thought she had damaged Harry Sprague's patrimony. But the author did not seem concerned with the vehicle's presentation. The faded-blue seats were ripped, the roof lining was cantilevered over the rear seat, and the air was heavy with must and decay.

Maya climbed into Laurel's seat and looked out the window. This is what Laurel saw. After a minute, Maya cranked open the door—at first it wouldn't give, filling her with dread—and moved over to the driver's side, Alex watching from the Escape. This is what Tim saw. She switched to the rear. She could barely slide in, so narrow the space there, and her pants raised a storm of dust as she slid across the shredded upholstery. This is what Max saw. She felt nothing—they were not here to be found, or she lacked whatever it was that would have made them feel present. Her imagination was not strong enough—she was not her mother's equal.

From the backseat, she saw, though it had eluded her when she was in front of it, that the glove compartment was so full of papers it wouldn't close. She returned to the front passenger seat and pried it open. There was a pocket notebook whose corners looked chewed by a dog, filled with notations and figures in a hand so minuscule Maya could not make out any of it; a receipt for a block of rosin; a page torn from the phone book (Ra-Re) with an addition scrawled over it; a fridge magnet with the calendar for 2004. Next, she pulled out a postcard—on one side was an antelope leaned into a gallop, on the other a picture of Laurel and a picture of Tim, glued to opposite ends of the card. They looked even younger than they had in 2004—they were yearbook pictures. Laurel was as pretty as Maya remembered, the yellow hair drawn in the middle. Tim, clean-shaven, looked embarrassed to be wearing a suit, its fit obviously clumsy even though only the shoulders were visible; the photographer had gotten him with his eyes just off the camera; they were piercingly blue even in the black-and-white photo.

There was an arrow drawn between the two pictures. Beneath had been written:

> *Most likely to be*
> *Joyous and free*
> *Especially*
> *If you marry me.*

Maya ran her fingertips over the photos. Perhaps Laurel was already pregnant with Max, only didn't know it. But don't all women know, even if they don't know? Maya didn't know. She studied Laurel's eyes. She was smiling—carelessly, widely, and freely. She had a beautiful smile. Maya did not get to see it when the two young parents came to deliver their child.

Maya returned everything she had pulled out save for the postcard. She looked at Alex, at the entryway to the house. Then she folded the postcard, wedged it into a pocket of her jeans, and stepped out of the Datsun.

15

‡

"I'm glad I'm drunk," Maya said. "I wish you were, too." Alex started the car, but they idled. "I'm glad we came," she said. "I know you're not, but I am. I'm sorry."

"I don't know what I thought they could tell us," Alex said. "It was a stupid idea."

"You were scared," she ventured.

He shrugged. "I'm sorry," he said.

They drove without talking, the nine miles to Adelaide now drawing the opposite desire from Maya: She wished to get back sooner, recover her son, as if the nonpresence of Laurel and Tim would somehow lead to his nonpresence also; it had been well over an hour, full darkness. There was no true darkness in Acrewood. Here, the darkness swallowed not only the road, but the mountains. The mountains blotted out Laurel and Tim, but the darkness blotted out the mountains. And Laurel and Tim blotted out the darkness. The Escape was like a dinghy sailing on a sliver of moonlight. Thin white flakes swirled in the beam of the headlights. She took reassurance from the steady rev of the engine, the night's only sound.

At the Dundee, their son was maneuvering between tables, in his hands a plate half as large as his torso, and the skirt steak in it even larger—the tips flopped over the edges. On this Wilma Gund did not skimp.

"Your son's earned you a free meal," she said as she dashed out of the kitchen. "I hope you don't mind," she said, meaning his conscription into table service. "We're slammed on Saturday nights." Max didn't seem to mind. He deposited the flank steak at a corner table, his shoulders rising after being relieved of the weight, and had his hair ruffled by the man who was about to consume it. Seeing his parents, Max waved. Maya walked quickly toward him and embraced him, the man at the table hesitant to cut into his steak while, next to him, a mother embraced her son as if he had been lost. Ovals of gratinéed potato were dominoed next to the steak—Max's doing. The sight of the food made her nauseous, but she was grateful for the din.

"Sit?" Wilma shouted from across the room. "I'll get you soon as I can."

"I'm not hungry," Maya whispered to no one. She took Max and walked back to the front of the restaurant. "It's my birthday tomorrow," she told Wilma.

"Can't offer much more than a free meal, honey," the proprietress said, wiping her forehead with a sleeve.

"Is there a Mr. Gund?" Maya asked. "Do you run everything by yourself?"

"I'd love to stay and chat," Wilma said. "You staying tomorrow as well? I forget. You can claim your meal then if you want."

"Which of your bars do you recommend?" Maya said.

"Why, this one," she said. "What're you looking for?"

"Music," Maya said. "Isn't there music?"

They were sent to the jukebox at the Stockman. Alex attempted to object on the grounds that it was no place for an eight-year-old, but the Stockman turned out to be as full of cowboy-hatted ranch men drinking steadily at the bar as children dashing between tables.

Thundering out of the jukebox was a pop song by a girl who was never going to love again that was on the radio out east. When it ended, the male half of another family of tourists shyly approached the jukebox and selected country music. The singer warbled as if through a mouthful of liquor, but his message was the same—he was done loving. How much were these promises worth?

They settled at a table and watched the dance floor fill with the tourists and an older couple, these eighty apiece. The tourists danced too much and the old ones too little, their hips limited. A waitress whose breasts were insignificantly penned by a halter top brought Maya a vodka neat, Alex a ginger ale, and another ginger ale for the cutie pie. Max swung his legs up and down—his stool was too high for him—but without his earlier anomie.

"I'm hungry," he said, adding to Maya's guilt about dragging the two of them to do what she wanted. And did she really want it? She wanted only to keep distracting herself. Tomorrow, she would think about the conversation with Harry—tomorrow, tomorrow, tomorrow. It was her birthday, after all. She would celebrate it by facing the truth. But there were hours and hours till then, an almost-endless collection of fifteen-minute increments. She was grateful to the booze for making it possible not to think of Laurel and Tim, and she was grateful to Laurel and Tim for the way they would push Marion out of her mind tomorrow. She had rigged it up ably.

"We'll just have this one and go," Maya said. "It's bedtime for you, soon."

"Happy birthday, Mama," Max said.

Stifling tears, she kissed his hair.

"Are you and Mama going to dance?" Max asked his father.

"Your papa isn't a very good dancer," Alex said. "And this is special music. You have to know how to dance to this music."

"They don't look like they know," Max said, nodding at the tourist couple, who clutched each other and swung back and forth.

Even though he came in and out of view due to the back-and-forth of the dancers, Maya knew she was looking at Marion Hostetler on the other side of the bar. Her expectations had been wrong every step of the way—no Laurel and Tim, nothing from Max—but of this she was plainly and brutally certain. Trying to do the right thing, she struck out, but the wrong—it was hers with ease and precision.

Maya looked quickly at Alex; he hadn't seen him.

"I don't want this," Maya said at her drink, nearly full. She saw

Marion looking at them from across the room. She made herself look away. "Max needs to get fed. Let's go."

Alex looked at her, puzzled. "You want to go back to the restaurant? Let's just get something here."

"Please, Alex," she said. "This noise is too much. I'm getting a migraine. Let's go."

"All right, all right," he said. "I'll flag her and pay."

"No, I'll pay," Maya said. "Please wait outside."

Alex stared, baffled.

"Alex, please, just go outside with Max. Right now, please."

Alex shrugged—it was no time to try to make sense of his wife. He slid off his stool and held out his hand for their son. Max gulped the ginger ale, hitting bottom before mother and father could get him to stop. He burped. Then he took his father's hand and they went outside. When the door closed behind them, Maya sprang out of her seat and crossed the bar.

"What are you doing?" she said.

"I don't know," Marion said.

"In front of my husband and son," she said.

"Now it's a problem?" Marion said.

"Marion," she said coldly.

"I didn't know how else to find you."

"So don't find me."

He glared at her. Then he set down his drink on the warped wood of the bar. It wobbled, and they both reached for it, but it held. "I'll go," he said.

"Wait," she held up one hand as she covered her eyes with the other. "I'm sorry, wait. How did you find us?"

"There's only one hotel in town," Marion said.

"Wilma? What did you say?"

"I said I wanted to surprise my brother for his birthday."

"Oh, hon, you're here now," the waitress winked at Maya. "One more vodka neat? Gentleman paying?"

Maya shook her head. Her palms were wet; the last drink had

taken her from a manageable looseness to unstable feet. She asked
for water. She wanted to be clear for this. She shivered as if she
were cold, though the bar was steamy with laughter and music. It
seemed like a nice place to hide out when the weather finally got
around to delivering. There were more couples on the dance floor
now. She felt for Marion's arm to steady herself. He was still wearing the plaid that was on her shoulders during the night.

"The girls?" she asked absentmindedly.

"We were going our separate ways anyway. They have school.
They're just being polite to their dad—their mind's on schoolwork
and boys. I turned toward home and then I drove past it. And kept
driving. And driving. You shouldn't have told me what town."

"I shouldn't have," she said. "I did, though." She turned pale:
"Are you staying at the hotel?"

"No, I wouldn't do that," he said. "I have a room in Sheff City.
It's fifteen miles down the road." He smiled sadly, his eyes nar-
rowing and then opening again, but a touch slower, as if he needed
rest. "It's too cold to camp tonight. It's going to snow tomorrow."

"Marion," she said, but had nothing to add.

"It was a mistake," he said. "I'll leave." He swallowed down the
last of his drink.

"Impressive work," the waitress nodded at the glass, but they all
knew what she was talking about.

"You must be new," he said, and put a ten-dollar bill into the
glass, the edge soaking up the final bit of the drink. "You'll buy
some discretion with the change." The waitress's eyes got big and
Maya felt vindication.

"Don't know why Wilma sent you to the Stockman," Marion
said.

"You've been here," Maya said. "You've been everywhere."

"I spent the summers near here when I was fifteen through
eighteen. They've always been rude at the Stockman."

"I told Wilma I wanted music," Maya said.

He nodded at the dance floor. "Some other time."

"Marion," she said. Marion, Marion, Marion. "I can't."

"You can't," he said. "I'm heartless for trying."

"No . . ." she started. "You must know . . ." She couldn't get out what she wanted to say in the pitiless amount of time before Alex became confused and came back inside.

"You go first," he said. "I'll settle your bill. Go."

She didn't move. "That I can't manage to either."

"Go, Maya," he said. "Go."

She walked away like a ghost.

The meal at the Dundee stretched interminably. Max exhibited the first signs of life since leaving New Jersey. He wanted the flank steak, though he ate only the part that flapped over the plate. Maya would have said no to such a large meal, but she felt too guilty. Alex finished it in addition to his own shepherd's pie. Maya's hands shook and she drank water even though she had no taste for it. Incredibly, Max asked for dessert. Max never asked for dessert. Even as Maya welled with relief at seeing her son recover his appetite and a measure of energy, it meant the protraction of her misery, more time until she could bury her head in a pillow and make herself fall asleep. She pleaded for tonight to be a night when, because of misery, she fell asleep instead of stayed up. Once upon a time, she had slept soundly, like her son when he was an infant. Could he have got that from her, in some osmotic way? Or was it a coincidence, and actually he owed it to something about his genes? Maybe Alex had been more right than wrong about that. She was condemned to ask herself questions like this for the rest of her life. Perhaps she should drink not water, but more alcohol. Obliterate herself to make sure she fell asleep as soon as her head touched the pillow. She would pay for it the next day, but that was the next day. She was willing to spend her birthday in pieces if it only meant this day would end.

Maya and Alex watched Max go at a sundae. He managed only a fraction. Maya was relieved, but Alex took on leftovers again, and they waited while he worked.

"She does okay, Wilma," Alex said, looking up from the empty plate and wiping his mouth. Misery made him hungry. Maybe he wasn't miserable. He was going home tomorrow.

The proprietress refused to take money. "That potato gratin went over like hotcakes," she said. "Things are usually slowing down this time, but I had my busiest night of the month. I had two fellows from up near Worth who ate their meals and then ordered second sides of the gratin on top."

Maya left a twenty-dollar tip on the table. She did not want to owe anyone anything. Alex looked at her disapprovingly, but did not interfere.

Maya felt vile undressing in the light, as if her betrayal was painted all over her. Max had been put to sleep in a little alcove next to the main room. It was just her and Alex, without the protection and distraction of Max. Alex seemed as if he had forgotten all about Laurel and Tim. So had she. That was Marion's gift. She'd never asked him about the paint flecks on his wrist. Was he a painter? A housepainter? She didn't even know what he did for a living. How could you come so close with someone without knowing what they did for a living?

"Maya," her husband called to her again. He had already climbed into bed.

She looked down at him vacantly.

"Are you thinking of them?" he said. He was trying to be thoughtful, and she tried to be grateful.

"Yes," she said. "What is it?"

"Switch off the light. I forgot the light."

In minutes, Alex was wheezing into his pillow as if he were at home. She lay next to him silently. She envied his comfort—and he was the one who had insisted it was uncomfortable here. She had been wrong—it would not be a night when she would drop into sleep. To avoid waking Alex, she tried to avoid moving. She was an odd prisoner, no bars but she couldn't move. So she lay, incarcerated in position, and wept silently at the ceiling.

The clock was past two A.M. when she allowed herself to slip from the bed. She tiptoed to the bathroom. The ventilator's rattle was shocking after the silence of the bedroom, and she closed the door too loudly. Heart beating, she listened to make out whether she had woken anyone, but no sound came. To get rid of the noise, she had to switch off the light, and was plunged into darkness.

She thought about climbing into the bathtub and letting hot water run over her, but the darkness of the room was so complete that she would make new noise. So she sat on the closed toilet in the darkness and stared at the wall. She was out of tears, and just stared.

Her mother had told her a story: Her own father had walked into the bathroom one night to relieve himself. He didn't like to turn on lights. But when he relieved himself, he relieved himself all over his wife, because she had had the same idea and then fallen asleep on the toilet. Maya stifled a mirthless laugh. The story was ludicrous.

It was not one of her mother's inventions; it was from life. And yet, the story seemed impossible, contrived, whereas the stories her mother told and invented felt true. Maya had been taken from her mother too soon to tell the difference well, though her mother hadn't helped; she hadn't drawn the line well. The natural relation between Maya and her mother, between children and parents, had been terminated by Maya's love affair with Alex. This was the true curse of the way she had emigrated, a curse Alex would never experience. At that moment, Maya was a child who wanted her mother.

Time had lost its shape. She rose—why now? why not ten minutes before? if she was not outside herself, she was not inside herself either—and maneuvered open the door. In the room, she stared at her clothes, hung neatly on the back of a chair, as if she could correct for the betrayal in her heart by being neat outside of it. She began dressing. The keys to the Escape were on Alex's nightstand. He had repurposed a small dish from the bathroom to double for the wicker basket at home, and her heart squirmed at fishing the keys out of the dish. Now she made noise. Now she wanted to be caught. But he slept.

Walking downstairs, she marveled again at the power of greater predicaments to diminish the lesser: She would have to drive herself down snow-flecked roads in the night, and yet she felt no fear, only numbness. It was useful. Sometimes numbness was useful. She was stunned to discover Wilma napping in a soft chair behind the reception desk. She stirred on hearing Maya's footfalls.

"You do all of it," Maya said in disbelief.

Wilma rubbed her eyes and stared at the clock. "I do all of it," she repeated drowsily and yawned. "Mr. Gund hasn't been with us for a number of years. What in God's name has you up at three thirty?"

"Where is Sheff City?" Maya asked.

"Sheff City? What do you want with Sheff City at this hour? Is everything all right?"

"I can't tell you," Maya said, holding back tears. She hoped Wilma would understand and not press.

"I see," Wilma said. "It's fifteen miles down the road. That way." She stuck out a chafed finger. It was raw with cooking, dishwashing, laundry.

"Is there only one hotel there, like here?" Maya said.

"Did you have a fight? I have other rooms. I'll give you one for free. No need to drive in the night."

"It's not that," Maya shook her head.

"There's three," Wilma said. "The Hansen place, Overlook, and Fish and Fawn. Sheff City's on the river there, so they got the angler business. Wait a minute—did your husband's brother find you? I just thought of that."

"It's him I'm going to see," Maya said.

Wilma gave her a long look. "I better not ask any more questions," she said. "You don't know his hotel?"

"He said only Sheff City."

"You sure he wants to be found?"

Maya shrugged helplessly.

"Well, he's probably at the Hansen. By the look of him, he's probably at the Hansen."

"Why the look of him?"

"Fish and Fawn is for the yuppie folks from California. The Overlook—that's a frat party. So I'd say the Hansen."

Maya remained in place, midway down the runner to the front door. "I admire you," she said finally.

Wilma waved her away.

"I'm sorry," Maya slurred. "It's hard for me to find the right words. I meant only that—if I lived here . . . I would enjoy seeing you."

Wilma gave her a wondering look. "Well, at least one of you can have a job in my kitchen whenever he wants. Now get out there, get your drive over with. It's getting cold."

"I'm sorry for waking you," Maya said.

Wilma waved her away once again.

Sheff City was in the direction of Laurel and Tim's home. Harry Sprague's home. Maya would not be allowed to forget. But she didn't wish to forget. She climbed behind the wheel, and, after a tottering start because she had pressed the gas too firmly, slid onto the road. There was not one car on the low-lit street; soon the streets ended and she was in pure, rural darkness. But the headlights were powerful and lit the way clearly. She pulled over carefully, tinkered with the controls by the wheel until she found the beams, and pulled back out, fingering the lever from time to time so she knew where to flick if a car was oncoming. But no cars were oncoming.

She stole looks at the odometer. When 8.9 miles turned to 9, she gazed off in the direction of Harry Sprague's house. There, shrouded in darkness, was the car that had delivered her son eight years before. That spot—all that remained of Laurel and Tim— would vibrate in her heart. Every time she saw a map, she would think of the distance to *that* spot. She did not have to be physically present for that to transpire. But it couldn't have without her seeing the place. That was the trick of it, at least for her—she had to see it to know.

She drove into the night, a driver at last. It turned out to be easy, the car sensible, wanting to be driven; she felt proud of herself. All this time she had feared the unnecessary. She had preferred to fear. Her fear of the idea had been so large that she had not bothered to wonder if the practical fear behind it was great; she took for granted it was. Alex occasionally groaned at having to drive her, but never pressed her to learn. Was this a kindness or unkindness? Both. But it was from him, in the afternoon, that she had got her first real lesson. She said thanks to him.

She thought about Laurel. Driving was like washing dishes, like weeding a garden—it busied your hands and gave your mind recess, like the parent expert at keeping a child distracted. And so Maya allowed herself to drift off. She allowed herself to imagine, finally, lights up ahead, coming. They were festive: What other person had business on this road at this abandoned, desolate hour? A secret meeting in the night, while everyone slept. As the cars neared each other—Maya slowed down to be careful; her heart was beating too fast and she was paying attention to too much at once—the other car came to a standstill and switched off its lights. It sat in the road strangely, like an animal killed in an unnatural place. Maya jammed the brake. She wasn't smooth with it, the car bucked, and she jumped a little in her seat. She stopped well ahead of the other car. Then, embarrassed to be shown for a novice, she crawled forward until the hoods were even. She turned off her headlights, killed the ignition, and waited in a ticking silence as the cold moon lit up the road. It was less dark with the lights off.

When Laurel got out of the other car, Maya scrambled out of the Escape. Laurel's car looked like the Rubins' Corolla, one of those sedans—Maxima, Altima, Sentra—whose name ended in a vowel and to Maya said: family. Laurel wore what the waitress from the diner wore when she went to the bank for the afternoon shift: a black skirt, a crisp white shirt, a black jacket. Panty hose, and heels with a strap: not fashionable, not dowdy. The hair was pulled up in a bun. It was the unblemished face eight years later—with some blemishes. They stood in the moonlight, staring at each other.

"It's you," Maya said like a fool.

"Is it?" Laurel touched her own face carefully, as if it were a mask. "The face cream I go through."

Maya's fingertips came up near Laurel's cheek, seeking permission. The younger woman nodded. Her skin felt puffy but smooth. Maya let go and closed her fingers, trying to hold the feel of Laurel inside them, but it was instantly gone.

"Won't you help me," Maya said.

Laurel cleared a strand of hair from one eye. "Do you know what my dad said once when I was little? I don't remember what kind of competition it was—shooting or riding. I was six? seven? You know how little girls get with their dads. God and Santa Claus rolled into one. He said, 'All these moms and dads saying 'good luck, honey,' 'good luck, honey.' Well, I ain't gonna wish you luck. You know why? 'Cause you're good luck yourself.' I didn't know what he meant. But I felt very special. Like a horse, for some reason. Isn't that funny? As sleek and strong and beautiful as a horse. Must have been riding, then. Anyway—I get it now. I use it back on him. He hasn't spoken to me in eight years and sometimes I talk to him in my head, and I say, 'I don't need you to answer—I'm all the luck that I need. I'm going to talk to you anyway.'"

"My father ever gave me only one piece of advice," Maya said. "'Ignore absolutely everything I say. Listen only to your mother.'"

They shared a small laugh.

"I am so much older than you," Maya said, "but I feel the opposite. Why is that? Maybe coming to America should count as zero? I would be twenty-five then. If I count from the year I met Alex, it's twenty. This is a good game. You can keep going until you explain why you don't know anything."

Laurel's mouth fluted into a look of impatience, setting off apprehension in Maya. "Did you call me here because you wanted to berate yourself in front of an audience?" Laurel said. The wind gusted between them, rattling their shoulders. Laurel drew her palms up her forearms—slowly, deliberately, like someone who knew how her body worked. She shivered. "I forgot this cold real quick once we moved."

"Tell me where you are," Maya said.

"Not here," Laurel said.

"Please," Maya said.

"We're okay. It's a little town near a big town that lost lots of jobs, so they made it real easy for young couples to settle. We were welcomed. Tim coaches track. Little gimpy for a track coach but the kids love him. We've got a nice house. If my parents knew what I made . . . they'd disown me all over again."

"You mean so little?"

"No—so much."

Maya nodded fervidly to cover her embarrassment at all the things the Rubins had allowed themselves to think about Laurel and Tim. "So you and Tim are together," she said.

"Why wouldn't we be? Didn't we give up enough?"

"I'm sorry," Maya said. "I didn't mean—"

"Won't you stop apologizing?"

Maya raked her fingernails across her chest, as if that would scrape off the unease there.

"Why was that, by the way, Mrs. Rubin?" Laurel said. "I brought you the child—I brought you Max—but you kept apologizing to me. What had you done wrong?"

"I'll talk with you about anything—only don't call me Mrs. Rubin."

Laurel gave a soft nod.

"I don't know," Maya said, falling back against the Escape. It was warm from the miles it had driven. She placed both palms on the frame. The car purred into her hands; it was glad to be held, and she didn't want to let go. For a moment, she forgot Laurel and stared at the dim outline of the peaks rising by the side of the road. She turned back to Laurel. "Did you ever . . ." she said, hoping she would be understood.

"Two," Laurel said. "A boy and girl."

Maya took a knuckle in her mouth. Laurel could give one up and still come out ahead. "Tell me," Maya said. "Please."

"Grant and Adelaide. Six and three. Against every odds, they get along. Tim named one, I named the other."

"Why 'against every odds'?" Maya said hopefully. She resented the family's fortune and relished the news of an obstacle.

"Because they're a boy and a girl. At six and three it's like sixty and thirty."

"I wouldn't know," Maya said, defeated once more.

"You know other things."

"How much time do I have with you?"

"I don't have any of the answers you want," Laurel said.

"This will make you angry with me—but it sounds like you don't think of him."

"I think of him. All the time. As your son."

"I'll find you. He needs to know you. Something about him can't rest until he knows about you. What is that called? There's a name for it."

"You're thinking of purgatory. Tim and I are Lutherans—we don't believe in that. Not that it matters. You didn't put us in purgatory. What Tim and I did—it either brings you closer to God, or it takes you away. For good."

"Then Max is the one lost."

"So find him."

Maya held her lips tight. Laurel took her by the forearms. "Now, will you let me go? It took so long to get out of here. I thought it was rodeo, or my dad, that made me want to so bad. And the whole time it was probably weather." Her eyes lit up with the small joke.

Maya listened to Max's mother's heels click the pavement. Then the sedan started up, a resolved, confident sound. Maya held up a palm in good-bye. The window rolled down.

"It's you who can't rest," Laurel said. "He sees you and can't rest."

"That's what my husband says," Maya said. "How do I switch it off?"

"You think that's what you ought to do?"

Maya heard the gearshift lurch inside Laurel's hand. It was easy to imagine her executing whatever duties required her to wear such an outfit, and draw the paycheck she did. Why did Maya feel like a fool next to Laurel? That evening eight years before, Laurel had been rock-faced with Tim, indifferent to Alex and Mishkin. Even Max had failed to move her when she walked past him for the last time. Because of this, in the years since, Maya imagined Laurel as some kind of adult who couldn't be pleased. But the girl had been only eighteen. If she hadn't turned herself to stone before crossing Maya's threshold, she would have gone up in flames with bereavement. But now Laurel was not playing at strength. Now she was—grown and strong.

"I'm happy he comes from you," Maya whispered, too quietly for Laurel to hear under the roar of her engine.

+

Sheff City was not a city—it was smaller than Adelaide, with only one real street, and bad cell-phone service. The Yellowstone River, which Maya could hear but not see, a silver rush in the darkness, explained why the town had three motels to Adelaide's one, and why the Hansen Motel could afford to make the Dundee in Adelaide look freshly renovated by comparison.

There was only one window that showed burning light. Unwilling to think harder, Maya walked to it and knocked softly. She turned around to see if she could recognize Marion's car in the parking lot, but realized she didn't know what he drove. There were only three cars in the parking lot. The season was ending.

She was about to knock again when Marion opened the door. He blinked repeatedly, like a child trying to waken.

"You were asleep," she said.

"It's not really a sleeping night," he said. "I don't know when I went under." He squinted. "You're standing in front of me."

"I'm standing in front of you. Whatever made you follow us to Adelaide, Marion—I hope it will also keep you from asking me to explain."

"You don't have to explain," he said. He moved so she could walk in.

It was the flower room. There were flowers on the wallpaper, the towels, the bedding, even in the air, industrial jasmine hitting the room from plug-ins in the sockets.

"I haven't seen a hotel room in ten years," Maya said. "And now two in one day. It's awful, this room."

"It's awful," Marion said.

She sat down carefully on the edge of one of the unmade beds; there were three in the room. Alex disliked street clothes mingling with sheets where they slept nearly bare. She marveled bitter-ly—in her lover's hotel room, she respected her husband's predi-lections. She wondered what her son had gotten from her, but she did not have to wonder what she had got from her husband. She was struck by the simple headlong power of twenty years together. She felt like a survivor.

"Can I fix you something?" he said. "Tea? Well, it'll be time for coffee soon." The clock said after four.

Maya's eyes filled with tears. She didn't bother to bring her hands over them. She couldn't bear to wipe down more tears. Soon, she would have hands like Wilma Gund, only because of sadness, not work. Marion sat down and covered her. She turned into him and cried harder, cried as she would have to her mother. She used him for her mother. She felt that he knew that and didn't mind. She loved him for that.

"You should sleep," he said. "A long day."

"I don't believe it will end," she said.

"Were the parents there?"

Maya shook her head, unclear whether she meant they were not or she could not bear to speak about it. He didn't press. She loved him for that, too.

"I don't want to sleep yet," she said. "I've been thinking of you since morning. You are the only person I've wanted to speak to all day. Even more than Laurel and Tim. How can that be? How can I be this person? And then you appeared."

"Come," he said. "Stand."

"Why? Look at your shirt, I've made a mess of it."

"This prize number?" he said. "Stand with me. You said you wanted to dance."

"Dance?" she said through her tears and laughed sourly.

"What kind of music do you like?"

"Please don't distract me. Alex is always steering me away. He thinks he's committing a kindness. I used to think so, too." She looked up. "I'm sorry to mention him."

"It doesn't matter if you mention him or not," Marion said. "And I'm sorry."

"I don't know what kind of music," she said. "The kind they played in the bar. The kind that was on when we spoke—not what they were playing at first."

Marion rose and pulled a little radio out of his duffel bag and played with the dial. He set it on the night table and held his hand out to Maya. She came close and he wrapped her up.

"This is going to be a disappointment if you expect much better than swaying," he said. "My last dance was at high school prom, thirty-five years ago."

She closed her eyes and shook her head; don't speak.

They swayed clumsily, though little by little they eased into it and found more of each other's rhythm. The radio station had no short supply of bluesy, wailing songs. Marion had not pulled shut the shades, and any passing guest could get an eyeful of two people slow-dancing. Marion called out the names—Gene Autry, Loretta Lynn, Johnny Horton—as they came on. They were just sounds to Maya, pure foreignness. But she felt calmed by the plaintive, twanging music, the gentleness with which the men and women sang of ungentle things. She couldn't make out most of the words, but what she caught did not suggest major happiness.

She opened the top two buttons on Marion's shirt and wedged the side of her face into the open space, up against his breastbone.

"You have a good one," she said.

"Do you know?" he said.

"It's beating fast."

"Cigarettes and dancing."

She removed her face and looked at him. "Will you lie down with me?"

He motioned to the three beds. "You choose."

"Why are there so many? Do people never come through here alone? I would come here alone and sleep for a year."

"You can put three snoring fishermen in here for fifteen dollars a person. Makes them feel like the away football game all over again."

"The one by the window," she said. The large, three-paned window was the room's only grace; the owner knew he could not compete with the landscape. You could see none of it now, only blackness swirling with motes of snow in the sharp triangle of light that fell from a streetlight somewhere above the motel. The motes settled like dust; evidently the wind had died down. The cold, antiseptic brightness of the fluorescent light was mellowed by the silver shadows given off by the dusting of snow.

Marion started to unfurl the bedspread, but she motioned against it. She was in street clothes and could not muster the force to remove them. She went down and he fitted himself around her. She smelled the wood smoke with sweat. They watched the snow.

"I'm so tired, Marion," she said. He laid his hand on her shoulder, and it fell under his touch. "Aren't you?" she mumbled. "Just for a minute."

"Shhhh," he said.

She dreamed of nothing.

+

She awoke with first light; the sun was difficult to imagine behind all the gauze in the sky, but even its gray hit her eyes with unfamiliar sharpness. The knowledge of what she had done worked its way through her with terrible force. The alarm clock was on Marion's side of the bed, but it didn't matter what time it was; it was light outside.

She slid from Marion's grasp and stepped toward the window. Now the mountains were visible; in the daylight, you could not look away from them.

"One thing you'll never be able to do," he said. She looked back—she had woken him. He was propped up on an elbow, the other hand rubbing an eye. "See yourself the way I can right now."

"What do you see?" she said.

He took his hand away and looked at her thoroughly. "You could stay," he said.

She turned back to the window and watched the snow settle. "After two days, you are ready for that?"

"You live for fifty-two years so you can know what you want in two days," he said.

"Twenty years later, don't we end up where Alex and I've ended up? Where you and Clarissa did? Doesn't it all come to the same thing?"

"In twenty years, I'll try to save you the trouble and be dead," he said. "But no—you are wrong about that. I can't prove it to you because I haven't lived it—I've lived the opposite. But I know."

She smiled weakly. "I could cook for Wilma," she said. "She needs the help. We could buy a motel—make it something it should be."

"Why didn't you open that café that you wanted?" he said.

She nodded, as if agreeing with something he'd said.

"Won't you tell me?" he said.

She watched him with pity. "What could be interesting about me, Marion?"

"I look for explanations only if I need explanations," he said.

She turned back to the window and looked out at the morning. "When I told them I wanted to do it, they looked at me as if I'd said I wanted to take Alex and move back to Ukraine."

"Which them?"

"My parents-in-law. Eugene—my father-in-law—said: 'So you mean on the weekends?' I explained again, but he still thought I meant I wanted to come work with him—he imports food. He thought I wanted to cook the food. 'But why? It's cooked already.' Finally, I got through. So he called a friend with a restaurant, and got me on the line for a day. He said, 'Why speculate? Educated people make decisions based on facts and experience.' My father-in-law, the logician.

"I had lead in my legs that day. Bricks in my hands and lead in my legs. I bumped the other cooks. I scattered an entire container of smoked eel on the floor. Smoked eel—it's burned into my mind. Nervous, I guess. It was different from the kind of food I wanted to make—heavy sauces, all that sugar. Of course, they didn't ask me back.

"Soon after that, Eugene gave me an ad in the newspaper. An opening in mammography at the hospital down the road. I would be home early enough to get Max from the school bus. I already had a semester of radiology from school, and he knew the department manager because he catered their holidays. He had found a way for me to try out at the restaurant; couldn't I try this out in turn? So I did. I intended to return the favor, and then go back to my plans. This is how I understood the new situation: I had new people to take into account; I had to try. But, you know, I liked the hospital. Because I was expecting so little? I liked being around all that sickness and death; I was alive by comparison. It was me and six or eight women, all older; Dominican, Italian, Greek, Cuban: I never had to bring lunch from home. I liked all that equipment in my hands: it was solid. I learned how to use it. I became good at it. At the end of the day, I didn't have to wonder what the day had been worth.

"I thought, maybe Eugene was right, and simply no one had cared about me deeply enough to open my eyes to the truth. Maybe I had been holding my breath for four years—I had come only for college, on a student visa; there are so many things you don't know about me, Marion. Maybe cooking was just a trance of some kind—because I missed my mother, I missed home. And now that I'd found a new family, it was over, and I had a new direction. Truthfully, I was relieved. A fear went out of me. I thought: So I will not get to do that. It was like saying good-bye to a complicated lover. The love went, but so did the heartache."

"You keep saying your father-in-law. What about your husband? What did he say?"

"He didn't say anything. I thought he was trying to respect me by not getting in the way."

Marion only nodded at something.

"It sounds so bad spoken out loud. I've never spoken it out loud before."

"Why?"

"No one's asked. But also I didn't tell anyone. Whom to tell? We have no friends. I have no friends. You're my first friend in twenty-five years in America."

"I don't want to be your friend."

"What about Max?" she said. "Have you thought of that?"

"He would be here, with you. Where he's from."

"He's not from here anymore," she said. "Max doesn't want to be in Montana. He wants to be wild in New Jersey. And I have to be where he is." She looked out the window again. "I have to protect him from his family."

"And where do you want to be?" he said.

Maya exhaled. "I can't stop looking at the mountains. It's so easy to go your whole life without seeing them. Without seeing anything, really. I wanted to know yesterday: Do they become invisible to you? In a month or a year, would they become ordinary?"

"Now you don't steer away."

She looked back at him with love. "I want to be here, Marion."

"So, we'll answer every question," he said. "I wouldn't say this—" he started and broke off.

"Go ahead. If you thought I loved Alex." She waited out a pause. "But I do love him. I thought I was marrying someone of ambition, creativity, power. The power to bewitch. He was awkward and tentative—so unlike the boys I had known. But he kept going—he kept after what he wanted even though it wouldn't come easily. Doesn't it count so much more that way? It did to me then, at any rate. Even though it wasn't right, even though I had a boyfriend—he kept going. He could not stop; it was passion. He bewitched me—in the last way I thought I would be bewitched. That felt so right—I thought I knew everything, and he showed me I didn't." She thought for a moment. "Is that a story I tell myself? Maybe it was much simpler than that, and I only wanted to sell myself to America. Once you start looking inside yourself in this way, there's no more hope of a clear answer."

She rubbed her fingertips on the glass of the window, as if trying to leave a trace of herself. "It was some time before I understood that the things that I loved were an anomaly for him. It wasn't what he loved about himself. Then I thought he wanted help getting back to them. I was wrong. And then we just . . . stayed that way. I wouldn't let go. Like letting go was another defeat—so young, and already so many defeats. My stubbornness about cooking—maybe I turned it into a stubbornness about us. I would change him—it would get better. And then Max . . . But the solution is not to ruin Alex's life—this family's. Not yet, at least. Don't I have to unfail myself before I fail him? I am not asking you to wait. All I can say is I don't know. And I love you. I do love you."

They sat with this miserable information.

"When I told you that Max was adopted," she said finally. "Did you think why?"

He worked at his lip with his teeth. "Was it that you two couldn't . . . ?"

"Yes," she said. "Did you wonder who?"

"No," he said. "I have children; that's not what matters to me."

"Do you want to know who?"

"It doesn't matter to me," he said. "Tell me if you want me to know."

"Alex can't have children. He has Klinefelter's—a syndrome. They discovered it when we tried to get pregnant. But his parents think it's me. They decided that I was infertile and that he was covering up for me, a gentleman. Little by little, that story became fact. A word here, a word there. It bothered me at first, but then you think, Who cares, anyway? If they knew their son was infertile, they would not sleep at night. They would feel as if life had laughed in their face. But I . . . they love me. In the way they know how. But I will always be the adopted daughter. So if it's me, they can go to sleep at night. Though I am sure they worry: Will Max inherit this blemish from Maya? And then they remember Max is not Maya's. And this helps them sleep. Max wouldn't exist in our lives without the blemish, but they couldn't sleep calmly if the opposite was the case, wondering if he would inherit it. The release is built into the flaw."

He watched her silently, absorbing the information.

She exhaled at the glass of the window, leaving a mark that then narrowed and vanished. She turned the shades so that the room was invisible to anyone outside, but, properly angled on the bed, one could still make out the mountains a little. Crossing her arms, she raised her blouse over her head. She shivered though the room had warmed up overnight. Her skin was paler than the snow outside. She removed her bra and her small breasts fell free. She stepped out of her pants, then her underwear—she had been wearing homely white briefs, but could not induce herself to feel shame. She lowered herself onto the bed. She had forgotten to take off her socks.

Marion was motionless on his side of the bed. She was seeing a new expression on his face, and she thought how much more there was to learn about him. If they had a life together, she would learn something new about him over and over. It would not end for many years, and perhaps ever.

She tried to fit him for the mask of death she had slipped so easily onto her mother, and herself, and Alex, and Max. But she could not picture Marion as anything other than there, his face taken up with a mournful amusement. He was older than her, but despite the slightly bent fingers, the tiredness around the eyes, and the loose skin she felt feeling his heart, it felt more difficult to imagine his death. Perhaps she knew him too little, had him too flimsily to be able to calmly let go. And yet, she felt she knew him. Some things, she knew. She knew that if he walked out of the room, she would love him. If he took off his clothes, but wore a condom, she would love him. If he didn't use a condom, but nothing came of it, she would love him. If he didn't, and something did, still she would. Every single outcome was the right one.

Her legs parted slightly from a slow-sweeping lurch in her stomach. She felt a dull furrow open, as if by a sledgehammer dragged by someone too young to lift it. It was her—she was dragging the sledgehammer. She was on Misha's farm, dragging the sledgehammer, everything still up ahead. From the furrow things wanted to spill. The sensation was of some sort of impending evacuation, and she turned over because it was all happening there. Her knees, pressed into the roughly starched cotton of the bedsheet, nearly buckled but she grunted and dug in. She pushed her face hard into the pillow so that no light came in—she wanted to be underwater without adequate air. She closed her fingers over the thin vertical iron slats of the headboard, such as it was, and dug her nails into her skin. She would love him if he walked out of the room, but if she heard the buckle snapping on his jeans, the flop and rustle of denim—she would love him a little bit more.

"Your son is wild because of you," Marion said.

She looked up at him insolently, and said: "Don't be frightened of me."

The first thing she felt were two fingers on the strong vein inside of her thigh. They ran down it, feeling it like an old scar. Then his hands moved to her ass, and he held it in his hands like two breasts, just holding, like a cat with tinfoil in its mouth. He spread the cheeks with his fingers, and she let out a soft groan while reaching for his jeans buckle. Working with one hand, she undid the button and zipper and pulled down the jeans around his thighs. He wore nothing under them. Sliding out from under his touch, she pushed her face into his groin, and inhaled around him. He smelled clean, human but clean, like the leaves that stay cool on the floor of the woods even though the sun is shining with force. His penis was warm on her cheek, and she pressed her head into it. They were oddly positioned, like two wrestlers in an impasse, no winner, he on the bed on his knees, she worked into him like a burrow. His hands scaled and descended her back, the two panels on either side of the spine like the wings of a book, firm board over soft flesh.

When they had enough of feeling each other, they rearranged themselves on the sheets, Maya under Marion, the blanket kicked around their feet. The room was submerged in a half gloom; Maya felt around herself a softly swallowing grayness broken only by the vague shape of his body. Alex came into her mind, but instead of shutting her eyes against him, she apologized to him for feeling none of the fault he wished she would feel—she would begin feeling it as soon as this ended, but she wanted to do this now, forgive me, my love—and waited until he went away. When Marion entered her, his hands levered on her hip bones below him, she kinked up her back, drove the crown of her head into the mass of pillows beneath it, and issued a low, satisfied grunt at the uneven ceiling. Then she clasped his arms and forced him down onto her. She wanted his weight.

Though Marion was only slightly taller, their bodies did not have the same rhythm; he pushed in while she was pushing out. Eventually, she smiled sheepishly at him, and he, licensed by her, at her. Uninstructed, he withdrew. She slid out from under him and pointed with a finger at the pillow, which now went under his head. His erection faltered, and he muttered sheepishly. She closed his mouth with her lips. It was their first kiss. It seemed so belated. There was so much else that they'd forgotten to kiss. There was old sleep on his tongue, but she wanted it. She wanted everything having to do with him. She lifted her lips from his for the second it took to say "I want everything having to do with you" and then covered his mouth again before he could answer, though his eyes answered her—with disbelief and rising desire. They kissed for so long that they forgot everything else.

In the night, the difference between one minute and four works differently, but they kissed for four minutes, not one. Then they stopped kissing and lay hidden in each other's mouths until Maya felt the outer edges of sleep. No. She withdrew herself from him, and pulled her lips down to his chest, covering one nipple with her teeth, her hair falling over his chest. Then the other. It stirred him—she felt him growing full under her. She unsealed herself from his chest with a long inhalation. Then she took his penis with her fingers, and worked it inside herself. The rhythm was better this way. Her back kinked again, she raised and lowered herself on him while their bellies took sweat from each other. Each lowering-down was a soft pop, her ass on his thighs. She preferred down, because she felt more of him. Now, some milestone having passed, she allowed herself to make noise—a long call, meant to travel. He was shyer than her, and it was several minutes before he forgot his reticence and moaned with an uncomplicated satisfaction.

She was consumed by his look of stupefied wonder—wonder at her. She had never seen a man more plainly happy. So even in the midst of all that was happening, plain happiness was available. She would not have dared to guess. She felt for his face, and scratched it with her fingernails. His neck, ribbed with age. She wished her fingerprints to become altered by him; she wished for some part of him to pass into her in a way that wouldn't dry and leak out. He warned her that he was close. She warned him to remain inside her. She needed just a little bit more. But he was already lost to new information. He clasped her ass in his hands, and cast himself into her with a force he counted on her to understand and forgive, one finger grazing the pleated spout of her asshole every time he pushed up. It accelerated her, and they came almost at the same time, him hitting the walls of her so forcefully that he cried out. She fell on him; they ran with sweat, running off them onto the sheets. And again, they lay hidden in each other. Until he was soft enough that he slid out of her in the wetness. And still they remained, drying and leaking out and memorizing the other. To no value because memory is nothing next to the thing.

16

They drove back to the Dundee in silence. The storm, which in the night had only dusted the pavement, seemed to have changed its mind, the slate-gray sky swirling with snow. Because of the weather, Marion had offered to accompany her; he would find a lift back. She agreed—for no reason having to do with the weather. Her heart wobbled at seeing another man in the seat Alex had occupied, and occupied responsibly, for two thousand miles.

The mountains watched her go the way she had come with neither pity nor shame nor sympathy nor regret. Marion, who sometimes regarded her with the same motiveless curiosity, kept his eyes on the road and said nothing. She relished the silence, the snow like the cotton damping a wound. The new skin over the ground was thin, and only briefly unblemished, but it worked for the moment; she was at the remove that she wanted. For instance, the Escape was past the turnoff for 2207 New Missouri Trail South before Maya thought of Harry Sprague and Sangu Sethi—she saw her: big-lipped, big-haired, big shiny white teeth with a gap: the lurcher of the family—caught up in each other in bed, the dogs at their feet. She knew this steadiness would desert her soon, but it was holding for now, and past this she decided not to think. They were pulled up at the Dundee, idling, before she fully noticed they were in Adelaide.

"I want you to go upstairs, get your family, and drive out of here," he said. "We're in the outer ring now—it's going to keep getting worse before it gets better. You have an hour to outdrive it. I'm not asking only for you."

She told him yes, even though she didn't know whether she was telling the truth. It was so difficult to tell the truth; it didn't line up neatly with love.

She felt his face with her hand. He closed his eyes against it. When he opened them, he was looking at her through the grid of her fingers. He reached up, closed her hand with his, and returned it to her side. Then he stepped out of her car and stood in the falling snow until she walked out on the passenger side and clicked the alarm, which rang as if it were supposed to say something for them as well. He smiled the forestlike smile, the wrinkles at his eyes marked by neither love nor hostility, rather the baleful amusement she saw there sometimes. But before he walked away, the amusement was replaced by something that did resemble love. He nodded slightly, and in that small motion, Maya felt a greatness of love. She almost cried out for him. Then Marion flicked up the sheepskin collar of his jacket, hiked up his shoulders, and strode away. She watched him go.

From the balcony of Room 31, wearing nothing but a shirt, a pack of cigarettes crumpled on the table next to him, Alex watched also.

+

Room 31 was blacked out, the heavy shades drawn in full. Max was asleep on the rollaway in the alcove; the bedding on the queen was a mess. The room was heady with the papery aroma of hotel coffee, so stale that Maya's eyes burned with new fatigue at the scent of it. She had not slept properly in three nights. How much longer could she endure? She stood looking at her son for a long minute, so that if he awoke, he would have been frightened, a spectral shape in the room. Carefully, Maya parted the shades and slid open the heavy balcony door. Alex did not turn around. He gazed ahead, his hand shivering as he brought the filter of a smoked-down cigarette to his lips. He dragged on it before she could speak, burned himself, winced, but continued to hold the cigarette as smoke trickled through his teeth.

She called for him, and he turned around. Little red flashes ran through his eyes, and underneath there were gray pouches of puffy, blown-up skin. He opened his mouth to speak, but nothing came out, and he turned around to face the street once again. You could feel the coldness of his skin without touching him. A half-drunk cup of coffee waited next to the cigarettes, and next to it the coffeepot, nearly full.

She went back inside, upset the bed by pulling off the blanket, returned outside, and draped it over his shoulders. He shuddered at her touch. She put her arms on his shoulders.

"You got caught," he said.

"I wanted to be caught," she said.

He leaned forward to be free of her touch. "What kind of person are you?"

"Please look at me."

"You are the last thing I want to look at," he said.

"We will have to look at each other for two thousand miles. Please look at me."

"I don't want to know," he said.

"Please don't say that," she said. "Please stop saying that. I want you to know. I need you to know. I can't live any longer pretending we don't know what we know." She lowered herself next to him and encircled his waist with her arms. "I came back, Alex. But not because you've been sitting here killing yourself. Killing me."

"People don't change," he said.

"I need you to fail trying," she said. "For fifty years or so. Then you can stop. We will do it together."

"Together," he said derisively.

"Stop that," she said. "Stop it. Please."

"What do you want?" he said to the street.

"I want to go, Alex. I'm ready to go."

Alex stared at the snowflakes settling on the railing of the balcony. In less than a week they had gone from their living room to the balcony of this motel in a lost Western town, staring at weather they had not seen since their childhoods in Russia. He had been right, too right—disorder awaited just outside the walls of your home, walls eternally in need of shoring up and defense. However, his wife wanted the disorder—that was equally inarguable. What does a person do when his life comes to this kind of dissent, when it takes back the promise it's made? He didn't know. Simply, he didn't know. Alex stood up unsteadily, stared at the coffeepot as if about to bus it, then decided to leave it outside, snowflakes melting with a hiss on the still-warm glass of the pot. When they stepped inside, Max, as apparently fond of beds outside New Jersey as unfond of them there, farted and clutched the pillow more tightly.

+

They were sliding down an artery to the county road when Maya saw the sign: the Last Gasp Rodeo & Pancake Breakfast at the Adelaide Fairgrounds, down an artery off the artery. Maya looked at Alex, who had no objection left in him. "Just for a minute," she said. She turned to the backseat, from where Max looked up with slit eyes. He had been rushed through a breakfast of cereal and juice from a vending machine. "One last stop before we go," Maya said. And then she asked Marion's forgiveness for not leaving when she promised she would.

The detour required backing up—the road was too slick with snow to reverse; Alex would have to turn around in poor visibility without sagging into the irrigation ditch off to the side; the driving lanes were so narrow—so there was a long moment of Alex sitting silently after he had slid to a stop and put on his hazards. But then he lowered the window, stared carefully in both directions, jerked the vehicle forward, back, and forward again, and soon they were negotiating the ruts of the washboard road that led to the back side of the Adelaide Fairgrounds.

She had imagined rodeo as a nighttime activity, with massive generator-powered lights flooding a field—that's what she had found online—but the Last Gasp was a morning event. A cement mixer was turning batter in a corner of the parking lot for the pan-cake breakfast.

"Come with me, Maxie?" she said to the backseat.

"But it's snowing," Max said.

"Please come with me," Maya said.

"What's going to happen?" Max said.

"The cowboys play with the animals," Maya said. "Do you remember how you played with those deer?" Max looked at her questioningly. "I'm not mad at you about that anymore," she said. "You don't know why you liked it—but you liked it. Well, the cow-boys like riding horses. And bulls. It's fun for them."

The arena smelled powerfully of cow dung and something greasy like motor oil. Cold air gusted off the packed earth. Maya held Max's hand tightly. A loud, grating bell went off and in past the bleachers she heard pounding hooves, the earth rippling slightly beneath her. The entire place—past the entry booth, a small hangar for the pancake breakfast, and beyond it, a partly covered arena surrounded by gym bleachers—vibrated with an air of unfamiliar ceremony. The ticket window held a potato-nosed ancient rubbing his hands in front of a space heater.

"Rodeo association is running a special for the last event of the season," he said, showing them a mouth of false, sterling-white teeth. "Beautiful ladies get in for free. And future rodeo stars get in for free. So your total is zero."

Maya huffed out a helpless smile.

The upper bleachers were empty, but the rows near the dirt were full, cameras bathing the astringent air with flashes of silver. She was reassured by the seeming indifference of the crowd to the storm gathering outside. A moan of bovine protest issued from somewhere in the arena, but it was halfhearted, the animal going through some ritual. The loud bell went off again, and now they could see. The lock slipped from the chute gate and the dirt was crowded by a blur of animals, the bell shrilling again before Maya could understand what had happened. The scoreboard said

3.0 seconds. A man was on the dirt—he wore a cowboy hat, a Western shirt with two frilled pockets at the chest, and sneakers— his arms around the neck of a collapsed steer, its eyes wide in stunned, peaceable terror. The cowboy let go, scrambled up on his feet, smiled shyly, and raised his arms toward the stands. "A tenth-second shy of venue record!" the announcer called out. Feet stomped the bleachers and cameras whirred.

She had to watch again—two gates opened, two horses emerged, and between them a steer. She couldn't determine the purpose of the second rider, who veered away to allow the first to slide onto the animal and wrestle it to the ground until by some unknown metric the event was judged complete.

Maya looked over at Max. He was squinting down at the arena. "Doesn't it hurt?" he said, meaning the steer.

"I don't know, honey," Maya said.

"I don't like it," Max said.

They stamped their feet in the cold. A fine film of dust settled over their jackets. The cold smell of hide and excrement mingled with the yeasty scent of pancakes being turned out in the main building. In a fenced-off area walled off from the chutes, the riders paced, or chatted, or rubbed their hands together in wild concentration. One was laid down on the dirt, his head on his saddle, and his cowboy hat over his eyes. Clean, unlined faces, a picture of vitality that did not translate to their bodies, which covered for injuries: they hobbled, waddled, and dragged. In the crow's nest, the announcer God-blessed America, and took the crowd through two bars of "America the Beautiful." "Ladies and gentlemen, this cowboy's only pay this morning is your applause." When a new event came up, he went through a careful explanation what was what—the rodeo was for experts and newcomers alike.

The events seemed organized by escalating violence. In the next, a horse rider cast a noose around the neck of a calf, the horse rearing up to keep it tight while the rider ran the length of the rope, slammed the calf on its side, and tied its feet up in the air.

The sight felt lurid and Maya turned away. She found herself wishing that the animal would wriggle out and stomp the man who had thrown it to the ground. If Maya had never felt especially close to Max's biological father, she had felt even less close to the animal that must have mangled his leg, even if it was responsible for a long process that ended in her acquisition of a son. But she felt a strong kinship with it now.

"Mama, let's go," Max said.

"Me too," Maya said.

The ground cover had increased in the brief time they'd spent in the arena—the snow cracked underfoot. Northeast snow slicked up and slushed, slurping under the feet, but this was the snow of Kiev. Maya's mother would finish her cigarette at the window and Maya her oatmeal at the table, they would take the rumbling elevator down, and crunch snow on the way to school for an endless fifteen minutes, a faint hint of smoke wreathing her mother's speech.

Maya closed her eyes and breathed deeply, Max waiting patiently. When she opened them, she wished desperately to see her mother standing in front of her. Maya looked down at her son and said, "I need to go see my mother." Did ships sail between continents any longer? No matter—she would go in the hold of a cargo freighter if she had to.

"Your grandmother," Maya said. This grandmother Max barely knew. Maya experienced deeply the distance that her husband had been remarking on since the start of the trip, only he was measuring to New Jersey and she, now, much farther. His constant remarking on it had tuned it out in her mind, but now she understood very well what he was speaking about.

"I don't remember the last time we built a snowman," Maya said. "Come."

Alex, who had remained at the wheel of the Escape, was summoned and asked to gather up snow, which he did with his feet, his hands in the pockets of his too-thin jacket, while Maya and

Max sculpted. Soon, they each had three balls, round as ice-cream scoops. "You're a natural, Maksik," Maya said. Max clapped his gloves.

A passing elderly couple unlocked arms to insist on photographing the handsome family in front of their winter creation, and the South-Central Montana Rodeo Association scrapbook for the 2012 Last Gasp still holds, next to an image of Curtis Purnell riding the bull Fat Chance to the highest score of the day, an image of the Shulman-Rubins of Acrewood, New Jersey, next to a pair of snowmen.

"My feet are wet," Alex said.

"Almost," Maya said.

She knelt before the snowmen and in the belly of the first drew a large T, in the other an L. Alex, sunk in a sullen, sleep-deprived reverie, stared at Maya from the edge of the snow pile.

Max looked up at his mother. "What do the letters mean?"

"Max?" Maya said. "Your papa and I have something to tell you."

Alex continued to watch his wife with a defeated hostility.

"Two things," Maya said. "The first is that we love you very much. So, so much. You will always be our boy."

"I know, silly goose," Max said. He clapped his hands.

"Do you remember we were looking at a photo album at home once and you wanted to know why there were a hundred pictures of you at seven weeks but none from before?" Maya said. "And we said it was because cameras weren't around yet, and we finally managed to get one when you got to be seven weeks?"

"I guess," Max said cautiously.

"We weren't telling the truth, honey," Maya said. "Please don't be upset with us. We want to tell you the truth. We want to tell you only the truth from now on."

"Maya," Alex whispered like a drugged person.

"The truth is that we are your second mommy and daddy," Maya said. "Another mommy and daddy had you in their belly.

Right where these letters are—it was you. But then, after you were born, they asked if your papa and I would take you. They really loved you but they couldn't hold on to you—they were too young to take care of a baby. They loved you so much. And they wouldn't give you away until they had found some people who they knew would love you even more."

Max stared at her, trying to understand. "So I wasn't in your belly?" he said, frowning.

"No, honey."

"You're not my mama and papa?"

"Yes, we are, darling, yes we are. I am your mama, and Papa's your papa. But you've been blessed. Only special kids get this kind of blessing. You have four parents instead of two. You have an extra pair."

Max blinked twice, and again. He was staring intently at her, his head pitched slightly forward. "But where are they now?"

"I don't know, my love. We tried to find them, and couldn't. That's why we came here. But if we ever find them—I promise, I will ask them to come and spend time with you."

"But why did they give me away?" Max said. He was trying not to cry and looked at his father. Alex gave his son a cracked smile, but didn't move.

Maya tried to embrace Max, but he wriggled out and stared at her. He was little, so little. "They loved you so much that they gave you away because someone else could take better care of you than they could," she said, her voice filling with tears. "That's how much they loved you. I know it's hard to understand—we'll keep talking about it. But if they stayed in touch, seeing you would remind them of what they had done. It was too painful. But it wasn't just them, honey—it was us, too. We wanted you to be ours so bad that we didn't ask them to stay in touch. And they got what they wanted and we got what we wanted, and only you didn't."

"I don't believe you!" Max shouted and ran off toward the car. Maya rose heavily and moved off after him, Alex watching them

with a dull resignation. Max got to the car first and began to beat
his fists on the locked door. At Maya's touch on his shoulders, he
spun out and ran to the other side of the car. Abruptly, he changed
his mind and ran off from the vehicle, stamping the snow with
quick little footsteps. He fell in the snow even before Maya caught
up to him. He was trying to get up when she threw herself down
over him and they both wept, Maya into Max's shoulder, and Max
into the snow. Alex stared at them from the side of the car like an
intruder. Finally, he approached and knelt before them. Maya did
not look at him. She heard only his voice, thin as a fallen-out hair
on a pillow: "You'll catch cold. Please."

As they made their stumbling way out of the fairgrounds,
Max cried himself to sleep. The Escape warmed up rapidly. Alex
blasted the heat downward at his feet and they climbed onto the
patchy white county road that led to the front of the fairgrounds
and would start them on the long road east. The snow was gust-
ing more thickly. As they rolled out of Adelaide, Maya heading in
Harry Sprague's direction a fourth time—she would call him; no,
fax him; ask him to become the boy's godfather; ask him to invent
for the boy stories of Laurel and Tim until she could track down
their real selves; for now, Harry was as close to them as her child
could come—Maya wondered if another three days in Adelaide
was a small price to pay for not driving in hideous weather. But
she had found her limit; she needed to go home. She would rest a
little and then get started again. She would find them. For Max,
she would find them.

Besides, those on the road want to keep moving. It is unnatural
to turn back, even if behind you are homes with lights and heaters
and food and before you a swirling white nothing.

It didn't take long for the road to vacate itself of human in-
trusion. What population advantage this part of Montana enjoyed
over the prairie had been erased by the weather. Maya consulted
the map—she remembered more towns along the county road be-

tween Adelaide and the interstate, where surely they were plowing, but the road had settled into an immense emptiness. Trying to make the map agree with what she was seeing, Maya had gotten turned around and in a panic found herself unable to tell where exactly was Sheff City. She swiveled wildly in her seat—she needed to know where she was relative to it, and to him—and then had to clamp together her teeth to keep back her tears.

At the wheel, where the plodding snow, the blowing heater, and his heartbroken morning had fused into a warm mash, Alex was fighting to keep his eyes open. "Maya," he whispered. The storm had suddenly turned feral, as if the level-straight lines separating the counties on the map could be for gradations of weather as well. The dun, bare peaks turned snow-streaked charcoal and the bruised-looking sky gleamed with vicious gray light. Maya flicked on the radio hoping for weather, but they were in a Christian zone, the talkers less concerned with the hazardous conditions of this world than the hazardless ones of the next.

"Bring *on* the fattened calf!"

"If you have been con*tam*inated—"

"Because God works through family radio—"

She turned it off and stared at the map with bewilderment she meant to conceal from the driver. She was grateful her son was asleep; she begged him to stay so. Briefly she thought about turning back but now they were almost as far away from Adelaide as to the interstate. If they continued down the county road, they would intersect with it in thirty miles. She looked over at Alex's speedometer—he had slowed down to a crawl; it would take them an hour. Now she believed Marion; now the next hour would bring down a foot.

She stared at the map, willing it to yield some thin capillary of a north-south shortcut that could slice down to the interstate. The windshield was drowning in snow, the wipers scrambling wildly and not keeping up. The road ahead was the color of ash, the lane dividers long vanished. The fluffy pellets that had seemed so benign early that morning and even at the fairgrounds were descending with bureaucratic resolve.

They slid by a green rectangle: Interstate 90: 29 miles. How could one be so close to one of the busiest roads in the world and yet so helplessly enshrouded by blankness?

A half hour's drive, now it would take them two hours. Alex was down to below twenty miles an hour, his shoulders up at his ears as he tried to make out the road through a small unfogged aperture in the windshield. There was so much snow pushing down now that two banks were building up on either side of the roadway. She remembered a country road driven as a child, willows rising from the sides of the road until they met above the roadway in a protective embrace. Now, she imagined the snowbanks multiplying until the three of them were sailing in a white tunnel, the sky as white as the walls of this borderless land that had suddenly turned airless and tight, and ran without end to the bluffs, the ridgelines, the buttes, the false beautiful names with which the people here marked the heartless world around them.

She found a capillary. She ran her hand across the map to make sure she wasn't imagining. "Alex!" she shouted. Two miles east of them, a local road cut south to the interstate at a length of nine miles. That they could cover in a half hour; maybe the road was plowed, though probably not. Alex's knuckles were white from clutching the steering wheel. His nose was pressed to its tip, squinting into the gloom. After a minute of silence, he said, "Help me look for it." He was blinking furiously.

Something dull and stonelike was taking up room in Maya's chest. She realized she was holding her breath. She tried the radio out of nervousness, but there was a sermon on, calm and unperturbed, already having accepted the death awaiting them all. They passed a placard of a prancing cow nailed to a split-rail fence—if there was a ranch somewhere here, she would knock on the door with no shyness. But where? Perhaps on the side road. Caps of

snow neatly crowned every rail of the fence, an imponderable harmony.

The turnoff was well marked, visible even through the fog and
smears of the windshield. Maya was cheered—logic dictated that
a significant turnoff would not lead to an insignificant road. And at
first, the side road—Alex asked twice that she verify on the map
that they were doing the right thing—proceeded in a flat ribbon
and felt more traversable than the county road. Perhaps it was in
the lee of some ridge, and therefore got less snow. Maya tried to
urge forward optimism.

Alex had nearly ceased trying to direct the vehicle, focusing
instead on keeping the speedometer from falling too far. From
somewhere beneath, the Escape squeaked. Car words sailed
through Maya's head—carburetor, chassis, axle, suspension. Beautiful words, connected to nothing. The once-black wave of the
road flung them around, whitecaps lashing the hull.

They were 3.7 miles down the shortcut—Maya was counting by tenths of a mile, surreptitiously awaiting each shift of the
odometer—when the Escape's wheels refused to take a snowed-
over incline. Maya shrieked as the car slid, Max flying awake. The
car remained on the bank like a slug clutched to a wall—the snow
was too heavy to climb over. Little by little, it had thickened as they
proceeded down the road, as if the leeward protection had ended.

Through the windows, it looked as if darkness was starting in on
the sky. No, it couldn't be time yet for darkness. But the weather
had cloaked the sky so thoroughly that it was all the same thing.
Max began to weep softly. Maya called to her son and asked him to
hold on; Mama and Papa would fix this, and then she would climb
in the back. He would have to hold on for a little bit longer.

"Alex, we have to turn around," she said.

"We just wasted a half hour on this," he said.

"We'll waste another getting back. But at least that road was flat."

"I can't turn around!" he yelled. "Look at what's happening out
there." Max began to wail more loudly.

"Please don't yell," she said.

Alex cast her a hopeless look.

"Turn it off," Maya said.

"Turn what off?" he said.

"The car."

"Maya . . ." he said. She sat next to a defeated man. She thought he would burst into tears.

She reached forward and flicked off the ignition. The engine died and the wipers collapsed in exhaustion. When the car was rumbling, more than half a tank of gas in its hold, the possibility that they would remove themselves from this bank was alive. Now, it was gone. It seemed odd to be still—a bad idea, surely, for the engine to grow cold. It seemed like they were giving up the pretense, like they were going to hunker down and hope they didn't get buried, slide off into some ditch, end up some animal's winter capture. They sat in silence. In twenty seconds, the windshield was covered.

Maya opened her door. Obediently, the car started dinging. Snow slapped her face. She was ready to be swallowed by the interminable, graying whiteness around her, and actually felt herself falling, and closed her eyes in fright. But she remained in place, and opened them.

The wind was slight, and the temperature actually seemed well above freezing—the situation outside felt nothing like the unnavigable misery that had loomed from behind the windshield. The air was mellow, unconfrontational. Maya blinked rapidly as snowflakes settled on her shoulders, inside her collar, on her eyebrows, her nose. She stuck out her tongue and tasted the cold crystal. The view above her was vast. She had been shivering, but realized it had been in anticipation, not because the weather demanded it. This was the world she had been born to, snow from September through April. She had been on sabbatical for twenty-five years, but she had found it again. If it all did end here, there was no better place.

She looked into the car and waved to Alex and Max to come out-side. A long moment passed during which she wondered whether Alex would attempt to coax the Escape into action so he could save himself and his son from the mad interloper among them. But after a long minute in her life, she heard one of the doors open. It was Max's door. Then her husband emerged.

Through her parka, Maya felt her midsection, soft and sticky under her sweater, her T-shirt—she was supposed to have show-ered, but hadn't; she was not supposed to have stolen a T-shirt out of Marion's bag, and had. Down there, the last vanishing evidence of Marion Hostetler preserved just a little bit longer because of the cold. Or maybe not last. You just didn't know. So much you just didn't know. But it didn't matter, if you were ready for all of it—if you were ready to call things by their name. It was comic to feel her belly three hours after he'd been inside her; this wasn't a fairy tale, least of all her age; but she felt anyway; because she wanted, and could.

Maya had asked Alex and Max outside because she had wanted to show them that the wretched magnificence all around was inno-cent, and not what they thought. That they would make it: some-way, somehow. They would lay down mats under the wheels, they would pirouette on the snow, they would coast back to the county road, they would inch forward. She took Alex's hand, then her son's, and stood with them staring at the brutal, mysterious splen-dor before them. She wanted them to see that it would take some doing to get out of this trouble, but the forecast was good, and the world full of wonder, and there was nothing to fear out there at all.

Acknowledgments

The original debt is to family: Anna Oder, Yakov Fishman, Arkady Oder, and in memory of Sofia Oder and Faina Fishman.

The contemporary debt is to friends and colleagues:

Alana Newhouse: I am so lucky to have your friendship.

Henry Dunow, Terry Karten, Elena Lappin: You are my golden triumvirate. Jane Beirn: You're a miracle worker, and it's been an honor to work with you. Special thanks also to Nikki Smith, Jillian Verrillo, and Stephanie Cooper: You're so good at what you do.

The readers: Ben Holmes, Amy Bonnaffons, Ellen Sussman, Jules Lewis, Susan Jane Gilman. You carried me down the last leg.

Margot Knight and the Djerassi Resident Artist Program, where this novel was begun, and Wayne Hoffman, Mark Sullivan, and the Horizontal Pines Artists + Writers Haven, where it was finished.

Those who took time to share their stories and educate me: David Politzer, Sari Siegel, Laura Summerhill, Mary Cherry, Laurence Sugarman, Kiro Ivanovski, Scott Summers, Susan Wise Bauer.

The Jewish Book Council, and especially Carolyn Hessel, which does so much for literature.

The evangelists, in no order: Joe Flaherty and everyone at Writers & Books, Bonnie Sumner, Miwa Messer, David and Sally Johnston, Bruce and Julie Blackwell, John King, Vanessa Blakeslee, Yossi Gremilion, Ida and Peter Sorensen, John and Joanne Gordon, Meredith Maran, Dan Speth and Cathy Clemens, Darlene Orlov, Juliette Ponce, Ellen Kaye and Seth Goldman, Carolyn Carr Hutton, Ella Shteingart, Stewart and Susan Kampel, and the many others who've gone out of their way to spread word. I wouldn't be nearly as far without you.

About the Author

Boris Fishman was born in Belarus and has lived in the United States since the age of nine. He is the author of the novel *A Replacement Life*, which was chosen as a *New York Times* Notable Book of the Year and a Barnes & Noble Discover Great New Writers Selection, and won the Sophie Brody Medal from the American Library Association and the VCU Cabell First Novelist Award. His writing has appeared in the *New Yorker*, the *New York Times Magazine*, the *Wall Street Journal*, the *London Review of Books*, the *New Republic*, and other publications. He lives in New York City.